Excelsior

Excelsior

by Randall Silvis

Henry Holt and Company • New York

Published by Henry Holt and Company, Inc.,
115 West 18th Street, New York, New York 10011.
Published in Canada by Fitzhenry & Whiteside Limited,
195 Allstate Parkway, Markham, Ontario L3R 4T8.

Library of Congress Cataloging in Publication Data
Silvis, Randall, 1950–
Excelsior.
I. Title.
PS3569.I47235E9   1987   813'.54   87–11838
ISBN 0-8050-0440-8

First Edition

Designed by Liney Li
Printed in the United States of America
10 9 8 7 6 5 4 3 2 1

ISBN 0-8050-0440-8

For Rita
and for Bret

Acknowledgments

My deepest gratitude to Arnold Goodman, for his faith and perseverance. To Rob Cowley, for his caring guidance. To Larry Dennis, for hewing a path through the tangle of academia. To my mother and father, for baby-sitting above and beyond the call of grandparenting. And to the Pennsylvania Council on the Arts, for its support during the writing of this work.

Although the city of Erie, Pennsylvania, actually does exist, it is not the same city as the one depicted herein. I have taken the liberty of rearranging the geography and of placing in it numerous undesirable characters and settings, none of which, I'm sure, could be found in Erie.

Part One

Part One

NOTHING is new, only freshly painted.

So thought Bloomhardt as he lay in bed, looked at the sunlight slanting in through the window, felt its April warmth across his legs, and felt his body ache. His body ached every morning with a comprehensive soreness to which he could ascribe no cause, a soreness more spiritual than anatomical. His body ached and his mouth tasted sour and he felt three times his thirty-four years old. It was 7:30 in the morning and this was the best he would feel all day.

Nothing is new, only freshly painted.

He scratched himself between his legs and listened to the ticking of the clock. His pubic hair was matted, but he could not remember why. Had he made love to his wife last night? Had he had a wet dream? Not the haziest memory of either event remained. Either way, though, it did not matter. Nothing mattered.

Downstairs in the kitchen, Annie, his wife, was making breakfast. He could smell the coffee and bacon, could hear a Tom and Jerry cartoon on the television. The noise rang like a gong inside his head. He was not hung over but wished he were, for then he would have an excuse for feeling this way.

"Turn that television down!" he shouted.

He lay in bed and scratched himself. Mornings were difficult for him because they heralded another day, a continuation of his monotonous life. If only he could awaken some morning to find that it was afternoon, or midnight, or to discover that the top of his house had been whisked away while he slept, or, while easing out of a sexy dream, look up to see a sad-faced priest administering last rites—maybe then he would have something to look forward to.

Reluctantly he pushed himself up on his elbows and examined the broad bar of sunlight that came slanting through the window to break across the foot of the bed. It was the same bar of sunlight he had seen yesterday at this time and it fell across exactly the same spot. "Nuts," Bloomhardt said, and slumped into the pillow.

Ten minutes later, Annie came in and sat on the edge of the bed. He looked at her pretty face, thin and worried, as she, smiling, stroked his forehead, her long brown hair falling over her shoulders as smoothly as water over round stones, her Ben Franklin glasses making her seem spinsterish. For a moment he felt the urge to pull her into bed and make love to her. On second thought, he was too tired for it, though he knew she would offer no resistance. If she *would* resist, he could find the energy for it. But Annie never resisted.

"Better get up, honey, or you'll be late again," she said.

"I don't care," said Bloomhardt. "Everybody's always late."

She laid a hand on his naked chest, then tickled her fingertips over his stomach and down between his legs. "I know how to get you up," she teased.

Gently he pushed her hand away. "That only works for a part of me."

She smiled apologetically. "Breakfast is ready," she said. "And Timmy is waiting to eat with you."

But Bloomhardt did not want to eat with his six-year-old son. His son made him nervous. "I don't think I'll go to work today. Call and tell them I'm sick."

She leaned forward to touch her lips to his forehead. "You don't have a temperature," she said.

"I don't have to have a temperature to be sick. People die without ever having had a temperature."

She smiled timidly, sympathetically.

"Come on, call me in sick."

"But, John, honey. I called you in sick on Monday."

"Tell them I've had a relapse. What did I have Monday, trichinosis?"

"No, that was last week. Monday you had conjunctivitis."

"Let's go with that one again," he said.

"My baby," she cooed while stroking his head. "You work so hard. I wish there was something I could do."

"You can quit petting me," he told her, and jerked his head away.

She drew her hands into her lap and looked down at them.

"Well, are you going to call me in sick or not?"

"If that's what you want me to do, I will."

"Of course that's what I want you to do. I'm nauseated, my head hurts, my eyes are bloodshot, and every bone in my body aches. Do you want me to go to work feeling like that?"

Annie reached for the telephone on the nightstand and began to dial the number, which she knew by heart. Suddenly Bloomhardt sat up and slapped his hand down on the phone cradle, breaking the connection. "Wait a minute, what day is this? This is Friday, isn't it? Never mind, Annie, hang up. I guess I can make it through one more day."

"I wish you had a job you liked," she said.

"There's no such thing." He swung his legs over the side of the bed. "Gotta hurry. Make sure breakfast is ready soon."

"It's ready now," she told him.

"But I'm not ready now," he said as he hurried, stiff and naked, into the bathrooom. Annie remained on the edge of the bed for a few moments longer, feeling guilty, responsible for his discontent, her hand absorbing the warmth in the indentation his head had made.

Under the steamy spray of the shower, Bloomhardt stood and watched the soap lather go swirling down the drain. The thought of another day in the accounting offices of Universal Steel filled him with dread. The only good thing to happen all week was that somehow, miraculously, Friday had arrived.

Though what did it really matter, he wondered, whether he went to work or stayed home? In either place he would be miserable, bloated with despair. At work he had to contend with the senseless monotony of his job, with delinquent coworkers, stale doughnuts, sabotaged coffee, and a padlock on the men's room door. At home it was a wife whose passivity and self-effacement drove him to acts of cruelty, to nasty barbs and taunts for which, moments later, he despised himself, for he truly loved Annie. And the more he loved her, the more he detested himself, and the more he acted out his self-loathing on his family.

To top it all off, he had a six-year-old son he was afraid of. He was afraid of him because he knew in his heart that Timmy despised him, despised him because he, Timmy, knew what Bloomhardt knew, that Bloomhardt was a failure, a flop as a husband, an unfit father.

Bloomhardt knew these facts about himself and his family, and this was what made him cling to his bed each morning. Plus a hundred other worries. This monstrous old house, for example. Nine rooms, each costing approximately seventy dollars per month. He and Annie had purchased the house as newlyweds, back when they had dreamed of furnishing it with a half-dozen children, a half-dozen Bloomhardts to romp and laugh and fill the world with joy. But that was how long ago? Ten years. Ten lost, irretrievable, irrevocable years. And instead of six children they had but one son, a frail and taciturn child, a child who in Bloomhardt's presence only stared at him and blinked behind the thick round lenses of his glasses.

Meanwhile, outside on the sidewalk the garbage piled up like Mount Rushmore, monument to another garbage haulers' strike. Stray dogs came in the night to shit on Bloomhardt's porch, or, worse yet, to hide their deposits in the tall grass of his front lawn, where he would invariably step on them. Tonight, no doubt, when he turned on the television, hoping to relax awhile, a fuse would blow. Maybe the refrigerator would be on the fritz. Next time he reached for toilet paper there would be none on the roll, no extra rolls in the house. Magazine and newspaper subscriptions would expire without notice. Taxes and insurance premiums would be raised, bank accounts overdrawn. The electric company would be granted a 4-percent increase. The neighbors were loud, prices high, beer cans rusted along the highway. Around the world there were wars and rumors of wars. Maniacs were in charge of four-fifths of the planet, imbeciles the rest. Constipation proliferated, as did hemorrhoids, eczema, halitosis, and dandruff, everything that made the human race uncomfortable and ugly.

And as if that weren't enough, Bloomhardt could not recall whether he had made love to his wife last night or had had a wet dream. Not that it mattered. Mox nix, nothing mattered.

Looking at himself in the bathroom mirror, his face shaggy with shaving cream, Bloomhardt smiled in spite of himself when he heard that fractured phrase in his mind. *Mox nix.* It was what his grandmother used to say, her translation of *es macht nichts*, picked up fifty years ago from the vendor who delivered her monthly load of coal. Bloomhardt remembered how he, as a child might spill his bean soup on the linoleum floor, or, climbing into his grandfather's lap, knock a glass of beer off the table, and his grandmother, tiny scarecrow of a woman, would scurry for the mop while reassuring him, "Mox nix, don't cry, the floor needed washing anyway."

Mox nix, Bloomhardt thought, and drew the razor down his cheek, nicking his chin, his blood pink when it mixed with the shaving cream. Mox nix: a good phrase. In two words, the state of the universe.

had it not been a Friday, Bloomhardt would have remained in his bed, faking illness, curled like a caterpillar beneath warm blankets. But Friday hinted of change and adventure, it dangled a Saturday in front of his nose. On Saturdays, Bloomhardt went to his second job, selling tombstones at Fenstermaker's Quality Memorials—another dead-end job, of course, but one that brought in thirty-five untaxed dollars each week, enough to pay the monthly mortgage on two rooms in his dinosaur of a house. And on Saturdays he was paid the additional fringe benefit of flirtatious advances from Myrna, Joe Fenstermaker's buxom, black-haired wife. Sometimes Bloomhardt would respond to her advances and sometimes not. Sometimes it was more fun just to tease her, to watch her claw at her breasts and gnash her teeth in a rutting frenzy. Joe's secretary-wife was always in heat, always eager to spread a tattered blanket over the bench in her husband's workshop, but Bloomhardt never knew from one week to the next whether or not he would indulge her.

Now, as he brushed his teeth, Bloomhardt felt guilty because he was looking forward to tomorrow. This guilt, in turn, made him resent his love for Annie. How could he love his wife so dearly and yet be unfaithful to her? The diversion Myrna supplied was such a trivial one, so short-lived in the overall scheme of things, that on a rational level he could see no harm in it. Yet it overwhelmed him with guilt. Even feeling good, it seemed, made Bloomhardt feel bad. And feeling bad made him very tired. He looked at himself in the bathroom mirror, clean-shaven, teeth bright, eyes bloodshot, and said to himself, because there was little else to say, "Mox nix."

Sometimes even a fresh coat of paint hides nothing.

Tucked up close to the kitchen table, Timmy lowered his head as his father approached. He was afraid of Bloomhardt, just as Bloomhardt was afraid of him. Bloomhardt accepted the cup of coffee Annie handed him, took a quick sip, and said, "Don't bother with anything else, I don't have time to eat."

"I made waffles and scrambled eggs," she said. "And you won't have to wait, it's ready now."

"I told you, I'm late."

He drank his coffee in gulps and stole surreptitious glances at his son. When Timmy raised his head unexpectedly and caught his father looking at him, Bloomhardt, not knowing what else to do, winked.

Timmy blinked twice, then stared at his empty plate again.

"Okay," said Bloomhardt. "Let's get going."

"Timmy hasn't eaten yet," said Annie.

"Ah, geez," Bloomhardt groaned. "You knew I was late, didn't you? So why didn't you feed him?"

Facing the stove, she answered meekly, "Yesterday you said we all had to eat breakfast together from now on. You said you didn't like having your breakfast alone."

"But couldn't you see that I'm late this morning? Don't you know how to read a clock yet?" Bloomhardt heard the anger in his voice, and thought, Maybe I'm possessed by demons. That possibility gave him a twinge of pleasure.

"I'm sorry," said his wife. "It's just that you were late yesterday morning when you said it."

"I'm late every morning, but not as late as I am today."

"I'm sorry," Annie said.

"Ah, geez," said Bloomhardt. "He'll just have to eat in the car. Don't they feed you at that school you go to?"

Timmy said nothing. He looked at his watery image afloat in the white plate.

"I'll walk him to school today," said Annie. "You go ahead or you'll be late."

"I'm already late! And you can't walk him to school, it's nearly two miles. Why didn't you put him on the bus?"

"You said you didn't want him to ride the morning bus anymore. You said you would drive him to school every morning."

"I said, I said! Good Lord, Annie, can't you tell when it's necessary to disregard what I've said?"

She stirred the scrambled eggs. "I only try to do what you tell me to do. I only try to make you happy."

Bloomhardt glanced at his scrawny son, who sat motionless, staring into an empty plate. "I'm sorry," Bloomhardt said.

Annie turned to face him. "I'm sorry," she said.

"Don't you be sorry, it's my fault. I don't know what's wrong with me."

"I'm sorry," she said.

"Damn it, Annie, stop that! I'm the one who's late, I'm the one who stayed in bed too long. Everything is always my fault. You know that, and yet all you ever do is say 'I'm sorry.' Why don't you tell me to shove it once in a while?"

"I try not to upset you. I know how much you hate your job."

"That's not your fault either."

"I know," she said. "I'm sorry."

Bloomhardt banged his cup onto the table. He grabbed a waffle off the plate, spooned scrambled eggs over it, then slapped another waffle on top. To Timmy he said, "You want ketchup on this?"

The boy shook his head no.

"Come on, then. Let's get rolling."

Timmy sprang out of his chair, kissed his mother on the run, and followed Bloomhardt outside. On their way to the garage, Bloomhardt handed him the waffle sandwich. "This is the latest thing in fast-food breakfasts. Don't get the car messy."

During the seven-minute drive to school, Bloomhardt stole secret glances at his son. Being alone with Timmy always made him edgy. He did not know what to say to a six-year-old child. You could not talk baby-talk and you could not discuss the rising crime rate or the probable cause of the decline of the family unit. The mind of a six-year-old was a puzzle to Bloomhardt. He wanted his son to love him, as any son must love the father who feeds and clothes him and has never once raised a hand to him in anger. But Bloomhardt knew that this son, his son, did not love his father. Nor could Bloomhardt think of any reason why he should.

"How's school going?" Bloomhardt asked.

Timmy, his mouth full of waffle sandwich, chewed quickly and nervously. He held the sandwich over his lap so as to spill nothing on the car seat. He blinked behind the thick round lenses of his glasses. When his son looked at him that way, his eyes going *blinkblink,* face expressionless, Bloomhardt felt alien, a freak.

"Fine," Timmy said.

Bloomhardt nodded. "What grade are you in now?"

"First," the boy said.

Bloomhardt nodded again. It seemed a very long two miles to school, the traffic unnaturally slow. "What kinds of things do you learn in first grade?"

Timmy swallowed a small bite of waffle and egg and thought carefully. He did not want to say anything that might cause his father to shout at him. But sometimes Bloomhardt would shout for no reason at all. "We make things," Timmy finally ventured.

"Oh? What kinds of things?"

"Things with clay."

"You make things with clay," Bloomhardt repeated, nodding. "What kinds of things?"

Timmy looked at his father. Was he going to start shouting? "Animals," said the boy. "And sometimes people."

"Unh-huh," Bloomhardt said, nodding. "Well, that's a good thing to learn. That'll probably come in handy some day." He drove silently for a few blocks, hands sweaty on the wheel. "Yep," he said, still nodding. "That's a very good thing to learn, making things with clay."

Bloomhardt heard himself and knew how foolish he must sound, even to a six-year-old. He did not want to sound foolish, he wanted to sound all-wise and knowing, but there were thousands of miles between himself and Timmy, and he sensed that no matter what he might say, it would always be gibberish to the boy. He wanted to fold his arms around his son and whisper how much he loved him, how he longed to say fatherly, endearing words, but how his mind always came up blank. He wanted to confess to Timmy his sense of ineptitude, his fears, his need to see the boy smile now and then. But Bloomhardt was afraid to say these things; he was afraid that Timmy would sit there stiffly, unresponsive, blinking. Because his son did not like him.

Bloomhardt brought the car to a halt in front of the elementary school. "You didn't eat much of your sandwich," he observed.

Timmy regarded the crumbs of scrambled egg dotting his lap.

"Well," said Bloomhardt, "don't tell your mother."

Timmy looked at him, waiting, while Bloomhardt searched for something wittier to say, something that would send the boy skipping happily into the schoolroom, filled with love and admiration for his father.

"Have a nice day," Bloomhardt said.

Timmy nodded, then pivoted to face the door. Afraid to let go of the half-eaten sandwich with either hand, he tried to open the door with his elbow. Bloomhardt saw the boy struggling and quickly leaned over him to reach for the door, but when his father's huge arm streaked in front of him, Timmy, startled, sat back sharply, and in doing so knocked his sandwich against Bloomhardt's elbow, smearing scrambled eggs over Bloomhardt's sleeve.

Jerking away too quickly, Bloomhardt whacked his hand against the dome light. "Ouch!" he yelped, and in reaction snapped back his head, banging it against the window. "Ouch! Goddamn it, ouch!"

Timmy kicked open the door and fled toward the schoolhouse. Bloomhardt, his head and hand smarting, watched his son disappear inside. Then he surveyed the mess on the car seat, his greasy sleeve and wrist. Groaning hopelessly, he pulled shut the door, which seemed to require nearly all his strength, yanked the gearshift into place, and lurched away.

Nearly thirty minutes late when he walked into the long gray office building at the Universal Steel factory, Bloomhardt winked sheepishly at the receptionist, a woman he hated because she had no respect for any of the accounting clerks' bladders, all of which would soon be aching. A baggy-skinned skeleton with nicotine-stained fingers, she sneered in response to his wink and rammed a plug into the switchboard.

As he tiptoed past the half-open door of the Boss's office, Bloomhardt peeked inside. The Boss, in his Naugahyde swivel chair, blunt pudgy feet resting on his desk, was reading last night's newspaper. Later in the day he would read this morning's paper. After lunch he would read magazines.

In the hallway outside the main accounting office, Bloomhardt paused to draw a cup of coffee from an urn on a coffee cart. First he checked his mug to make sure there was nothing in it. Sometimes he would find a plastic spider in his cup, sometimes a dead fly. Once there had been a wad of chewing tobacco, already well-chewed. Another time a hard gray dog turd, so old that it had begun to grow hair.

But this time his mug was empty and clean, which immediately made him suspicious. He lifted the lid off the urn and eyeballed the coffee. By all appearances it was safe to drink. He drew a cup and sniffed it. Nothing unusual abut the taste, unless you expected the fresh, rich flavor of well-made coffee, which Bloomhardt did not.

Such circumspection was routine at Universal Steel. Inside the office, seated at his desk, Bloomhardt would be even more cautious. More than once he had grabbed a ringing telephone only to discover too late that the inside of the receiver was smeared with mustard or oil or some other slimy substance. More than once he had reached for his pencils, only to find them glued to the desk. He could not count the times the screws had been removed from his chair, so that when he leaned back to stretch, the legs collapsed. If he had a dollar for every time his calculator tape had been set on fire or deliberately jammed, he could buy his wife a pair of diamond earrings.

Most of the five men with whom Bloomhardt shared an office were neurotic, chain-smoking, alcoholic pranksters. How else to survive the monotony of pounding an adding machine day after day? It was the anticipation of this prank-riddled monotony that filled Bloomhardt with dread as he lay in bed each morning.

Now he peeked into the office and saw two empty chairs besides his own. The two most dangerous men, Goathead and Smitty, were not at their desks. Tensed, ready to duck any projectile that might come flying his way, Bloomhardt walked inside. But no one spoke to him as, prior to sitting, he checked his desk and chair for sabotage; no one looked up. Calculators and typewriters clicked, pencils scribbled. On his desk was a stack of pink bills of lading, which he soon began to thumb through, sorting according to date. He yawned, and a paper clip flew into his mouth. Coughing and choking, he spit it out, then looked at Roomy, the basset-faced clerk whose desk faced his, who was eyeing him sourly.

"This job starts at eight o'clock," Roomy growled. A middle-aged man with sad brown eyes, a bulbous nose, and thinning hair dyed unnaturally black, he spoke with a feminine lilt in his voice.

"This job starts when I get here," Bloomhardt answered.

"Then you'd better start getting here on time. Seems like I'm the only guy in this place who knows his position anymore."

"I know a good position for you," Bloomhardt told him.

"Oh, suck it off."

"Jazz me."

"Drill me."

"In your ear."

"Oooh la la!" Roomy sang in falsetto, grinning good-naturedly.

Bloomhardt smiled and shook his head. Nothing had changed since yesterday. In this accounting office, no hellos were ever offered, no how-are-you-this-mornings. If someone spoke, it was to deliver an insult, tell a racy story, share a bit of gossip, or beg for a loan. There was no camaraderie in the usual sense, there were no bosom buddies here. Wisecracking and dirty tricks were the order of the day, just as they had been for as long as Bloomhardt could remember, ever since his first hour in this office three years ago, when he had been hired to replace a clerk named Mickey, a man who, the day before, had shot himself in the men's room, and whose ghost, the next morning, found itself imprisoned behind a padlocked door, where it now flitted like a moth against the cool tile walls.

After checking his desk for booby traps, but finding none, Bloomhardt scooped up a handful of pencils and went across the room to Smitty's desk, where the pencil sharpener was mounted. Smitty, typically late, had not arrived, so Bloomhardt sat in his chair. He had sharpened only a few of the pencils when Smitty came staggering through the doorway, eyes bloodshot, sandy hair uncombed, shirt and trousers wrinkled. He walked unsteadily, swaying on his heels, dragging one foot after the other.

Because he was barely five and a half feet tall and as muscular as a bantam weightlifter, Smitty appeared at first glance much younger than he actually was. He was forty-five but on good days could pass for thirty. This morning, as he wobbled from side to side while leaning against the desk and squinting down at Bloomhardt, he looked closer to sixty.

"Who shit in my chair and put legs on it?" he asked.

Bloomhardt smiled as he turned the crank on the sharpener. "You look like yesterday's lunch, Smitty."

"I've got no time for your flattery, Bloomie. Just hurry up and make some room so that I can fall down."

Roomy clicked his tongue. "You might not feel so bad if you didn't stay out whoring all night long."

Because it was too painful to move his head, Smitty regarded Roomy out the corner of his eye. He opened his mouth to reply, then decided not to waste the energy. "Either move it now, Bloomie, or get ready to catch me, cause I'm coming down."

As Smitty started to fall, Bloomhardt grabbed his pencils and slid out of the way. With a moaning sigh, Smitty flopped into his chair. Bloomhardt had taken only one step toward his own desk when he screamed and jumped, pencils flying, as Smitty raked a ruler between his legs.

"And a goosy good morning to you too!" Smitty cackled.

"I can't believe you're still dumb enough to turn your back on him," Roomy said, chuckling with delight as Bloomhardt gathered up his pencils. "Nobody's balls are safe around him."

Nelson, hulking and slovenly, with long hairs curling out his nostrils and ears, looked up from his desk near the window and barked, "Knock it off! You guys are always screwing around. Some of us have work to do, you know."

Smitty spun in his chair, grabbed himself by the crotch, and jabbed his hips in Nelson's direction. "Here, work on this awhile," he said. Nelson snorted, grunted, gritted his teeth, and returned to his paperwork.

Petey, the other man in the office, smiled amiably, enjoying the show. He seldom joined in the horseplay but watched it with interest, blue eyes sparkling. He was a tall, long-limbed, strong, and healthy young man who did not drink or smoke and was never late for work. Only thirty years old, he already owned a hundred acres of farmland and was saving toward the purchase of another sizable tract. It was a mystery to Bloomhardt how Petey could work so smoothly, unperturbed by the vulgarity of the others. His life seemed to flow along at its own steady pace, tranquil amid the turbulence Bloomhardt felt helpless to escape.

The Goathead, the senior clerk, was now more than forty minutes late. But this too was more or less typical. He was probably hiding in the lilac bushes outside, his breath Jim Beam—warm as he waited for the Boss to make his 8:45 visit to the ladies' room. Alfred Drumbacher, dubbed the Goathead because of his plume of white hair that resembled the beard of a billy goat, had been with the company for twenty-eight years and knew the Boss's routine by heart.

The Boss was an oval-shaped man, five feet nine inches tall, around whom lingered a discordant symphony of smells. His cologne had a strong spicy scent of cinnamon and pine, his deodorant that of a funeral parlor, his hair cream, which he wore in overabundance, that of a poorly ventilated whorehouse. All day long he sucked on breath mints. Every morning and afternoon he sprinkled foot powder into his shoes, so that little clouds puffed around him when he walked. He kept a can of air freshener on his windowsill and used it frequently. He wore dark suits, and his white shirts smelled as if they had just come from a Chinese laundry where they had been starched with green tea.

The Boss arrived at exactly 7:59 each morning. After spraying the room with air freshener, he would settle down at his desk with the previous night's newspaper. On occasion he would make a phone call or two, pass along the previous day's production figures to his supervisor in another city (these figures awaited him on his desk each morning, left there by one of his employees, he did not know who), do the crossword puzzle, visit the ladies' room, then return to his office and wait for lunch. He knew nothing about the business and did not care to learn anything. By some perversity of fate, twenty-five years had passed and brought him unwittingly to this position of power, and with only a few more years until retirement, when he hoped to catch up on his reading, he was not about to jeopardize his security by getting involved in a business whose workings he could not comprehend. Things were humming along just fine as they were. Somehow, he reasoned, he must be doing what he was meant to do.

So it was a typical morning, the nine o'clock calm strained and tense. Nelson grunted as he ran his thick fingers over the calculator, punching out numbers. Smitty, seated behind the typewriter, trying to catch up on last week's work, groaned as he made yet another typing error. Roomy, cross-checking totals from his accounts-receivable invoices, appeared single-minded and intent, but at any moment might scream and throw something. Smitty, without notice, might leap from his chair to knock Roomy across the ears for breathing too loudly. And Bloomhardt, already tired, already bored, would yawn again, but this time with mouth closed, and try not to think about the senselessness of his work.

Earlier in his career at Universal Steel, he had tried to make some sense of it, to understand its subtleties and nuances, but had had small success. How could he believe that his efforts were of value when he had never actually seen the commodities he inventoried, had never stood beside the railroad cars whose contents he audited daily? How could he believe, when he had never glimpsed the hundreds of thousands of dollars in freight charges he apportioned each day? For him, everything was reduced to a number on a sheet of paper; that was Bloomhardt's reality. Figures were fudged and no one was ever the wiser. Money flowed in and just as invisibly flowed out. Mox nix, it was all just numbers, just graphite scribblings and inky hieroglyphs. It was enough to drive a man insane. But it paid well.

From his seat near the door, Bloomhardt looked across the room to the window, through which he could see pigeons flying over the hills of dolomite ore piled in the ore yard. With the sun climbing over their peaks, those bulldozed mountains looked like breasts arching to the sky. They made him think of Annie, though her breasts were small. He thought of her fine strong legs, the grip of her thighs. He fantasized that she was resisting him, squirming beneath him and trying to knee his groin while he, pinning her arms to the floor, ripped off her blouse with his teeth.

But, ah, too bad; in real life, Annie never resisted, and Bloomhardt knew, sadly, that she never would. And her selflessness was killing him. He could make the most ridiculous of demands and she would kill herself to satisfy them, then beg his forgiveness if she fell a trifle short. Her love flooded over him without an ounce of effort on his part. He deserved none of it.

Bloomhardt watched the pigeons as they wheeled through the sky, their bodies gray in the shadow of the ore pile, stark white in the sun. They rose on whim and drifted on caprice, they sailed and glided and soared. Seeing them strutting along a sidewalk or preening on a rooftop, he would have thought them dirty, clumsy things, but seen through the window across the room, with three desks full of unimaginative paperwork between him and them, they were graceful, beautiful, pure platinum birds. They were free, and he was in prison. He was thirty-four years old and he ached for either youth or death.

by twenty minutes past ten the day was in full swing, a day like any other. Out in the hallways, people ran from office to office. Information poured into Bloomhardt's office via telephone, teletype, messenger, memorandum, and long-distance scream. He and the other clerks were expected to make some sense of it all. Everybody had a question, and if he received an answer it was in the form of another question. If the business moved ahead, there were twenty men eager to take credit for it, but no one to claim responsibility for even the most routine blunder. Pass the buck, that was the name of the game. If the buck stopped at your desk, look incredulous and lie through your teeth. All that mattered here was survival. All that mattered was the five o'clock whistle.

The disorder of the place staggered Bloomhardt. Even after three years he was unaccustomed to it. Needing to urinate, needing to flee, he stepped into the hallway. The only quiet place in the building was the bathroom, but there was still a heavy padlock on the men's room door, just as there had been for the past three years. He hurried up the hall to the ladies' room, but found it locked from the inside.

"Occupied!" called the receptionist, when he rattled the door.

Bloomhardt trudged back down the hall. Knowing it would do him no good, he kicked the door to the men's room, then yanked on the padlock. He had been doing this several times a day for three years, but the door never opened, the lock never broke.

No one could enter the men's room because it too was occupied, for the rest of eternity, it seemed, by Mickey's ghost. It had been so occupied since the day Mickey walked inside, locked the door, faced the mirror, pulled out a Smith & Wesson .45 from wherever he had it concealed on his bowling-pin body, and put a bullet through his forehead. Roomy, who had been filling his coffee cup at the time, was the first person to enter the men's room after the echoing, coffee-spilling shot. With a manliness that surprised even himself, he had kicked open the door, then rushed inside and pulled Mickey away from the wall and saw Mickey's brains tumble out the back of his head like Jell-O from a Teflon-coated mold.

The next day, Bloomhardt received a call from his employment office. He took a day off from his job as an attendant at the Lake Erie Cherry Street Marina, put on his only suit, and reported to Universal Steel for an interview. The Boss glanced at Bloomhardt's résumé and said, "I see that you have a degree in accounting."

"Liberal arts," said Bloomhardt.

"Wonderful. We could use someone around here who really knows his accounting. What we do, though, is all pretty basic stuff—adding and subtracting, that sort of thing. Oh, I won't deny that you might be called upon to do a little multiplication and division from time to time, but don't worry, you'll have your very own calculator for that. And typing, you'll have to type a report now and then. You do type, don't you?"

"Well . . ." said Bloomhardt.

"Fine," said the Boss. "I like a man who knows his way around an office. I never learned to type myself, couldn't see much need for it in my field. How does eighteen thousand to start sound to you? Ten paid holidays, fifteen sick days, four personal days, full insurance coverage, free admission for you and your family to the annual company picnic. You are a family man, aren't you?"

"Eighteen thousand?" Bloomhardt said. At the marina he had earned less than twelve thousand a year and was forced to ask his parents for a loan every three months or so.

"All right, all right," said the Boss. "You're really backing me up against the wall, but I can go as high as eighteen six. That's pretty generous for an entry-level position, but for a man with your qualifications, a certified public accountant who knows his way around every office machine in the book like the back of his hand, I think the salary is justified. So, is tomorrow at eight A.M. okay with you? Hey, how about those Cleveland Indians?"

The next morning, his mind still reeling, Bloomhardt found himself seated at Mickey's desk. Two hours later he discovered the lock on the men's room door. No one seemed to know where it had come from or why it was there. Bloomhardt suggested that the lock be removed, but no one thought that a good idea. Weeks passed before Bloomhardt learned that he was the successor to a suicide. Only gradually did he come to understand that everyone in the building revered the memory of Mickey, a gentle and unassuming man, and that they feared contracting his madness from his ghost. Everyone, that is, except Bloomhardt himself, who resented the inconvenience to his bladder that Mickey's suicide caused.

at 10:45 the Goathead still had not arrived. His telephone rang insistently, but the other clerks were too busy to answer it. Roomy, reaching across his desk for a page of figures, knocked over the cup of coffee he had poured an hour ago but had not yet found time to drink. Nor did he have time now to mop up the mess, not if he wanted to light another cigarette, and he needed a smoke far more than he needed a dry desk. Smitty squirmed in his seat, his bowels groaning. But there was no time to run to the toilet now; he would have to settle for a fart and a belch. There were shipping statements to catalogue, invoices to verify, incoming and outgoing trains to inventory, bills of lading, waybills and progress reports, typewriter ribbons to change. There was too much to do and there were too few men with too little time to do it.

Into the midst of this turmoil, unannounced, the Boss suddenly appeared. Something must be seriously wrong, Bloomhardt thought, to shake him out of his nest before noon. Each of the clerks felt the Boss's presence, smelled him standing in the doorway, but no one would look up. Finally the Boss cleared his throat. Above the steady clacking of calculators and the ringing of a telephone, he asked, voice quivering, "Who's got the incoming freight today?"

Without taking his eyes off his calculator, Roomy answered, "Alfred does."

The Boss glanced at the Goathead's empty desk and, keenly observant, remarked, "He isn't here."

"He was here just a minute ago," Smitty lied. "He must have gone to the john. Or, in our case, the jane."

But the Boss did not smile. Because Bloomhardt's desk was the closest to the door, it was into his face that the Boss shoved a list of scrawled numbers. "As soon as Alfred gets back," he said, straining for a tone of authority, "have him track down this train. Find out if the cars are on a siding somewhere. The Home Office has been on my ass about this all morning long."

Bloomhardt took the paper from the Boss's trembling hand. "What's the problem?"

"They're lost!" the Boss cried. "We can't find them!"

"We lost an entire train?"

"Ninety-four cars of grade-one nut ore. Lost between Pittsburgh and here. Have Alfred call every agent at every station along the line. I want that train verified in our yard today."

"This could take forever," Bloomhardt mumbled.

"I need it by noon!"

Shaken by his own display of command, the Boss scurried back to his office. Bloomhardt looked at Smitty, who shrugged apologetically. "I suppose you're too busy to help?" Bloomhardt asked.

"Is the pope horny?"

"Damn that Goathead," said Bloomhardt, as he scanned the long list of lost cars. "We'll be all day trying to straighten out this mess."

"We ought to turn him in this time," said Smitty. "No more covering for him. Go ahead, Bloomie. Go tell the Boss."

"You think the Goathead knew about this lost train?"

"Knew about it? Christ, he's probably the one who lost the frigging train in the first place. He probably did it on purpose, for a joke!"

Bloomhardt and Smitty stared at one another across desks overflowing with unrecorded invoices, manifests never posted, unanswered inquiries, unnoticed notices, stale doughnuts, and spilled coffee. "Ah, what's the use?" Smitty moaned, and threw up his hands. "It's crazy, it makes no sense, we work, work, work and never get ahead! I swear, if I had Mickey's gun right now . . . ."

"With two bullets," said Bloomhardt. "Don't leave me out."

"Three bullets! Because the first one goes in the Goathead!" Smitty glanced around the room. "All right, you numbskulls, don't play coy. We're in a bind here, so everybody pitches in. Roomy, you fairy, grab a phone or you're gonna be wearing your nuts as earrings."

Bloomhardt tore the paper into three pieces and handed a list of numbers to Roomy and another to Smitty. Somehow, Petey found time to offer his assistance. Only Nelson refused to help.

"It's not my problem. I keep my nose clean."

"You keep your nose shoved up the Boss's crotch," Smitty corrected.

"Ahh, go jerk off."

"The only jerkoff around here is you," said Roomy.

"Who asked you, you faggot homosexual?"

Bloomhardt, Smitty, and Roomy all turned to Nelson and shouted in perfect unison, "Shut the fuck up!" Across the hall, the secretary clicked her tongue in disgust and recorded this exchange of obscenities in a leatherbound notebook she kept in her purse.

Nelson scowled and muttered for a while, then, as the other clerks busily made one telephone call after another in an attempt to locate the missing train. At five minutes before twelve, the Boss appeared in the doorway again, his face ashen. "Well?" he asked.

"Well," said Smitty, ready to throw in the towel and fink on the old man, "it's like this—"

Bloomhardt banged down his telephone receiver and interrupted, giving Smitty a wink. "Alfred said," he told the Boss, "that as far as he can determine, this train is fictitious. It doesn't exist."

"What does he mean, it doesn't exist?" the Boss yelped. "How can it not exist? And where is Alfred, anyway?"

"He had to go to the john again," said Bloomhardt. "But he asked me to tell you that these ninety-four cars were recorded as loaded in Pittsburgh, but instead of being loaded with grade-one nut ore, they were actually loaded with scrap and sent somewhere else. Michigan, he thinks. Which means that as far as we're concerned, the train doesn't exist. We can scratch it off the books."

Smitty, Roomy, and Petey, who were hearing this news for the first time and thought it an extemporization, looked admiringly at Bloomhardt. The Boss, less impressed, began to quiver.

"As far as we're concerned," he sputtered, "that train *has* to exist. I've already authorized over thirty thousand dollars in shipping charges, so we had damn well better have that commodity in the yard or somebody's feathers are going to get singed, and they aren't going to be mine, you can bet on that! So you go pull Alfred out of that bathroom and tell him to locate that train. I don't care if he has to walk to Pittsburgh and load every last car himself!" Shaking uncontrollably, eyes brimming with tears, the Boss turned and fled.

"Where in the world did you come up with a story like that?" Smitty asked Bloomhardt.

"It's no story, it's true. This is only a paper train."

"Kee-rist," said Smitty. "That Goathead has really put our asses in a sling this time. What the hell are we supposed to do now?"

Smitty, Roomy, Petey, and Bloomhardt stared hopelessly at one another.

"Screw you guys," said Nelson. Reaching into a desk drawer, he pulled out his lunch bag, stood up and headed for the door. "It ain't my problem. I'm going to lunch." The four others sat very still for a few moments, unspeaking, then they too grabbed their lunches and raced up the hall to the infirmary.

The infirmary was a cool oasis available to them only during the lunch hour, when the first-aid officer drove into town for a sandwich and a Moosehead beer. It was a room free of cigarette smoke, free of the scents of coffee and sweat and overheated machines. While still stumbling down the corridor, Smitty wolfed down two slices of cold pizza, then in the infirmary he flopped out on a cot and immediately fell asleep. The other clerks gathered their chairs around him and chewed their sandwiches in silence. Roomy, when he finished eating, put his feet up on the cot, leaned back in his chair, and closed his eyes. Nelson, always campaigning for a promotion, just happened to have a dozen extra chocolate-chip cookies, and left to share them with the engineers and the cost analyst. Petey stepped outside to stretch his legs and clear his lungs. Bloomhardt went to the window, put his hands to the glass, and stared at the sky. He remembered himself as a boy brimming with life and energy, full of enthusiasm, anxious for adulthood. He watched that boy playing baseball, discovering girls, running fast and loose with his youth while doing all those wonderful, innocent things he did not really believe he had ever done.

He was startled out of this trance by the scrape of a chair across the tile floor, and turned to see Roomy slouching back to the office. He glanced at his wristwatch: 12:58. "Nuts," said Bloomhardt. He went across the room and shook Smitty by the shoulder.

Blinking and groaning, Smitty sat up. "Christ, Bloomie, is it time already? I just now dozed off."

"Let's go," Bloomhardt told him. "We've still got to find that lost train or we'll be paying for it out of our own pockets."

Together they trudged down the hall, shoulders bumping as Smitty, still unsteady on his feet, lurched from side to side. "Boy, oh boy, I have got to clean up my act," he said. "If I don't lay off the women and booze, I'm gonna be dead within a year."

"I've heard that story before," Bloomhardt said.

"But this time I mean it, I swear to God."

They walked in silence for a few steps, then Smitty said, "By the way, Bloomie, you doing anything tomorrow? I got a couple of hot ones lined up. Thought maybe we could take them out to the lake and do a little pearl diving."

"It's not even June yet," Bloomhardt said. "The water will be like ice. Anyway, I can't. I work at Fenstermaker's tomorrow."

"Who said anything about getting in the water? But listen, since you have to work, I'll tell the girls to wait till Sunday. They won't cool off much by then."

"Thanks anyway, but I think I'll pass. I've been meaning to spend some time with my little boy. Maybe I can get him to like me a bit if we start doing things together."

"Don't count on it," Smitty said. "But hey, if you want him to like you, bring him along to meet the girls! It's about time you got him started on the important things in life."

Bloomhardt threw out an elbow and knocked Smitty against the wall. Smitty, after recovering his balance, hurried to goose Bloomhardt before he could sit down, but both men came to a sudden halt just inside the doorway. Seated at his desk was the Goathead. He looked up at them and grinned impishly, then turned his attention downward again to the fat Bermuda onion he was slicing into four thick wheels. He then placed the onion atop a slice of rye bread spread liberally with Limburger cheese, sprinkled it with salt and pepper, and pressed another slice of bread on top.

Roomy, standing with his arms crossed behind the old man, said to Bloomhardt, "He sneaked in while we were at lunch."

Bloomhardt said, "We're in a hell of a bind because of you."

The Goathead took a huge bite from his sandwich, then asked, eyes twinkling, mouth full, "What's the problem?"

Yanking a sheet of paper from beneath the Goathead's hand, Roomy then waved it in the air. "Here are those ninety-four cars we've been busting our guts trying to locate! Apparently there was some problem with routing, so our ore was loaded onto two different trains. These cars have been in our yard for three days, and this old Goat knew it all the time!"

"All you had to do was ask," the Goathead said.

Smitty yelped and dove into the room, grabbed the old man in a headlock, and beat him softly about the head and shoulders, the Goathead chuckling as he tried to stab Smitty in the groin with a letter opener. Roomy swept up the old man's pencils, broke them over his knee, then yanked out the calculator tape and sent it rolling across the floor. Bloomhardt, shaking his head, sighing, slumped into his own chair, exhausted.

His cheeks bulging with onion and bread, the Goathead cackled gleefully. Roomy snapped a last pencil in half, flung it at the old man's head, and retreated to his desk.

"He's drunk again," Smitty announced, worn out and breathless. "There's no use punching him if he can't even feel it."

"Don't think that sandwich covers up the booze on your breath," said Roomy. "It just makes you stink twice as bad. And someday your drinking is going to catch up with you."

"The sooner the better," said Smitty. "Ain't that right, Bloomie? Tell the old Goat what a disgusting lowlife he is."

"You're a disgusting lowlife," said Bloomhardt.

The Goathead howled with delight.

"Knock it off!" Nelson barked. "Why don't you clowns try doing some work for a change? Romper Room is over."

at one minute before five, Smitty sprang to his feet, stepped to the door, and began to blink the lights on and off. "Roll down your sleeves and pull up your pants!" he announced. "It's five o'clock on Friday and the drinks are on me!"

One by one the accounting clerks dropped their pencils and switched off their machines. They stood, stretched, yawned, and filed into the corridor. Smitty fell into step beside Bloomhardt as they headed for the exit.

"Bloomie, old pal. What about those two ladies I mentioned earlier? How's about if I call and have them meet us downtown?"

"No thanks, Smitty. I just want to go home and relax. Maybe I'll take Timmy out to a movie or something."

"Let him watch television, it's more educational. Come on, you can't afford to pass up action like this."

"Take Roomy, he'd love to go with you."

They had come outside now and were crossing the long yard to the parking lot. Smitty turned and looked critically at Roomy, who had been eavesdropping from two steps behind.

"Sure, I'll go," Roomy said, as he stepped up beside them. "My wife's in the hospital for some female thing, so I can stay out all night if I want to."

"I don't think so," Smitty told him. "These girls are too sassy and energetic for you. You'd only end up embarrassing yourself."

"Take Petey, then," Bloomhardt suggested. "He has more energy than the rest of us put together."

Petey, a few feet to Bloomhardt's left, merely smiled.

"Don't you have the milking to do tonight?" Smitty inquired. "Another forty acres to plow, something like that?"

"As a matter of fact, I do have plans for tonight."

"There, I knew it. Not that these girls wouldn't have flipped over you, Pete. You're a charming guy, but a bit too clean-cut for the likes of them. What these girls need is someone like me, someone with the proper balance of charm and corruption."

"Nelson has charm," Bloomhardt said.

"Eat a turd," Nelson answered, and broke away to head for his car. Petey and Roomy did the same, Petey smiling as Roomy muttered angrily under his breath.

Only the Goathead, who had been trailing a few yards behind, did not turn away, but continued to where Smitty and Bloomhardt stood at the edge of the parking lot. Grinning in anticipation, the old man cleared his throat.

"Here's your answer," said Bloomhardt as he threw an arm around the Goathead's small shoulders. "This man has more charm and corruption than he knows what to do with."

"You have got to be kidding," said Smitty.

The Goathead puffed out his chest. "What's the matter, ain't I good enough for your girls?"

"You ain't good enough for my cocker spaniel," Smitty said.

The Goathead's face flushed scarlet and his hands tightened into fists. He was the same height as Smitty, but Smitty was muscular where the old man had gone soft. Smitty laughed and punched him lightly on the arm. "Go on, you old fart. Go home and play with your belly button. That's about all the excitement a cadaver like you can stand."

The Goathead stared at him a few moments longer, then pivoted sharply and stomped to his car. He got in, slammed the door, and drove away, his tires squealing and throwing gravel.

"That was the right word, wasn't it, Bloomie?" Smitty asked. "Cadaver, that means like a corpse or something, don't it?"

"Right," said Bloomhardt. "But I don't think you should talk that way to him. He's got feelings too, you know."

"Him? His feelings have been pickled for the past forty years. He don't feel a thing."

"I still don't think you should talk to him like that. To Nelson maybe, but not to the old man."

"Ah, he knows I love him. Besides, Bloomie, I don't want nobody with me tonight but you. You're the one I can always count on. I mean, what am I supposed to do with two sex-starved girls on my hands?"

"You've got two hands, don't you?" Bloomhardt slapped him on the back. "Have a nice weekend, Smitty. Don't hurt yourself."

"What about the lake tomorrow? I'll have the girls pack a picnic lunch. We'll bring the wienies, they'll bring the buns."

"Can't," said Bloomhardt as he walked to his car. "Have to work."

"Sunday?"

"Family day."

"Since when?"

"Since this Sunday."

"I don't like it, Bloomie, you passing up a sure thing like this. I'm starting to worry about you!"

Bloomhardt waved goodbye and climbed into his car. As he drove away, up the long asphalt drive that joined the highway, he glanced into his rearview mirror and there saw Smitty kneeling in the middle of the road, hands clasped in prayer, still pleading with Bloomhardt to reconsider.

during the ride home, back through Erie to its suburbs on the other side, Bloomhardt felt himself shrinking, growing comfortably smaller. With each mile he shed more of the day, its frenzy, vulgarity, and tension. He felt, as he did at this time every Friday, that he was molting, leaving the old skin, thick and insensitive, behind, so that by the time he pulled into his drive, his need for toughness, for the relief of crude horseplay, had vanished. What he needed now was love and gentle laughter, human warmth, a few kind words.

Into his living room he walked, full of hope. On the floor in front of the television sat Timmy, watching the Three Stooges. Bloomhardt looked at the boy's small curved back, the spine and shoulder blades as sharp as thorns beneath his shirt, and immediately he felt himself stiffen, felt his viscera shiver. He was afraid of the boy, scared to death. What do you say to a son who does not like you?

"Hiya, sport," Bloomhardt ventured. Timmy pivoted from the waist and looked up at him, his face expressionless, his eyes going *blinkblinkblink* behind his glasses. Bloomhardt grinned, feeling stupid, and hurried into the kitchen.

Annie, standing at the sink, turned to meet him and, still with a wooden mixing spoon in her hand, slid her arms around him and kissed his cheek. "Another lousy week," Bloomhardt sighed. He felt the warmth of her body seeping into his as she rubbed a hand over his back in quick, soothing strokes.

"It's over now, though. You've got the whole weekend to relax."

"And then another lousy week after that."

"Try not to think too far ahead."

He kissed her neck. "Something smells good. What's for dinner?"

"Broiled chicken," she answered nervously. "Is that okay?"

"Great," he said, and pulled away from her to go to the sink, where he turned on the water and began to wash his hands.

"I made peas and sweet potatoes too," Annie said, still apprehensive. "And biscuits. And a marble cake for dessert. Will that be enough?"

"Plenty," he said. He let the water splash over his hands and wrists, he scooped it into his face. The tone of Annie's voice, so whining and small, irritated him, and he tried to wash that irritation away with a flood of tepid water.

"Or you can have ice cream instead of cake," she continued. "Or both. Whatever you want."

He turned the tap on full and held his face under it. Stop it, he thought. Just stop it right now or I swear I'll bite this sink in half.

Annie saw his shoulders tighten at the mention of ice cream and cake, and she tried quickly to think of another dessert. "Peaches!" she said. "We have those peaches I canned last summer. I could make a cobbler, would that be all right?"

Bloomhardt lifted his head out of the sink. Cold water dripped off his face, ran down the back of his neck. He stared at the faucet and felt an urge to rip the plumbing out with his bare hands.

"If there's something else you'd rather have, I'll run out to the store and get it," Annie said. "Just tell me what you want . . . so that I'll know. . . ." Her voice faded away in an uncertain whisper.

Bloomhardt put his hand on the shiny faucet, and squeezed. He squeezed until his knuckles ached, until he thought his veins would pop. He felt like Dr. Jekyll in transition to Mr. Hyde. "No chicken," he growled, amazed as always to hear this voice, which sounded so much like his own but was the voice of a stranger.

"But . . ." said Annie meekly.

"I don't want chicken, I want a steak. I want a steak and fried potatoes. And I don't want any dessert. None. Period."

Not moving, staring at his back, Annie said nothing. A part of her wanted to tell him that he would eat what she had cooked or nothing at all. Another part feared that if she did, he would never love her again.

Bloomhardt, clenching his teeth, felt fangs straining to burst through his gums, felt claws poking at his fingertips. But he hated this beast and was determined not to let it appear. He turned to his wife and, forcing a laugh, ready to tell her it was all just a joke, saw the tears glistening in her eyes, which so infuriated him that he was momentarily speechless.

"Is sirloin all right?" she asked, sniffing, as she turned to the refrigerator and pulled open the freezer compartment door.

Bloomhardt hated himself. No, hate was far too weak a word. "Annie, honey, wait a minute. Geez, baby, you didn't think I was serious, did you? Couldn't you tell I was only kidding?"

Still holding the door open, she looked at him shyly. A tear sparkled on the side of her nose. "Honest," he said, "I was teasing. Why do you take me so seriously all the time?"

She smiled and sniffed once more and then let the freezer door fall shut. Bloomhardt, too full of self-loathing to meet her gaze for long, grabbed a dish towel off the counter and dried his face and hands. Then he crossed to the threshold and, peering into the living room, called, "Let's go, sport. Time for another wonderful dinner!"

At the table, Timmy ate with his head lowered, but now and then sneaked a glance at his father by peering over the rims of his glasses. Bloomhardt had piled his own plate high with food, taking twice what he could comfortably eat so as to show Annie his appreciation for her efforts. He was no longer hungry and had to force each mouthful down. "Mmm-mmmm," he said. "Deeelicious!"

Between bites he peeked guiltily at his wife and son. Timmy, he knew, hated him. Annie didn't, but should. Why is my love so clumsy? he wondered. So dumb? He felt a huge constriction in the middle of his chest and knew that it had nothing to do with the food. Annie noticed that he had become motionless, was staring blankly at his fork, and asked, "More chicken, John?"

He looked up. "I'm sorry, did you say something?"

"Can I get you anything? More chicken? Dessert? Coffee?"

Bloomhardt regarded his plate, the mountains of food. Damn Annie for being so damn good to him. "More white meat," he heard himself say. He was possessed, no question about it.

Annie glanced at the untouched chicken breast still on his plate, but said nothing. She probed for more white meat on the platter. Finally, timidly, as if she had committed a grievous sin, she said, "There isn't any white meat left. I'm sorry."

Bloomhardt smiled to himself and felt a perverse chill of glee. Could Annie not see the burlesque of his demand? How far would he have to push her before she finally showed that she was human, before she flipped a spoonful of peas in his face or mashed a sweet potato on his head?

"You have some white meat," he told her, and nodded toward her plate. She looked down at the chicken breast, then, contritely, skewered it with a fork and passed it to him.

"That isn't enough," he said.

"But . . . a chicken only comes with two."

"Then you'd better start buying your chickens somewhere else."

"There's a wing and a drumstick left," she said.

"I want white meat," he told her. "You never make enough white meat. Sometimes I think you buy scrawny chickens on purpose, just so I won't get enough white meat. I think you must tell the butcher to give you the chicken with the smallest breasts, don't you?"

While saying this, Bloomhardt kept thinking, Any time, any time now. All he wanted from her was an indignant shout, maybe a projectile he would have to duck. But even the tiniest of gestures, a snarl, a muttered curse, would have sufficed. God, how he would adore her if only she would fight back!

"I'll make two chickens next time," she told him.

"Knowing you, they'll be all legs and necks."

Half-smiling, he thought, Come on, this is ridiculous, how absurd do I have to get? The butter dish was but a few inches from her hand, why didn't she ram it in his face? And she was clutching a knife, wasn't she? Would he blame her if she lunged forward to stick him in the throat? No, certainly not, he would sit still for it. He would get down on the floor and kiss her feet if only she would *do something*!

He watched one tear, then another, plop into her buttered peas. "I'm sorry," she said. "I can't do anything right."

"Aggghhhhh!" Bloomhardt screamed as he banged his fist onto the table. He stood, wiped his mouth, threw down the napkin, and stormed outside. Twenty seconds later the back door squeaked open again and, remorseful, full of self-loathing, he poked his head inside. "Uh, Timmy," he said smiling stupidly, sheepishly, "how about coming outside for a minute when you've finished eating? And Annie, sweetheart, by the way, I was just teasing about the chicken. Dinner was delicious, really. Fit for a king."

Idiot, he told himself, and ducked outside again.

On the steps of the back porch, Bloomhardt sat and stared at the sinking sun. From inside the house came the warm clink of silverware and dishes being loaded into the dishwasher, the inviting gurgle of the garbage disposal. From inside himself came the noise of his self-loathing, a steady *thhppthh-ppthhpp* as relentless as a sneering metronome.

Timmy came outside and, holding on to the doorknob, stood with his back against the door. Bloomhardt, sitting on the top porch step, looked at him over his shoulder. Be gentle, he cautioned himself. Be nice. "What took you so long?" he asked.

"I was helping with the dishes."

"Oh. Well . . . how about coming over here beside me for a minute?"

Timmy did not move. He looked at his father. He blinked.

"Come on over and sit down beside me," Bloomhardt said.

"I have a lot of homework to do."

"They don't give homework in first grade. Come on, come sit with me so that we can talk man to man." Bloomhardt smiled and patted the porch.

Timmy came forward three tiny steps, but stopped just out of reach of his father's hand. "I'm not going to do anything, Tim," Bloomhardt said. "I just want you to sit with me awhile. So that we can talk. Father to son."

Half a minute passed. Then, apprehensively, Timmy moved to the edge of the porch. As he bent his knees to sit, Bloomhardt's arm came out and swept up the boy's legs and pulled him off the porch. Bloomhardt sank to his knees on the ground and very gently rolled Timmy onto the grass, giving him a quick, furtive squeeze before releasing him. Timmy lay there in a compact ball, an armadillo that did not move and scarcely appeared to breathe, his face tucked into his thighs, arms clutching his knees.

"Loosen up," Bloomhardt said as he nudged the boy's shoulder. Timmy rocked back and forth on the curve of his spine. "Come on, loosen up," Bloomhardt said, nudging him again. "Get up and wrestle with me."

Timmy flopped onto his side, his back to his father. With his mouth turned toward the grass, he said, "I don't like wrestling."

"Why not, Tim? It's fun. And it's great exercise."

"I'll get hurt," Timmy said.

Bloomhardt felt a sharp stab of pain in his chest. "I wouldn't let that happen," he said.

"I always get hurt."

Another stab of pain, deeper and hotter. "I think you're exaggerating a little bit, Tim. You don't *always* get hurt. Anyway, you can't go through life rolled up in a ball like that. So get up and wrestle with me, okay? I won't even use my hands, I'll keep them behind my back. How's that sound?"

"You're bigger than me, it wouldn't be fair."

"Well, sure, I'm bigger than you, I'm your father. You wouldn't want your father to be a little shrimpy guy, would you? Like maybe twelve inches tall?"

"Six inches," said the boy.

Bloomhardt lay flat on the ground, out of breath. He rolled his head to the side and looked at the sun, which was now nearly set, halfway below a crimson-streaked horizon, sinking from blue sky into the deeper blue coolness of Lake Erie, eight miles away. He envied the sun's ability to do that, to disappear with a quiet, elegant flourish and then reappear reborn, brighter and stronger.

To Timmy he said, "Okay, we won't wrestle. But if you don't unroll soon, you're going to miss a beautiful sunset."

Timmy said nothing, still coiled in his armadillo ball.

"Boy, oh boy, that just might be the prettiest sunset I have ever seen."

A minute later, after no response from his son, Bloomhardt added, "Yes sir, this has got to be the sunset to beat all sunsets, if you ask me."

He watched carefully and a few moments later saw Timmy's intertwined fingers begin to slip apart, the knees opening to create a slender peephole.

"It looks to me," said Bloomhardt, "almost as if the sun were melting. Like it's a giant balloon filled with liquid gold, and the gold is leaking out and spreading across the sky."

Timmy's head rose by half an inch. Soon his black-rimmed eyes peeked out from beneath a thin arm. "The balloon would break," he said.

"You think it would?"

Timmy released his knees and, keeping his legs tucked, lifted his head by a few more inches. "The sun is burning hot. It's a burning star."

"That's right, son, it is. But how did you know that?"

"I learned it in astronomy class."

"You have astronomy class in first grade?"

Fearful that he had said or done something wrong, Timmy turned his head a few degrees and out of the corner of his eye regarded his father.

"Hey, that's great," Bloomhardt quickly told him. "Geez, I wish I had studied astronomy when I was in the first grade. The only thing I learned was the alphabet."

"I learned that when I was three," said the boy.

"I remember," Bloomhardt said. Slowly he rolled onto his side so that he faced the child's back, and even more slowly inched a hand toward him, but then stopped, a fingertip away from contact.

"It almost looks like the sun comes down and sits on the land," Timmy said. "Then the land gets hot and catches on fire."

Holding his breath, Bloomhardt eased his hand onto Timmy's shoulder. He felt the boy stiffen as if he might roll away, but kept the touch very light, his hand unmoving, and eventually Timmy relaxed. "The sun doesn't really touch the land anywhere," Bloomhardt told him, filled with love.

"I know. It's way out there in the sky. Ninety-three million miles away."

"Wow," said Bloomhardt. He moved his hand in a slow, weightless stroke up and down the boy's arm. He wanted to seize and embrace him, to wrap his arms and legs around him and press the boy to his chest. He wanted to kiss that small face, to taste his eyelashes and nose and mouth and neck and ears, something he had not done since Timmy was an infant and too young to see through his father. He wanted to blow trumpet noises on the child's belly and hear him squeal and laugh. He wanted to get to know this boy who was such a stranger to him, had always wanted to know him, but had somehow become unacquainted back when infancy gave way to childhood.

Bloomhardt longed to hug his son, but feared that Timmy would stiffen and repel him, so instead he gave the boy a playful shove and said, "Let's do something."

Timmy rolled away, out of range. Suspiciously he faced his father. "What?"

"Anything, it doesn't matter. What would you like to do?"

"We could go in the house with Mommy and read a book."

"Naw, I mean let's do something physical. A couple of he-men like us should do something athletic, don't you think? Besides, neither one of us gets enough exercise."

"We have exercise period at school," Timmy said.

"When I was your age, Tim, I never stopped moving. I was always running and jumping and playing and climbing trees."

"Mommy said not to climb trees."

"She just meant that you have to be careful whenever you do."

"She said not to climb them."

"Well, that's because she's a girl. She doesn't know the kinds of things that boys are supposed to do."

"She said not to."

"I *know*, Timmy, but she meant when you're alone. She didn't mean you couldn't climb one when I'm here to help."

"But I don't want to climb a tree."

"Sure you do. Every little boy loves to climb trees."

"Not me, I never climbed one. Mommy said not to."

"You don't mean that tree behind the garage, do you? You've climbed that one, haven't you? The one with your tire swing on it?"

"It's too big to climb."

"It only looks big because you never climbed it, Tim. Anyway, the bigger the better, right? So come on, let's go climb it."

Slowly, Timmy began to retract into his armadillo ball. "I don't know how," he said.

"Well, that's what I'm here for, Tim," said Bloomhardt as he slipped his hands beneath the boy and scooped him up. "I'm going to teach you how."

"I'll get hurt."

"How could you get hurt? Daddy's here, isn't he?"

"That's what I mean."

Bloomhardt tried to ignore the prick of pain that raced through his hands and into his knees. Carrying Timmy like an oversized infant, cradled in his arms, he went to the rear of the garage and stood beneath the giant black oak whose branches stretched thirty feet in all directions. On the bottommost branch, eight feet from the ground, a thick rope with a tire attached to it had been hung.

Bloomhardt, standing beside this swing, gazed up at the thick branch and asked, whispering so that his wife could not hear, "You've never shinnied up this rope and climbed into this beautiful tree, Tim?"

Clinging to his father's arm, peering up fearfully, the boy answered, "It's dark up there."

"It's not dark yet, son. It just looks dark from down here."

"Let's do it tomorrow."

"Okay, sure. But as long as we're here, how about a little test climb?"

"I don't have the right clothes on."

"Sure you do," said Bloomhardt. Then, as he hoisted the boy into the air, "Alley ooop!"

"Tomorrow," Timmy moaned.

"No time like the present, sport." Extending his arms high above his head, Bloomhardt bumped Timmy against the branch, the boy turned now so that he faced the ground, clinging desperately to his father's wrists and cringing each time his shoulder scraped the underside of the limb.

"Come on, Tim, grab the branch. I can't keep holding you up like this all night."

"Nobody asked you to."

"My arms are getting very tired, sport."

"Then put me down."

Bloomhardt settled on his heels for a moment, took a deep breath, then again went up on his toes, stretching harder than ever and finally maneuvering and pushing the boy until his left hip and shoulder rested obliquely along the top of the limb. "There, you're on it. Now grab hold."

Timmy, with eyes squeezed shut, sank his fingernails into his father's wrists.

"Now, Timmy, listen," said his father. "I want you to act like a big boy. I'm going to count to five and yank my hands away, so you had better be holding on to that branch."

"I won't," Timmy said.

"One."

"Don't."

"Two."

"Daddy, please."

"Three."

With his right hand Timmy snatched at the limb, at the same time wrapping his feet around his father's arms. "Don't let me fall," he pleaded.

"You're not going to fall, honey. Just hold on with your other hand too, and you'll be fine."

"I'm going to fall, don't let me fall."

"Four," said Bloomhardt.

"Don't let go of me!"

"Five."

With one quick jerk of his body, Timmy was astride the limb, hugging it with face, chest, stomach, hips, arms, legs, hands, and feet. "There," said Bloomhardt, looking up proudly. "That wasn't so hard, was it?"

"I'm going to fall," Timmy said.

"There's another branch right above your head, Tim. Reach up and grab it and let's see how high you can go."

"I'm going to fall out!"

"Shhh, not so loud, or Mommy might wonder what we're doing out here."

"I'm not allowed to climb trees, Daddy."

"Yes you are, I said you could. So just try to relax and enjoy it. Now tell the truth, don't you feel proud of yourself for having climbed this big old tree?"

"Yes. Now let me down."

"You can come down anytime you want."

"You have to help me."

"But if I help you, Tim, you won't learn to do it by yourself."

"That's okay."

"No it's not, Timothy. I'm very sorry, but it's not."

As Bloomhardt waited beneath his son, torn by conflicting desires to embolden and mollify him, Annie stepped out onto the back porch. Unable to see them behind the garage, she called out, "Timmy! Time to come in now!"

Bloomhardt shouted back at her, "We're playing hide and seek!"

"He should come in now," Annie said. "It's getting dark."

Bloomhardt ran to the corner of the garage and showed himself to his wife. "Go inside," he said, and motioned her away with his hands. "You'll give my position away."

She went inside the house but remained at the door, peering

out, while Bloomhardt raced back to the tree. "You must want me to fall out," the boy said when his father had returned.

"You don't really think I'd ask you to do something that could hurt you, do you, son?"

"You have before."

"Those were accidents," Bloomhardt said, but felt his resolve evaporating.

A minute later Annie called out again from the back door.

"Leave us alone!" Bloomhardt shouted. "We're catching fire-flies!"

"I'll catch fireflies with you," the boy said meekly after the screen door had clapped shut.

Bloomhardt sighed. "I'm really sorry, Tim, if this is scaring you. It hurts me to see you afraid like this."

"Then help me down."

"That's just it, I can't. I want you to grow up and be brave and strong and not afraid to try things on your own."

"Why do I have to do it all tonight?"

"Timmy, please. Can't you just trust me and do what I ask?"

"It's too dark to see anything."

"The rope is right beneath your chest, sport. Just slide your hands back and grab the rope and swing your legs off the branch. And don't be afraid, because it's not very far to the ground, it's only a couple of feet."

"It's taller than you are!"

"It just looks high from up there," Bloomhardt said. "Now come on, grab hold of the rope and swing down. I'll be here to catch you in case you fall."

"I thought you said I wasn't going to fall."

"You're not. There's no way you can. Because even if you accidentally lose your grip, I'll catch you."

"You'll drop me."

"I will not. Would I drop my one and only son?"

"Then stand right there and don't move."

"I'm not going anywhere," Bloomhardt said. He knew his son was going to do it now, and he felt a surge of love and pride for him. He'll be so proud of himself when he gets down, Bloomhardt thought. And maybe he'll trust me from now on and start to like me a little bit. I think maybe I finally did something right with him. Maybe I'm not such a terrible father after all.

"Good," Bloomhardt said as he watched the boy slide his hands along the bough to the knotted rope. "Very good. Now just slide off the side and swing your legs down."

"What if I'm not strong enough to hold on?"

"You're stronger than you think, sport. You're one of the toughest little guys I know."

"Don't let me fall."

"I've got my hands up already."

Very slowly the boy uncrossed his ankles, then began to ease his left foot higher, to scrape it delicately over the top of the branch. Just then, Annie came onto the porch again and called, "John! Honey, it's late! Timmy should come in now!"

Not wanting to rush the boy or be deprived of his triumphal landing, Bloomhardt sprinted to the corner of the garage and told his wife, "Damn it, Annie, go inside!" He had barely finished when he heard a shrill yelp, then a thud and a louder yelp, and racing back to the tree he found Timmy sprawled face up on the ground, the tire spinning above him.

"Are you all right, son?" Bloomhardt asked hoarsely as he knelt over him.

Timmy blinked. "I got down."

"Why didn't you wait for me?"

"I thought you were there. You said you wouldn't move."

"Ah, geez," said Bloomhardt. "I'm sorry, sweetheart. You didn't fall on your head, did you?"

"I hit it on the tire. But it didn't hurt much."

"What does hurt?"

"My leg."

"Right or left?"

"Both," said the boy.

Tenderly, Bloomhardt leaned over him, trying to see in the darkness as he gently examined the thin legs. Annie came up behind them and gasped when she was close enough to see them, her husband bent over their son. She knelt on the opposite side of Timmy and laid both hands on his cheeks, turning his face toward hers. Before she could ask anything, Bloomhardt answered, "He's okay, he just . . . tumbled off his swing."

"Tell mommy where it hurts," she said as she kissed the child's forehead.

"I'm okay," Timmy said.

"Heck, it would take more than a little tumble to hurt this guy," said Bloomhardt, too ashamed of himself to meet either the boy's or Annie's eyes, his heart thrashing in his chest, his face feeling as red and sore as a bruised tomato.

"Let's all go inside now," Annie said soothingly. "It's too dark for you to be playing out here."

"Sure," said Bloomhardt as he patted the boy's foot. "We were coming in anyway, weren't we, sport?"

Annie helped Timmy to stand, then led him away, limping, while Bloomhardt remained on his knees beneath the tree. He listened as the back door squeaked open and then fell shut. Suddenly angry, he grabbed the suspended tire with both hands and shoved it away from him as hard as he could. It swung out, the tire spinning, then shot past him again, so close that he felt the breeze of its movement on his face. On its return trip, it whacked him squarely across his back.

"Oooooopfff!" he said as he sprawled onto his face.

He lay with his cheek to the cool, footworn ground and felt the tire spinning and swinging above him. He wished it were a swinging broadax so that he could lift his head and slice his painful thoughts away.

joe Fenstermaker was a burly, amiable man in his late forties, a smiling, trusting man with thick fingers and strong arms, with clear, honest eyes, prominent ears, an aquiline nose, and a head as round and bald as a polished apple. On Saturdays he traded in his work overalls for a three-piece suit and made his rounds to various funeral directors throughout the city, courting the goodwill of those who could promote his product. On these same Saturdays, Bloomhardt worked as Joe Fenstermaker's salesman. In his own three-piece pinstripe suit, Bloomhardt would lounge about the office with Myrna, Joe's insatiable, black-haired secretary-wife. With his feet propped on the corner of her desk, he would flirt and sip coffee and inhale the dizzying redolence of her musk-scented perfume, while at the same time keeping an eye out for the occasional customer.

As soon as Joe had climbed into his car and driven away each Saturday morning, Myrna's campaign of seduction would begin. "Johnnie," she might say to Bloomhardt at the first opportunity, "would you mind filing these papers for me?"

"Sure thing," Bloomhardt would reply. But as he stood at the filing cabinet, his back to her, he would suddenly become aware of warm hands dipping into his trousers, long-nailed fingers kneading his buttocks.

"You've got the cutest little bum I've ever seen, Johnnie."

"Myrna, please, I'm a married man."

"And I'm a married woman. Let's have a honeymoon."

"Don't you ever feel guilty about this?"

"Guilt is for the Catholics, honey. I'm a Scientologist."

At 10:15, after waving goodbye to the first customer of the day,

Bloomhardt might turn back toward the office only to find Joe's wife blocking the doorway, her ample breasts leaving little clearance for him to squeeze through. "Come on in, Johnnie. What are you waiting for?"

"I'm waiting for you to stand aside and give me some room."

"Since when have you been afraid of touching me? They haven't bitten you yet, have they?"

"They haven't, but you have."

"You know, honey, I'm beginning to think you don't like me anymore."

"I like you very much, Myrna. In fact you're driving me crazy, standing there like that. But I'm trying to turn over a new leaf and you're not making it very easy."

"Maybe you just need some encouragement to make your new leaf sprout."

"Jesus, Myrna, don't touch me like that out here! Aren't you afraid that somebody might see us?"

"Then let's close up for lunch and go back to Joe's workshop."

"Honest to God, you are the horniest woman I have ever known. Doesn't Joe keep you satisfied?"

"Can you tell that I'm not wearing any panties today? I don't have a stitch on underneath this dress."

"And that's another thing, Myrna. Maybe you haven't noticed, but we have some male customers who keep coming back week after week just to get an eyeful of you in those low-cut dresses you wear. You keep this up and we're going to get raided."

"Then raid me now, honey, and beat the rush."

At eleven o'clock, Bloomhardt might step into the rest room for a moment of peace. But while standing before the toilet he would hear a key turning in the lock, and before he could yank up his zipper, Myrna would be upon him.

"For God's sake, Myrna, it's not even noon yet!"

"I can't help it, I skipped breakfast."

"Myrna, please. Think of my wife. Think of your husband."

"I'd rather think about this, honey. And, ooh, look, there's more to think about already."

"All right, all right! Put out the 'Closed for Lunch' sign and lock the door and I'll meet you in the back."

"I'm way ahead of you, Johnnie. It's all taken care of."

"And what if a customer comes?"

"Unless I come first, the hell with him."

Seldom was there a significant change to this routine. Myrna might play coy and keep her hands off Bloomhardt for an hour or even two, but this only served to arouse both of them more. Sometimes, Bloomhardt managed to delay the workshop rendezvous until the afternoon, and on rare occasions even succeeded in returning home with his virtue intact for that day. In most instances, however, the final outcome was as predictable as the sunrise. Nothing was new, only freshly perfumed.

Despite the ambivalence of excitement, fear, and guilt these liaisons aroused in him, Bloomhardt looked forward to Saturdays. He thought of them as a kind of joke he played on the rest of the week. He did little for his pay, and as a bonus was treated bountifully to the boss's wife. What made this even more of a joke was that Bloomhardt truly liked his boss. Though of plodding and limited intelligence, Joe Fenstermaker was a kind and generous and patient man. He often gave Bloomhardt sound and practical advice about such things as car engines, hot-water heaters, and customer relations. He never failed to praise Bloomhardt's potential as a salesman. So Bloomhardt could not help but feel an apostate's delight when he deliberately cheated Joe out of a sale, when he talked a customer into buying a cheaper tombstone, or when he overcharged and pocketed the difference.

This particular Saturday was nothing less than the zygotic twin of all Saturdays that had preceded it. In the morning an elderly couple arrived to browse among the display of marble and granite stones. Bloomhardt walked two steps ahead of them down the neat, narrow rows.

"As you can see, Mr. Fenstermaker is not only a craftsman, but an artist. Take a look at the bas-relief work on that one, for example. Impeccable."

"We're partial to pink marble," the old woman said. Her husband, feebler than she and hanging on her arm, licked his rubbery lips and nodded in agreement.

Bloomhardt smiled. "I knew the moment I saw you two that you were pink marble people. *Haut monde,* I said to myself. Only the best for these two."

The old woman blushed and hid her cheap plastic purse behind her back. "We had in mind a marble pedestal," she said. "With two angels. Holding a wreath between them."

"On their toes," said the old man.

"Pardon me?" said Bloomhardt.

"He means that the angels are standing on their toes," explained the wife.

"With a foot in the air," said the old man.

"Yes, each angel is standing on one foot, on his toes, with the other foot in the air."

"Like this," said the old man, and, to demonstrate, lifted his right foot off the ground. He immediately fell against his wife, who would have tumbled over had Bloomhardt not caught her by the arm.

"I understand," said Bloomhardt as he helped to put the old man upright. "You want the angels frozen in a kind of *jeté.*"

The old man smiled wistfully. "We were dancers once."

"And still amazingly nimble," said Bloomhardt.

"We would like the entire arrangement to be no less than five feet tall," said the woman.

Bloomhardt nodded as he contemplated his pitch. This was a lovely old couple, and he did not wish to cheat or offend them. Holding the woman by an elbow, he drew her, and consequently her husband, down a side aisle, out of view of the office window.

"I'm sure we could come up with an arrangement like that," he told them. "But I think I should warn you that it will be expensive—very, very expensive. And in my professional opinion, and please remember that I'm an expert in this area, I think the design you suggest would be, well, just a bit . . . déclassé."

The old woman raised her eyebrows and stared at him open-mouthed. Her husband tried to stammer, but only a thin thread of drool trickled out. Bloomhardt held the woman by her elbow and gently guided her down the aisle, gradually leading them back to their car parked at the curb.

"I hope I haven't offended you, but I want to be honest. I know why you think you want that particular design. You've been together a long time and you love each other dearly, and you want those marble angels to be a lasting testament to your love. It's a beautiful sentiment, really, a lovely idea, but when it's all said and done, how much solace will you derive from a five-thousand-dollar hunk of marble looming over your heads? Me, I'd be afraid it would come crashing down on top of me. And I don't have to tell you what the pigeons will do to it. And no one to shoo the pigeons away, because both of you will be sealed up in four-thousand-dollar caskets. You've already spent thirteen thousand dollars, and that doesn't even include the price of the plot. My point is, will you enjoy what you've done for each other? Will your beautiful gesture of love be appreciated by anyone?"

Near the sidewalk now, the old man had stopped moving and was staring at his feet. Bloomhardt took hold of his arm and, progressing a few inches at a time, steered him closer to the car.

"Now think about this," said Bloomhardt. "Think about what you could do right now with all that money. You could fly to Europe and visit all the great cathedrals and museums, you could watch ballet from Lisbon to Leningrad! You could establish an endowment, *in your names*, to help talented young dancers further their training. Now *that* would be a memorial to love, wouldn't it? A memorial to life instead of to death. And in the meantime you could order a lovely bronze plaque for yourselves. I mean, look at you, a dignified couple such as you are. Would you really want to erect an ostentatious display of pink marble as your final statement to the world?"

By now the old couple could only stand there, speechlessly gumming their words, eyes glazed. Bloomhardt went to the car, opened the door, and ushered the old man inside. As he buckled the seatbelt, he told them, "Don't make your decision today, take some time to think about it. You kids have still got a lot of life left in you, so go have some fun."

He closed the old man's door, then turned to the woman. With his arms around her shoulders, he escorted her to the driver's side. "Listen," he said softly, "don't start looking forward to death just yet. You two keep moving, okay? Keep dancing. Make death take you from behind." And with that he gave her a little pat on her fanny.

She said nothing as she slid in behind the wheel. Bloomhardt closed the door, stepped back to the curb, and smiled encouragingly. The old woman, still a bit dazed, started the engine. As the car began to pull away, her husband looked back at Bloomhardt and gave him a rubbery grin.

Bloomhardt felt very good about himself as he headed back to the office. He had cheated Joe out of a big sale, it was true, but on the other hand he felt that he had contributed a dash of zest to the old couple's lives. He was smiling when he threw open the office door and strolled inside, and so was taken by suprise when Myrna leapt out from behind the curtain, naked but for the tattered gray blanket she held around herself. She pounced upon Bloomhardt, encircled him in the blanket, and, with a desk stapler in her right hand, quickly stapled the ends of the blanket together, sealing him in her cocoon.

"Myrna," he groaned. "You don't play fair."

She giggled and, with with her free hand, locked the door. "If you don't like it, Johnnie, complain to the boss."

"Never mind," he said, and shuffled with her into the back room.

On Sunday morning, Bloomhardt mowed and raked the yard while his wife and son were at church. Timmy played alone in his room throughout most of the afternoon. Annie and Bloomhardt sat side by side on the sofa, his arm around her shoulders as they watched *The Mouse That Roared* on television. He felt inadequate in his love and undeserving of her loyalty, and he tried without success to take his own advice and not think about death, which for him was another Monday and just around the corner.

The evening dinner began quietly and too politely. Bloomhardt did not look at Timmy except when Timmy was not looking at him, for he could not help noticing the small blue bruise on the boy's forehead, evidence of the accident and of Bloomhardt's paternal ineptitude two nights earlier.

Annie asked Bloomhardt if the roast beef was tender enough, if there was too much salt in the gravy, if the potatoes needed extra butter. Bloomhardt, having already eaten his fill, heard himself asking for Annie's blueberry tart. She gave it to him gladly, which infuriated him. Timmy excused himself and went to his room. Annie apologized for making Bloomhardt angry, Bloomhardt resisted calling her a fool. She apologized for failing to bake an extra blueberry tart. He stood up and threw down his napkin. "Annie," he said, and then stopped. He squeezed shut his eyes and took three deep breaths. "Dinner was delicious," he told her, and left the room.

He turned on the television and lay on the sofa and listened to Annie cleaning up in the kitchen. Now and then he heard her sniff and knew that she was crying, blaming herself for being a poor wife. The television newsman said that a car bomb had blown up an

American embassy in the Middle East. There was rioting in Belfast, London, Chile, and South Africa. Several pounds of plutonium had disappeared from a nuclear power plant in Utah. A new strain of venereal disease, resistant to all known treatments, was rapidly migrating across the country.

Bloomhardt pushed his face into the sofa and pulled a pillow over his head. Another week ended, another week began. His heart felt as raw as a peeled onion.

It was a few minutes before ten, and the Goathead smelled like a distillery. He sucked his teeth and muttered to himself as he worked. Smitty paused to rub some focus back into his eyes, and Roomy took the opportunity to zing him with a paper clip.

"You walking abortion," said Smitty, and retaliated with a half-eaten doughnut.

The Goathead, wanting to get in on the fun, fired a paper wad at Roomy's bulbous nose. Nelson muttered, "What a bunch of morons," and picked a gob of wax from his ear. Petey leaned back in his chair and watched a barrage of unlikely projectiles zipping from desk to desk.

It was such a familiar routine that the day might have been the previous Monday, a morning last November, a day at the beginning of time. Mox nix, nothing ever changed. Bloomhardt went into the corridor and, leaning against the coffee cart, imagined that the intermingled din of office machines and horseplay was actually a million auger-nosed mites burrowing into his skull to copulate and procreate and fill his brain cavity with mucilaginous larvae. He rubbed his eyes, which seemed permanently inflamed. He stretched his jaw, which felt rusted in place.

Knowing what he would see but unable to resist a fleeting

tremor of hope, Bloomhardt glanced toward the men's room. There it was, the padlock on the door. He started for the ladies' room, but the receptionist saw him coming and scooted out of her glass cubicle and into the washroom ahead of him.

"Bitch," he muttered as he banged on the door with his fist. The receptionist, laughing softly from the other side, lit a cigarette.

Smitty had been watching from down the hall, and upon Bloomhardt's sullen return told him, "She does the same thing to me. You have to sneak up on her when she's busy with the switchboard."

"I have been here for three years," said Bloomhardt, "and I haven't once been able to empty my bladder in peace. Three years!"

Smitty chuckled. "Relax, Bloomie. Accept things as they are. The rest of us have."

"How can you accept something as silly as this? Right over there is a perfectly good rest room going to waste!"

"You keep agitating yourself like this and you're gonna have an accident right here in the hallway."

"I'll tell you what I'm going to do, Smitty. I'm going to talk to the Boss and demand that that lock be removed."

Smitty grinned. "You're pissing into the wind, Bloomie."

"It's better than not pissing at all," said Bloomhardt, as he went up the hall again. The door to the Boss's office was closed, so he rapped on it sharply. He heard the Boss inside, sinking down in his chair, trying to disappear behind a magazine. Bloomhardt knocked again, then turned the knob and pushed the door open a few inches. Peering through the crack, he saw the Boss peeking out from behind a copy of *Sports Illustrated*. Suddenly the Boss tossed down the magazine, snatched up the telephone, and began to mumble into it.

Bloomhardt pushed open the door. "Have a minute?" he asked.

"Well," said the Boss, looking nervous, "this is a very important call. Long distance. Person to person."

Bloomhardt knew there was no one on the line. "I don't mind

waiting," he said, and leaned against the door frame.

The Boss nodded, swallowed once, thought for a few seconds, then said into the telephone, "George, listen, something has come up, something important, employee relations, that sort of thing. I'll have to get back to you later." He slammed down the receiver, looked up at Bloomhardt, and smiled anxiously. "Come in," he said. "Sit down."

Bloomhardt knew better than to look for a chair. There was only one in the room, and the Boss was sitting in it. Bloomhardt walked to the front of the Boss's desk, put his hands on the edge of it, and leaned forward. The Boss leaned back.

"I was wondering," said Bloomhardt, "if there is any reason why we can't take the padlock off the men's room now."

The Boss's eyes grew large. He filled his cheeks with air, then exhaled in short, noisy puffs. "Well," he said. "Nobody can find the key. And believe me, we've looked. Everywhere."

"You could cut the lock off," Bloomhardt suggested.

The Boss pondered this for a moment. "Well, yes, yes, I suppose we could. But we would rather not ruin the lock, you see. I mean, why ruin the lock if we don't have to, right?"

"That lock can't be worth more than a couple of dollars. I would be happy to provide a replacement."

The Boss thought about this and nodded. Bloomhardt nodded in return. They nodded at each other for a full fifteen seconds. "So okay," said Bloomhardt. "I'll call out to the mill and have one of the welders come in with a cutting torch."

"Now, now wait a minute." said the Boss. "Let's not go off half-cocked on this. I don't think that's something we want to just jump right in and do, not at this point in time."

"How else would you suggest we get it off?" asked Bloomhardt.

"Well, let's just think for a minute. Let's just put our heads together on this and see what we can come up with."

Bloomhardt waited half a minute. "I can't think of anything else. Can you?"

"Well, yes," said the Boss. "Yes, I can. Have you considered using the ladies' room?"

"I've been using it for three years. On rare occasions."

"It's awfully nice in there," said the Boss. "They have vinyl benches and big mirrors and a little dispenser of perfumed soap. And cloth towels. Now that's something I would truly hate to have to give up."

"Me too, but the women won't let us use their rest room. They don't like us being in there. They run inside and lock the door whenever they see one of us coming."

"Oh, I don't think so," said the Boss. "Are you sure? That's never happened to me, and I use it all the time. Ten or twelve times a day, in fact."

"Nobody does it to you because you're the Boss."

The Boss smiled and nodded. It was nice to hear someone acknowledge his authority. "Have you thought of doing what you have to do in the morning?" he asked. "Before you leave home?"

"It's a long day," said Bloomhardt.

"Well, yes, I know it seems that way sometimes. But there's really nothing I can do about the length of the day. That's something for your union representative to bring up at the next contract negotiation."

"What I mean is, it's a long time to go without using the rest room. We drink a lot of coffee, and some of it, well . . . has to come back out."

"Too much coffee isn't good for you," the Boss said. As far as he was concerned, that said it all.

"This is terribly inconvenient for everybody," Bloomhardt said.

The Boss looked up. "Was there something else?"

"No, not something else, the same thing. Take the lock off the men's room door!"

Fidgeting uncomfortably, toying with a roll of breath mints, the Boss glanced about, searching for a diversion. He looked out the window, but there was no reason out there to change the subject.

He stared at the telephone, but it did not ring. He studied his watch; too early for lunch. Finally, trapped, he looked toward Bloomhardt again but kept his eyes darting from side to side, up and down.

"Well," said the Boss, "to be perfectly honest with you, Bloomhardt, to tell you the truth, with all due respect . . . I think that this is a very sensitive subject and one that should be discussed only in private."

Bloomhardt went to the door and pulled it shut, then came around the desk and faced the Boss again.

"Oh," said the Boss. "You want to talk about it now?"

"I think we should."

"Oh. Well, then, all right. Fine. But the thing is, Bloomhardt, just between you and me, I really don't think the time is right just yet, so soon, I mean so early, to have the lock, you know, removed."

"It's been three years," Bloomhardt said.

"I know it seems that way to you, yes. But you're a young man. It's different for the rest of us."

"I'm not sure I understand."

"You see, that's my point, exactly my point. How can you understand? Nobody expects you to. But if you did understand, you would see what I mean. I hope that helps to clear things up a bit."

"No sir, it doesn't."

"Because you don't understand, you see? That's my point. It was a tragedy, that's what I'm trying to get across to you. Something none of us here can forget."

"I don't want anybody to forget it, sir. I just want to use the bathroom."

"I'm sure that if I spoke to the women, if I asked them nicely, they would promise to let you men have your fair share of the ladies' room."

"They'll lie to you," Bloomhardt said.

"Well, yes," said the Boss, looking down, "yes, I suppose they might."

"So?" said Bloomhardt.

The Boss looked up. "So?"

"So we can have the padlock removed?"

"Well, no," said the Boss. "But I will speak to the women on your behalf."

Bloomhardt held his breath for ten seconds, then exhaled loudly. The Boss rolled his breath mints back and forth. Bloomhardt stared blankly at the edge of the desk. Very quietly, whispering, the Boss asked, "Bloomhardt?"

"Hmmm?"

"You're not afraid? Not at all?"

"I never knew him. We never met."

"You would have liked him. We all did."

"I'd like him better if he'd let me use the rest room."

"Well," said the Boss as he looked down again. "Yes. Certainly. Of course. I'll be sure to speak to the women about it."

That was the end of the conversation, and Bloomhardt knew it. The Boss was already reaching for a magazine. Bloomhardt, feeling beaten, stepped into the hallway. Huddled close to the Boss's door were Smitty, Roomy, and the Goathead, all of whom crowded around Bloomhardt, snickering, as he trudged back to the office.

"Get away from me," he told them. "If you're so interested in what went on, why weren't you in there with me?"

"Are you crazy?" Smitty asked. "We don't want to use the men's room."

"You never knew poor Mickey," said Roomy. "One of the sweetest guys in the world, and that's his crypt in there, his tomb."

"Yeah," said the Goathead. "So how would you like somebody taking a crap in your tomb?"

Just outside the accounting office, Smitty pulled Bloomhardt aside and let the other men pass. "You missed a fine time this weekend, Bloomie. I've half a mind not to tell you about it."

"Congratulations. Your brain power has increased a hundred percent." He tried to walk away but Smitty grabbed his arm.

"I had to take both of them on by myself!"

"Life can be so cruel sometimes, can't it, Smitty?"

"I swear, Bloomie, one peek at those girls and you'd be happy to die on the spot. And friendly? Cooperative? Even a guy with your imagination couldn't come up with fantasies enough to tire them out."

"Why do I get the feeling you're lying through your teeth again?"

"Because you always expect the worst of people, that's why. But listen, I told the girls all about you, about how you're a secret writer and all that. They're dying to meet you! I told them how you're always writing little notes and stuffing them in your pockets and how you're going to write a blockbuster someday, and how if they play their cards right and treat you extra nice you just might put them in your book."

"How did you know about the notes?"

"Hey, I got eyes, don't I? All you ever do anymore is stare out the window and scribble notes. I didn't want to say anything about it, Bloomie, but you've been doing so much daydreaming of late that we're all a month behind in our work."

Bloomhardt shook his head. "You're right, Smitty, and I'm sorry. I don't know what's wrong with me, but I can't seem to keep my mind on my work anymore. It just seems like life is passing me by all of a sudden, like it's a merry-go-round that's spinning too fast for me to jump on."

"That's why these girls are perfect for you, Bloomie! They make time stop, I swear. Besides that, they'll blow your socks off and make you see stars, and if that doesn't get your juices flowing, you're already dead. So how's Saturday night sound?"

"Thanks, Smitty, but I want to spend the weekend with my son."

"Hey, that's another thing. Why this sudden interest in being nominated for father of the year? Christ, give the kid a weekend off, he's probably sick of seeing you around all the time. Or am I wrong, Bloomie?"

Smiling crookedly, Bloomhardt shrugged.

"Yeah, that's what I thought. So give him a break and spend the weekend with me and my girls. Believe me, God will bless you if you do."

"I don't know," said Bloomhardt. "Maybe you're right."

"You're damn right I'm right." Smitty slapped him on the back. "Now let's try to get some work done before Nelson goes running to the Boss."

Bloomhardt had no desire to spend his weekend with a boozing satyr and his two nymphs, but neither did he want another weekend like the last. At his desk again, settled into his own Chair of Forgetfulness, he stared longingly out the window. If he were a successful writer, he might be deserving of Annie's admiration, and then would not have to think so poorly of her for thinking so highly of him. But he had never written more than fifty words at a time. He filled his pockets with impressions and observations and then emptied these fragments into a shoe box at home. Sometimes, late in the evening when his wife and son were in bed, he would sit in the living room and hold the shoe box on his lap, rubbing it like a magic lamp, waiting for the inspiration that would bring a masterwork gushing out. The inspiration never came.

So now he stared out the window at the ore piles. A headache beat like a jackhammer between his ears. His jaw was stiff from a morning of grinding his teeth, and his eyes burned from the smoke the Goathead and Smitty blew in his direction. His spine felt sore and out of whack, as twisted as a shillelagh. He wondered where his youth had gone. He thought fondly of his grave. The calculator clicked the only song it ever played: *nothing is new, nothing is new, nothing is new.* . . .

On Friday, Bloomhardt weaseled out of his date with Smitty and the two lascivious girls. Smitty ranted and swore, he stomped his feet and punched the air, but Bloomhardt knew that, come Monday, all would be forgiven, that Smitty would again tantalize him with the bawdy details of his debauchery.

On Saturday, Bloomhardt went to work at Fenstermaker's and fornicated with Fenstermaker's wife. At home in the late afternoon he mowed the yard and washed the car, took down the storm windows and put up the screens, cleaned out the garage and swept the basement and changed the filters in the furnace. And despised himself.

Early Sunday morning he crept up to Timmy's bed and shook the boy awake. "Rise and shine, Tim. Up and at 'em."

Timmy, blinking sleepily, squinted up at his father. Without the broad black frames of his glasses, the boy seemed more delicate and fragile than ever. "What's the matter?" he asked.

"Nothing's the matter, we're going to have some fun today, just you and me. We're going to the YMCA!"

Timmy, it seemed to Bloomhardt, sank down into his pillow.

Bloomhardt peeled the blanket away from his son. "Let's go, tiger," he said. The sight of the boy clothed in only his underwear, that narrow sunken chest, those skinny limbs, brought a lump to Bloomhardt's throat. His son was so small, so sleek, so creamy-skinned, as fragile as a newt. Bloomhardt longed to gather the boy in his arms, cuddle and stroke him. But he restrained himself. Restraint was the order of the day.

"I have to go to church with Mommy," said the boy as he sat up and reached for his glasses on the nightstand.

"You can miss church this time, Mommy said it's all right. So come on, hurry up and get dressed. Breakfast will be ready in two minutes. Pack your gym bag with your swim trunks, tennis shoes, shorts, and a sweatshirt. Boy, oh boy, are we going to have fun today!"

Timmy, blinking like an owl, stared at his father.

"Move it, move it, move it!" said Bloomhardt, and slapped him lightly on the thigh. Timmy scrambled off the bed and ran to the bathroom. On his way downstairs, Bloomhardt paused to listen outside the bathroom door. The sound of water tinkling in the toilet filled his heart with joy.

at breakfast he noticed something unusual about his wife; she fidgeted and picked at her food, she dropped her fork twice. Several times she opened her mouth as if to speak, but at the last moment turned away, silent. Bloomhardt nonchalantly buttered his toast and stirred ketchup into his scrambled eggs. Her uneasiness had not escaped him, but he was resolved to keep quiet about it. From this morning on, he was going to be a new Bloomhardt: patient and understanding, tolerant, nondemanding. He was not going to point out, for example, that the eggs were too dry, the toast too brown. He was not going to remind Timmy to pull his chair closer to the table. Bloomhardt was proud of himself. Henceforth, anyone who wished to hear him utter a critical word would have to beat it out of him.

"Tim and I will be gone for three or four hours," he said. "What do you plan to do after church?"

"Nothing special," said his wife. With her fork, she gave a sausage link a tour of her plate. "Maybe I'll clean the bathroom, or wax the kitchen floor."

"How about putting on a new roof and painting the house while you're at it?" he asked. She looked up, uncertain.

"Come on, smile, I was kidding. Why don't you go shopping or something? Buy yourself a new pair of shoes."

Surprised, she said, "We really can't afford them, can we?"

"If you want new shoes, buy them. In fact, buy yourself a new dress to match your new shoes. You deserve it."

Annie, like Timmy, blinked a half-dozen times. She knew that at any moment her husband was going to complain that the coffee was bitter, the orange juice sour. To test him, she said, "I was thinking about going out for an hour or so today."

"Good! You need to get out more often. You keep yourself cooped up in this house far too much, you know."

"It's just next door. To Helen's place."

Bloomhardt winced when he heard his neighbor's name. Helen Krakow was big-breasted and brassy, pushy and loud. The mere thought of her made his throat constrict, trapping a bite of toast, so that he had to fight to keep from gagging and then quickly washed the toast down with coffee. *Restraint,* he reminded himself, and, ten seconds later, forcing a smile, said, "That sounds nice."

"She, uh . . ." Annie mumbled, averting her eyes.

"She, uh?" said Bloomhardt.

"She's having some of her friends from class over. For brunch. And she wanted me to meet them."

"Good, good. What kind of class is it? Arts and crafts, that sort of thing?"

Annie shook her head, a quick, nervous shake.

"Is it painting? Pottery? Cake decorating? Quilting?"

Another no, her eyes riveted on her plate.

Bloomhardt turned to Timmy, who was watching carefully for warning signs of the old Bloomhardt's return. "It must be dog training," Bloomhardt said with a wink. The boy, expressionless, blinked in return.

"Either that or turtle breeding," Bloomhardt said. He arched his eyebrows and flicked an imaginary cigar. "Which is bound to be a shell of an experience." Was that a smile beginning on Timmy's mouth?

"Or perhaps it is the highly regarded Japanese art of bug squashing. Ahh so!" he said as he stomped a heel on the floor. Timmy's smile widened by a millimeter. Annie blushed and kept her head down.

"Or wiener rolling," said Bloomhardt. "Or olive stuffing. Which do you think it is, Tim?"

The boy, his mouth curving upward in a slight but bona fide smile, answered, "Maybe it's a class in banana peeling."

Bloomhardt howled. "That's it, that's it!" he cried as he seized his wife's hand and squeezed it. "Timmy's right, isn't he? Banana peeling, of course! Boy, oh boy, leave it up to Helen to think of something like that."

Annie gave no answer or any other indication of life for such a long time that gradually the smile faded from Timmy's lips. Bloomhardt leaned closer and tried to peer into her eyes, but she tucked her chin into her chest and shyly looked away.

"Hey," he said softly, giving her hand another squeeze, "we were just teasing, sweetheart."

"I know," she said.

"Then tell us what kind of class it is. We're interested."

"It's for women," she mumbled.

"Well, I'm relieved to hear that. I thought for a moment it was just for male sumo wrestlers." Again he winked at the boy; Timmy's mouth twitched.

"Is it something you'd rather not tell us?" Bloomhardt asked.

Annie shrugged, a tiny, meek gesture. Then, with a kind of oscillating movement, she drew herself up straight, pushing back her shoulders, lengthening her neck, lifting her chin into the air. She still could not bring herself to look at her husband, so she spoke to the refrigerator instead.

"It's a class in assertiveness training."

Timmy saw how his mother had steeled herself for this, saw too the surprised look that crossed his father's face. He saw his father draw slowly back and sit up straight. The boy did not know what assertiveness training was, but he knew that this was probably a good time to get out of firing range, and so he eased himself down in his chair until his eyes were level with his plate.

But Bloomhardt's response surprised even himself. "Well, gee. You know, that sounds like . . . like a darn good idea."

Annie looked at him out of the corner of her eye.

"No, really, I mean it, I think it's a good idea. I wouldn't want you turning into another Helen Krakow, of course, but haven't I always said you'd be better off with a little more backbone? Honestly, honey, I think it might do all of us a lot of good."

Annie was stunned breathless. Timmy blinked in double-time. And Bloomhardt actually seemed embarrassed by his admission. He had as much as told her that she had a right to disagree with him sometimes, that he was not a demigod but a fallible human. And that, he realized, was all he had ever really wanted, to have his fallibility acknowledged, so that he would not have to feel so guilty about being imperfect and would not have to act so beastly just to wrench that acknowledgment from her. Yes, life would be so much more enjoyable if Annie would recognize her husband for the shit he was. It would take a lot of pressure off him.

After a few moments he pushed back his chair and stood up. "Well, son, let's you and me hit the road." He went to Annie and, with his hands resting lightly on her shoulders, bent forward to kiss her cheek. "I love you," he whispered.

Annie, motionless but for the tears that began to well in her eyes, was incapable of reply.

Bloomhardt turned away quickly, grabbed his gym bag off the counter, and hurried out the door. He walked briskly so as to keep a step or two ahead of Timmy and have time to pull the tears from the corners of his own eyes, where they seemed to be stuck.

At the shallow end of the YMCA swimming pool, with blue water circling his hips, Bloomhardt anxiously waited for Timmy to jump in. The boy, his toes curled over the pool's edge, arms locked at his sides, shivered. His teeth chattered. Across the bridge of his nose was a tiny white bandage, and beneath the bandage a small cut, made when his glasses had snapped in half when struck by the basketball thrown too enthusiastically by his father thirty minutes earlier in the gymnasium upstairs. The glasses, patched with black electrical tape, now lay on the bench against the blue-tiled wall. Without his glasses the boy saw his father, only four feet away, as a faceless, fluid creature— half blurry man and half bottomless pool.

Bloomhardt moved forward a step and held out his hands. "Okay, sport, you don't have to jump in. Just let me hold you in the water and I'll teach you to dog-paddle."

As Bloomhardt came forward, Timmy backed up.

"Timothy, you stay right where you are. What's the sense in coming here if you won't even get wet?"

"I'll get wet in the shower," Timmy said.

"But that's not the same as swimming, is it?"

"I don't know how to swim."

"I *know*, and that's why we're here. But how can I teach you if you won't even get in the water?"

"You can just tell me."

"It doesn't work that way, Tim."

The boy shivered. He needed to urinate and wanted to squeeze his penis, but his father had already cautioned him that he should not do that in public. So he pushed his fingertips into his thin legs, squeezed his ankles together, and blinked.

"You won't be so cold if you get in the water, son."

"I'm not cold," said the boy, lips blue, teeth chattering.

Bloomhardt patted the water as he thought of what to say. "Timmy, listen. When Mommy and I go swimming in the lake this summer, don't you want to be able to go in with us?"

"The waves knock me down."

"Well, yeah, they did last year, but you're bigger now. Besides, it won't matter if you know how to swim."

Timmy ran his fingers over the goosebumps on his arms.

"You've been standing there for over twenty minutes now," said Bloomhardt. "Just look at everybody else, Tim. See how much fun they're all having?"

Timmy said nothing. He knew, without seeing, that everyone was watching him, whispering, sneering at his cowardice.

"Ah, geez," said Bloomhardt. He sloshed to the edge of the pool and climbed out. For a moment Timmy thought the ordeal was over, they would get dressed now and go home. But then Bloomhardt grabbed the boy from behind and lifted him off the tiles and held him suspended over the water. Timmy gasped and went stiff; he dangled like a wooden puppet from his father's hands. Three seconds later, Bloomhardt set the boy down again.

"I'm sorry, Tim," he said. "I shouldn't have done that and I hope it didn't scare you, but I'm getting kind of upset with you, son. I might understand if there were any chance of your getting hurt, but there isn't. None. And besides, swimming is one of the most important things a little boy can learn. Especially when he lives only a few miles from Lake Erie. Can't you see how important that is, Tim?"

The boy stared straight ahead, only now getting his breath back. No matter where he looked, he saw only a colored blur, a floating mist of unpleasant noises and odors, of air that grew more frigid by the minute.

"Tim, please," said Bloomhardt. "Sweetheart, don't be afraid." He reached out to touch his son between those tiny tight wings of his shoulder blades, to comfort and reassure him, but the touch of a cold fingertip against his spine startled the boy; he threw back his shoulders and arched his hips forward and began to fall, tumbling like a domino.

Timmy felt himself falling, but was too paralyzed to save himself. He did not throw out his arms to simulate a dive, but kept his hands locked against his thighs, even as the water smacked his stomach, hard and sharp and cold, and in the next instant slapped his face.

Almost immediately, Bloomhardt was in the pool and hauling the boy to the surface. "Timmy, open your eyes! Timmy look at me, are you all right, are you okay?"

Like a waking child, the boy opened his eyes and blinked three times. "Yes," he said.

With one arm, Bloomhardt held his son around the waist, his knee between the boy's legs, and with the other hand brushed back the wet hair and wiped the water from Timmy's face. "Why did you fall in like that?" he asked. "You're either supposed to jump in feet first or dive in with your hands in front of you."

"I think somebody pushed me," Timmy said.

It was such an innocent remark, said not as a condemnation or complaint, that Bloomhardt felt doubly deplorable. He wished the water would turn to concrete so that he could climb to the ten-meter platform, the highest, and, with hands clasped behind his back, dive off. Out of breath, suddenly weak, Bloomhardt said to his son, "Well, at least you got wet. So what now? Do you want me to teach you how to swim?"

"I want my glasses back," Timmy said.

Bloomhardt nodded. He carried the boy to the edge of the pool and lifted him out, then climbed out himself, retrieved the glasses, and, while Timmy waited, hugging himself and shivering, rubbed him dry with a towel. "Would you like to go to the video arcade for a while?" Bloomhardt asked. "Or maybe go get some ice cream or see a movie?"

Timmy said, "I want to go home."

Again Bloomhardt nodded. He wrapped the towel around the boy's shoulders. "Let's go," he said.

In the shower room, Bloomhardt positioned his son underneath the first shower jet, then he himself went to the sixth, afraid that if he stood too close he might accidentally bump into Timmy and cause him to slip and fall, or he might lose his grip on a bar of soap and squirt it into the boy's eye. He held his face up to the steaming spray, accepting the punishment of water that was too hot. A man like me should be born sterile, he thought. Better yet, a man like me should have a father who was born sterile.

Later, Bloomhardt turned to take the spray on the back of his neck, which was stiff with tension. The boy, he noticed, was staring intently at his father's crotch. Every few seconds he would wipe the moisture off his glasses with his fingertips. When he became aware that his father was now looking at him, Timmy turned away and walked back to the locker room.

Quickly, Bloomhardt lathered himself with soap, rinsed it off, shut off both showers, and followed his son. He rounded a row of lockers to find Timmy standing there beside the bench, still wet and naked, looking down at his stubby, hairless penis as he held it between a finger and thumb. Soon Timmy looked up, saw his father, released himself, and blinked. Bloomhardt came forward and handed a towel to him. "Better hurry and get dressed before you catch a chill," he said.

He was aware, though, that Timmy, while drying himself, kept sneaking glances in his direction, his gaze never higher than Bloomhardt's waist. Finally, Bloomhardt turned to him again. Were those tears sliding down Timmy's cheeks, or merely water dripping from his wet hair?

"Tim?" he asked. "You okay?"

The boy nodded and sniffed. A tear fell from his chin to the carpet.

"Hey," said Bloomhardt as he sat on the bench, then touched his son's elbow. "Honey, what's the matter? Do you still hurt somewhere from falling in the pool?"

Timmy sniffed again and shook his head no.

"Does your head hurt where the basketball hit it?"

No again.

"Then what is it, sport? Tell Daddy what's wrong."

"I can't do anything," the boy said. His shoulders had begun to tremble, so Bloomhardt wrapped the towel around them, and with his own towel dried the boy's hair.

"What do you mean, Tim?"

"I can't climb trees and I can't play basketball and I can't swim. And I don't . . . I don't have . . ."

"Whoa, wait a minute, sport. It's not your fault if you can't do those things, it's mine. You're just a little boy, honey, but I'm the father, I'm supposed to teach you. So I'm the one who's to blame here, not you. Geez, it's not your fault that your old man's such a flop."

"I don't think you're a flop," Timmy said.

Bloomhardt's heart did a happy somersault. "Well, gee, it makes me awfully glad to hear you say that, son. And I'm going to try extra hard not to be a flop anymore. It's just that I'm not always sure what's the right thing to do."

"Neither am I," said the boy.

"Then maybe we could teach each other, huh? You teach me the things you know, and I'll teach you what I know, okay?"

Timmy nodded and sniffed. "What about that?" he asked.

"What about what, honey?"

Shyly, the boy pointed at his father's naked groin. "I don't know how to do that either."

"What, my penis? I don't understand, Tim. You have to tell me what you mean."

"I don't know how to make it look like that. With hair. Nobody ever told me."

Bloomhardt gazed down at his son's stubby penis and bald scrotum and he, too, wanted to cry, "Ahh, Timmy," he said as he held the boy by his shoulders and pulled him closer. "Honey, you're not supposed to have hair there yet, you're just a little boy. When you get older you will but not for seven or eight years yet."

"Then will you show me how to do it?"

"I won't have to show you, son. When you're ready for it, it will grow all by itself. The same way the hair grows on your head. Heck, you'll even get some here," and he tickled him under the arms. "You might get some here too," and he squeezed the boy's tiny nipples. "Wherever you're supposed to get it, that's where it will grow."

"Won't I have to do anything to make it grow?"

"Nope. It'll grow just like a flower. You won't even have to water it."

Timmy, still holding his own penis between finger and thumb, looked at it a moment longer. Then he looked up at his father and smiled.

"Okay?" Bloomhardt asked.

Timmy nodded.

"Okay, sport. Let's get dressed and head for home."

"Or we could get some ice cream first," said the boy.

Bloomhardt felt so swollen with love and gratitude that he could not see straight. He leaned sideways and kissed his son's damp head. "Whatever you say, sport."

Choked with emotion, he faced his open locker again. He reached for a sock and pulled it on. He smiled to himself. For the first time in a long time, he felt like a father.

Those few moments of intimacy shared with his son in the YMCA locker room made the week that followed a wonderful week, made Bloomhardt feel like a puzzle man who, his pieces once scattered, was now made whole. As a result, even the days at Universal Steel were tolerable. He no longer felt boxed in by the anarchy of his office, but, like Petey, was amused by it, entertained. Several times that week, Smitty caught him smiling to himself and demanded to know what he had up his sleeve. Bloomhardt, in answer, would glance at Petey and wink, as if the two of them shared a secret.

At home Bloomhardt was, if not a model husband and father, at least an aspiring one. He lavished Annie with so many compliments that she lay awake at night worrying that he had a brain tumor. Each time his arms ached to roughhouse with the boy, to wrestle or tickle or twirl him in an airplane spin, Bloomhardt thought twice, three times, and, knowing his capacity for inflicting injury, settled for a game of Parcheesi instead, a shared bowl of popcorn, a gentle good-night hug. And as each day passed, he imagined he was seeing his family in a clearer light, that now in their eyes there was a sparkle of hope where only apprehension had been.

Then Saturday came. At breakfast he promised his wife and son a Chinese dinner and a movie that night, an evening on the town. Annie looked at him as if he were dying, making deathbed promises. To show how healthy he was, he beat his chest and did a Tarzan yell. Timmy actually giggled! Minutes later, as Bloomhardt headed out the door, he heard Timmy ask his mother, "Is something the matter with Daddy?"

"I don't know," Annie said. "But as long as it isn't fatal, I hope it lasts."

What Bloomhardt had was not fatal, not unless it was truly possible to die from happiness. He felt so good that he thought he might live forever. The morning was bright, the June air warm and clean, and Bloomhardt, humming as he drove, promised himself that nothing would ever go wrong again.

Myrna was frowning as Bloomhardt threw open the office door and stepped inside. He had already decided to waste no time in telling her that their affair was off, over, ended, kaput, and he hoped she was not going to be unpleasant about it. He also hoped she was not going to be too pleasant, for she was wearing a low-cut yellow summer dress, glossy red lipstick, and his favorite perfume.

"Ah, Myrna, my little morning glory. You're as lovely as—"

"Shhhh!" she told him, brow furrowed, a finger to her lips.

"Okay, I'm going to come right to the point. It's time that you and I had a—"

"Shhhh!" she interrupted again, rising halfway out of her chair. "Joe's still back there in the shop. He wants to see you."

There was something in Myrna's voice, something more than mere disappointment, that sent a chill up Bloomhardt's spine. "What's up?" he asked.

"All I know," she said, arching her painted eyebrows, "is that he said to send you in as soon as you got here."

Bloomhardt straightened his tie. "Fine," he said, feigning insouciance. "This will give me a chance to ask for a raise."

As he walked past her desk, Myrna oozed to the side and grabbed him around the waist. Pressing her breasts into his back, she dipped a hand down the front of his trousers. "I'm the one in charge of raises," she whispered hotly.

"Holy cow, Myrna! Joe could come walking out here any second!"

"I can't help it, I've been thinking about you all week. I want it so bad that I'm ready to erupt."

He pried her hand free and, pushing her away, said, "Not now!" When she came forward again, he put a hand against her forehead and held her at arm's length. "Myrna, geez, get control of yourself. This is crazy. It's dangerous!"

"That's why I like it so much. Wouldn't it be fun to do it now, right here against the wall, with him just a few feet away?" Giggling and panting, she grasped the edge of the filing cabinet for support, then lifted her left foot between his legs, hooked it behind his buttocks, and tried to pull him closer.

"We'll talk later," he said as he pushed her away, a bit too roughly.

"No talk," she answered, bouncing off the filing cabinet, then coming at him with both hands groping. "Action."

Making a crucifix with his fingers, he thrust his hands in front of her face, halting her momentarily as he, walking backwards, ducked into the short corridor that led to the workshop. Inside the shop, straddling a low bench as he leaned over a block of granite on which he had been carving an inscription, was Joe Fenstermaker. Instead of the three-piece suit he usually sported on Saturdays, this morning he was dressed in his work clothes, a grimy T-shirt, dusty, stained overalls and suspenders, and a pair of plastic goggles. He bent close to the tombstone and, waving an air hose back and forth, chased dust from the newly chiseled lettering.

Bloomhardt, standing two feet away, looked down at the broad, thick musculature of Joe's back and shoulders, his stout arms, bull neck, and tanned bald head glistening with perspiration, and he thought of Myrna bubbling and steaming in the front office, and he realized for the first time that he liked Joe more than he liked Joe's wife. If I wasn't such a coward, he told himself, I'd drop to my knees right here and now and confess and beg him to forgive me. Then he looked again at Joe's strong arms and thick powerful hands. Lucky for me I'm a coward, he thought.

Soon Joe leaned back to survey his work and saw Bloomhardt standing there, smiling sheepishly, looking for all the world like a little boy who knew he was about to be punished but hoped it would not hurt too much. Joe raised the air hose and gave him a squirt of warm, stale air in his face.

"What's up?" said Bloomhardt. "Did you forget it's Saturday today?"

Grinning, Joe asked, "What's so special about Saturday?"

"Oh, nothing, I guess," Bloomhardt answered, and tried not to look guilty of anything.

"What are you looking so nervous for?"

"I'm not nervous."

"You sure look it."

"Well, I'm not."

"I bet you think that as long as I'm not going out today, you can take the day off."

"Well, that thought had crossed my mind." In fact, it had not crossed his mind until that very moment, but it seemed a splendid idea. He could get clear of Myrna and her volcanic body and maybe treat his family to a picnic on Presque Isle.

"Forget it," said Joe. "I've got lots for you to do today."

"Oh?" said Bloomhardt. Why was Joe grinning at him like that?

"You know that overgrown cemetery out on Old Pike Road? It belongs to the Sisters of Mercy, and they've hired me to get it cleaned up again."

"Yeah?" said Bloomhardt, relieved.

"There's an acre or so at the far end where they want a little meditation retreat for themselves. You know, hedges and marble benches, seraphim on pedestals, that sort of thing. So I need you to go out there and clear away the scrub brush for me."

"Gee, I would really love to do that, Joe. But as you can see, I'm hardly dressed for physical labor."

Smiling, Joe got up and went across the room to a battered locker, from which he pulled a pair of oil-stained coveralls and work boots. "Uh-uh," said Bloomhardt, shaking his head. "I hired on as a salesman, Joe, not a Japanese gardener."

"Hey, I'm only thinking of you," Joe said as he returned to the bench. "I mean look at you, you're a young man and already you're getting flabby around the middle. And just look at the color of your skin. When was the last time you spent an hour in the sunshine?"

"So give me the day off and I'll spend it lying on the beach."

"Sure, you'll lie on the beach and drink beer and stuff yourself with junk food. Naw, what I have in mind will be so much better for you, John. Besides, you'll be doing God's work."

"What union does God belong to?"

"Okay," said Joe, laughing. "You're not obligated to do this, I know. I just thought you might like to use your muscles for a change. You sit in an office all week and never lift anything heavier than your dick, right? It's no wonder your hair's falling out."

"Look who's talking," said Bloomhardt, and wondered if Joe had been insinuating anything with that comment about his dick.

"Sure, and do you know why I lost my hair?"

"Termites?" Bloomhardt asked.

"It's because when I was your age I spent every day in an office too. No fresh air, no vitamin D, just smoke, coffee, and anxiety from morning to night. I had a heart attack when I was thirty-five, did I ever tell you that?"

"No, because you just now made it up."

"Ask Myrna," said Joe.

Reminded of her, Bloomhardt thought it might not be such a bad idea after all to be out of range of her perfume and passion. "I don't suppose you'll reconsider and just give me the day off?"

"Nope," said Joe. "If you don't want to work outside, that's up to you. You can stay here and push tombstones, same as always."

Bloomhardt considered this for a few seconds, then yanked the knot from his tie. "I'll probably get snakebitten," he said.

"Naw, God'll protect you. Hey, maybe I can get you an honorary membership in the Sisters of Mercy for this. How'd you like to be an honorary nun?"

Unbuttoning his shirt, Bloomhardt said, "How'd you like to kiss my honorary ass?"

Minutes later, dressed in baggy coveralls and heavy boots, Bloomhardt hung his pinstriped suit in the locker. Joe told him, "You'll thank me for this at the end of the day. You'll feel like a new man."

"Right. A new man dead from sunstroke and snakebite."

Joe chuckled. "The truck's all gassed up and ready to go, the equipment's in the toolbox, the keys are in the ignition."

"And all's right with the world," said Bloomhardt. "So listen, while I'm out there hacking my way through the jungle and getting a double hernia, what are you going to do—lounge around back here and fondle your air hose?"

"Oh, I don't know. Maybe I'll get my secretary back here and let her do the fondling. You think she'd go for it?" When he said this, Joe did not smile as broadly as Bloomhardt would have liked.

"Hey, don't ask me. I'm just an ignorant, underpaid peon."

Joe gave him a long, half-smiling look. He knows, thought Bloomhardt, and began to sweat inside his coveralls. Oh God, he knows. But no, he can't, he'd kill me if he knew.

"To tell the truth," said Joe, "as soon as I finish with this stone, I'm going to take another look at the books. Something is screwy somewhere."

"Oh?" asked Bloomhardt as perspiration trickled down his spine. He tried to lower the zipper on his coveralls, but it was jammed near the collar.

"What are you squirming around like that for?" Joe asked.

"The zipper's stuck."

"So leave it stuck awhile. You'll be wearing those things all day, you know."

"Jesus, I'm roasting to death. It's like a sauna in here."

"I thought it was nice and cool," said Joe. "I have the air conditioner set at sixty."

Bloomhardt wiped his forehead with the back of his hand. "Must be my imagination," he said.

"Must be," said Joe. "Now take a hike. And on your way out, tell Myrna where you're headed. She'll have to watch for customers till I finish up back here."

Bloomhardt nodded uncertainly and shuffled away. In the front office he told Myrna what her husband had said, while she, with a perfumed handkerchief, blotted the beads of perspiration on his face.

"At least it's not as bad as I thought," she answered. "I thought he was going to send you home for the day, and then we wouldn't be able to have our little party."

"Our little party is off anyway," he replied.

"No, it isn't, honey. I'll sneak out to the cemetery later and join you."

"Don't you dare! I think Joe is onto something."

Myrna giggled and pinched his hip. "Oh, he's too dumb."

"I mean it, Myrna, this is it for us. No more touchie-feelie, no more anything, not here or anywhere else. I'm trying, for once in my life, to be a good husband. So won't you please give me a break?"

Pouting, Myrna looked up at him with doleful eyes. "Oh, all right," she conceded.

"Thank you," said Bloomhardt, and turned to go out the door. He had his hand on the knob when Myrna seized him about the waist and bit his left buttock. He spun, sending her crashing against the wall, then yanked open the door and bolted outside. He was sweating again, but this time it was a cold sweat, a leg-stiffening, scrotum-shrinking sweat of fear, as he made his way to Joe's pickup truck, climbed in, and sped away. He was not absolutely certain, but believed with enough certainty to set his teeth chattering, that when he had spun to throw Myrna off, he had also glimpsed, in the open doorway of the corridor that led to the workshop, the fleeting glint of a shiny bald head as it ducked out of sight.

abandoned for fifteen years, the cemetery on Old Pike Road was little more than a deserted field of tall grass and scraggly bushes, goldenrod and milkweed, Indian tobacco, sumac, and low-crawling dewberry brambles. Here and there a time-beaten stone stuck up from the grass like an old tooth in a mouthful of hay. Other stones lay facedown, others leaned precariously forward or back, still others were broken in half or crumbling to dust. Bloomhardt walked through this graveyard with a sickle, moving slowly, occasionally beheading a weed. He was calmer now and no longer fearing for his life, and the seclusion of the cemetery, with its buzz and hum of insects and twitter of birds, soothed him even more.

He read the faded inscriptions on the stones and wondered abstractly about the individuals asleep beneath his feet, whether they were in any sense aware of him, whether they were at peace. A crow called from the distant woods, and another crow, nearer, answered. Gazing across the field, Bloomhardt admired the measureless blue depth of the sky and realized that this place was already perfectly suited for meditation. Why desecrate it with landscaping, with plaster saints and angels? Though he knew he would lose his job as a result, he decided not to cut another weed. In fact, he was going to lose his job anyway, one way or the other. If Joe did not fire him, he would be forced to quit; that was the only way to avoid Myrna and her incorrigible lust. For Bloomhardt knew that, no matter how noble his intentions, he was too weak to hold her off.

To get her out of his mind, he returned to the truck and tossed the sickle in the toolbox. In the truck's glove compartment he searched for a pencil and a sheet of paper, thinking he might compose a line or two of verse, an ode to Annie. Instead he found a dog-eared paperback of *The Adventures of Huckleberry Finn*. He was delighted by this discovery, as much by the book as by the knowledge that Joe Fenstermaker, who had never once alluded to any interest in literature, was a secret reader.

Book in hand, he headed for the shade of a young pin oak tree, and now more than ever regretted that he had cuckolded Joe. He wished there were a stream nearby so that he could wash the scent of Myrna's perfumed handkerchief off his face; every time he caught a whiff of the fragrance, his heart fluttered and his body twitched. He hated the lust that gnawed at him and wondered if there was any way, short of castration or lobotomy, to rid himself of it.

But no longer, thought Bloomhardt as he tramped down the tall grass and then sat against a headstone. As of this moment I begin anew. Later he would need to look for another second job, but for now he was going to celebrate his rebirth by enjoying his favorite passage from *Huck Finn*. He thumbed through the book to a section he knew well, a section that, when he had read it as a teenager, set him to dreaming of his own adventures. With the first few words, Bloomhardt was caught up again in the story. He could smell the thick fog and the dark night as Huck and Jim drifted downriver, one in a canoe and the other in a raft, whooping and hollering as the currents spun and carried them nearer, apart, closer, farther away. They could not see or locate one another because the fog dismantled their voices and sent them ricocheting into unknown places. And then, unexpectedly, the fog cleared and the two men came together. It was a beautiful, mystical passage, and Bloomhardt read it a second time. Only then did he realize that this was the story of his life, that his two selves had been disjoined, one black and one white, swirling through a fog of confusion. But now the fog had lifted and he was whole again—or perhaps for the first time ever.

He laid the book aside, stretched out on the ground, and stared at the sky through the interlocked branches of the pin oak. Yellow sunlight, broken by the gentle fluttering of new leaves, trickled over his face. Mox nix Universal Steel, he thought, where all is chaos and mayhem, every man for himself. He could tolerate it five days a week, he could rise above it. Mox nix Joe Fenstermaker, mox nix Myrna. Mox nix the warm scent of perfume he breathed and the throbbing erection it bred.

Comfortable in his baggy borrowed coveralls, stretched out on the roof of a friendly stranger, the tombstone as headboard, Bloomhardt closed his eyes and envisioned cool white fog on a river, a cool white perfumed fog. He eased himself into that fog and drifted slowly through it, gliding smoothly, floating down a river of quiet to a secluded island of sleep.

Waking with a start, Bloomhardt assumed that either he had slept all day or the bright sky had suddenly been blacked out, for he could see nothing and there was a great weight pressing upon his chest. He thought that perhaps the grave beneath him had collapsed, that he had fallen through and now supported half a ton of turf along the length of his body, its grassy matting tickling his face. But field grass, he soon realized, was seldom redolent of musk. Nor did mere dirt often press its wet mouth to yours, or squirm and moan and dig its hand between your legs.

"Holy fuck, Myrna," Bloomhardt mumbled as he pushed her black hair out of his eyes.

"Ooooh," she moaned, and ground her breasts against him, "that's it, honey, talk dirty. I love it."

"I'm not talking dirty, I'm asking a question! What in the world are you doing here?"

"Guess," she said before she flicked her tongue in his ear.

"Aghh, stop it, cut it out! And please get off me and let me breathe again."

She bit his neck, growling, then pushed herself up and sat across his hips.

"Good Lord, Myrna, you're naked!"

"Am I?" she asked innocently. "Oops!"

"Oops, my ass. You get up and get dressed. Or at least get off me so that I can get up and get the hell away from you. What if somebody comes along and sees us like this? What if Joe does?"

"He won't. He's still back at the office, trying to figure out why the books won't balance." She reached behind herself and grabbed a handful of Bloomhardt's thigh. "Besides, I told him that I was going to treat myself and go out for lunch. Yum yum yum."

"Myrna, please. You're making this very difficult for me."

"Yes, but am I making it hard?"

Bloomhardt groaned and fell back against the ground. This isn't fair, he told himself. I tried to resist, I really did. But a man would have to become a eunuch to survive something like this. And that, in my opinion, is asking a bit too much.

"Let's get these coveralls off you," Myrna said as she yanked at the zipper.

Weakly he told her, "I'm going to ask you one more time, Myrna. Please let me up."

"From the looks of things, honey, you're already up."

"For God's sake, Myrna."

"Johnnie, honey, relax. As soon as I get this damn zipper down . . . what is wrong with this thing? Anyway, I can't leave until I've had my lunch, remember? I'm just starting on the appetizer now, but before I go I plan to have everything. From soup," she said as she bounced atop his hips, "to nuts."

Bloomhardt sighed. "Myrna Fenstermaker, you are a very crude woman."

"Crude as in oil?" she asked.

"Exactly."

"Then hurry up and drill me, honey, 'cause I'm getting ready to gush."

Short of violently bucking her off, which he was in no mood to do, Bloomhardt had little alternative but to lie beneath her as she struggled with his zipper. "It won't budge," she told him. "Damn! I'll tear this thing out with my teeth if I have to."

"Try yanking it up and down," Bloomhardt suggested, now nearly as anxious as she.

"You do that, honey," she said gasping. "I've got another idea." She slid off Bloomhardt and, kneeling between his feet, slipped an arm up his trouser leg. He had managed to jerk the zipper up, closing it over his Adam's apple, but there it stuck and would not come down.

"Now I'm choking to death!" he cried.

Myrna pushed the cuff of his baggy trousers over his knee, hoping irrationally to uncover at least those few inches of flesh she sought so feverishly. She succeeded in getting a hand on only the head of his prick, but even then it lay pressed tightly against the inside of his thigh, pointed at his foot, pinned in place by the roll of his trouser leg. An unlikely position, no matter how she considered it. "Johnnie, do something!" she begged.

"I'm choking," he answered hoarsely. "How's that?"

Lunging forward, she bit into the cloth at the top of his inseam. Snarling, tossing her head back and forth, she attempted to chew a hole through the coveralls, but with little success.

"The toolbox!" Bloomhardt gasped. "Look in the toolbox in the truck! Get a screwdriver or something!"

In an instant, Myrna was on her feet and sprinting toward the truck. Three seconds later she returned with the sickle, its curved blade gleaming. She stood over Bloomhardt again, straddling him like a randy buxom Colossus of Rhodes, and as she lowered the sickle toward him she cautioned, "Lie still. This blade is sharp."

"Be careful, Myrna."

She slipped the tip of the blade into the fabric just below his crotch. "Be *damn* careful," he said.

As the pointed tip penetrated the cloth, Myrna jerked the blade forward, working the cool outside edge of the sickle over Bloomhardt's stomach and chest. With a delighted yelp she then tossed the tool aside, fell to her knees, and tore the coveralls open from hips to collar. Wriggling free, Bloomhardt shed the outfit as if it were a split cocoon. He pulled off his boots, a feat that took longer than necessary because of the way Myrna was pawing at him hungrily, then skinned off his underwear and kicked it into the weeds.

"How am I going to explain those coveralls to Joe?" he asked.

Myrna threw her arms around him and dragged him to the ground. "Just say that a bear attacked you."

"A horny bear," said Bloomhardt.

"Grrrrr," she snarled as she clawed his back.

Bloomhardt tried not to worry—about the ruined coveralls, about cuckolding Joe again so soon after promising himself he would not, about betraying Annie—but he was only partially successful, the pleasures of the flesh being strong but not strong enough to silence the guilt that incessantly clucked its tongue at him.

He would have felt even less amorous had he suspected the reasons for his sudden assignment to the cemetery: had he known, for example, that more than one customer had complained to Joe that on Saturdays the "Closed for Lunch" sign could be seen hanging from the office door at wildly inconsistent hours, sometimes as early as 10:00 A.M.; or that Joe had long been puzzled by Bloomhardt's sales record, with its erratic fluctuations; or that, on the previous Sunday, while sweeping beneath his workbench, Joe had discovered one of Myrna's hairpins; or that at that very moment, even as Myrna squirmed and moaned in utter disregard of the grass stains and stone bruises accumulating on her buttocks, Joe was creeping toward them with a murderous glint in his eyes.

Having abandoned his car a hundred yards down the lane, Joe had tiptoed to where the other two vehicles were parked suggestively close to one another. Finding no one in either vehicle, he had surveyed the top plane of grass for signs of movement below. It did not take him long to pinpoint their position, marked as it was by Myrna's occasional shriek. With every muscle tensed, he inched toward them, heavy beads of perspiration rolling down his forehead and stinging his eyes.

Bloomhardt heard a twig snap. He froze for a moment, then lifted his head. "Don't," Myrna groaned as she pulled on his shoulders, "don't stop yet."

"Shhhh, I think I hear something."

"It's just a rabbit. Come on, Johnnie, come on."

"Shhhh," he said again.

"It's *nothing.*"

"I hear something. I know I do."

"What you hear," said Joe Fenstermaker as he picked up the sickle, "is the sound of your pecker coming off."

By the time Joe finished this statement, Bloomhardt was already out of Myrna's leggy embrace, already on his feet and vaulting a tombstone. *Swssssh!* went the curved blade behind him, only inches from his tensed and tucked glutei maximi. Bloomhardt spotted a taller tombstone and frantically dove behind it.

"Now, Joe," he said as he and the other man circled the granite marker, "take it easy. This isn't what it seems."

"You weren't fucking my wife?" asked Joe.

"Well, gee, at first glance it might have looked that way . . . ."

Swssssh! went the scimitar in front of his nose, so close that Bloomhardt could smell the oiled metal. "And I suppose you haven't been fucking with the account books, either," said Joe. "You've been screwing me left and right, haven't you?"

Bloomhardt held out his hands in supplication. "Joe, it wasn't intentional. I guess I'm just not a very good bookkeeper."

"That's your job!"

"I'm incompetent! Is that my fault?"

Intent on pursuing Bloomhardt, Joe had stepped over his cringing wife without so much as a glance. Now, as he swung again at Bloomhardt's neck and instead sent chips of chalky granite flying, Myrna scrambled to her feet, scooped up her clothes, and ran to her car. Bloomhardt continued to work his way from one tombstone to another, never more than half a step ahead of Joe's whistling blade. He thought that if he could get close to the lane he would make a dash for the car when Myrna came speeding by, that she would stop long enough for him to dive inside. He knew that, as much as he meant to her, she would never leave him stranded there, naked and defenseless at the mercy of her frothing husband.

But she did. As the car approached, Bloomhardt ran toward it, leaping high over tombstones, dressed in nothing but his thin argyle socks. Myrna did not even slow down for him, but went roaring past with her foot jammed on the accelerator. She did, however, swerve at the last minute so as not to run him down, and left him standing in the middle of the lane, screaming and waving his arms, as the dust swirled around him.

"Heeheehee," Joe tittered, eight feet away. He held up the sickle and turned it so that the sun glinted off its blade. Thirty yards behind him were Bloomhardt's clothes and the pickup truck.

Bloomhardt chuckled nervously. "This is sort of a funny situation, isn't it, Joe?"

"Yep," said Joe as he came slowly forward. "And if you think that's funny, then think about this, think about life with just a stub for a pecker. That oughta really give you a laugh."

"Now, Joe," Bloomhardt began, but had to leap into the weeds again as Joe lunged at him. *Swsssh!* went the blade as it lopped off the goldenrod cluster. Bloomhardt put on a burst of speed and began zigzagging this way and that, bounding from one tombstone to another, with Joe close on his heels and grunting each time he swung the sickle. Bloomhardt tried to work his way back to the truck, but was always cut off and had to reverse direction. Thorny vines slashed at his legs, nettles and cockleburs stabbed his sticky groin. He ran through a stand of milkweed plants, and their pods exploded against his stomach and chest, smearing him with their viscous milk. He heard the sickle slicing off weeds, and imagined what it would do to his flapping, shrinking appendage. The horror of this thought gave him renewed strength, so that he turned and made a desperate dash for the woods three hundred yards away, where he hoped at least to find a sturdy branch with which to defend himself.

As the woods drew nearer and Bloomhardt pushed himself harder, his lungs burning, he suddenly realized that he could no longer hear Joe wheezing and swearing. He veered sharply to his right and, still running, glanced over his shoulder. Joe had stopped more than fifty yards back. He was bent double and gasping, but still furiously shaking the sickle. Bloomhardt stopped and faced him. Now he too was bent double, hands on his knees as he gulped huge swallows of air. His lungs and throat felt raw, and for a few moments he thought he might faint.

Half a minute later, Joe pushed himself erect. He stared at Bloomhardt for a while longer, as if trying to decide whether or not to continue the chase. Please, God, Bloomhardt prayed, I'm going to die anyway, so can't it please be with my body parts intact?

Finally, Joe turned and headed back to the vehicles. Bloomhardt looked to the sky. "Thank you. I won't forget this."

Wheezing and panting, Joe Fenstermaker returned to the circle of trampled grass beneath the oak tree. He gathered up the split coveralls and Bloomhardt's underwear and shoes. At the pickup truck he yanked the keys from the ignition, popped the hood, and pulled off the distributor cap. Every rag and shred of cloth, the tarp from the toolbox and even the rubber floor mats, anything Bloomhardt might conceivably use to cover his body, Joe removed. Carrying all this, he returned to his car. As he drove away, he honked the horn and waved.

From his chest down, Bloomhardt's body was a scarlet road map of scratches and minor punctures. Gingerly he plucked a thorn from his testicle, another from between his toes. He unwound a slender spiked vine from around his ankle. Beads of blood glistened like tiny rubies on his skin. He trembled, even though his body was shiny with perspiration. He realized how close he had come to death, to castration by a gardening implement, and he dropped to his knees, his legs suddenly too shaky to support him. But he also felt strangely alive and energized, somehow triumphant, a wildebeest that had wrenched itself free of the lion's jaws. Every naked, stinging pore seemed alert, quick with a fiery pride. Kneeling there in nothing but his torn socks, bleeding from a hundred small wounds, Bloomhardt could not help but smile.

Stepping lightly then, he picked his way back to the gravesite. There he sat on the trampled grass and plucked the nettles from his socks. But for the beaten-down weeds and the crisscrossing paths Bloomhardt had made as he ran, there were no indications of human life here, no sign of human failings and struggles. Even the copy of *Huck Finn* was gone. The paths through the weeds could just as easily have been made by animals, Bloomhardt told himself. And this bed of flattened grass by a family of nesting deer.

It pleased him that they had left nothing behind but animal signs, for that was exactly how he felt—wild, inspirited, a lively, quick-footed creature. He had no idea how he would get home again, how he would travel six miles in nothing but a pair of socks, socks now as flimsy as lace. He had no idea how he might explain his condition to Annie, or what additional recourse Joe Fenstermaker might seek. The only thing he knew was that all of this uncertainty was exhilarating. A part of his life, at least, had changed.

Something was new.

Until nightfall, Bloomhardt hid among the weeds and crumbling tombstones, by which time he could count a hundred insect bites along with his hundred other small wounds. It was nine o'clock before the darkness grew deep enough to conceal him and he felt it safe to emerge from the cemetery. Following the narrow macadam strip of Old Pike Road, he kept to the fields and wooded areas, scurrying from bush to tree to weed patch, bobbing and ducking like a furtive wood nymph. Whenever the headlights of a passing car swung toward him, he dove to the ground, always praying that he would not land upon a rabbit or snake or even a field mouse, in which case he fully expected to have a heart attack. The moon was full but the sky cloudy, and only occasionally did Bloomhardt find himself stranded in the open when the moon broke through the clouds, his body gleaming like an alabaster statue as he flattened himself in the grass.

After forty-five minutes of this, including frequent pauses to work yet another thorn from his flesh, Bloomhardt spotted the lights of a farmhouse. Thirty yards or so away from the house was the barn. He made his way toward it through what proved to be a cow pasture, a discovery his right foot made only seconds after he had crawled beneath a barbed-wire fence. He shook the cow dung, still warm and pungent, from his foot, then ran in a low crouch to the building. At the wide front entrance he lifted the heavy latch and slid open the door just enough that he could squeeze inside.

The barn was as dark as a cave, dry and warm, redolent of new hay. From high in the eaves and rafters came the soft coo of pigeons, the flutter of wings. From one floor below came the rustle of cows ruminating in their stalls. The barn was so well constructed that only slivers of gray light penetrated from the outside, and these were too high in the rafters to cast illumination where Bloomhardt stood. But in a matter of seconds his senses of hearing and smell became acute. He smelled machine oil and grease and knew that there was a tractor somewhere in the darkness, off to his right. That tiny pattering sound was a mouse scurrying across the floorboards. A squawk and flutter followed by a frantic beating of wings told him that two pigeons had mated.

It was all so pleasant that under other circumstances he might have climbed into the hayloft for the remainder of the night. But Annie had probably telephoned a dozen taverns and hospitals by now, and was probably sick with worry, so he continued to feel his way along the wall, searching for something with which to cover himself. The first object he encountered was a bridle dangling from a nail. He held the bridle to his waist, but no matter how he turned and twisted, it concealed nothing. Next he discovered a pitchfork, which he did not pause to try on. Next he found some empty feed sacks, which made his heart leap gratefully, for if he could find nothing else he would tear holes for his arms and legs and put on the sackcloth, a fitting outfit, he thought, for the return of a prodigal husband.

Next he found a coil of thick rope, then an aluminum lawn chair. And finally—ah yes! just the ticket!—a horsy-smelling raincoat made of a heavy rubberized material. Quickly Bloomhardt slipped it on and buttoned it. The coat hung to below his knees and felt as if it weighed twenty pounds. In one of the deep pockets he found a pair of rubber gloves, which he stretched on over his stinging feet.

Creeping back along the wall, he retraced his steps to the door, eager now to be outside and on his way home. In his haste he knocked the pitchfork off its hook. It clattered to the floor and clanged against some other metal object, a bucket perhaps, which immediately sent all the dozing pigeons into the air, their wings beating, it seemed to Bloomhardt, as loud as thunder.

Outside, a dog began to bark. Soon it was answered by another. Before long, the voices of four yelping dogs were raised in alarm. Running like a blind man, face to the wall, hands pounding the boards, Bloomhardt bolted for the door. Across the road then he sprinted, stepping high, the fingers of the rubber gloves slapping like swim fins until, as the porchlight snapped on at the farmhouse, he dove behind a curtain of alfalfa.

Crawling on his hands and knees, the stalks of grain lashing his ears, Bloomhardt kept moving. Since none of the yelping dogs was yet tearing chunks of meat from his flanks, Bloomhardt assumed that the beasts were chained or penned up, but it was not until several minutes after the barking had ceased that he allowed himself to pause, rise to his knees, and peek back toward the farmhouse. The porch light was out again, and all was quiet. From his kneeling position Bloomhardt offered up a short prayer of thanks to the patron saint of adulterers. He then stood and, still trembling, resumed the long trek home, his hands and knees black with damp earth, ears on fire, feet ensconced in rubber gloves and making sloshing, sucking noises with every step.

Two hours later he entered the town. He kept to the unlighted sidestreets and back alleys and tried to appear nonchalant. To make less noise, he peeled off the rubber gloves and walked in his bloody, perspiration-soaked socks. He was out for a bit of exercise, that was all—his evening constitutional. The sky was cloudy, so he wore a raincoat—who could find fault with that?

After a half hour more, he was creeping toward the side of his own house. Never before had the sight of that nine-room monster so delighted him. The front porch light illuminated a wide path through the yard, but on all other sides the house was dark. Whistling softly, Bloomhardt strolled onto the front porch and tested the door. As he had feared, it was locked; Annie would expect him to have his key. The back door was locked too. Should he ring the bell and wake his wife? "I was on my way home from work, Annie, when the strangest thing happened. My car stopped dead, right in the middle of the road, and when I got out to see what was wrong, I heard a whining noise in the sky and looked up and there was a spaceship hovering over me! And the next thing I knew . . ." No, not even Timmy would believe that one. Better to sneak in quietly, if he could, and face the music in the morning.

He stood in the shadows at the side of his house and peered up at the small bathroom window above the back porch. He knew from experience that Annie seldom remembered to lock that window before she went to bed, having opened it during her nightly shower so that the mirror would not fog. At least twice a week he had to reprimand her. "It's an open invitation to burglars!" he always said.

Now, feeling like a burglar himself, he prayed that the invitation was still open. Stepping onto the porch, he grasped the metal pole that braced the roof, then pulled himself up hand over hand until he could grab the edge of the roof and swing his legs up over the rain gutters. Then, on his hands and knees, he inched across the canted roof to the window.

The window was closed. "Nuts," he muttered. But had Annie remembered to lock it? He dug his fingernails into the wooden sash and yanked outward. The window opened easily. He giggled, pleased with his ingenuity and excited that his ordeal was about to end in triumph. In fact, he almost wished that it had been more of a challenge. He had barely had time to chase this thought from his mind when, just as he was preparing to crawl through the window, the porch light blinked on next door. He dropped to his stomach and flattened himself against the shingles. His neighbor, Helen Krakow, stepped out onto her porch. Wearing a bulky pink robe and fuzzy pink slippers, she clutched in her right hand a tennis racquet, her arm cocked menacingly, eyes alert for any sign of movement in the shadows.

I didn't make *that* much noise, Bloomhardt thought. She must have radar screens for ears.

She came to the edge of her porch and surveyed one side of her house, then moved cautiously to the other side. Bloomhardt held his breath. Through a bay window whose curtains were open he could see Helen's husband, Bud, dressed in striped pajamas and asleep in a recliner chair, the flickering light from the television dancing colorfully over his face.

"Bud!" Helen hissed through the screen door. "Bud, damn it, there's somebody out here!"

Bud Krakow grumbled and rolled his head to the side.

"Bud, up and get out here right now! And bring a flashlight!"

A few moments later he sat up and rubbed his eyes. "If there was anybody out there," he said over his shoulder, "one glimpse of you and he's in another state by now."

Bloomhardt stifled a giggle.

"Very funny, ha ha. But I know he's still here, damn it, because I can hear him breathing!"

I'm holding my breath! Bloomhardt thought, his lungs ready to burst.

"Damn you, Bud, act like a man for once in your life. Get out here and do something!"

Bloomhardt watched through the window as Bud wearily pushed himself up and disappeared into another room. A minute later he came out onto the porch. In his right hand he carried a twelve-gauge shotgun, in his left a bowling ball. He wore a saucepan on his head and had a fat cigar clenched in his mouth. A long-handled flashlight was stuck in the waistband of his pajamas.

"Is this manly enough for you, Helen?"

Bloomhardt felt a rush of fondness for his neighbor, a man he rarely spoke to and seldom saw except through the bay window.

"You're pathetic," Helen said.

"No, dear, I'm tired. And you're hearing things again."

"Like hell I am." She snatched the shotgun from his hand. "Turn on that flashlight and shine it around the yard."

He set the bowling ball on the porch, slipped the flashlight from his waistband, and flicked it on. "Don't shoot until you see the whites of their eyes," he said.

Bloomhardt tried to make himself flatter against the roof. His armpit itched fiercely and there was something tickling his nose, but he was afraid to move as he watched Bud playing the flashlight beam across the Krakows' yard.

"I know this is a major disappointment," said Bud, "but there simply aren't any perverts out here, Helen. Just our luck to live in a pervert-free neighborhood."

"Shine it in Annie's yard," said Helen as she stepped down off the porch. "I think I hear something over there."

She hears my skin itching! Bloomhardt thought. He could stand it no longer; he rubbed his nose on a shingle and slid a hand into his armpit.

"There, there it is again! Don't tell me you didn't hear that."

"All I hear is my pillow whispering my name," said Bud.

"Shine the light up the side of Annie's house."

"So that's who's out there, eh? The Human Fly?"

Helen grabbed her husband's wrist, pulled him down off the porch, and directed the flashlight beam to Bloomhardt's porch, then up one of the support pillars, then onto the roof. A second after the light fell upon him, Bloomhardt heard the horrifying click of the shotgun's safety being released.

"Don't shoot, don't shoot!" he whispered hoarsely as he rose to his knees and threw his hands into the air. "It's just me, just your friendly next-door neighbor!"

Bud Krakow held the light in Bloomhardt's face and followed his wife as she moved closer to Bloomhardt's house, the shotgun still trained on his chest. "It's just Bloomhardt," Bud said. "How you doin', Bloomhardt?"

"Good, Bud, good. And how's everything with you?"

"Oh, comme ci, comme ça. You know how it is."

"Yeah," said Bloomhardt, "I know."

"What are you doing up there?" asked Helen.

"Well . . . I, uh . . ."

"She was hoping you were a pervert," said Bud.

"Sorry, I'm not."

"That's okay, it's not your fault," Bud told him. "And don't worry, one'll come along sooner or later. Helen can wait, can't you, dear?"

"Why don't you shut up and go to bed?" she answered.

"A lovely idea," said Bud. "John, it's been nice chatting with you like this. We'll have to do it more often. My roof next time?"

"I'll be looking forward to it," Bloomhardt said.

Nodding and smiling, Bud Krakow turned away. Helen grabbed the flashlight from him and pointed it at Bloomhardt, who, still kneeling, now lowered his hands to shield the light from his eyes. Bud retrieved his bowling ball and went back inside the house.

"I'm waiting for an answer to my question," Helen said. "Just what are you doing up there?"

"Something you could never be accused of," Bloomhardt told her. "I'm minding my own business."

"Monkey business, if you ask me."

"If you must know," he said as he crawled to the edge of the roof, "I'm cleaning out the rain gutters." He dipped a hand into the gutter, pulled out a fistful of soggy leaves, and threw them to the ground.

"At midnight?"

"Why not? I'm no slave to time."

She moved a few steps closer and shined the light up and down his body. "In a raincoat? With nothing, it seems, underneath?"

"This is dirty work, Helen. Leaves are dirty, you know. Dirty and wet and slimy. See for yourself." He dug out another handful and flung it down at her.

Helen stepped out of the way. "Don't think for one second that I believe you, because I don't. I think you've been up to no good again."

Bloomhardt picked the sticky pieces of leaf off his hand.

"Helen," he said, "I just had a brilliant idea."

"I doubt that."

"No, really, I did. And my idea is this. Why don't you go bother somebody who actually cares what you think?"

"Like Annie, you mean?"

"My wife is getting her beauty sleep right now. Something you've obviously missed a good deal of."

"Then maybe I'll have a little talk with her in the morning."

"Gee, sounds like fun. You bring the doughnuts, okay?"

"You won't think this is so funny in the morning."

"Well, until then," he said as he stood up. "As always, Helen, you've been a scintillating conversationalist. Tragically, though, our time together has come to an end. Toodle-oo, toots." He went to the bathroom window and started to climb through it headfirst.

"Why not use the door like any normal man would?" she asked.

He paused to look at her over his shoulder, the flashlight still bathing him in its gauzy light. "Because then," he told her in a half-whisper, "I would be deprived of the pleasure of doing this," and he flicked up the tail of his raincoat as he crawled through the window.

She did not flinch or gasp or extinguish the light when presented with this full view of his naked buttocks, but merely scoffed, as he twisted and squirmed through the narrow opening, scraping skin from his thighs. "Just as I always suspected—you're half-assed."

Bloomhardt snorted, but said nothing more. Stretched horizontally, his hands in the lavatory basin, he slowly drew in his knees to rest one foot and then both upon the windowsill. Shifting his weight onto his hands, he sucked in his stomach and gingerly lowered his right foot toward the floor. And directly into the turquoise water of the toilet bowl.

bloomhardt stuffed his raincoat, rubber gloves, and torn socks in the clothes hamper, where he could retrieve them in the morning for secret disposal. He was amazed that the house was still so quiet, Annie and Timmy still asleep. After a quick shower to rinse away the multitude of odors he had acquired, he daubed iodine on his wounds and salve on his insect bites, all the while searching his mind for a convincing alibi, but with little success. Even so, he told himself as he wrapped a towel around his waist and flicked out the bathroom light, a lame excuse is better than none, and he settled on the least ridiculous explanation he could think of, that he had been mugged, knocked unconscious, and stripped and rolled into the bushes, and he had only recently recovered consciousness.

On sore and tender tiptoe he made his way down the hall. In the first bedroom on his left, its door ajar, Timmy lay sleeping. In the dim glow of the night-light the boy's face looked so peaceful, so innocent, that Bloomhardt had to fight down the urge to creep inside and lay a kiss upon his cheek. Instead he sent him a silent one from the doorway, then progressed down the hall. With every squeak of the floorboards, he winced. He felt like the sneaking pervert Helen had hoped he was. This house is too damn big, he told himself. The room at the end of the hall seemed a mile away.

On the threshold of his bedroom he paused. He thought he could hear Annie's soft breathing, but his heart was pounding so violently that he could not be sure. His goal was to steal into bed without disturbing her, so that in the morning, when she awoke snuggled in his arms, she might be more amenable to his lamebrain explanation.

He tiptoed to his dresser, eased open the top drawer, and rummaged inside until he was able to identify by touch a pajama top and bottom. If they were not a matched set, too bad, but color coordination was not his primary concern at that moment. He unwound the towel from his waist and let it slide to the floor. As he lifted a foot to pull on his pajama trousers, Annie sat up in bed and switched on the light.

"Geez!" Bloomhardt said when he had come back down from his

startled leap. "Christ, Annie, you almost gave me a cardiac."

She said nothing. Sitting against the headboard, still wearing her glasses, eyes red and puffy, she brought her gaze down slowly from Bloomhardt's face, over his chest and stomach to the streaks of iodine painted on his legs and toes, his pubic hair stained orange with it.

Softly, guiltily, foolishly, he laughed. "You're not going to believe what happened to me tonight, sweetheart." He pulled on the pajama bottoms, then went to the bed and crawled in beside her. She stared straight ahead for a few moments, then eased onto her back and rolled away.

Should I try to explain myself now, he wondered, or let it pass until morning? Let it pass, let it pass, he told himself. Looking at the back of her head, he felt very small, deplorable. What he really wanted was to lean over and kiss her shoulder, to blurt out his sins and purge himself through confession, to beg her forgiveness. Why did he continually hurt this woman whom he loved so much that each time he looked at her, his heart clenched? Because you're defective, he told himself. You've got the soul of a bacterium, the character strength of mold.

But no more, he vowed. Never again. If I make it out of this one alive, I will be the consummate husband from now on, the ideal father. I'll be her goddamn slave, that's what.

Pleased with his good intentions, he leaned over her and reached for the light switch. As he did so, he happened to glance across the room. There, on a wire hanger dangling from the knob of the closet door, was his pinstriped suit. Bloomhardt, his hand still reaching for the light, felt his testicles shrivel.

Annie remained with her face buried in the pillow. Another sixty seconds passed before Bloomhardt finally switched off the light and lay down. He stared at the ceiling, seeing nothing. After what seemed to him a very long time, Annie took off her glasses and laid them on the night table. She, too, then stared blankly at the ceiling. His body as stiff as a plank, stinging from a hundred small wounds and itching from a hundred more, he tolerated the quiet as long as he could.

"Well?" he whispered, his voice hoarse.

There were ten seconds of breathless silence. Then Annie pulled the covers over her head.

In the morning he hid in bed and feigned sleep, his head wrapped in a pillow. Now and then he peeked out at Annie, who, getting ready for church, sat at her vanity table, wearing only a white satiny slip as she tried to mask with makeup the dark circles under her eyes. The sight of her half-naked back and arms, the sheen of the slip as it curved around her hips, the delicate scent of her perfume, all made Bloomhardt want her there beside him. Had he not been still rigid with suspense, he might have sprung from beneath the covers to drag her back to bed, but for now he could only lie there cowed, wanting her, wondering, both relieved and fearful of the worst when finally, without a word, she left the room.

An hour later he sat alone at the kitchen table and drank the coffee Annie had left for him. It angered Bloomhardt that she had been so considerate as to make him a fresh pot; the least she could have done was to spike it with a dash of arsenic. Wasn't she going to do *anything* about last night? Did she intend to close her eyes and cover her head forever?

She knew all the details of his infidelity, he was certain. Joe Fenstermaker would not have bothered to return Bloomhardt's suit but for the opportunity of filling Annie in on the rest of the story. No doubt he had painted for her a colorful portrait of her husband running naked into the bushes while squealing like a rabbit. Yes, Annie knew everything, she knew more than the truth; of that Bloomhardt had no doubt.

What troubled him most, however, was her response to the incident. At the very least, she might have wailed and torn at her hair and heaved his suitcase into the yard. It was what any good wife would do. He deserved it, didn't he? Yes, he deserved to be tarred and feathered, circumcised without benefit of anesthesia.

Bloomhardt expected to be made to suffer, he wanted it, he demanded it! She had no right to be so inconsiderate of his needs. He was a whoring, lying bastard and he was entitled to be treated like one.

Bloomhardt sipped his coffee. Maybe, after Annie returned from church to denounce and reprove him, after he admitted his worthlessness and successfully begged for one last chance, maybe he would cleanse himself with a long hike in the sunshine today— down to Fenstermaker's to retrieve his car before that duplicitous fink could have it impounded. Or maybe he would haul his old ten-speed racer out of the basement. A little tightening of the spokes, a bit of grease on the sprockets, and off he would go on a fifty-mile ride to sweat the gunk and guilt out of his pores. Too bad his bike had no rumble seat, or he would take Timmy along. Too bad there was no second bike so that Annie could join him, a family outing. Too bad this, too bad that. Mox nix, it was a sunny day, ripe with the tease of summer, and starting today, after the necessary catharsis of tears and recriminations, he would be on a solider footing with his family, it would be a new beginning. It was what he had yearned for all along. All he had ever needed was the chance to repent.

Down in the musty basement, he dragged his bicycle out from behind a tower of rotting cardboard boxes. He dusted off the frame and seat and then hauled the bike to the front yard, where he flipped it upside down. He oiled the chain and greased the sprockets, tightened the brake cables, checked the pads for wear. With his old hand pump he inflated the tires until they felt as hard as stone, then adjusted the derailleur and listened with pleasure as the gears clicked crisply into place.

Working on his bike made Bloomhardt feel like a kid again, clean and innocent. On this same vehicle he had pedaled his way through college, commuting from his parents' home to the campus, by bicycle on dry days and by car on wet, though it was the two-wheeled journeys he remembered most: spring mornings when he rode through a veil of fog; autumn days when gold and scarlet leaves crackled under his wheels; moonlit summer nights when he sailed home on a liquid machine, his heart buoyant with love, his stomach heavy with beer.

Remembering these gentler times, days and nights whose edges had been smoothed away from frequent tumbling through his thoughts, he was abruptly startled back to the present by the sound of his name, which seemed to come crashing toward him from half a block away. "Bloomie!" Smitty yelled, waving, as he broke into a trot. "Bloomie, my pal, my buddy, my friend!"

So vivid and comic was Smitty's appearance that Bloomhardt wondered for a moment if he were watching a cartoon come to life. Grinning broadly as he ran, arms pumping, Smitty was a flat-footed splash of unnatural colors. His cutoff denim shorts, frayed just above the knees, were of faded orange with green patch pockets. His fluorescent yellow T-shirt had a huge decal of a beer can stenciled on the front. He wore white knee socks, striped red and blue at the top, and black canvas basketball shoes. A pair of mirrored sunglasses rode atop his head.

"Have I got a treat for you!" Smitty said as he slapped Bloomhardt on the back. "Where's your old lady?"

Trying not to laugh, Bloomhardt answered, "In church."

"Good. That's just where she oughta be on a morning like this."

"Is that where you're headed?"

"In a manner of speaking, yes. Because I come to you now as a missionary. I'm gonna show you the way, sinner."

"The way to what—the funny papers?"

"Sure, go ahead, insult me. But keep it up and I might not introduce you to my two altar girls, who, by the way, are sizzling in their bikinis in my car. I left the car around the corner just in case your wife was about. Didn't wanna be the cause of any marital spats."

"Thanks for the consideration, Smitty, but I'm already in dutch."

"Oh-ho, out on the town last night, huh? Well, good for you, so was I. In fact, me and the girls haven't even been to bed yet, which is why I came looking for you, if you know what I mean. So come along without an argument, Bloomie, and I won't have to hurt you."

"Thanks," said Bloomhardt, chuckling. "But I've got plans for today."

"Yeah? Like what, tinkering with this piece of junk?"

"This piece of junk is very near and dear to my heart, Smitty."

"Looks ready for the junk heap, if you ask me. Come on, man, you want something to ride? I've got something for you to ride, and you won't get your hands greasy doing it."

Bloomhardt smiled and shook his head.

"For Christ's sake, Bloomie, don't make me beg, we're wasting precious time! These girls are so hot that there's steam coming from between their legs. You oughta see my seat covers—holes burned right through them!"

"It's Sunday, Smitty. The day of rest."

"So what's more restful than a hot fuck on a warm afternoon?"

"Sorry," said Bloomhardt. "But listen, as long as you're here, maybe you can do me a favor. There's a slight chance I might need a place to stay for a day or so."

"You really are in the doghouse, ain't you? No wonder you're keeping a low profile."

"It's not definite yet. I just thought that as long as you're here . . ."

"No sweat. *Mi casa es sewer casa.*"

"That's *su casa.*"

"Sue who?"

"Never mind," Bloomhardt said. "I might be coming over as

early as this afternoon. Right after Annie gets home from church."

"Hey, the sooner the better. I'll try to keep the girls bottled up till then, so they don't lose none of their fizz."

"I don't want any fizz, Smitty. Just a place to hole up for a while."

"Say no more. It'll be fun sleeping with a guy for a change."

Bloomhardt looked at him askance.

"Just kidding, pal. I mean, come on, do I look like a fruit to you?"

Bloomhardt chose not to answer that question. "You sure you have room for me?"

"Man, I've got so much fucking room that I don't have room for any more. You know where I live, don't you?"

"I've never been there, but I know the address. South Holland, right?"

"Right, one-fifty-six. Apartment number five, it's on the top floor. The door's unlocked."

"You always leave your door unlocked?"

"Not usually, no. But last month I got drunk and lost my key, so I kicked the door in. But hey, don't worry, it's a very safe building. And who knows? You might like it so much you won't ever want to leave."

"I really appreciate this, Smitty."

"Like I said, no sweat. What'd you do, anyway? Come home with a bag on?"

"Oh, just a little disagreement, that's all. It'll blow over in a couple of days. In any case, thanks for the hospitality. I'll pay you back for this someday."

"Don't worry, I'll make sure you do. You can come visit me in the hospital when this fast life I'm living finally catches up with me. Which probably will be any day now."

"Then why don't you settle down?"

"Naw, I'm still storing up memories for my golden years. But hey, don't look now, your old lady and kid are coming up the street. Time for me to vamoose."

"Thanks again, Smitty. I'll probably be seeing you soon."

"I'll tell the girls to put a cap on it for a while." He winked, started back down the street, then paused for a moment to call out loudly, so that Annie would be sure to hear, "It was a pleasure conversing with you, Bloomie! See you at work tomorrow. Gotta get back to my jogging now!" He waved to Annie and Timmy, then trotted away, arms pumping wildly.

As Annie came into the yard, her purposeful stride seemed to falter. Bloomhardt thought she was about to say something, but at the last moment she lowered her head and hurried into the house. Timmy, in a blue seersucker suit, lingered behind. He stood on the opposite side of the bicycle and stared at his father through the spokes.

"Just getting the old bike back in shape," Bloomhardt told him. Timmy laid his hand on the front tire and gave it a spin.

"This bike is older than you are," Bloomhardt said.

Timmy blinked. He watched the spinning chrome of the rim reflecting the sun. Bloomhardt felt awkward, as if his face were polka-dotted with guilt. Timmy put his hand on the foot pedal and ran his finger over the teeth of the serrated edge.

"Hey, sport," Bloomhardt began. "About last night."

Timmy gave the pedal a single crank.

"I'm sorry about that Chinese dinner and movie I promised you. It really stinks to make a promise like that and not carry through with it. I hope you're not too mad at me."

Timmy watched the wheel spin. "Mommy said you had to work late."

"Did she? Well, yeah, I did. I did have to work late."

Timmy leaned over and plucked a dandelion from the grass, then held the yellow flower against the turning spokes, decapitating it. "Doing what?" he asked.

"Huh? Oh, you know. Going over the account books, that sort of thing."

"That man brought your suit back," Timmy said.

"Man?" said Bloomhardt, suddenly too dumb to think.

"That bald man. He brought your suit back."

"Oh. Yeah. Well, uh . . ."

"Mommy said you were probably doing something dirty and you didn't want to get it on your suit."

"That's right, I was, I was doing something dirty. I mean something with dirt in it. I mean . . . I mean after the books, after I finished up there . . . I did some work in the workshop."

"But you didn't have any clothes on."

"Oh sure, I had a pair of coveralls. You know, work clothes. For that kind of thing like . . . I was doing."

Timmy did not nod or smile, offered no indication of belief or disbelief. He gave the wheel another spin.

"Did you, uh . . . hear what Mr. Fenstermaker said? I mean, you know, when he gave my suit to Mommy?"

"No," Timmy said.

"No?" said Bloomhardt. "You didn't hear anything?"

"He was smiling and he said, 'Your husband seems to have misplaced this.' Then Mommy said, 'I don't think I understand.'"

Bloomhardt, who had been kneeling beside the bicycle, fell sideways onto his right buttock. It was not a voluntary movement. "Then what happened?" he asked.

"The man just kept smiling at her. Mommy asked him to come in and she told me to go to my room, then after a while she came up and said we couldn't go to a movie, then I went over to Helen's and Mommy went someplace in Helen's car."

"She did? In Helen's car? Do you know where she went?"

Timmy shook his head no.

To hire a lawyer, Bloomhardt thought. Or a contract killer. Thinking this, he felt the hair stand up on the back of his neck and he quickly scanned the area for the glint of a gun barrel, the reflection from a telescopic sight. He was about to throw himself to the ground when he told himself no, there was no sniper about, Annie was not the murder-for-hire type. He looked at his son, who was staring at him expressionlessly. I'm such a fool, Bloomhardt thought. To blur Timmy's view of him, he gave the wheel a hefty spin. To drown out his own thoughts, he began to speak.

"Yes sir, this is a fine old bike, sport. When I was in college I used to dream about riding this bike all over Europe, just riding and writing, sleeping in open fields, seeing all the places that men like Hemingway and Fitzgerald and Joyce and Dos Passos saw. . . ."

Timmy did not know any of those men, but he liked the sound of his father's voice now, he liked watching his father's face through the whirring spokes, liked the duet of soft voice and spinning, clicking wheel.

"Boy, I was in great shape back then," said Bloomhardt, remembering. "Not stuck behind a desk every day like I am now. Always out riding, pretending I was tooling along a canal in Amsterdam or up a cobblestone street in Paris. Watching the fishermen along the Seine . . . going round and round in Piccadilly Circus. . . ."

For several moments after Bloomhardt finished speaking, both he and Timmy were silent. Bloomhardt felt calmer now, the way he sometimes did after a long confessional prayer. And Timmy, when his father's voice had that rare quality of repose, was no longer afraid of him.

"Can we go there?" the boy asked.

Bloomhardt looked up. "What'd you say, sport?"

"Can we go there?"

"To Europe? Geez, I wish we could. But considering the mortgage payments and car payments and insurance payments I have to make, plus the utilities, groceries, taxes, and clothes, and more taxes and more taxes, I'm lucky just to be able to send you and Mommy to church every Sunday." And just like that, his mood darkened again. He fingered the bicycle chain, its new oil shining blue-black in the sun.

"Speaking of church," Bloomhardt said, "how was it today?"

"Fine," said the boy.

"How did Mommy like it?"

"Fine," he said again.

"She didn't by any chance stay after church and have a private little talk with the minister, did she?"

"No. About what?"

"Oh, nothing. I was just wondering."

"She didn't," Timmy said. He ran his hand along the inside curve of the handlebars then, felt the smooth plastic tape and the slender brake cables, trailed his hand along the crossbar to the sharply contoured seat and back to the front wheel, where his fingers stroked the spokes as if they were harp strings.

"You really seem to like this old bike of mine," his father said.

"It's nice," said Timmy.

"Well, I'll tell you what. If you can ride it, you can have it."

Behind the thick lenses of his glasses, Timmy's eyes grew wide. He spun the tire, but gently.

Bloomhardt stood and flipped the bicycle right side up. After selecting the proper wrench from the dozen scattered at his feet, he quickly adjusted the seat to its lowest position. "There," he said as he tightened the nut. "Climb on up here and we'll see if your legs are long enough."

Timmy had already retreated by several steps.

"Come on, sport, it won't hurt you. Just sit on it and we'll see if your legs reach the pedals."

"I like my bike," Timmy said.

"Well, sure, it's nice, but don't you think you're getting a little too big for it?"

"I'm only six years old."

"You'll be fine, I promise. Come on, act like a big boy. There's nothing to it."

Hesitantly, Timmy advanced a single step.

"You'll like it," Bloomhardt said.

Timmy came another step forward.

"You'll feel like the king of the world sitting up here."

Three more steps and the boy was beside the bike, terrified. "Alley-oop," said Bloomhardt as he scooped Timmy up and set him on the seat. Nearly horizontal as he leaned forward to grip the handlebars, Timmy sat frozen in place, legs clutching the frame.

Bloomhardt pried one of the legs free. "I think if you stretch you can reach the pedal," he said.

But only by sliding off the seat and listing to his left, the crossbar snug in his crotch and the nose of the seat rubbing his spine, could Timmy stand on one of the pedals. His knuckles were white and his teeth clenched.

"There, I knew you could do it," said his father. "Now how about a turn or two around the yard, just to get the feel of it." Stiffly, rigid with fear, Timmy shook his head no.

"Here we go," said Bloomhardt. With both hands gripping the seat he rolled the bicycle forward, intending to push it all the way around the house. But after only a few yards, with Timmy jerking the handlebars from side to side, his elbows locked, Bloomhardt came to a halt, his face white. For just an instant he had witnessed a horrifying vision. He had seen Timmy lying in the middle of the road, had heard tires squealing, car horns shrieking. He was knocked breathless by this mirage, this dreadful picture that flashed through his brain, and barely had the strength to lift his son off the seat and ease him gently to the ground.

"That's enough for today, sport," he said, voice and body trembling.

Timmy looked up at him and blinked several times. He knew that he had disappointed his father again. Bloomhardt was staring at him and breathing very hard and there was not the hint of a smile on his face. Timmy's chin began to quiver. He took one step away from his father, then two, then turned and ran sobbing into the house. Bloomhardt stood there panting, trying to get his breath back, trying not to fall.

Twenty minutes later, nearly recovered from the terrible vision that he now attributed to his own guilt-ridden imagination, Bloomhardt peeked in through the kitchen window and saw Annie setting the table for lunch. He eased open the door and stepped inside, noticing, when he entered, that her shoulders tightened, that her hands stopped laying out the silverware for just a moment, and that she faced the window above the sink again without even glancing in his direction.

Gingerly he pulled a chair away from the table and sank into it. "If I had a tail," he said softly, "it would be between my legs right now."

Annie stared out the window at the driveway and the garage, at the oak whose branches spread like gnarled umbrella leaves toward the house. Bloomhardt picked up a salt shaker and turned it around and around in his hands. "I made him cry again," he said. "Seems like that's all I'm able to do anymore. When all I really want is for him to know how much I love him."

"He does," she answered.

He hoped she would say something more, that she loved him too, but she said nothing, she did not move. Bloomhardt felt an icy shiver trickle down his spine. Half a minute later he inhaled slowly, reluctantly, as if just to take another breath compounded his sins. "What about . . . what happened . . . last night?"

Still she did not answer. Cautiously he lifted his head, just enough to see her hands gripping the edge of the sink, shoulders trembling, and he knew that she had begun to cry. When she spoke, it was in a tiny voice glutinous with phlegm and aimed at the drain in the sink. "I went looking for you," she said. "In Helen's car."

So that was where she had gone. He forced a laugh and said, "I'll bet she advised you to make a hit-and-run, didn't she?"

Annie sniffed back her tears. "I didn't tell her where I was going, but I think she suspected that it had something to do with you. She asked if I wanted to borrow her pruning shears too, just in case I wanted to cut somebody's you-know-whats off."

Wincing, he covered his crotch with a hand. "She's a generous woman, all right."

He waited a long time for Annie to continue, to get the ball of punishment rolling. Any second now, he thought, she's going to turn on me and raise the roof with anger. He was determined to sit with downcast eyes and accept it all, the ridicule and emasculation, the condemnations so long overdue. He was a lowlife, no-class louse and he was ready to face the music. The moment she threw him out, he would begin his campaign to win her back. After a few days, maybe a week, of roses and love letters and a singing telegram or two, she would relent and allow him to come home again. It was all going to work out fine, and would be just the kick in the pants he needed to change his life.

But now, strangely, she began to cry more lustily than ever. "I felt so sorry for you," she told him. "All alone and without any clothes on. I think he could at least have left you your shoes! I tried for hours to find you."

Bloomhardt did not like the sound of that. "I had been with another woman," he reminded her. "His wife."

Very slowly, then, she turned to face him. She stood with her back against the sink, shoulders hunched, arms hugging herself. Tears ran down her cheeks and splashed onto the floor. "I'm sorry," she moaned. "Whatever I did to make you do that, I'm sorry, John, I didn't mean to. Just tell me how, and I'll try to be a better wife for you. I'll do anything, I promise, just please forgive me, don't leave me, I'll die without you!"

Bloomhardt held to the edge of the table as he pushed himself erect. "Oh, no you don't," he said shaking his head. "Uh-uh, no way, you are not going to get away with this, Annie. Damn it, I'm the one in the wrong, not you! Throw a plate at me, why don't you? Come on, come after me with a frying pan, I won't even cover up my head. But no way am I going to let you stand there and cry and beg for forgiveness, Annie. That's what *I* was going to do!"

She stared at her feet. "If I were the wife I should be, you wouldn't need to go to somebody else."

"I'm rotten!" he shouted. "Don't you realize that yet? Tell me to go to hell, tell me to take a flying leap! But for Chrissake don't stand there and ask *me* to forgive *you.* You're an angel, Annie. A goddamn saint."

"All I want is for you to love me as much as I love you."

"Jesus, I do. That's why it's breaking my heart to see you acting like such a wimp. Aren't those assertiveness classes of yours doing any good at all? Hell hath no fury like a woman scorned, don't you know that? Well you've been scorned, woman, so get infuriated! God knows, I'm ready and willing to take what's coming to me—just give me the chance!"

She looked at him over the rims of her glasses and, wringing her hands, said, "Just promise you won't leave me. I'll die if you say you're going to leave me."

He slapped his forehead with the heel of his hand. "I am not going to let you steal my punishment from me, Annie. How am I supposed to get clean of this thing if you don't make me suffer for it? No. No, unless you give me what I deserve, and do it with sincerity, then I *am* going to leave. I'll throw myself out if I have to!"

"I'll do anything you ask. Anything. Just tell me!"

"Not like that, damn it. You're supposed to hate me for what I've done. At least for the rest of the day, anyway. So look me straight in the eye and tell me that you hate me. Tell me that you'd rather swallow puke than look at me."

"I love you," she said.

He moved closer, took her chin in his hand, and brought her eyes up to meet his. "Annie, listen to me. If you want to salvage this marriage, you'd better learn how to fight, and learn quick. I betrayed you, for God's sake. I cheated on you. Now think of that, think of how I've humiliated you, and tell me to go to hell."

"Please," she whimpered. "Don't ask me to swear at you."

"Tell me to go fuck myself!"

She lowered her chin and kissed his hand.

"Agghhhh!" he cried. He pulled away from her, went to the knife drawer, and yanked it open. He grabbed a bread knife with a long serrated blade, then stepped back to Annie and forced the handle into her hand.

"Stab me!" he said as he threw back his arms to expose his chest. "Right here, right in the heart!"

Horrified, she dropped the knife to the floor.

Bloomhardt snatched it up again and pressed the tip of the blade to his shirt pocket. "I'll hold it in place. You just smack it with your hand."

She put both hands over her eyes.

"Just bump it, for Chrissake! A goddamn flesh wound!"

She spun away, put her head in the sink, and covered her head with her arms. Bloomhardt threw down the knife, grabbed her by the shoulders, and pulled her around to face him. "Throw a pot at me," he begged. "A coffee cup, a banana, anything! Please, Annie, please, don't be like this."

Weeping, her glasses beginning to fog, she sniffed and said, "I'm sorry. I can't help it."

"Okay. Okay, you don't have to throw anything at me, you're not the throwing type. But can't you at least *say* something, make an obscene gesture, something like that?"

She looked up lovingly and gently stroked his cheek. "I guess I'm not that kind either," she said.

"You're impossible!" he screamed. "How do you expect me to live with someone so damn perverse and forgiving all the time?

Can't you learn to be like everybody else? Show a little compassion, can't you? I've got needs too, you know. Ah, Annie, come on, just this once, okay? Stick your tongue out at me, can't you at least do that?"

Tentatively, she slipped the tip of her tongue between her lips, but it was a playful gesture, teasing. "You're smiling!" he cried. "That does it! That's all I can stand!"

He turned on his heels and strode out of the room. Annie chased after him, following him up the stairs and from room to room as he stuffed a suitcase full of clothes, scooped his shaving kit and toothbrush in too, snapped the suitcase shut, and tromped down the stairs again.

"Don't," she pleaded, sobbing. "John, please, sweetheart, give me another chance. I can be mean, honest. I'll learn how. You can teach me."

Bloomhardt jerked open the front door, paused for a moment, then turned to face his wife. "When you can tell me to go fuck myself," he said, "and really mean it, then and only then will this marriage be worth saving."

Timmy, standing at the top of the stairs, listening, held his breath. His mother said, "I can," as she clutched at Bloomhardt's sleeve. "I can do it now."

"Then do it. Say it. And mean it."

She stared at him with wet, shining eyes. When finally she opened her mouth to speak, no words came out. Bloomhardt pulled away and stepped outside. He was halfway across the yard when Annie came running out to the edge of the porch and cried, "Wait!"

He turned. "All right," he said. "Say it."

"Go ff-ff . . ." she said, hands clenched in tight balls and beating against her breasts.

"Say it!"

"Go . . . go . . ." She threw her arms out, hands open. "Come back!"

Grimly, Bloomhardt shook his head. He took two steps backward, spun to face the sidewalk, and fell over his bicycle. Quickly
he rolled onto his hands and knees and glanced toward the house,
where he saw Timmy on the uppermost porch step, blinking, Annie running through the yard with her arms outstretched. Next
door at the Krakow house, the front door banged open and Helen
came flying out, a huge wooden mixing spoon in her hand.

She's planning to stir me to death, thought Bloomhardt. But he
did not wait to find out. He jumped to his feet, snatched up his
suitcase, and ran.

Part Two

BLOOMHARDT'S car had not been towed away and was exactly where he had left it in Fenstermaker's lot. Nor, he discovered with his heart beating wildly and his pulse thrumming in his temples, had it been rigged to explode when he started the engine. The only evidence that anyone had been near his car was the folded sheet of paper tucked under the windshield wiper. He opened it with trembling hands and read: *Tuesday night is free. Call me. Love, M.* He ripped the note into four pieces, stuffed it in the ashtray, and sped away.

Although he missed his wife and son already, Bloomhardt was in high spirits as he drove toward Smitty's apartment. With the window open and warm air bathing his face, rock music blasting from the radio, he felt convinced that this brief separation would do wonders for Annie, would prove to her once and for all that she could not get away with being so good to him all the time.

He tried not to let his spirits sag when he pulled up in front of Smitty's apartment building in an unattractive part of the city, close enough to the tire factory that the air seemed curdled with the smell of burning rubber. Surrounded by ramshackle clapboard houses whose scraggly yards were littered with dismembered toys and automobiles, Smitty's building stood out as a masterpiece of squalor. There was evidence, albeit faint, that the structure had once been painted white. Maybe the faded I LIKE IKE bumpersticker peeling from a second-floor window could recall the exact date. Several of the windows were cracked or broken, some patched with metallic duct tape, others with cardboard, plywood, or thin sheets of transparent plastic, also torn. The roof sagged. Four courses of bricks were missing from the top of the chimney.

The front porch no longer existed, having rotted and collapsed to leave a leap of six feet between the door and the ground.

On the left side of the house, an open stairway zigzagged to the third floor, every fifth or sixth step missing. Bloomhardt, carrying his suitcase, smiled uncertainly as he approached the fat woman lounging across the bottom step. She squinted at him through sullen, sleepy eyes and brushed back her hair, displaying through the rent armhole of her muumuu far more of her pendulous breast than Bloomhardt cared to see.

"Don't touch that," she said as he put a hand out toward the safety rail.

"Excuse me?"

"It ain't nailed on good. You touch it and it'll fall off."

"Oh," he said. "Thank you." Balancing the suitcase on his head, he stepped over her heavy legs to the next available step.

On the second-floor landing he nearly tripped over an uncovered chamber pot. From inside the building, through the open doorway and down the short corridor, came the sound of a man and woman screaming, heating the air with obscenities. By the time Bloomhardt reached the third floor he was already dizzy, reeling from the sights and sounds and odors of putrescence.

He located Smitty's apartment not by its number, which was missing, but by the splintered lock on the door. Tentatively he pushed the door open with his foot. The apartment consisted of one large room and was furnished with a sway-bellied sofa, a scattering of *Penthouse* and *Hustler* magazines, a console radio, and, next to the dirty window, an unmade bed with clumps of stuffing leaking from the mattress. At the opposite end of the room was the kitchen—a square little refrigerator with a hot plate atop it. On a card table nearby were dirty cups and glasses, saucers overflowing with cigarette butts, a trash basket crammed full of empty beer cans. In the bathroom, which Bloomhardt did not have the nerve to investigate, were more dirty dishes, dirty clothes, and dirty magazines stacked in the bathtub.

The linoleum bulged along each of the walls, and in the center of the room it was worn through to bare wood. There were more odors than Bloomhardt could identify, none of them agreeable. Through the thin walls came a symphony of discord—babies wailing, a woman swearing at the top of her lungs, a radio playing so loud that the glass in the window hummed.

Bloomhardt did not take another breath until he was safely inside his car again, all windows and air vents tightly sealed. He rested his forehead against the steering wheel and tried to conjure up the sweet scent of Annie's skin, the delicious silence of Timmy curled up in a chair, reading a book. But if he returned home so soon, less than two hours after throwing himself out, what good would that do? What lesson would Annie learn from that?

Again he regarded Smitty's apartment house. The fat woman at the bottom of the stairway sat leaning forward, picking at her toes, her sloppy breasts about to spill from her dress. Bloomhardt had a frightening vision of what would happen if they did: two huge walruses of flesh thrumping toward him, capsizing his car, burying him forever beneath a mountain of sour odors.

He sped away as fast as he could and did not look back.

Without knocking, he opened the front door of his parents' home and stepped inside. He had left his suitcase, for the time being at least, in the car. Quietly listening, his back to the door, he could hear his mother two rooms away, in the kitchen, washing dishes. When he thought of his mother these days, that was always where he pictured her. When he envisioned his father, he was in the backyard, tossing the football to an energetic boy, a boy who was now a man and who felt as energetic as a loggerhead turtle under heavy sedation.

Here in this living room, as elsewhere in the house, everything was orderly and clean, the sofa cushions fluffed, the bric-a-brac without a trace of dust, the pictures straight. It was not difficult for him to peer twenty years into the past and see the living room of his youth. And yet he felt out of place here. It was no longer home. The house seemed darker than he remembered, as though not as much sunlight penetrated it now as when he was a boy. And there was a faint odor of staleness, of accumulated time, of hours, weeks, and years stacked layer upon layer like old furniture wax to darken the wood and absorb the light.

Not wanting to face his mother just yet, he tiptoed up the stairs to his old bedroom. Surely he would find something there to lighten his mood. He sat on the bed in the room that was now his parents' guest room, though there were never any guests, and saw that all of the discards of his youth his mother had saved. The room was much as it had been on that day so long ago when, shortly after his graduation from college, he had married Annie and moved into his own house eighteen miles away.

Hanging from a nail in the wall was his straw sombrero, survivor of a trip to Tijuana fifteen years ago, the hat caved in now, the straw brittle. Propped against the dresser was his first guitar, three of its strings missing, the neck badly warped. And standing in the corner was his pool cue, also warped, the one that had kept him in debt from playing nine-ball. Even his worn-out golf spikes, looking newly polished, seemed to have been awaiting his return.

Easing back on the bed, he let his head sink into the feather pillow. He had always liked this bed, its size and firmness. It was the best bed in the house. Maybe staying here for a few days would not be so bad after all; maybe it was just what he needed.

A few moments later, refreshed, he pushed himself up and left the room. At the end of the hallway he turned the corner to the stairs and came face to face with his mother, who, crouching, brandished an enormous gleaming meat cleaver in her hand.

"I thought you were a burglar," she explained, chuckling,

after he had gasped and stumbled back against the wall.

Sheepishly he answered, "It's only me, Ma," and held out his arms to her as she came up the last two steps, tears already sliding down her cheeks. She could cry faster than any other woman he had ever known.

Hugging her, he thought that she had put on a few pounds since his last visit, had added more gray to her hair, more pallor to her complexion. In truth, she had looked like this for quite some time, a woman in her sixties, but it always took him a minute or two to juxtapose the two images, mother remembered and mother now. He looked down at her hand as it squeezed his arm: the veins across the back of her hand stood out, thick blue welts. He wanted to press that hand to his lips and apologize to her for the unfairness of growing old. Despite her additional weight, she seemed fragile in his arms, as if her increased size, like that of the puffer fish, was all illusion, a bluff of swollen emptiness and air.

He kissed her cheek and then pulled away. "Let's go down-stairs," he said.

In the kitchen they sat at opposite ends of the tiny rectangular table, sipping coffee. He tried to pay attention, to smile and nod as she filled him in on a month's worth of news, but frequently found himself staring at the wall clock, the toaster, the paper-towel dispenser. She talked quickly, nevously, as if her words were a rope she could coil around him to keep him in his chair. She told him about the increased school taxes, the noise the water heater made, what was going on in Ethiopia, Iran, Ireland, and Holly-wood, a hundred things he did not wish to know.

"How's Dad?" he asked.

Just fine, fine, except for his back problem, his sciatica. He was at Herman's Deli at the moment, had walked over for a newspaper and some cold cuts for lunch, he should be home any second now, you're going to stay a while, aren't you? By the way I saw an old friend of yours the other day, that Jake what's-his-name, the one with the beard, the odd one, and I hope your father remembers to pick up a jar of mustard, he never pays attention to anything I say—

"Jake?" Bloomhardt interrupted. "Jake Speers? What in the world is he doing back in town?"

Jake, said his mother, was teaching at the university now, and oh by the way speaking of teaching had he heard about those monkeys that had been taught to speak sign language, wasn't that just the craziest thing? and what about the coming ice age? and oh, your father killed a mouse in the basement last Wednesday, and oh my god the boy down the street went and got his cousin pregnant!

It was all Bloomhardt could do to keep from banging his head on the table. Would he be able to stay here a few days? He felt as if he had already.

He stood up. "Well, I hate to leave, but I've got to be going. Tell Dad I'm sorry I missed him. Give him my love."

His mother followed him to the door. "Why rush away, you just got here. Your father will be so disappointed. Can't you at least stay long enough to have a sandwich with us?"

Bloomhardt squeezed the doorknob. "I really have to be getting back, Ma. I just came out for a little drive, thought it would be nice to pop in and say hello. But dinner is at two, roast beef, and geez, Annie won't like it if I'm late."

"You should have brought Timmy with you, we haven't seen him in months."

"Well, yeah, I know, I'm sorry. . . ."

"Our only grandson is growing up right under our noses, but it's more like he's on the other side of the world from us."

"I'll bring him over, Ma, someday. . . ."

"Your father's always saying that we should just jump in the car and go visit you, but I tell him no, that you don't want us old folks hanging around and interfering with your lives."

"Ah, Ma, it's not like that. . . ."

"So we just sit here and wait and hope you'll drop by or call, and when you finally do, your father isn't even here to say hello."

"Tell you what," Bloomhardt said, halfway out the door. "One of these days we'll have a picnic at the beach, okay?"

"Oh, that would be so nice! Your father would like that. When can we do it?"

"Well, that depends. Maybe in a week or so."

"Well, you just tell me what to bring and I'll bring it. You always loved my potato salad, remember? And it will do your father good to get out, he doesn't have much interest in anything anymore."

"Goodbye, Ma," Bloomhardt said as he started down the porch steps. "See you soon."

She followed him onto the sidewalk and to the car. "You don't know how much your father misses you, you should try to visit a little more often, let him watch his grandson growing up. It isn't like it's a five-hour drive from your place to ours, is it?"

Bloomhardt, inside his car now, leaned across the seat as his mother put her head through the open window on the passenger side. He kissed her cheek. She wrapped her arms around his head and squeezed so tightly his ears popped.

"Give Annie our love," she said as he pulled away from her to start the engine. "And little Timmy. Tell him that Grandma and Grandpa love him. What's that suitcase doing in the backseat?"

"Laundry," said Bloomhardt, "it's just laundry. Now step back or I'll run over your feet."

"But it's Sunday, where are you taking laundry on Sunday? Is there something wrong with your washing machine? Do you want your father to come out and fix it?"

"This is dry cleaning, Ma. For tomorrow. So I won't forget to drop it off. I gotta go now. 'Bye!"

Eight miles south of town, in a bucolic setting deodorized by breezes that swept off Lake Erie, was Bloomhardt's alma mater, the state university he had attended fifteen years earlier. Here on a bench in the middle of the Oak Grove he sat. Two squirrels and a chipmunk, long accustomed to handouts, played at his feet. Every now and then another coed would walk by, dressed for church, looking heartbreakingly beautiful simply because she was so young. Two bulky young men in shorts and football jerseys sprinted past, stirring last year's leaves with each meaty stride.

Nothing, it seemed to Bloomhardt, had changed since he and Jake Speers were fraternity brothers here. The trees had new leaves on them, of course. The acorns scattered on the ground were not the same nuts Bloomhardt had known. The benches had been painted a deeper shade of green, though not recently. There was a new dining hall under construction across from the library. And the students—they, of course, were not Bloomhardt's class-mates, looking as they did all fresh from the egg. But these changes were mere façade to him, just window dressing. What remained unaltered was the ambiance of the campus, that quiet tingle of expectation he felt, then as now, whenever he visited the Oak Grove. Whether the tingle was caused by the microwave vibrations of so much knowledge compressed into one place, or by a similar compression of youthful sexuality, he did not know. He only knew, then as now, that the tingling gave him an erection.

But even more exciting was the information Bloomhardt's mother had dropped so cursorily, that Jake Speers, Mad Jake, the scourge of Theta Xi, was teaching here. The odd one, his mother had said, the one with the beard. That described Jake to a T. As sophomores he and Bloomhardt had grown beards in the hope that whiskers would gain them easier entry in the local taverns. Bloom-hardt's beard had been a failure, sparse and uneven, the antithesis of Jake's woolly, unmanageable red mane. The girls had teased Bloomhardt so unmercifully that he finally shaved off his scraggly growth, shaved it, in fact, in Jake's room at the frat house, where Bloomhardt, a commuter, often spent the night. He recalled how good he had felt the day the beard came off, how clean and pure, as if he were starting anew. He wished he could feel that way again.

Good old Jake, thought Bloomhardt as he pictured that toothy grin. Mad Jake, always ready to lend a hand or a bit of unwanted advice, always free and easy with his money, generous to a fault. An energetic and outspoken student of psychology, though a not particularly handsome one, he had had his pick of the girls. Bloomhardt, shy and tongue-tied, had relied on Jake's overflow for his own dates. In fact it was through Jake that he had met Annie.

"She's not right for me," Jake explained before introducing Bloomhardt to his future wife. "She's bright and pretty and has perky little tits, but Christ, Bloomstein, she won't smoke dope, she'll only drink wine, and she's not very keen on the idea of oral sex. Now what the hell kind of a girl is that for me? You take her. Maybe if you don't bore each other to death, you might hit it off."

It was when Jake went away to graduate school that Bloomhardt had lost track of him, their stream of correspondence slowing to a trickle after a few months, then eventually drying up. Now, more than a decade later, Bloomhardt was struck by the realization of how sorely he missed Jake's company.

In the basement of Babcock Hall, the building housing the psychology department, Bloomhardt located Jake's office across from the water fountain. DR. JACOB SPEERS, ASSOCIATE PROFFESSOR read the nameplate on the door. On a magazine subscription form he ripped from the bulletin board, and with the stub of a pencil rescued from the dust beneath the water fountain, Bloomhardt scrawled a note: *Jake, you big ape. Welcome home! Call me at . . . .* At where? he wondered. Where do I go from here?

Call me at the YMCA, he wrote, and signed it *Bloomstein.* He slid the paper under the door, then started back up the hall. He had taken only four steps when there was a slight rustling noise behind him and he turned to see the slip of paper in the middle of the hallway.

This time he folded the paper in half, folded it a second time, and slipped it under the door again, pushing it hard so that no draft would suck it back out into the corridor. He waited twenty seconds. Nothing happened. He turned and walked away.

Again the paper rustled behind him. He looked over his shoulder and saw it lying in the hall. Now he went to the door and tested it, and to his surprise the door clicked open. Bloomhardt peeked inside, but the room was empty. Jake's desk, facing the door, was piled high with books and magazines and loose papers, the chair vacant. Bloomhardt laid the note upon the desk and weighted it down with a stapler. He turned to leave and was immediately seized in a bear hug and hoisted off the ground, his scream cut short by the woolly wet kiss Jake planted on his mouth.

Bloomhardt coughed and sputtered as he pulled his face out of Jake's beard. "Put me down, you're breaking my back!"

"Shut up and kiss me again!"

"How about a kick in the balls instead?"

"Anything! Anything! Just show me that you care!"

Finally Jake dropped Bloomhardt and stood there grinning at him. Bloomhardt, gasping for air, said from his knees, "You haven't changed a bit."

Jake grabbed him under the arms and dragged him to a chair. "Sit, my liebchen, sit. Relax, unwind, take a load off. Good God, Bloomers, you're looking awful."

"What do you expect?" said Bloomhardt, still breathing hard. "I've just had the life scared out of me."

Jake sat on the edge of his desk, grinning broadly. "God, it's good to see you. Let's compare peckers."

Massaging his ribs, Bloomhardt tried not to laugh. "What are you doing in here today? Don't you know it's Sunday?"

Jake nodded toward the window near the ceiling. "Sunday is when the girls from the dormitories go to church, no?"

"So you sit here and look up their dresses as they walk past."

"It's my way of paying homage to our Creator," said Jake.

"You saw me coming down the sidewalk, didn't you? That's why you weren't surprised to see me."

"Nothing about you ever surprises me, Bloomstein. But you've lost a little hair, haven't you? And you're not as scrawny as you used to be. And I heard from your mother that you and Annie have a Junior Bloomstein now."

Bloomhardt nodded. "A little boy. Six years old."

"Well, if he has to be little, that's a good age to be. Is he anything like you, or is he normal?"

"He's a terrific kid."

"Takes after his mother, eh? Speaking of which, how is my favorite nonpromiscuous woman?"

"As wonderful as ever."

"You mean she hasn't gotten wise to you yet?"

Bloomhardt only smiled.

"And the writing, Bloomingway? Are you still at it? Whatever happened to that novel you promised to dedicate to me?"

Bloomhardt looked at his hands. "I don't write much these days," he admitted. "I mean sometimes a little, but . . . you know."

"Still an undisciplined dreamer, eh?"

"Hey, look who's talking. A Sunday-morning voyeur who kisses men on the lips."

"Not all men," said Jake, affecting a lisp. "Just the cuties like you."

"You're as demented as ever," said Bloomhardt.

"And do you think, at our age, that that doesn't require discipline? Listen, it wasn't easy screwing up three marriages in less than ten years."

"No kidding, Jake? You've been married three times?"

"Hard to believe, isn't it? Each of my wives felt the same way. But yep, I've even got a little girl somewhere from the first one. Unfortunately, her mother thinks I set a bad example as a higher primate, so I haven't laid eyes on the child for about eight years, five months, and thirteen days. Not that I care, you understand."

But Bloomhardt spotted a glimmer of sadness in his friend's eyes before Jake lowered his head. Bloomhardt felt his own throat clog with emotion. "Time sure changes things, doesn't it?" he said.

"I think that's why time was invented, Bloomers. But hey, look at us now. Here we sit, just like a million years ago. And I bet that in about five seconds we'll start talking about going out to find some fresh young tail."

"Not me," said Bloomhardt. "But if I know you, that's the reason you came to work here in the first place, isn't it?"

"Listen, I've spent a third of my life hearing the confessions of assorted fruits and nuts day after day, so this job is a well-deserved sabbatical. Besides, I consider it my patriotic duty to keep the sexual revolution rolling. And don't laugh, because I know you, and I know you can't walk across this campus without getting lumpy pants, right?"

But Bloomhardt did laugh, and the laughter nicked his heart. "I'm really glad you're back in town, Jake. Things won't seem quite as bad now with you around."

Jake pulled at his beard. "Okay, lay it on me."

"Hmmm?" said Bloomhardt.

"Come on, don't be shy, I know that look of yours. You've got something to unload, so let's have it. Herr Doktor is in."

Slowly Bloomhardt pushed himself to his feet, then crossed to the bookshelf. With his back to Jake, he pulled out a book at random and opened it. "The truth is," he said as he turned a page, "things aren't so hot at home."

"I surmised as much," said Jake, "considering the note you slipped under the door. But for Godsake, Bloomers, the YMCA? The Young Men's Cocksucking Association? And please don't tell me you've come out of the closet. I mean, holy frijoles, hombre, we used to sleep in the same bed!"

Bloomhardt smiled, but wistfully. He closed the book. "I was with another woman. Annie found out."

"And she threw you out of the house?"

Bloomhardt turned to face him. "Hell no, I wish she had. But no, not Annie. No, my wife begged *me* to forgive *her* for making *me* be unfaithful!"

Jake looked at him quizzically, and then began to laugh. He laid his hands on his belly and threw back his head and roared, a deep, resonant, echoing laugh. He laughed so hard that he had to wipe the tears from his eyes.

"Not a sympathetic bone in your body," said Bloomhardt.

Jake howled. When he was able to speak he answered, "Still the same old dipstick!"

Bloomhardt's face reddened.

"Now, now, don't get mad." Jake slid off the desk and swung his arm over Bloomhardt's shoulder. "Your wife loves you, Bloomy-tunes. She's insecure and afraid and she doesn't want to lose you. And this bothers you? What's the matter, you got something against love?"

"Well, no, but—"

"But nothing. Listen, trust me, you're a dipstick." He squeezed Bloomhardt's shoulder, then took him by the arm and led him into the hallway. "I only speak to you like this because I love you, you know." He pinched Bloomhardt's cheek. "Mein schatzy."

Bloomhardt slapped his hand away. "You're cracked."

"Maybe so," said Jake as he kicked the door shut. "But that's not a very nice thing to say on a Sunday. This is, after all, God's day. So come on, let's go get drunk and compare peckers."

The following morning, during breakfast in Jake's bright kitchen, Jake insisted that Bloomhardt move in with him.

"You need a few days to decompress," he said. "And so does Annie. My sofa was good enough for you last night, wasn't it?"

"It was fine, very comfortable, but I don't want to impose—"

"I'm never here anyway, what's the difference? So if you're worried about privacy, forget it. You'll have all the privacy you can stand."

"Gee, I don't know. . . ."

"Wonderful! So tonight after work you can stop at your house and pick up whatever you'll need for the next week or two. You might give your son a word of reassurance while you're at it. Kids tend to blame themselves for things like this, you know. Here's an extra key; just make yourself at home. Come and go as you like. And, oh yeah, I'd better warn you: if you happen to come home sometime and hear strange animal noises from my bedroom, just ignore them. Unless of course I give three bloodcurdling screams in a row, in which case you should remove your pants immediately and come join the fun."

at Universal Steel, it was a Monday like any other. The Goathead, still saturated from a weekend binge, sneaked to work fifteen minutes early and glued down everybody's telephone receiver. While he was at it he sabotaged the calculators, jamming the paper so that the readouts appeared as solid black lines of indecipherable numbers. As a coup de grace, he painted the underside of Smitty's drawer handle with mustard. Later, when Smitty yanked the drawer open in search of his missing pencils, he grabbed a handful of yellow slime, which he felt compelled to clean off by rubbing his hands in Roomy's hair. Roomy's revenge, when the Goathead staggered to the coffee cart for another doughnut, was to slip a dead caterpillar, preserved in wax paper for several days, into the old man's coffee.

In the meantime, telephones jangled, calculators clicked like chattering teeth, the hallway resounded with obscenities. Nelson scowled, Petey smiled, Bloomhardt stared out the window at the ore piles.

"Hey, Bloomie," Smitty asked after Bloomhardt's first abortive trip of the day to the ladies' room. "What happened yesterday, my neighbors scare you off? I knew you wouldn't stay. Why do you think I invited you in the first place?"

The minutes lurched by, the hours stumbled past. Bloomhardt hated his life. Beneath the surface, nothing was new.

In the evening he parked his car two blocks from his house and crept guiltily up the sidewalk. In the half-light of dusk, as the streetlamps began to buzz and glow, he felt that he had done and was about to do something despicable, that the taint of his soul was as obvious as a purple birthmark splashed across his face.

From behind the hedge that enclosed the park across the street from his house, he scanned the windows for a sign of life. He saw no one, no shadowy movement behind the curtains. He did not know why he was being so secretive. You make the mortgage payments, don't you? he reminded himself. You haven't killed anyone, you haven't sold heroin to toddlers or supplied terrorists with machine guns. So why do you feel like such a criminal?

He did not know why, but even as he tiptoed through his yard, even as he unlocked the front door and ducked inside, that was precisely how he felt. And when, upstairs, he stuffed a shopping bag full of underwear and socks, shirts and trousers and toiletries, he felt that he was stealing something not rightfully his.

In the bathroom he noticed that Annie had left the window open again. He pulled it shut and locked it. Where is she? he wondered.

Have I driven her to something rash? On his way downstairs, his questions were answered by the sudden appearance of Helen Krakow.

Bloomhardt's neighbor was not a big woman except in regard to the dislike she aroused in him. Broad-shouldered, big-breasted, and lantern-jawed, she looked, with her wide hips and skinny legs, like some kind of wingless bird, part emu, part duckbill platypus. At the bottom of the stairway she stood, blocking his descent, legs spread, hands clamped to her hips.

"Come to borrow a cup of sugar?" Bloomhardt asked.

"You ought to be ashamed of yourself."

"These are my clothes, Helen. I'm entitled to them."

"Do you even care that she's going through hell right now? I sat up with her the entire night, and she hasn't stopped crying yet."

"She always was a marathon crier, Helen."

"You're a cold sonofabitch, aren't you?"

"Ah, come on, lighten up. We need a few days apart, that's all. Everybody goes through this kind of thing. A week from now we'll be back together again just like nothing ever happened."

"Not if I can help it, you won't."

"What's that suupposed to mean?"

"It means that you don't deserve a woman like her, and I'm determined to make her realize that."

"Excuse me," said Bloomhardt as he squeezed past her. When she raised a hand to brush a strand of hair out of her eyes, he flinched and ducked, thinking she was about to give him a karate chop to the throat. At the front door he paused, then turned to face her.

"Where's Annie now?" he asked. "And where's Timmy?"

"At my house, where they belong. With people who care."

Bloomhardt had an urge to throw his shopping bag over her head and kick one of her skinny legs out from under her. He looked out the door; the night was dark now, nothing visible in the grayness but the dim blue streetlamps. The shopping bag tugged at his hand, bulging with despair.

"Do me a favor," he said softly. "Tell Timmy I'll come by soon to see him."

"I wouldn't dare. It would give him nightmares."

Bloomhardt's face grew hot, his spine stiffened, and his knees locked. It would be so satisfying, just once, to sock her in the jaw, a crisp left jab. He imagined her going down, thumping onto her bony knees, then toppling forward, breasts flattened to pancakes, nose wedged in the carpet. Picturing her like this, he was able to smile again, and said, "Anyway, thanks for looking after them."

Wearily he pushed open the door and went outside. As he walked toward the sidewalk he glanced to the left, where Bud Krakow, smoking a fat cigar, lay stretched out on a chaise longue on his front porch. Inside the house, Annie was at the window, looking out. Bloomhardt stopped for a moment and blew her a kiss. Bud Krakow raised his hand and waved. Annie kissed the palm of her own hand and pressed it to the glass. Bloomhardt started toward her, took two steps and then broke into a trot, but suddenly there was another woman at the window, pulling Annie away. An instant later the curtains were drawn. Bloomhardt stood in the middle of the yard, shifted the heavy shopping bag to his other hand, and stared at the shrouded rectangle of light.

"Evening, neighbor!" Bud Krakow called. "What a night, huh?"

"Right," said Bloomhardt. "What a night."

bloomhardt blinked, and days sneaked by. He yawned, and weeks sprinted past. Before he could muster the nerve to visit his family again, it was the Fourth of July. In the meantime he had sent Annie and Timmy dozens of greeting cards—funny ones, sentimental ones, imploring ones—because a part of him feared that if he did not continually remind his wife and son of his existence, he would be forgotten.

Several times he had telephoned, but on the rare occasions when Annie and not Helen or some other woman answered, he, struck dumb by guilt and choking on emotion, was unable to speak, and quickly hung up. But on the morning of July Fourth he declared his independence from all misgivings. He did not announce his visit but walked boldly through the front door of his house, all anxieties hidden behind a smile and an armful of gifts.

"Hiya, sport," he said when his son, who had been watching cartoons on television, looked up at him, surprised. He leaned toward the boy's upturned face and laid a kiss on his forehead. "How's my number-one son?"

"Fine," said Timmy.

"That's good. Now reach into this bag, I brought you a present."

Hesitating, Timmy looked from his father to the bag and back again.

"Go ahead, it's not a pit viper."

Timmy parted the mouth of the bag and peered inside.

"Take it out," said his father. "It's a soccer ball."

After another look at his father, Timmy cautiously reached into the bag and pulled forth the black and white ball. He turned it over in his hands. He looked at his father. He blinked.

"Do you know what soccer is?" Bloomhardt asked.

"Yes."

"Good, because that's a soccer ball. Regulation, just like the pros use. Maybe today I can show you how to kick it, okay?"

Timmy turned the ball back and forth and examined its geometric stitching, the alternating panels of black and white leather. "Do you like it?" his father asked.

"Yes," said the boy. "Thank you."

"My pleasure," said Bloomhardt. Did other fathers and sons talk this way, he wondered, or just those few who were strangers? "Where's Mommy? In the kitchen?"

Timmy nodded.

"Is anybody out there with her?"

"No."

"Okay, sport. You stay here and get the feel of the ball, and I'll be back in a couple of minutes."

Walking warily, flinching with each creak of the floorboards, Bloomhardt approached the kitchen. Annie, standing at the table, was stirring mayonnaise into a large bowl of macaroni and diced vegetables. When Bloomhardt crossed the threshold she was already looking in his direction, eyes glittery with tears.

"Hi," he said.

"Hi. I . . . I thought that was your voice I heard."

"Is that why you're crying?"

She shook her head and looked down. "It's the onions."

Bloomhardt nodded. He came a step closer. "I've missed you."

She answered without looking up. "I've missed you too."

"I never meant to stay away so long," he explained as he set his packages on the table. "But it seemed that every time I came by, Helen was standing guard."

"She's been helping us out," his wife said hoarsely. "She's been a good friend."

"I guess so. Except that she said if I really cared about you and Timmy, I'd stay away forever."

"She's only trying to help. She just wants what she thinks is best for us."

"Fuck Helen Krakow," Bloomhardt said.

Annie looked at him over the rims of her glasses, her frown slowly evolving into a smile, a tear trickling down her chin. "Oh, John," she said.

He came around the table and stood behind her, circled her waist with his arms, and nuzzled her neck. She pressed her cheek to his. The scent of her hair made him dizzy, made him want to faint into a delicious stupor. "You and Timmy are the most important people in the world to me," he said. "You know that, don't you?"

"I know," she said, and turning to face him added, "You're basically a very good man."

"I'm basically a dolt," he told her.

She smiled. "I'm so happy to see you again."

"Hey, wait a minute, I almost forgot about the present I brought you." In one of the packages on the table was a small, velveteen-covered box, which he quickly opened and held out to her. Inside, on a velveteen pillow, was a heart-shaped gold locket on a slender gold chain.

"I know you've always wanted one," he said. "It's eighteen-carat gold. The best I could find."

She lifted it from the box and held it to her mouth and tried to stop crying. Bloomhardt took the necklace from her and fastened it around her neck, then remained behind her, squeezing her tightly as she trembled, his mouth pressed to her ear.

"I lied about the onions," she said, sniffing. "I started to cry the moment I heard your voice in the living room."

"That's probably the first lie you've told in your entire life."

"Probably."

"Well, good for you. At least now I know that you're human."

She flinched at that, and drew an inch or two away from him. "What's in the other packages?"

"Fried chicken, wine, potato salad, baked beans, and a chocolate cake. All the fixings for a Fourth of July picnic."

"Today?" she asked.

"No, I thought we could do it sometime in December, when the beaches aren't so crowded."

"It's just that, well, I already have plans for today."

"Are they more important than our reunion celebration?"

"It's just that it's all been planned. Helen and some of her friends are coming over."

"I should have known."

"And some of my friends from class."

"What class?"

"The assertiveness class, remember? You wanted me to go."

"So that's what's happened to you," he said. "I've been standing here trying to figure out what's different about you, and now I know."

"I don't slouch like I used to, do I?"

"And you've even looked me in the eye a couple of times."

"You always said I needed a little more gumption."

"And it looks wonderful on you, sweetheart. You even sound different. You're like a whole new woman."

"You don't mind?"

"Mind? I think it makes you sexier than ever." He took her hand and pressed it between his legs. "Can't you tell?"

"You don't mind about the picnic?" she asked, suddenly short of breath.

"Who's thinking about the picnic?" He licked her ear and cupped her breasts in his hands.

"Don't," she said, giggling. "Timmy might come in."

"Let's go upstairs." Turning her farther so that they were face to face, he slid a hand between her thighs and slipped his tongue into her mouth. For a few seconds she savored the contact, then drew away. "Timmy," she said, breathing hard.

"Okay, okay, I'll be right back." After a quick kiss, he strode briskly into the living room, where Timmy stood waiting at the front door, bouncing the soccer ball.

"How about if you go outside and practice kicking the ball against the garage for a while?" Bloomhardt told him. "Mommy and I are going upstairs for a discussion. As soon as we're finished, I'll be out to play with you, okay?"

The turn of the boy's mouth and the slant of his eyebrows told Bloomhardt nothing. How can I love him so much, he wondered, and know him so little? "Don't worry, sport," he said as he tousled his son's hair. "I'm not going to hurt you this time. Feel how soft the ball is."

Timmy poked at one of the black panels. The ball had been deliberately underinflated and yielded easily to his touch. Bloomhardt gave him a swat on the behind and said, "You practice for fifteen minutes or so. I'll be out before you know it."

The moment Timmy stepped off the porch, Bloomhardt ran to the kitchen threshold, said, "Let's go!" and ran back through the living room and up the stairs, taking the steps three at a time.

The softness of the bed and the smooth, clean touch of the sheets made him lightheaded. He pushed his face into the pillow, he inhaled the lingering scent of Annie's perfume, the sweet clean odors of her hair and skin. He watched her undress and thought he had never seen anyone so beautiful, so perfect. She slid in beside him and he nearly cried out at the touch of her skin against his, the taste of her mouth, her fingers rediscovering the bumps of his spine. They rolled together, shivering, their teeth chattering although the room was warm with golden sunlight, and clung to one another as, outside, the soccer ball banged arrhythmically against the garage.

In the afternoon, Bloomhardt and Timmy kicked the ball back and forth in the shade of the pin oak tree, Bloomhardt making certain that he did little more than tap the ball with his instep. Once he pretended that the boy had kicked the ball very hard, and after catching it and grunting, Bloomhardt fell onto his back, feigning unconsciousness. Timmy ran to him, wide-eyed with fear, and, after hovering over him for a moment, jabbed his father's cheek with a fingertip. Bloomhardt stuck out his tongue, opened and crossed his eyes, and sang, "Cuckoo! Cuckoo!" When Timmy smiled, then giggled, Bloomhardt thought his own heart, swelling with miraculous joy, must inevitably burst.

Inside the house, Helen Krakow and her friends took turns peering out the kitchen window, as if hoping to catch a glimpse of Bloomhardt and hex him with a murderous stare. When, chasing an errant ball, he came into their view, he grinned and waved.

Later, he and Timmy sat against the side of the garage and balanced paper plates on their laps, the plates piled high with the food Bloomhardt had brought. Occasionally the boy would look up at his father, blink once, twice, and look away. Bloomhardt was well aware of this scrutiny; even so, his son's innocent query caught him off guard.

"Where have you been?" Timmy wanted to know.

Bloomhardt choked on a bite of chicken, then pounded on his chest until he coughed it up. "Ah, excuse me?" he said.

"Where have you been for so long?"

"Oh. Well, I, uh . . . I've been staying with a friend."

"Why?"

"Well uh . . . I haven't seen this friend for a long, long time." He wished his son would quit looking at him like that. "I'll bring him to meet you one of these days, sport. His name's Jake and he's a little bit loony. He's like a big, funny red bear."

Bloomhardt took another bite of chicken, but his mouth was dry and he could not swallow, and finally washed it down with a long gulp of lemonade. The boy was staring into his own plate now, looking shy again, which gave his father courage. "Didn't, uh, Mommy tell you why I was gone, sport?"

"She just cried a lot," the boy said.

Bloomhardt nodded. "How about you? How'd you feel about it?"

Timmy skewered a baked bean on a prong of his fork, placed it in his mouth, and chewed. Bloomhardt heard him blink. "I like my new ball," the boy finally said.

Unable to restrain himself, Bloomhardt leaned toward his son and lightly kissed the top of his head. Then he stood quickly. "Be right back," he said, already walking away. "I need more food."

In the kitchen he fought down the thick lump that had risen in his throat, then leaned against the refrigerator to eavesdrop on the twenty or so female voices that could be heard in the living room. Helen's voice was easily distinguishable from the others, shrill and authoritative, affecting him like fingernails dragged over a blackboard, but he could not understand enough to piece together what she was saying.

Annie surprised hm when she stepped into the kitchen, a tray of empty coffee cups in her hand. "Oh," she said, as startled as he. She opened her mouth as if to say more, but then walked past him to the coffee urn on the counter.

"What's going on in there?" he asked.

"We're voting on officers," she said as she refilled the cups.

"What kind of officers? Are you getting up a firing squad to shoot me?"

She felt an urge to smile, but checked it. "We're forming our own chapter," she told him.

"You mean that feminist thing of Helen's?"

She nodded, inordinately intent on filling the cups.

Stepping up behind her, Bloomhardt put a hand on her arm. "Annie, what's wrong? Why won't you look at me now?"

"I have to get this coffee," she said, eyes downcast.

"Let them get their own coffee. Come on, what's going on? Have they turned you against me again?"

"Please," she whispered. "Just let me refill these cups. We can talk later, okay?"

"Maybe I'd better just march in there and tell Helen Krakow to mind her own damn business," he said.

"Don't!" said Annie, finally turning to look up at him. "Please, don't say anything. I think they're going to nominate me for secretary."

"Secretary?" he said. "Jesus." He studied her a long time, those round, wet eyes pleading behind thick lenses. "This is important to you?" he asked.

"Very," she said.

Bloomhardt took a deep breath and released it slowly. "I'm becoming a stranger in my own house."

Smiling, she brushed her fingers over his cheek. "Not so strange as to forget where the bedroom is, I hope."

This, he thought, is my wife? It might have been funny, the way she was changing, were it not for an unpleasant feeling that the joke was on him.

"All right," he told her. "Whatever you want." Grabbing the bucket of fried chicken, he trudged outside. After plopping a drumstick onto Timmy's plate, he sat beside him again and gnawed on a wing, and a few bites later set his plate aside, leaned back against the garage, and closed his eyes.

"Are you going to sleep?" his son asked a minute later.

"I think I'm asleep already," Bloomhardt answered, not wanting to open his eyes, afraid that if he did he would see that something more had changed, the color of the sun, the texture of grass, the tilt of the earth.

The boy leaned against him and rested his head on his father's arm. "Me too."

Bloomhardt smiled. He felt like crying. "Pleasant dreams," he said as he pulled the child close.

bloomhardt dreamed that a caucus of caterpillars had gathered on his face. He felt their wispy feet and heard their low conspiratorial murmur. He awoke sneezing, and saw that it had been Timmy's hair tickling his face. His sudden movement awoke the boy too, and together they discovered the small delegation of women standing nearby, watching them and whispering.

Helen Krakow reached for Timmy's hand and, as she pulled him to his feet, said, "Your mommy wants to see you, honey."

The boy looked back at his father.

"Go ahead," Bloomhardt told him. "Go see what she wants."

With Timmy gone, the women moved two steps closer to Bloomhardt. "You must be the firing squad," he said groggily.

Helen Krakow smiled. "What a pleasant thought."

Bloomhardt yawned and tried to look bored. "Let's get on with it, Helen. You're interrupting my siesta."

"And you are interrupting Ann's evolution. You're holding her back."

"Really? Back from what?"

"From becoming a total person."

"She has two arms, doesn't she? Two legs and a head? All the necessary internal organs? How much more total can she get?" Chuckling, he picked up his glass of lemonade and raised it to his lips, but stopped when he saw the half-dozen black ants dog-paddling amid the ice. "Do me a favor, Helen," he said as he set the glass between his legs. "Try something new. Mind your own business."

"The dehumanization of one of our sisters *is* our business," said a willowy brunette on Helen's right.

Bloomhardt groaned. I bet she put the ants in my drink, he thought.

"Listen, John," said his neighbor. "Ann is our friend. We care about her. So we will not permit you to turn her back into the kind of person she used to be."

"And what kind was that?"

"You should know, you called her a jellyfish often enough, didn't you?"

"No," he said uncomfortably, "not that I recall. But even if I did once or twice, how would you know? Do you have my house bugged?"

From behind Helen, a woman whose face he could not see answered, "The only bug in that house is you, insect."

Bloomhardt put his hands flat on the ground and pushed himself up straight. He did not want to show any weakness, so he stared at the bridge of Helen's nose and imagined a bull's-eye painted on it. "Ladies," he said evenly.

"Women," the brunette corrected.

"Whatever," he said. "In any case, what my wife and I do is none, and I repeat, *none* of your business. But I do appreciate your point of view, and I promise to give it a great deal of thought. In return, there is something I would like all of you to do for me."

"And what's that?" Helen asked.

"Go fuck yourself with a hand grenade."

Helen, he noticed, did not flinch, though a woman nearby actually growled. "You're a destructive man," Helen told him. "Your son is a perfect example of that."

"For your information, there is nothing wrong with my son."

"You didn't throw him in a swimming pool before he knew how to swim? You didn't drop him out of a tree?"

His spine stiffened, his buttocks dug into the ground. "What the hell have you been doing, giving him the third degree? And no, of course not, I never did any of those things."

"You've terrorized that child long enough," she said.

"Terrorized? I guess you didn't notice how he was sleeping in my arms before you and your bonbon army chased him away."

"Familial instincts," she said. "He can't help himself. Ann is struggling against those instincts too, but she's mature enough to realize that it's a healthier atmosphere for both of them when you aren't around."

"Those are your words, Helen, not hers."

"Have you asked her lately?"

He sprang to his feet and strode confidently toward the house, terrified. Annie, biting her fingernails as she watched from the kitchen window, met him at the screen door. Behind her was another wall of women. Helen and her phalanx closed in behind Bloomhardt.

"Annie?" he said, and touched her fingertips through the wire mesh. She looked at him sorrowfully, tears dripping from her chin. "Sweetheart? Tell them, okay? Tell them you don't want me to go away again."

She looked down then, and when she spoke it was so softly that he had to strain to hear, her voice fluttering like tiny wings. "Maybe just a little while longer," she said.

"In my opinion," Jake said, "they did the right thing."

"Are you nuts?"

"Listen, Bloominski. All Annie needs is a little more time to figure out who—or is it whom?—she is. I told her that myself in our last counseling session."

Bloomhardt choked on his beer. Coughing and sputtering, he jerked his feet off Jake's coffee table and sat up straight. Jake, in the kitchen stirring a pot of chili, chuckled.

"I've only met with her six times so far," he continued. "But she's making remarkable progress. She no longer blushes when I bring up the subject of oral sex."

Jake expected to be answered by an aboriginal scream from the living room, but when he heard nothing except the slow crinkling of a beer can in Bloomhardt's fist, he peeked around the doorjamb. Bloomhardt's face was the color of a ripe plum, his eyes large and bulging, his mouth working silently open and shut.

"April fool," said Jake. "So take a breath before you pop a vein." He tasted the chili, then spooned it into two bowls, which he carried into the other room to set on the coffee table. "Actually," he said as he returned to the kitchen for crackers, spoons, a block of

Swiss cheese, and more beer, "I've only met with her once and that was just to let her know you'd be staying with me. We talked for a couple of hours that day, and boy, oh boy, was she a wreck!"

Breathing again but still dazed, Bloomhardt mumbled, "She never mentioned this to me."

Jake shrugged and pulled a chair close to the coffee table. "I guess she didn't want you to know," he said as he sat and reached for a spoon. "Come on, eat up. My chili is guaranteed to give you strength. Not to mention heartburn."

"I'm not hungry," said Bloomhardt.

"Listen, I didn't slave over a hot stove for the last five minutes for nothing, pal. Pick up that utensil and eat."

Bloomhardt reached for the spoon, but he did not dip it into his bowl. Instead he stared at his distorted reflection in the metal. He did not like the looks of himself. A few seconds later he tossed the spoon onto the table. "Your chili smells like dirty socks," he said.

"That's strange. I thought for sure I used clean socks." Jake grinned merrily and crushed a handful of crackers into his bowl. "Seriously," he said. "This separation from your family is good for me too, Bloomers. It gives me the chance to be with a man whose intellect and creativity and *savoir-vivre* I have always admired."

"You mean someone who listens to your psychological crapola and eats your slop and washes your dishes every night."

"That's another way of putting it."

"Right. But unless I dozed off, which is easy to do when you're talking, I haven't yet heard how all of this is benefiting me."

"What's your ambition in life, Bloomingway?"

"You mean other than a painless death?"

"Take, for example, that pile of note cards accumulating on my desk. Which gives me a pretty good idea of how you spend your evenings when I'm out. You pace the floor and stare out the window and squeeze your balls and try to summon up the Muse, correct?"

"I don't squeeze my balls," said Bloomhardt.

"Really? You should try it. It always works for me."

"I think we have different muses, Jake."

"Probably so. But my point is this. How much writing did you do at home? You sat half-conscious in front of the television every night while Annie made popcorn and opened beer cans for you. Tell me if that's not true."

"That's not true."

"No?"

"The popcorn was for Timmy. I ate cheese curls."

"Ahhh, well. So anyway, when you see your wife and son now, you're more patient and affectionate with them, aren't you? Because now, at least part of the time, you're free to do what you really want to do. Here at my place you don't feel guilty about doing something as impractical as writing. Again, tell me if I'm wrong."

"You're wrong," said Bloomhardt, but wearily, without conviction.

"So the time has come for you to take advantage of the situation, Bloomers. Seize the moment!"

"I don't want the moment. I want my family back."

"All in good time, my friend. But for now, why not accept this separation and make the most of it? Go to Paris, why don't you? Or Tahiti. Go anywhere, it doesn't matter. Just go somewhere and *write!*"

"I've always dreamed of going to Paris," Bloomhardt said.

"Don't I remember? In college, that's all you used to talk about."

"But I'm not a boy anymore, Jake. And the cost, geez, it would kill me. I'm still paying for a house I don't live in, and I send most of what's left to Annie. I'm lucky if I can afford a bottle of imported beer."

"Blah blah blah blah blah," said Jake.

"Oh, sure. That's easy for you to say."

"It'll be on me, then. My treat."

"No way. Besides, I still have a job, remember? No matter how much I hate it, I do have to make a living."

"Didn't you tell me you have two weeks of vacation coming in September?"

"September? Are you crazy? I'll be back home long before that."

"Give it some time," said Jake. "If you really love her, you'll give her a chance to grow."

"Why can't she grow with me in the same house? What am I, crabgrass?"

"Just give her a little space," said Jake.

Bloomhardt looked at him sourly. "You and Helen Krakow are going to wreck my marriage, you know."

"I'm trying to help a friend, that's all."

Slumping back against the sofa, Bloomhardt held the beer can to his forehead. "Some Fourth of July this has been," he said. "I didn't even get to see any fireworks."

Jake grinned. "Just wait until my chili starts working on us."

Over the summer, Bloomhardt made periodic visits to his house on Fairfax Avenue, but he rarely found Annie and Timmy alone. His wife had been elected secretary of her organization, which subsequently turned the living room into its headquarters. With each visit, Bloomhardt had to wade through more and more pamphlets and flyers, more posters, signs, petitions, and boxes of ERA buttons. He began to think of his house as an enemy camp.

Throughout the entire first week of August, while crouched behind the hedge across the street, he watched his driveway. In that driveway was a battered blue Volkswagen, its fenders riddled with rust, the engine hood as dimpled as a golf ball. Why that car seemed permanently parked in his driveway, he did not know. But he had a good idea.

His wife had taken a lover. Bloomhardt even believed he knew what kind of man her lover was. To own such a car, such an automotive blemish, he was probably an impoverished college student, a virile but witless stud in need of a haircut. He had been handed down to Annie by one of her so-called sisters who had grown bored with his limited, albeit athletic, sexual repertoire.

On the other hand, maybe Annie's lover merely wanted to create such an illusion. Maybe he was actually a sly Machiavellian businessman. A sales rep. Twenty years older than Annie, with a wife and four children on the other side of town. He dyed his hair and wore it swept back in an air-puffed pompadour to conceal its thinness. He came in the morning, while Timmy was at school, arriving and departing by taxi. The blue rustmobile was used to convey Annie and him incognito into the country, where he would spread a child's sleeping bag atop the grass, ease the cork from a bottle of cheap domestic wine, and proceed to make methodical but effective love to Bloomhardt's wife.

Bloomhardt could not stop such notions from clouding his mind. He loathed that Volkswagen as he loathed its owner, whom he vowed to destroy, to run off the road and bury them both, if necessary, in a heap of twisted metal and shattered glass.

But the owner of the car never showed himself. The blue Volkswagen remained parked in the driveway, as humiliating to Bloomhardt as if a used condom were fluttering from the mailbox flag.

All that week, at the end of each workday, Bloomhardt raced back to Fairfax Avenue and the concealment of the hedge. Occasionally he observed that the car had been moved slightly in his absence, that it was now parked to the right or left of its previous position, that there was fresh mud on the fenders. But as for Annie's lover, that elusive, smarmy cad, Bloomhardt failed to catch even a glimpse of him.

For six nights in a row, Bloomhardt seethed and fumed. When

not behind the hedge, he huddled in his car a block from the house, where he gulped down his dinner, greasy hamburgers and french fries, bitter coffee from a Styrofoam cup. Now and then he would reach beneath the car seat and pull forth a sixteen-inch length of steel pipe and rap it repeatedly against the palm of his hand.

On the seventh night he could not stand the thought of another greasy hamburger. The palm of his hand was red and sore from banging the pipe into it. He's moved in with her, Bloomhardt thought. That's why he never bothers to show himself. He must be a poor college student after all, too poor even to go to college. So he lies around all day and watches *my* television and drinks *my* beer and fucks *my* wife, with *my* poor little son locked in his room just a few feet down the hall. He probably has them all snorting cocaine by now! He probably has Timmy blinking like a pigeon, trying to read his picture books through a blue cannabis fog!

Armed with the pipe, Bloomhardt jumped out of his car and sprinted up the street. A minute later, soaked with perspiration but shivering with anger, he unlocked the front door and crept upstairs. He would catch the bounder in the act and bash him to a bloody pulp while Annie watched from bed, too horrified to scream!

It was well past midnight; the house was dark. At Timmy's room he paused outside the door, which was slightly ajar, and heard the boy's sibilant sleeping breath. With luck, Bloomhardt thought, he won't awaken to the bloody havoc I'm about to wreak.

Outside the open door of Annie's bedroom, he paused again. He clenched his teeth to stop their chattering, then wiped his hands, first one and then the other, on his trousers. All of a sudden he thought of being sent to prison for what he was about to do, he thought of the electric chair, of a metal cap screwed to his head, a lightning bolt zipping through his body. The image so terrified him that he nearly dropped the steel pipe.

Maybe instead of bashing in Annie's lover's head, he would merely dent it a little, give him a concussion. And knock out a few of his teeth, that would be a nice touch. What jury could fault him for that?

With this plan in mind, Bloomhardt felt around the doorjamb for the light switch. Finding it, he took a deep breath, counted silently to three, flipped on the light, and leaped inside, the pipe raised menacingly above his head. Annie, blinking nearsightedly, sat up in bed. There was no one beside her. She reached for her glasses on the nightstand and put them on, then gasped when she saw Bloomhardt, frozen in his stunned position, and pulled a pillow to her chest.

"What are you *doing* here?" she whispered hoarsely, eyes flitting from his to the long steel pipe he held to the ceiling.

"Hmmm?" Bloomhardt replied.

"I said what are you doing here?"

Slowly he lowered the pipe to chest level, but kept his arm tensed and ready. He went to the foot of the bed and peeked on the other side, he sank to his knees and peered beneath it. At the closet he yanked open the door and rummaged through the hanging clothes. Finally he faced his wife again.

"All right, where is he?"

"Where is who?"

"The guy who owns that Volkswagen out in the driveway. Where's he hiding?"

"I own that Volkswagen," she said.

"Huh?"

"I bought it for a hundred dollars from one of my friends. I need some kind of transportation, you know."

Bloomhardt smiled wryly. "You don't honestly expect me to believe that, do you?"

"Have you been drinking?"

"If that car is really yours," he said, "what's the number on the license plate?"

"I have no idea. What's yours?"

He could not remember. Suddenly he felt gormless and small, as stupid as a slug. "It's a nice car," he told her.

"What were you going to do with *that*?"

"This?" he said, and looked at the pipe as if he had only now discovered it. "Oh, listen, did you lose this? I, uh . . . I found it out in the yard."

"You found it out in the yard," she said.

"I, uh, I didn't want you running over it with the lawn mower, so I, uh, thought I'd better, you know . . ."

"Bring it in to me?" She glanced at the clock on the nightstand. "At ten after one in the morning?"

"Well . . . I didn't want you running over it with the lawn mower."

She looked at him a while longer and tried not to smile, the corners of her mouth twitching. Then she took off her glasses, returned them to the nightstand, and sank back against her pillow. "Turn off the light on your way out," she said.

He walked backwards to the door and switched off the light. Motionless, his hand still raised to the wall, he felt as weak as a shadow. As Annie stretched out in bed and rolled onto her side he heard the bedsprings creak, a delicious, nostalgic sound. The scent of her came to him through the darkness like an old memory, so dizzying that he leaned against the doorjamb for support. He would have cried had he been able, if the tears would come, so stupid and helpless did he feel. But as always the tears refused to emerge; they flooded his sinuses and dripped inward upon his heart, a Chinese water torture.

For several minutes he stood there in the darkness and imagined himself shriveling like a raisin. Then he whispered, "Annie?"

She did not reply.

"Annie? Sweetheart?"

"What?" she finally said.

"Can I stay tonight?"

So much time passed that he began to wonder if he had actually spoken or only thought of doing so. Then he heard a feathery rustling as she folded back the covers. "Don't bring the pipe," she said.

He undressed quickly and slid in beside her. He tried not to sleep, wanting to lie awake all night to preserve the feeling of her body against his, the silky, perfumed warmth. She fell asleep easily, her hand in his. When he awoke in the morning to find her no longer beside him, he felt cheated, duped by his own weariness, and he had to dress hurriedly or be late for work. He sneaked out the front door just as Helen Krakow was coming in the back, and jogged down the sidewalk to his car, shoelaces dragging.

O ver the course of the summer, Annie became a different woman. She seemed taller, she laughed more freely. On those occasions when he was able to infiltrate the bedroom, which he now thought of as solely her own, she did not cling to him after they had made love, but went downstairs to work on her column for the monthly newsletter. She changed her hairstyle, had it cut short and curled, the chestnut color highlighted with tawny streaks. She discarded her narrow granny glasses for over-sized lenses in translucent brown frames.

More than once she looked at her husband disdainfully and told him he was full of shit. Her self-assurance thrilled and frightened him. Sometimes she looked as if she had been crying, her eyes red, her mascara smeared, but she denied it and told him to go away. She seemed to change a little more each time he saw her. Reassuringly, though, she continued to wear the gold chain and locket he had given her. When he could, Bloomhardt kissed it for luck.

Though it was a strain on his budget, he bought Timmy an expensive microscope. Together they huddled over it, taking turns peering at a hair, a bubble of saliva, a dead fly. But the following week, when Timmy referred to the cobwebby filaments on a piece of moldy bread as mycelium, the aromatic blue mold as *Rhizopus*, Bloomhardt complained of eyestrain and coaxed his son outside to kick the soccer ball.

Later he gave the boy a telescope, but discovered an intense disliking for astronomy when Timmy corrected his father's identification of the craters Tycho and Kepler, his confusion of the Sea of Tranquility with the Sea of Serenity. Bloomhardt, neither tranquil nor serene, insisted they play with the soccer ball instead.

Not surprisingly, Timmy's agility with the ball soon increased. He showed his father how to lift the ball with his toes, how to bounce it from knee to head and catch it with his foot again. He was being tutored, he innocently explained, by one of Mommy's friends, a young woman who had played professionally in Europe.

The feminist organization grew like a promiscuous amoeba, endlessly splitting and increasing. A different committee convened every night. Dues and contributions flowed in from all corners. Annie, as secretary-treasurer and landlord, collected rent from the organization. She opened a separate bank account and paid herself a salary and instructed Bloomhardt to cut his support payments in half, but he continued to send the full amount, which Annie dutifully logged in her account book.

In his spare hours, Bloomhardt wrote voluminous notes; he filled one shoe box after another with his thoughts and observations. He told himself and Jake that he was working up to something bigger. In the meantime he scoured the newspapers for announcements of upcoming lectures by well-known feminists, and on the nights of these lectures, when he knew that Annie and her friends would be in attendance, with Timmy having been turned over to a feminist baby-sitter somewhere, he would sneak into his nine-room house and walk wistfully from room to room, a ghost in search of his former self.

Only occasionally did he beg Annie to let him come home. Every now and then she permitted him to spend the night, but come morning he was chased from the house two steps ahead of the arrival of Helen Krakow. Bloomhardt bristled at the mere thought of his neighbor, whom he had come to regard as his archnemesis, a ubiquitous dragon who filled his castle with poisonous smoke and with whom he must sooner or later do battle.

One Saturday morning early in September, Bloomhardt awoke with the feeling that the worst was behind him. There was no practical reason for such a thought, nothing had changed, and for five minutes he sat on the edge of Jake's sofa and waited for his sunniness to darken, but it did not. There was something in the air, a scent of newness, of regeneration. Bloomhardt sniffed it eagerly, quivering like a hound about to be sprung from his kennel.

"Don't tease me, God," he prayed.

Answered by no celestial guffaws, no cosmic giggles, he dressed and slipped away before Jake awoke. So in tune with the morning did Bloomhardt feel that he decided to walk to his house on Fairfax Avenue, a mile and a half away. Soon after, he began to jog. He felt his pores dilating like gills, gulping the sweet air. Let everything stale roll off me, he thought as he jogged away the stiffness. Let it trickle off my skin in an ambergris sweat. Even the tingle of his heels as they jarred against the concrete he found enjoyable, the itch of his skin and the tight, hot stitch in his side.

Two blocks from his house, he spotted the crowd milling around it. His first thought was of an accident, a house fire, a furnace explosion, something gruesome enough to attract the hundred people trampling his grass. His heart squealing with every step, he broke into a run. Then, eyes watering, he saw the sign planted near the sidewalk: BIG YARD SALE TODAY! He saw the card tables sagging with castoffs, saw a half-dozen posters proclaiming SUPPORT ERA! He saw big-breasted Helen Krakow presiding over the whole affair like a circus ringmaster.

Panting and itching, walking stooped over as he tried to catch his breath, he searched for Annie in the crowd. He spotted her in a far corner of the yard, seated at a table stacked high with feminist literature. She was flanked by eight other women, four on each side. Annie was speaking intently to a timid-looking teenage girl who kept up a steady rhythm with her nodding. The women seated around Annie were smiling. Never had his wife looked more attractive to him. Never less accessible.

Still lightheaded, he wended his way toward her, weaving between cardboard boxes and wobbly tables and chattering customers. He came upon a woman wearing a yellow bathrobe and black slippers who was examining a large green plastic Buddha, and immediately Bloomhardt recognized that Buddha as the one he had won for Annie at a carnival eight—or was it nine?—years ago. Now there was a strip of masking tape stretched across its navel, with a price marked on it: *50¢*.

"This is mine," said Bloomhardt as he snatched the plastic deity from the woman's hands. "It's not for sale."

She stared after him for a few seconds as he marched away, then announced to a friend standing next to her, "I didn't want it anyway. It was plastic, for God's sake. I wouldn't have paid more than a quarter."

Next, Bloomhardt recognized a box of his college textbooks, ten cents a book. On the same table was his twenty-year-old first baseman's mitt, the leather split, the threads broken. In the same box was a deflated basketball, a Ping-Pong paddle, a kazoo. He lingered over each item and remembered when they, and he, had been young.

"These aren't for sale," he muttered. Then, still clutching the Buddha under his arm, he shoved each of the other objects beneath the table. "These aren't for sale!" he shouted to the crowd. "Don't anybody buy them, because they're mine and they aren't for sale!" Hugging the green Buddha, he turned to confront Annie, but took only two brisk steps before Helen Krakow blocked his path.

"You," he said. "You put her up to this, didn't you?"

"Good morning, John," she answered smiling. "I was hoping you'd show up today. There's a man here that you should meet."

"This is my goddamn Buddha, Helen. It's not for sale."

"Fine," she said, and patted his arm. "You keep it, okay? But wait right here for a second, I'll be right back."

She turned and made her way toward a stocky young man in a crisp tan suit, who, several yards away, was engaged in conversation with another woman. Helen spoke to him, then took him by the arm and led him back to Bloomhardt.

"John," she said, "I'd like you to meet David Hughes. David, this is John Bloomhardt, the man you've heard so much about."

"This Buddha is not for sale," Bloomhardt told him.

Hughes smiled. As he reached inside his jacket he said, "I'm not interested in your Buddha, but I do have something I'd like to give to you." He brought forth a large manila envelope, which he then wedged between Bloomhardt's chest and the plastic statue he clutched.

"By the way," said Helen, "David is Annie's lawyer. His wife is vice-president of our organization. And in case you don't feel like reading that document just now, what it says is that Ann is suing you for divorce. The grounds are adultery and mental cruelty."

Bloomhardt blinked. His lips began to twitch. It was a joke of some kind, it had to be. He stared at Helen's grinning mouth and felt his eyes begin to cross, felt his internal organs breaking free from their moorings to slide down his legs and gather like wet socks around his ankles.

"You conniving bitch," he muttered.

"Now, now," cautioned the lawyer. "Let's not say anything that might very well result in litigation."

Bloomhardt looked toward Annie and saw that she had risen from her folding chair and, poised on her toes, was watching. Their eyes met, held for five seconds. Then she looked away. But what was that expression he had seen flash across her face? he wondered. Her familiar half-smile of apology, as if to say *Forgive me, I can't help it?* Or had it been something else—a smirk, a sneer?

He took a step toward her. The lawyer put his hand on Bloomhardt's arm. "I would advise against any further contact between you and your estranged wife until your lawyer and I have—"

"And I," Bloomhardt interrupted as he turned to face him, "would advise that you take your hand off me, or you'll be wiping your estranged ass with a bloody estranged stump."

Helen's eyes grew wide; she grinned expectantly. But slowly the lawyer withdrew his hand, and as he fumbled for a retort, Bloomhardt strode away. Annie, however, had disappeared now; her chair was empty. He spotted a knot of women moving toward the house, and from its center a flash of yellow, the same yellow as that of the blouse his wife was wearing.

"Annie, wait!" he screamed as he elbowed people out of the way. "Goddamn it, Annie, just wait one fucking minute, for Chrissake!"

But the front door opened and closed again before he could reach the steps. He bounded onto the porch and yanked on the door. It was locked. "Annie!" he shouted, and, dropping the Buddha, pounded the wood with both fists. "This is my house, damn it! Somebody open this door!"

The glass in the windows rattled as he pummeled the door frame, but the door remained locked. Out of breath, he sagged against it. Seconds later he remembered the crowd in his yard and turned to find everyone motionless, two hundred staring eyes.

"This is my house," he told them. "And that is my yard. And if any—hey, you! Get your hands off the bicycle, that's mine!" He kicked the plastic Buddha and sent it sailing over their heads, then leaped off the porch and, while running toward the man who had been examining the bicycle, screamed, "Don't anybody buy *one goddamn thing,* because it's all mine and it's not for sale!

"Give me that!" he snarled as he yanked the ten-speed racer away from a startled middle-aged man. Taped to the bicycle's frame was a cardboard sign that read *$10.00.* Bloomhardt ripped the sign off and kicked it high into the air. Then, holding on to the handlebars, he ran through the crowd, zigzagging erratically toward the street.

"Not for sale!" he cried. "Go home! Get out of my yard! This is my life and I want it and it's NOT FOR SALE!"

Nearing the sidewalk, he set his left foot on a pedal, swung his right leg up, and landed heavily on the seat. He bounced over the curb, grazed a parked car with his knee, and veered onto the street. Pedaling fiercely, he steered to the left and rode away, his eyes watering as he cut one last glance toward his house. There on his porch, standing like an Amazon sentinel, was Helen Krakow, her arms crossed triumphantly.

Bloomhardt leaned over the handlebars. Teeth clenched, legs churning like pistons, he rode down the center of the street, defying another vehicle to get in his way.

bloomhardt neither knew nor cared where he was going. What difference did it make? Mox nix. He pedaled hard, until every muscle and joint in his body seemed aflame. Three miles later, exhausted, he released a long moaning breath, leaned back to coast, and uncurled his spine.

The word DIVORCE popped into his head and nearly knocked

him off the bike. He saw it printed in tall black letters on the screen of his skull, set against a fluorescent orange background and surrounded by exclamation points of light. To regain his equilibrium and fight off nausea, he breathed deeply and pedaled hard, he immersed himself in the scenery and the strain of his aching muscles, in the pitted concrete and its fading painted lines. Only by such concentration could he stave off sickness. He heard every crack of his knee joints, every slip of the gears. He felt the long nose of the seat sniffing his crotch, felt the smooth tape of the handlebars growing slick beneath his sweaty hands.

Somewhere in this self-hypnosis, his consciousness made a quiet exit. A super-consciousness arose in its place, a massive awareness that acted not as filter but as synthesizer of all sensations. He felt the city slipping away behind him, felt himself being drawn toward the North Magnetic Pole. There was oil in his blood now, his perspiration the grease to lubricate his sockets. He and the bicycle were a single fluid unit, a twentieth-century centaur of man and machine.

Far to his left lay Lake Erie, flat and sprawling, its curtain of morning fog slowly rising. To his right was farmland—a white clapboard house, a patch of woods, a cluster of cream-faced Holsteins agraze in the pasture. He filled his lungs with country air, he smelled his own nostrils. On his tongue he tasted himself, his saliva, his fluids, a mouth rubbery and stale. He opened his mouth and bathed his tongue in the breeze of his movement. He stripped himself of thought, he sailed along on liquid wheels, man and machine and nature joined in a hymn of mindlessness.

Ten-speed racer with your whir of spokes and your gear-shifting clicks, you take the bass, sing it low, sing it low. And Nature, with your drone of insects and chirp of birds, you take the lead because you wrote the song. And you, unthinking man, you who are nothing and a part of everything, vibrate in harmony, hum with your heart, keep a steady beat with the thumping of your pulse.

Crouched low over the handlebars, Bloomhardt pedaled at an even pace, locked in tune. The wheels sang and the road slipped by beneath him and the warm wind of movement brought soothing water to his eyes. It was a September morning painted with a Technicolor palette, and he was a part of it. Each blade of grass had been daubed deep green, lime green on the milkweed stalks, viridian on the hemlocks. The dandelions had delicate gray coiffures, a killdeer whistled at his pumping legs. Out in the field, a rusted harrow lay with its knuckles sunk in the dirt. Swarms of gnats streaked by, a wren shat from a telephone line. A distant rooster crowed and was answered by a dove. Flies surveyed the topography of a decaying rabbit carcass that had been flattened by yesterday's traffic. A butterfly crossed Bloomhardt's path and dabbed its tissue wings against his cheek. Now and then a small cloud licked the curve of the sky. Now and then a dog barked, a breeze blew. Now and then the word DIVORCE lighted up in Bloomhardt's brain and nearly tumbled him onto his head.

Like a yogi striving for Nirvana, he submerged himself in the day. There was a dog rolling in the grass beside the road, playing with a bone. Bloomhardt could hear the bone clacking against the dog's teeth. He peered over the front wheel at the prow his shadow made and recognized himself in it, that watery splotch of black skimming along the highway. Everything was fine, was it not? Simply dandy. The world was a nuthouse, and he was just another acorn.

In this manner Bloomhardt rode, the riding a meditation for him, a necessary transcendence until he could pass safely beyond the point where the intensity of his anger and despair might ignite his spirit and incinerate it like cellophane. He pedaled with a savage disregard for pain, working up one good metaphysical sweat after another.

Up ahead, a single lane of asphalt snaked invitingly to the left. Like a racer on a track, Bloomhardt banked into the steep turn and glided through it. Good-bye two-lane country road, hello blacktop frontier. Now he was truly free, no cars zipping by, no honking horns, no distractions to shake him from his trance.

It was not long before the road began to slant downward. As his bicycle, his extended self, rolled faster, Bloomhardt ceased pedaling and fixed his eyes on the blur of pavement. The decline grew steeper, and for an instant he thought of the long push he would have when he turned for home, but then told himself, Mox nix, watch the road, see the strobe of sunlight through the trees, hear the world whirring by. He even closed his eyes for a moment to more completely submerge himself. But when he opened them again, a realization struck him: *Good God, this is dangerous!* He was traveling fifty, maybe sixty miles per hour now—at any rate too damn fast for a puny man astride a hollow bar of metal. He leaned forward and squeezed the handbrakes. The pads squealed as they hugged the tires, but the bike slowed only a little. And what was that sign he had just passed, a bold black L on a yellow background?

Ninety-degree turn! his consciousness screamed. *Slow down, fool!*

He squeezed the brakes until his knuckles burned, but knew that at even half his present speed, he could not negotiate the turn. With legs stuck out like a balancing pole, he steered the bicycle off the edge of the road and onto the soft dirt. Instantly he lost control and crashed into the steep bank, up the bank and then down and then into it again as the handlebars were yanked spinning from his hands. Bucked off the seat, he rode the wheel for a moment before flipping backward to the ground, where he rolled and tumbled and slid, clawing and grasping, until, twenty-five yards later, he bumped to a halt facedown on the side of the bank, feet above his head. The bicycle, which had somehow gotten behind him, crashed down squarely upon his back and thumped a tire against his skull.

For a long time he lay motionless among the leaves and weeds. His legs were entangled in the bicycle and he could not tell where they ended and the machine began. He breathed heavily, smelling the humus he had plowed up with his nose. Finally a thought came to him. *I survived, I'm alive.* It was not a particularly gratifying thought. Because now he knew that the pain would begin, and yep, there it was, ouch, owww, oooh geez damn does that ever hurt!

Gingerly he disentangled himself and sat up, arms and face burning with bleeding scratches, knees cut, trousers shredded, one ear lacerated, both elbows already purple. Three fingers on his right hand were jammed, half the nail on his thumb torn away. His nose felt as if it had been introduced to a swinging sledgehammer, and he could not seem to uncross his eyes. His scrotum felt as if it had been caught in a revolving door.

Of his vintage Italian racer, the transport of his youth, what was not bent or twisted beyond repair was broken. He stared at the bicycle as if it were a corpse, and had his own discomfort not been so overwhelming, he might have uttered a few words in eulogy. But mox nix, what good were words? There was no solace in this world, no harmony. Why waste on words the energy needed to stave off pain?

For another fifteen minutes he lay motionless, hoping for a car or truck to happen by. But none came. Finally he pushed himself to his feet and, moving uncertainly, began the long ascent. His bicycle he left where it had fallen, because he did not have the strength to carry another broken body. With each shuffling step he felt his soul leaking out through his wounds, hissing like air from a punctured balloon. He felt his empty body caving in upon itself, his heart collapsing around his spine. The word DIVORCE exploded in neon inside his skull and then flashed with the beat of his pulse. Flesh and metal and love, he told himself. It all gets broken in the end, it all falls apart. He walked stiffly, gingerly, bent in pain, and listened to the echo of tears as they plunked into the hollow where his soul had once been.

at a farmhouse near the top of the hill, he telephoned Jake and awaited his arrival. "Aren't you a little old to be doing Evel Knievel stunts?" Jake asked as he helped Bloomhardt to the car.

"It was an accident. I wasn't paying attention. I was distracted. Sorry if I've ruined your afternoon by nearly killing myself, Jake, but Annie is going to divorce me!"

"Hey, you didn't happen to notice any nubile little farm girls in the area, did you, Bloomers?"

"Boy, oh boy, you're a professional through and through, Jake. I sure am glad I came to you with my problems."

"Since when have we been on a professional basis? We're friends, and as a friend I'm telling you to relax. Don't panic until you see the mushroom cloud."

"You just don't understand."

"Right, I am but a dumb chauffeur. So where do you want to go—home or to the hospital?"

"Back down the hill to pick up my bike."

"I thought you said it was demolished."

"It is. But I want it anyway."

Unfortunately, all Bloomhardt could find of his bicycle was a scrape of red paint on an overturned rock. "What kind of degenerate would steal a broken bike?" he asked hopelessly, kicking through the dead leaves.

"A real sicko," said Jake. "Let's hurry home and alert the FBI and Scotland Yard. This sounds like the beginning of another reign of terror, if you ask me."

"Damn it, Jake, I'm serious. That bike meant a lot to me." He

163

gazed down the road, then screamed at the top of his lungs, "Bring back my fucking bicycle, you thief!"

"Geez, Bloomers, take it easy. It was just a hunk of metal, you know. And a useless one at that."

"No, it wasn't. It was my past, my youth. It was all the good times I can remember."

"Well," said Jake as he climbed back into his car, "tell it good-bye."

Later that evening, Bloomhardt lay stretched out on the sofa in his underwear, an ice bag to his forehead, his wounds painted with iodine, his body stinging from the inside out. Jake leaned against the wall and sipped a beer. "It's good to see you relaxing," he said. "You'll need to be fresh when you start your European adventure next week."

Bloomhardt shifted the ice bag to his shoulder. "That trip to Europe was your idea. I never agreed to it."

"So who asked you to agree? You've got to take your doctor's advice, whether you like it or not."

"A few hours ago you said you weren't my doctor, just my friend."

"I was off duty then. Besides, I already bought your ticket. Economy class, of course."

Bloomhardt shook his head. "Forget it, I'm not going."

"Ahh, do I remember my first trip to Europe! The botanical gardens in bloom, the meat pies and cheese, Belgian girls with their long hairy legs . . ."

"Jake, listen to me. I do not—"

"You do not know how to thank me, I know. But you can begin by not chewing on my ice bag, and stop looking so betrayed."

"But what if—"

"What if you don't go? You'll regret it the rest of your life, that's what. Yep, I can see it all now—there you are, Monsieur Bloom-bloom, working on your first novel in a little café in Montmartre, sipping a Pernod and blackberry brandy while you write. Later you'll stroll up to a pissoir and watch all the pretty schoolgirls walk by. That night you'll have dinner with a tubercular but beautiful streetwalker with perfumed armpit hair, and maybe she won't even charge you for her favors because she's falling in love with you. In the morning you'll awaken with the sun and go back to your novel, which, of course, will be a runaway best-seller, soon to be a major motion picture."

Bloomhardt kept shaking his head. "No no no no no no no."

"Listen to you, blubbering already. Well, don't even try to thank me, because words aren't sufficient to express your gratitude. By the way, remember that passport you got a few years back for the belated honeymoon you never took? I had Annie check to make sure, and guess what—the passport is still valid."

"She's in on this?" he asked, nearly choking on his surprise.

"And very happy for you, I might add. Yep, you get Europe and she gets two weeks of peace and quiet. So that's it, pal, I've taken care of everything. All you have to do is pack your bags. Take my advice and travel light."

Bloomhardt's body felt incapable of any travel, light or heavy. Nor did he have the strength to argue, for he knew that he could not possibly outlast Jake. Holding the ice bag to his elbow, he stared at the floor and blinked stupidly.

"That's my boy," said Jake. "Just sit there and dream about all the fun you're going to have. I need to go out for a while, I have an appointment with a perky little astronomy student who's having trouble distinguishing Labia Majoris from Labia Minoris. Very painstaking work. So don't wait up for me, I won't be home until the cock crows thrice. Toodle-oo!"

Jake flashed him a hairy grin and disappeared out the door. Bloomhardt stared at the doorknob until he could hold his head up no longer, then fell back onto the sofa with the ice bag on his chest. He drifted off to sleep and into a dream of men and women who, squabbling in a language he could not understand, had stolen the corpse of his bicycle. Dressed in animal skins, they huddled around a campfire and roasted his bike until it was nothing but a skeleton of charred bones. Then they ripped the skeleton apart and gnawed on the bones and made loud slurping noises as they sucked out the marrow. Bloomhardt was seated inside the circle of Europeans, dangerously close to the fire, naked and shivering, hugging himself as his stomach rumbled hungrily. One of the cannibals wiped a hand across his greasy lips and, grinning like a devil, reached into the fire to pluck out the last of the bones. Bloomhardt saw that it was his bicycle's needle-nosed seat, but in the cannibal's hand it turned into a skull. The cannibal tossed the skull to Bloomhardt, who caught it faceup. Now it was Timmy's head and all fleshed out, but the lenses of his glasses were shattered and there was blood oozing from his mouth. Bloomhardt began to scream and woke himself and sat there still screaming, clutching the dripping ice bag, until someone from the neighboring apartment pounded on the wall.

Part Three

THE DAY . . .
The night . . .

The day . . .
The night . . .

Bloomhardt felt each moment of his life slipping through him, as sharp as a knife, as wide as a house. All during the week that followed, when he called Annie or attempted to visit, he seldom got beyond Helen Krakow, who threatened him with a writ of harassment, a restraining order. Only once was he allowed to speak with his son, and even then he was made to wait on the sidewalk until Timmy was ushered out to him. Kneeling at the edge of the concrete while the boy stood on the edge of the lawn, with four women poised ten yards back, arms crossed over their chests, he reached out to hold his son's hands.

"How's it going, sport?" he asked.

"Fine," Timmy said, his face expressionless. Bloomhardt could not remember when this awkwardness, this distance, had crept back between them, but there it was again, a wedge of formality that held them apart despite the joining of their hands.

"How's school these days?"

"Fine."

"Are you learning anything new?"

"Le chien, le chat, l'homme."

"Gee, that's terrific. What does it mean?"

"The dog, the cat, the man."

"Boy, that's really something. Hey, do you still play with the soccer ball I gave you?"

"It broke."

"It did? How'd that happen?"

"Somebody kicked it over in Helen's driveway and she ran over it with her car."

Bloomhardt clenched his teeth. He took a deep breath and slowly released it. "Well, don't worry, honey, I'll get you another one."

"Helen already did."

"Oh."

"I still have yours, though. Helen put it in the garbage can, but I took it out. She doesn't know I have it. It's under my bed."

A wave of gratitude washed over Bloomhardt. His breath felt heavy and difficult to control. "So," he managed, "how's everything else? How are you feeling these days?"

"Fine," said the boy.

"That's good. I miss you a lot, you know. All the time."

Timmy pushed his glasses up over the bridge of his nose. He blinked.

"Well, gee, I guess I'd better let you go back in the house now. It was really nice to see you, sport. You be good, okay?"

"I will."

"Do everything Mommy tells you to do."

"I do."

"I know, you're a good boy." Bloomhardt leaned forward and kissed his cheek. "Well, goodbye, son. You run back inside now. I wouldn't want you to catch cold."

"Goodbye, Daddy," said the boy. Bloomhardt was happy to see that his son did not sprint back to the house, he walked, he walked slowly, and twice glanced over his shoulder as his father waved good-bye. Surely that counted for something.

After that, the nights turned cold. Bloomhardt felt his soul, like a maple leaf losing chlorophyll, turning brittle and brown. When not at work, he sat dully in front of the television set in Jake's apartment, a can of warm beer in his hand. Sometimes Jake would speak to him and receive no answer, would speak again, and again receive only silence, then would shake his head and walk away.

On Saturday night, Jake invited a young woman to his apartment for dinner, so Bloomhardt, feeling unfit for human company, pulled on his jacket and went outside. He drove to Fairfax Avenue, parked the car, and climbed out. Considering himself as insubstantial as a ghost, and therefore invisible, he walked up to the living room window and peered inside. Annie and Timmy were seated cross-legged on the sofa, facing one another, a jigsaw puzzle on a board between them. Bloomhardt realized that he could, for a change, enter the house without interference, but he found himself unable to do so. The picture of his wife and son seemed complete without him. He watched them a few minutes longer, then returned to his car. At midnight he crept back to Jake's apartment. Wrapped in a blanket, he lay on the sofa and listened to the squeak of Jake's bed and the gasping moans of Jake's guest. He covered his head with a pillow and hoped he would fall asleep and smother himself.

Bloomhardt did not climb off the sofa until the following afternoon, long after Jake's guest had departed. He then staggered to the kitchen, drank half a glass of warm water, and dropped into a chair at the table. Jake, who was standing at the stove, and adding spices to a pot of bubbling spaghetti sauce, told him, "Good afternoon, Bloominski. By the way, you look pathetic. You look the way my brother did the time he broke his dick. Did I ever tell you that story?"

"No, and please don't. I'm depressed enough already."

"Good God, man, why? You've got the world on a string, you're sitting on a rainbow, got the string around your feeeng-ger . . .!"

"Knock it off, Jake, okay? I'm not in the mood for a serenade."

"No? So what are you in the mood for?"

"Suicide would be nice."

"Ah, I see. Tired of living, sick of trying—that sort of thing?"

"Exactly."

Jake licked the mixing spoon and then laid it aside. "This is far more serious than I thought," he said. "Have you actually been contemplating suicide?"

"Only every waking hour."

"Might I suggest, then, that you spend more time asleep?"

"Believe me, I've tried. I'd sleep forever if I could."

Jake thought about this for a moment, then covered the pot of sauce and turned off the burner. "Get dressed, Bloomers. It's a perfect afternoon for you and me to take a walk."

Bloomhardt glanced out the window. "It's cold and gray and rainy, Jake."

"You see? Perfect!" Taking Bloomhardt by the arm, he hauled him to his feet and into the bedroom, then sat on the bed while Bloomhardt, protesting, lethargically dressed.

"I don't want to take a walk," Bloomhardt grumbled as he pulled a sweater over his head. "I've got too many things on my mind right now."

"No, you don't. It just feels like that because your brain's all clogged up with self-pity. By the way, your socks don't match."

"So what?"

"That's the spirit!" Jake jumped to his feet and went to the closet, from which he pulled a tan trench coat and a hooded yellow rain slicker. As he tossed the slicker to Bloomhardt, he said, "Button up, Bloomless. Wouldn't want you to catch pneumonia before you kill yourself. Die healthy, that's always been my motto."

"Why can't I wear the trench coat?"

"Because you're the one with the long face, and long faces look better in yellow. Don't you have any fashion sense?"

Ruefully, Bloomhardt shrugged on the slicker. "I don't suppose you'd consider telling me where we're going?"

"What? And ruin the surprise?"

Twenty minutes later they were twelve blocks from Jake's apartment, their faces shiny with rain as they stood beneath the faded maroon canvas canopy of the Louis P. Irving Funeral Home. "I guess you think this is funny," said Bloomhardt.

"Hey, this is no joke. It just so happens I have some business here today."

"Sure you do."

"I do! And the truth is, I thought a little fresh air and exercise might do you some good, so I dragged you along to keep me company. Okay?"

"I can't remember when I've enjoyed myself more."

"Me too. So come on, let's get this over with and then go grab a beer somewhere. Lucky for us, there doesn't appear to be a stiff-in-residence today. I'd hate to have to crash a private party."

With Bloomhardt in tow, Jake went onto the narrow porch and rang the bell. Bloomhardt stood to the side and tried to remain invisible. The man who answered the door was dressed in a black velour jogging suit and yellow sneakers, stood five feet eight inches tall, was slight of build but with a round, pixieish, big-eyed face.

"Mr. Irving?" asked Jake.

"No, Mr. Irving isn't in today. I'm his assistant."

"Igor?" said Jake.

"Pardon me?"

"Just kidding. Listen, I hope this isn't a bad time, but I'm doing some comparison shopping today and I was wondering if I might take a look at your merchandise. You do have a display room, don't you? A couple of floor models, at least? Something we could test-drive, so to speak?"

"Well, yes, we do, but—"

"Fine," said Jake. "You don't mind if we step inside for a minute, do you? This won't take long." He grabbed Bloomhardt, who was inching his way to the street, by the tail of his coat and dragged him inside past the startled assistant mortician.

"By the way," said Jake, "my name is Pithonus, and this is my friend Bloomhardt. The coffin is for him, sort of a going-away present. He's going to commit suicide any day now."

His eyes bigger than ever, the assistant looked at Bloomhardt, who, smiling wanly, shook his head and said, "And his name is Speers."

"Right," said Jake. "Speers Pithonus." He seized the assistant's hand and pumped it enthusiastically. "Pleased to meet you, how do you do."

"Pithonus?" the assistant asked.

"Right. It's like Piss-on-us, but with a lisp. Now then, which way to the showroom? Over here?"

"No! That's the Blue Room, where friends of the deceased gather prior to the service."

"Blue Room," said Jake, chuckling. "Cute. So where do you keep the demos?"

"I'm not really going to commit suicide," Bloomhardt said.

"Sure he is, he's just being modest. I'm hoping to get it all on videotape, make a documentary, call it *Bloomie Bites the Dust*. Hey, don't look so surprised, there's quite a market for this kind of thing."

"Really?" asked Igor.

"No shit. Listen, I've already been nominated for an Oscar three times, I'm surprised you never heard of me. Hey, I just had a wild idea. Picture this, Bloomie: Igor as your costar. Sort of a before-and-after docudrama? Chills, right? Shit, it'll be fabulous, a classic, I've got goosebumps just thinking about it."

"Really?" said Igor. "And my name is Robert. Robert V. Schnell."

"Glad to know ya," said Jake. "Listen, V—you don't mind if I call you V, do you? That's a great stage name, by the way. What's it stand for, Vivisection?"

Robert looked as if he might giggle. "Vance," he said.

"I'd like to go home now, Jake," said Bloomhardt. "Let go of my arm, please."

"Let's see the merchandise first, okay? Which, V, is where?"

"Through this door," said Robert as he led the way. "About this movie, Mr. Pithonus. Exactly what would you want me to do in it?"

"Just be yourself, V. Be your own beautiful and charismatic you.

Oh, maybe a little embalming, bloodletting, slice-and-dicing—death from the inside out, get the picture? All the local color. Holy squat in a bucket, Bloomie, look what they got in here!"

Jake dragged Bloomhardt into a large open room, a room furnished with antique brass lamps, tapestries, and colorful lithographs hung on buttercup-yellow walls, a plush umber carpet, and half a dozen shiny caskets resting on the wheeled tables that are known as church trucks.

"This isn't amusing," Bloomhardt muttered.

Jake shoved Bloomhardt and Schnell face to face. "Hey, you guys are going to be the stars of this epic, so get to know each other whilst I peruse the inventory, okay?" And before Bloomhardt could protest, Jake was out of reach.

"This is very exciting, isn't it?" asked Schnell.

"Very," said Bloomhardt.

"Nothing like this has ever happened to me before."

"Lucky you."

"I'd never even considered being an actor, but Mr. Pithonus makes it all sound so interesting. Tell me, do you really think I'm right for the part?"

"A natural."

"And are you really going to commit suicide?"

"It seems more and more likely."

"Hey, V!" Jake called from across the room. "What's the sticker price on this little runabout here?"

"Oh, that's a very popular model. That one goes for just under eighteen hundred."

"Nice," said Jake, "very nice. But to tell you the truth, I think what Bloomie needs is something with a little more zip. Got anything with tailfins?"

"Tailfins?" said Schnell.

"Yeah, and sport mirrors on the sides." Standing at the head of the casket, Jake began to push it toward them. "Vroom vroom vroooom!" he said. "Maybe a six-cylinder, two hundred horses under the hood? Hey, what kind of mileage can we expect from one of these babies? I don't see any bucket seats, are those optional? How about air bags? AM-FM? How about trunk space? We take a lot of ski trips."

"I'm, uh . . ." said Schnell. He looked to Bloomhardt again, who merely smiled and shrugged.

"What kind of warranty comes with this?" Jake asked. "How about Ziebarting? We don't want Bloomie to start oxidizing after a decade or two, do we? I mean, what if we decide to do a sequel?"

Schnell stepped closer to Bloomhardt. "He's putting me on now, isn't he? No one else has ever asked for those things."

"It's the union," Bloomhardt explained. Despite himself, he was beginning to enjoy Jake's antics. "Actors' Equity. They can be real sticklers sometimes."

Schnell nodded. He turned to Jake again and saw that he had climbed into one of the coffins and was sitting upright with his legs stretched out comfortably beneath the half-closed lid. "Mr. Pith-onus, please! Please, you mustn't, I can't let you do that, please come out!"

But Jake cut him off by breaking into song. "Sailing, sailing, over the bounding main!" he sang in a loud basso, while rowing with an imaginary oar. He winked at Schnell and called, "Your turn in the apple barrel tonight, matey!"

Schnell looked to Bloomhardt for help. Bloomhardt smiled helplessly.

Now Jake began to sing in a lisping falsetto, "Oh, we sailed on the good ship Venus, with a ball and a half between us. The fig-urehead was a boy in bed and the mast was an upright penis!" In his basso voice he added, "Ho ho ho, and a bottle of Old Spice!"

Timidly, Schnell touched him on the arm. "Mr. Pithonus, please. I'm afraid you might damage the lining."

"Sure, sure," said Jake as he climbed out. "Just rehearsing a scene from the movie, seeing how it would play. I'm thinking of doing a musical version. You do sing, don't you?"

"Well . . ." said Schnell, and cleared his throat.

"I knew it! Bloomie, get this man a contract!"

He threw his arm around Schnell's shoulder, drew him close, and steered him back toward Bloomhardt. "Listen, V, there's just a couple more things I need to know. You do women too, right?"

"Excuse me?"

"You know, down in the embalming room, or whatever you cut-ups call it. You work on women too, right? An Equal Opportunity systems-flusher?"

"Well, yes, of course."

"Uh-huh. So tell me, do you ever get the urge to, you know, explore their options?"

"I'm not sure I understand your question, Mr. Pithonus."

"Don't try," Bloomhardt warned.

"Come on, V, you know what I mean. Ever doink one of them?"

Schnell froze for a moment. Then he tried to pull away, but Jake, with an arm hugging his shoulders, held him close. "Hey, don't take the question personally, I'm doing research for the movie. Right, Bloomie? Listen, I didn't mean to imply that there was anything funny going on. I mean, geez, just the thought of that kind of thing gives me the willies."

Schnell's body became less rigid. He exhaled through his nose, then nodded solemnly.

"Unless she was real young," Jake added. "Like fourteen or so. . . . Okay, okay, you're right. What does age matter, just so long as she's got big bazooms, right, Bloomers?"

Bloomhardt rolled his eyes. Schnell, his face drained of color, stared incredulously at Jake.

"Now then, about rigor mortis," Jake said. "What I need to know is, do the jugs get hard too? Hey, there's no way to self-induce that, is there? 'Cause I know some ladies who could really benefit from that procedure."

Bloomhardt laid his hand on Jake's and tried to peel it off Schnell's shoulder. "Enough, Jake. Tell the nice man good-bye."

"Come to think of it," Jake said. "I know some men who could use a lift from localized rigor mortis. Hey, if we could get the patent on this, we could all be zillionaires overnight!"

"Turn it off, Jake. Enough already. Just stop it."

"But women," Jake mused. "That's where the big money is. You find a way to turn tits to stone, and *bam!* Easy Street."

Bloomhardt threw his hands into the air. "Aaaggghhh!" he cried as he turned and fled the room.

Jake patted Schnell's shoulder. "He can't stand talking about tits," he explained. "When he was a baby, his mother refused to breast-feed him. His father had to do it. Bloomie never got over it. But hey, thanks for the test drive, V. You'll be hearing from us soon. Ciao!"

Jake finally caught up with Bloomhardt less than six blocks from the apartment. "Christ, Bloomers, slow down. You want me to have a heart attack?"

"I think total paralysis would be more fitting."

"What's the matter, you think it's wrong to doink a corpse?"

"Why do I listen to you?"

"I once doinked a girl who was unconscious. She'd had too much to drink. I told her all about it as soon as she came around. She didn't seem to mind, so I doinked her again. She was better unconscious."

Bloomhardt could not help himself, he smiled. "How in the world did a man like you ever get a Ph.D.?"

"I guess you don't know what Ph.D. really stands for."

"I guess maybe I don't."

"It stands for Pull Hard on Dick." Jake threw an arm around Bloomhardt's shoulder. "So there, you see? Life's not so mysterious after all, is it?"

"Not with you around to explain things, Jake."

"Glad to hear it. So, then, still plan to commit suicide?"

"I guess I could put it off for a while."

"Good choice." Jake reached into his pocket and brought forth a long brown envelope. "Here. Enjoy."

"What's this?"

"Can't you read? It's a one-way ticket to Luxembourg. Plus three hundred dollars in mad money."

"Oh no," Bloomhardt said, vehemently shaking his head.

"Oh yes," said Jake. "We agreed on this last week, remember?"

"*You* agreed."

"Same thing."

"Forget it, Jake. I'm not going."

"Yes you are, Bloomers. Tomorrow morning, in fact. Ten A.M. All you've got to do is pack a bag, get drunk, climb on the plane, and pinch the stewardess's ass. Everything else has been taken care of."

"Jake, I can't, I can't, I just can't—"

"Yes, you can, can, can. And perhaps I should repeat that it is a one-way ticket you're holding. Which means that the responsibility of getting home again will be yours. Maybe you'll use your mad money, maybe you'll stay there forever, maybe you'll pull a chicken-enshit move like wiring your parents for the money. But the thing is, my friend, you will have to do *something*. Which is a lot more than you've done lately. And frankly, mein schatz, I'm fed up."

Bloomhardt stared at the envelope. "And what if I refuse to go?"

"Then I will compliment you on your decisiveness, I will shake your hand, kiss your mouth, boot you out of my apartment, and take the trip myself."

"You mean . . . ?"

"I mean *au revoir*, Bloomburger. *Adiós.* Good-bye."

Bloomhardt's pace grew slower and slower. Blinking dazedly, staring at the brown envelope, he finally came to a halt. Good-bye, he thought. It sounded so conclusive, so terminal. Good-bye was what you said to a moldering loved one when you went to Robert V. Schnell's Blue Room. It was what you said to a flattened soccer ball before sliding it into the gloom beneath your bed.

"Well?" Jake asked, but gently. "What's it going to be?"

Very slowly, Bloomhardt lifted his head. He looked down the rain-slick street, gazed up at the gray sky. He felt as top-heavy as a hewn tree that has yet to fall.

he rang the bell and waited. Annie opened the door, smiling, dressed in red corduroy slacks and a cream-colored sweater, her hair loose, her feet bare. His mouth went dry when he saw her.

"Hi," he said.

"Why did you ring the bell? The door wasn't locked."

"I never know anymore if it's safe for me to come in."

"The house isn't mined, if that's what you mean."

He peered over her shoulder. "Are you alone?"

"Just Timmy and me," she said. "So relax, okay? You're safe. For the time being, anyway."

For another thirty seconds he stood there looking at her, marveling at her confident smile, her poise. "Don't you want to come in?" she asked.

Awkwardly, feeling like an intruder, he stepped inside. As she closed the door she brushed against him and he nearly swooned from the familiar scent. Then, as she walked away, she said, "We're putting together a jigsaw puzzle. Come and help."

"Is it the same one—" he began, but caught himself.

"Is it what?"

"Nothing. Never mind."

As Bloomhardt entered the dining room, Timmy, seated at the end of the rectangular table, looked up. Bloomhardt smiled and winked, a cheerless, rueful gesture. "How's it going, sport?"

"Fine," the boy said.

His son's gaze made him uncomfortable, as did Annie's, both so forceful and penetrating that he could hold neither for long. He faced the living room and said, "Boy, it sure is quiet here today. Where is everybody?"

"We had to decentralize," Annie told him as she sat beside the boy. "Our organization, I mean. We outgrew this house, and besides, Timmy and I wanted our privacy back. So now only my committee and one other one meet here. Two days a week."

"You have your own committee?" Bloomhardt asked.

"I'm the coordinator of all recruitment activities. I supervise all the local seminars and membership drives."

"Wow," said Bloomhardt.

"We have over two hundred active members now. A few months ago there were only ten of us."

"You lost a husband but gained an empire," Bloomhardt muttered.

"Don't start," she said.

He stared at the wallpaper. "Well, anyway, I just dropped by for a minute. I guess you know that I'm leaving for Europe in the morning."

"So we heard," said Annie. She leaned close to Timmy and whispered something in his ear. He pushed back his chair, stood, and, with a quick look toward his father, left the room.

"What's the matter?" Bloomhardt asked.

"Nothing. He's going upstairs to get something for you."

"Oh." Bloomhardt shifted his weight from one foot to the other and watched as Annie fitted several puzzle pieces into place. Then, as if doing something for which he might be punished, he slowly drew a chair away from the table and lowered himself into it.

"You don't seem terribly excited about your vacation," Annie said.

"Can't wait to get started," he told her.

"I know you've always wanted to do something like this."

"All my life."

Now Annie too seemed to grow uncomfortable. She worked on the puzzle and said nothing more until Timmy returned. The boy stood beside his father and handed him a small package wrapped in gold foil.

"What's this?" Bloomhardt asked.

"You don't have to open it now if you don't want to," said Annie. "It's nothing special. Just an electric shaver."

"It runs on batteries," Timmy said.

"Because the current is different in Europe," Annie explained. "Or something like that."

Bloomhardt had to clear his throat before he could speak. "Thank you very much." He had not used an electric shaver in years, preferring instead the plastic disposable razors he bought by the bagful. Annie had apparently forgotten this, but still he was grateful. At least she had not presented him with a cyanide tablet or an exploding fountain pen. Surely that counted for something.

"I think Timmy has a present for you too," she said.

Bloomhardt looked at his son. "Do you, sport?"

Solemnly, Timmy reached into his pocket, clasped something in his hand, and then extended it to his father. In his palm lay a clay coin the size of a half-dollar, the edges scalloped like a clam shell, a picture etched onto the convex surface.

Bloomhardt picked the coin out of his son's hand. "This is beautiful," he said. "Did you make this, Tim?"

"Yes," said the boy.

"Tell him what it is," said Annie.

"It's for good luck," Timmy answered. "To carry in your pocket."

"It's wonderful," said Bloomhardt. A lump the size of a billiard ball was bobbing in his throat. "And you made it all by yourself?"

"Mrs. Kamer baked it."

"His teacher," Annie said.

"But I'll bet you made this picture all by yourself, didn't you, sport?"

"Yes," said the boy. The picture was of a stick man, a stick woman, and a stick child, the child in the center and holding hands with the two other figures. "On the other side too," he said.

Bloomhardt turned the coin over, and there, scratched onto the surface, was *245 Fairfax Avenu*. "There wasn't room for it all," Timmy explained.

"That's okay," said his father.

"So in case you want to send a postcard but forget where."

Bloomhardt turned in his chair until his knees were straddling the boy's legs. He took his son's hands and told him, "Daddy would never forget where you live, sweetheart. Never."

"But it's so far away."

"Not by airplane, it's not. On an airplane I could go there and come back all in the same day."

Timmy looked up at him and blinked, and suddenly Bloomhardt saw something amazing. He saw that his son was just a child after all, just a boy, a tiny creature caught in the middle of a world he could not control. That expressionless mask of his, that owlish stare, it did not reflect, as Bloomhardt had always assumed, disdain for his father, not scorn or even disinterest, but fear, a child's fear, an apprehension of the world and his place in it as genuine as any adult's and perhaps twice as disabling because he was only half as large. Why had Bloomhardt never seen that before?

"I won't be gone long, son. Just two weeks, that's all."

"Why do you have to go?" Timmy asked.

That one caught Bloomhardt off guard. "Well, uh . . . I don't really have to. . . ."

"Then you should stay home," said the boy. And before Bloomhardt could think of a reply, Timmy turned away and marched upstairs.

Bloomhardt stared at the emptiness where his son had been.

Slowly he turned to face Annie, who had remained silent. Were those tears he saw glinting behind the lenses of her glasses? Or only reflections from the overhead light? Before he could decide, she pushed back her chair, stood, and went into the kitchen.

What was he supposed to do now? he wondered. Had that been a signal for him to tuck his tail between his legs and slink away? He did not understand his wife anymore. What he expected was either the old Annie or a clone of Helen Krakow, but what she gave him was an unpredictable mix of the two.

A minute later she returned with two mugs of coffee. She set one in front of him, then returned to her chair. "What do you think of Timmy's present?" she asked.

"I almost started crying," he said.

"I saw it, but I didn't believe it. You've never cried in your life."

"Maybe I've just never let you see it."

"You should have," she said. She looked at him intently, as if trying to perceive minutiae she had not observed before. "The last time you were here, Timmy asked me if you were sick."

"Why would he ask that?"

"He wanted to know why you were being so nice to everybody."

Bloomhardt stared into his coffee cup at the reflection of light trembling on the black liquid. Without looking up he said softly, meekly, "Don't divorce me, Annie."

She did not answer quickly. "We have some time to think about it."

"Things are different now," he said.

"What things?"

"You."

"Thank God for that."

"And me. I've changed too."

"I'm not so sure I believe that. You can be awfully tricky sometimes."

She smiled when she said this, but even so, Bloomhardt was

amazed that she could think of him as conniving or manipulative, in control. He thought of himself as a kite on a broken string.

"You're still wearing the gold chain I gave you," he said.

She realized then that her hand was at her neck, that she had been toying with the locket. As she lowered her hand she told him, "It's a pretty necklace, why shouldn't I wear it?"

Her uneasiness gave him confidence. "Tell me you never miss me."

She did not answer.

"Tell me that Helen and all those other women are enough for you, that you never want me lying beside you at night."

She leaned forward and pointed a finger at him. "Watch it, John. Those people are very important to me, so don't you dare say anything bad about them."

"All right, I'm sorry. I understand. I just want *you* to understand how important you and Timmy are to me. I need you like I need air. Without you I'll die, I'll suffocate."

She looked at him for just a moment, her eyes soft. Then she looked down at the table.

He stood and went to her and put his hands upon her shoulders. At first she stiffened, but as his hands slid down her arms and he pressed his mouth to her ear, some of the resistance dissolved. Encouraged, he kissed her neck and cheek and gently turned her in his arms. He covered her mouth with his, and when he tasted her lips he felt all the breath go out of him. She did not pull away or resist, and when the kiss ended, she smiled.

"Now go," she said.

"Upstairs?"

"Out the door."

His hands, which had been inching over her breasts, stopped moving. "Huh?"

"If you really love me, you'll go now."

"I think I missed something somewhere."

"I don't want this to happen now, John. I'm not ready for it."

"You feel ready enough to me. And geez," he said as he took her hand and pressed it against him, "you can see for yourself that I'm certainly ready."

"All right," she said. "You can be selfish and keep kissing me, and five minutes from now we'll probably end up in bed together. It all depends on which is more important to you—my wishes or your gratification."

"In that case, there's no contest. Take your clothes off."

She went rigid and tried to jerk away, but he held her tight."I was kidding," he told her. "Of course I'll do whatever you want."

"You'll go? Really?"

He kissed her lightly on the cheek, then released her. "You want space?" he said. "Fine. I'll give you four thousand miles of space. And if that isn't enough, send me a telegram and I'll keep going, all the way to China if necessary."

She watched, surprised and smiling, as he walked backwards toward the door. "And if that still isn't enough," he said, "call Cape Canaveral and book me a window seat on the next shuttle mission. No-smoking section, please."

He opened the front door, took one step over the threshold, and paused. "Tell Timmy I love him, okay? And tell him that I agree, I think I should stay home too. And that as soon as the welcome mat goes out, I won't ever leave here again."

He stepped onto the porch and pulled shut the door. As he was going down the steps he heard the door squeak open, and looking back, he saw Annie in the doorway. "Call me when you get back from Europe," she said.

"Count on it. Two weeks from today."

"Jake said you might stay longer. He said you might decide never to come back."

"Jake is my friend, not my travel agent."

Annie smiled. "Have a good time."

He tapped his pocket. "Thanks for the electric shaver."

"Don't cut yourself. You're awfully clumsy, you know."

bloomhardt spent the rest of that day feeling wonderful. That night he roamed the streets of his old neighborhood and enjoyed the familiarity of the houses, yards, and sidewalks. "Soon," he told them affectionately. "Soon I'll be home again."

Afterward, filled with love and longing, he sat in his car and stared at the darkened windows of his nine-room house, the unlighted porch, the roof's silhouette against a half-moon sky. It was his house, and he was content for now just to imagine himself inside, Annie cuddled in his arms, Timmy at his side.

He fell asleep in his car and was awakened by the heat of the morning sun as it streamed across his eyes. He still felt wonderful but a bit silly, and drove away before any of the neighbors might notice him. At a coffee shop in town, he cleared his head with a jelly doughnut and four cups of coffee. It was after nine when he returned, feeling more wonderful than ever, to Jake's apartment. Jake met him at the door.

"Christ, Bloomers," he said as he pushed a suitcase at him. "I go to all this trouble for you, and you act like it's no more important than a stroll down the street."

"Huh?" said Bloomhardt.

"Huh, my ass. Are you going to take hold of this suitcase or do you want me to hang it on your ear?"

Bloomhardt reached for the suitcase, then stood there looking down at it. "I packed everything," Jake told him. "Passport, ticket, two pairs of underwear, and even a dirty magazine for you to read on the plane."

Bloomhardt lowered the suitcase to the floor. "Uh, geez, Jake, this is really nice but—"

Jake gripped the door frame with both hands, blocking Bloomhardt from stepping inside. "Pick up your bag, Bloomschmuck. Paris awaits."

"But Jake, I can't, not now. Look, Annie gave me an electric shaver as a going-away present."

"So go away, why don't you?"

"And Timmy made this for me. Look at the picture on it."

"Cute," said Jake. "It's all very touching, electric shavers and little clay Frisbees. So put them back in your pocket and move your ass!"

"Jake, come on, be a friend. One more lousy week and Annie will welcome me home with open arms, I just know it."

"Fine, I hope she does. And in the meantime, where do you plan to stay?"

"Well, gee, Jake . . ."

"Well, gee, Bloomers. Have you forgotten what I told you? You let me down and you're out in the cold. Or, in this case, out in the cool."

"You're really going to throw me out, just like that? I thought you were my friend."

Jake looked at him and sighed. "Bloomytunes, you've been living here for how long now—three months? You've slept on my sofa, you've eaten my food and drunk my beer, I've even offered once or twice to let you fuck my friends. And why did I do all this? Because I'm just perverted enough to like you, that's why."

"Wait a minute, Jake, I know what—"

"Don't interrupt, Bloomski, you can't spare the time. Anyway, I take you in, I become your patron, all because that pitiful soul of yours is crying out for creative expression. I give you the run of the place, for Chrissake, and what do I expect in return? An epic? A magnum opus? Hell, no—a lousy one-page vignette would have sufficed!"

"But Jake, I—"

"Shut up, I've got my blood hot now, and I'm not through yet. So what do I get from you? A pile of scribbled note cards, that's what. Well, they're in your suitcase now, and I hope they do you some good."

Bloomhardt stared at the floor. "I have to stay, Jake. I have to be ready when she changes her mind."

"Just hang around twiddling your thumbs until she whistles you back, is that it? Like some raggedy beggar that's willing to grovel at her feet."

"I am willing to grovel at her feet."

"And from that position she'll walk all over you. Because what she really wants is somebody just as strong as she is."

"I am," said Bloomhardt.

"You're about as strong right now as wet toilet paper." Jake waited a moment, then laid a hand on Bloomhardt's shoulder. "Listen, why do you think God in his infinite wisdom gave you me for a friend? Would I send you away like this if I weren't convinced it would be the best thing for everyone?"

Bloomhardt shrugged. "I guess you wouldn't."

"For once in your life you guessed right. So stand up straight and quit looking so forlorn. You're not going off to war, boy, you're off to new adventures in wine, art, and hairy-legged women!"

Reluctantly, uncertainly, Bloomhardt reached for his suitcase. He felt too weak to carry it. Jake slipped a hand into Bloomhardt's jacket and removed his car keys.

"Take the bus to the airport," he said. "I'll drive your car over to your house, where it'll be safer. I have to be in that neighborhood anyway, I have to counsel a cheerleader with nymphomaniacal tendencies. She can drive us back here, which is where I do my best work. Rah rah, sis boom bah!"

Bloomhardt gave him a doleful look. "Jake, I'm just not sure—"

"You're not sure why a mere mortal like you should be blessed with my friendship, I know. And to tell you the truth, neither am I.

It's just another one of life's little mysteries, Bloomers. I'll bring it up for discussion at my next Rosicrucian meeting. *Au vol!*" He gave Bloomhardt a shove, stepped back inside the apartment, and slammed the door.

Bloomhardt heard the lock click. After a while he turned and trudged downstairs and outside, then shuffled toward the bus kiosk on the corner. As he walked he listed heavily to his right, feeling off-center, misaligned, the suitcase as heavy as a tombstone.

In the airport he stood in line at the ticket counter, moving forward only when jostled to do so, watching all of the other people hurriedly coming or going, specific destinations in mind, excited to be leaving, happy to be home. But he was not one of them. He did not belong here.

When his turn came he stepped forward and dropped his ticket packet on the desk. "I have to cancel," he said.

The agent, a thin young man with a sparse brown mustache, had a nervous habit of rolling his upper lip down over his teeth, which made him look like a rabbit chewing grass. He examined Bloomhardt's ticket, rolled his lips a few times, and said apologetically, "The second boarding call has already been made."

"My wife died," Bloomhardt said. He had not planned to say this, nor did he know why it came to him now.

The agent bit his lip. "Your wife?"

"Three hours ago. In childbirth. I just now found out."

"I . . . I'm sorry, I . . ."

"How can I take a business trip now? The hell with business. The hell with my life. I need the ticket money to pay for her funeral. I'm poor, I need a refund."

The agent chewed his lip as his eyes turned glassy. Finally he gave Bloomhardt a crisp nod, stepped to the computer terminal, punched in some information, moved to another machine, and soon returned with the refund check.

"Thank you," Bloomhardt said woodenly. He turned and walked away.

He rode the bus back to his old neighborhood, then walked the last four blocks to his house on Fairfax Avenue, resolved to throw himself on Annie's mercy, confident that she, a compassionate woman at heart, would not turn him away. Everything, he knew, was going to work out fine. He could feel it in his bones.

His car, already delivered by Jake, was parked in front of the house. Unfortunately, it was but one of many parked at the curb. Even his driveway was clogged with cars. Annie's blue Volkswagen, however, was nowhere to be seen.

Not without some trepidation, he mounted the front porch steps. Just as he reached for the door, it popped open. Helen Krakow, wearing blue jeans, a bulky gray sweater, and a smirk, filled the doorway. "Christ, Helen," he said. "Don't you ever turn off the radar?"

"I smelled you coming," she answered. "Anyway, aren't you supposed to be in the clouds by now? Dr. Speers brought your car by just a minute ago." She still had the keys in her hand.

"Where's Annie?" he asked as he set his suitcase on the porch.

"Not here."

"I don't believe you."

"Then come in and see for yourself," she told him, but did not move aside to let him pass.

He stood on his toes and peered over her shoulder. In the living room were at least two dozen women seated around card tables, some of the women folding colored sheets of paper and stuffing then into envelopes, while others sealed the envelopes and addressed them.

"What's going on? I thought you people didn't meet here anymore."

"Special monthly meeting. Our newsletter goes out today. You wouldn't care to read it, would you?"

"Right, I wouldn't. So where *is* Annie?"

"She's giving a lecture at the high school."

"A lecture? In front of people? My Annie?"

"Our *Ann.* Your *Annie* was a wimp, which is something she obviously picked up from you."

"Don't get carried away, Helen. Remember that this is my house and I can have you all booted out of here if I feel like it."

"You must be forgetting about that restraining order I promised."

"You couldn't make it stick. In no way have I harassed or threatened her. By the way, Helen, this is a residential area. It's not zoned for corporate meetings. How about if I walk to the nearest phone booth and notify the zoning board?"

"Try it, and I'll have Ann transferred to our headquarters in Pittsburgh. Timmy, of course, will go with her."

"What makes you so sure she'd go?"

"What makes you so sure she wouldn't?"

Bloomhardt took a deep breath and looked away from her. He gazed out across the yard. The grass needed cutting. God, how he had missed that grass! A few moments later he faced her again. "What works against you, Helen? Garlic? A stake through the heart? Holy water? *What?* How do I get rid of you?"

"Easy," she told him. "Just take some of your own advice and go fuck yourself."

"If it was a choice between that and you, I'd certainly try. Failing that, I'd rather be celibate."

"You're a dickless worm," she hissed.

"Don't confuse me with the man of your dreams," said Bloomhardt as he picked up his suitcase. "I don't suppose my son is home either?"

She braced herself against the door frame. "It's your house—come check for yourself."

"Just tell him I was here and that I love him, okay?"

"Why scare an innocent child?"

"Just tell him, Helen. For once in your life, do the right thing."

Before she could reply, he turned sharply and went down the steps. At the bottom he looked at her. "By the way, I'll take those keys you're holding. Unless, of course, you'd rather be arrested for auto theft?"

She threw the keys at his face, exactly as he knew she would. He caught them neatly in his left hand. "I'll be back, Helen. Two days, two weeks, I don't care how long it takes, but I will get my family back. Your days are numbered."

Bloomhardt went to his car and tossed the suitcase into the rear. The car reeked of Jake's after-shave, which made his already jittery stomach nauseous. Where to now? he wondered. His castle was still a stronghold of harpies and ogresses, and despite his confident posturing he doubted that he would ever evict them. He felt hollow and weak, a man made of eggshells already dangerously cracked.

Out the corner of his eye he glanced toward the house to see what kind of obscene gesture Helen might be sending him. But the porch was empty. Nor could he see anybody watching from the windows. It was as if they knew he was no threat; they were so self-assured that they had turned their backs on him.

Enjoying your vacation? Bloomhardt asked himself as he sat on the edge of his parents' sofa, knees bumping the coffee table, a cup of steaming coffee in his hand. Out in the kitchen, his mother was putting together a sandwich he did not want. He could take it here for two lousy weeks, he told himself. Sure, why not? Upstairs in his old bedroom he would lie around and listen to the radio, read a few books, concoct wild tales of

European adventure with which to regale Jake. As for postcards: Well, gee whiz, Jake, I'm sorry, but I was too busy eating and drinking and fornicating to send you one. Jake would certainly appreciate that.

Maybe someday Bloomhardt would even admit to Annie where he had actually spent his vacation, but why rush into it? That was the nice thing about truth, it was durable, it did not rust.

So all that remained for him now was to break the news to his mother. His father was not home again, he had walked down the street, she had explained, to watch the traffic go by. "Mustard or mayonnaise?" she called from the kitchen.

"Hmmm?" asked Bloomhardt.

"Mustard or mayonnaise? On your sandwich."

"Uh, I don't care. Mustard, I guess."

"We have both."

"Mustard will be fine."

"You always used to take mayonnaise, didn't you?"

"Okay, whatever. Make it mayonnaise, then."

"But that doesn't mean you can't have mustard now."

"Either one, it doesn't matter."

"I have both jars right here in front of me."

"Mustard," he said. "Make it mustard."

"Brown, yellow, or the kind with the seeds in it?"

He did not answer. Would every meal in this house be an inquisition? He set his cup on the coffee table, stood, and went quietly up the stairs. In his bedroom he lay supine on the bed and dangled his feet over the edge.

He had been in this position, he remembered, when his youth sneaked away. This was the position for long stretches of daydreaming, for lying awake in the damp palm of a summer night and listening to his father's resonant snores, for lying awake in the trembling uncertainty of an autumn afternoon while his mother bustled about below, the vacuum cleaner whining, sucking up his wasted time. From this position on Saturday mornings he had tried unsuccessfully to stop his ears to the growl of the lawn mower beneath his window, his father haranguing him to get his lazy ass out of bed and do something. This was the position for smelling cabbage and corned beef boiling in a pot, for conjuring up gossamer visions that were so hard to hold, long silky legs slowly parting, a hard round ass, coquettish smile, firm pointed tips of budding breasts. . . .

His mother called from the stairs, and Bloomhardt immediately sat up, covering his erection with his hands. Sheepishly, then, he stood and tugged the wrinkles from his trousers and walked down the short hall to the stairs.

On the sofa again, his mother beside him, he lifted his bologna sandwich off the plate and, not the least bit hungry, took a bite.

"Well?" said his mother, looking hopeful.

"Well what?" he asked, mouth full.

"How do you like it?"

"Great. It's great."

"I used yellow mustard."

"I can tell."

"And mayonnaise on the other side."

"Excellent choice."

She nodded, pleased, and then began to talk. Bloomhardt had but a vague awareness of her voice as he chewed dryly on the sandwich. He stared at a broad shaft of light slanting through the window, thick with slowly swirling dust motes, tiny planets pulled by the gravity of the carpet and doomed to a shaggy oblivion. That carpet, a pine-green one he had lain upon a thousand times, was showing its age; a wide path of worn nap stretched from one end of the room to the other. Even the bar of sunlight looked faded and thin, well-trod. Bloomhardt swallowed the last of his sandwich and felt it plop heavily into his stomach.

"I can't stay, Mom," he said, interrupting her soliloquy, of which he had heard little. "Just dropped by for a minute to see how you're doing."

"Would you like another sandwich?"

"No, thanks a lot. That one really hit the spot."

"Your father should be home any second now. This is the time of day when the traffic starts thinning out."

"I wish I could stay, but I told Annie I'd be right back."

"I wish you had brought Timmy with you," she said, looking at her hands. Bloomhardt looked at them too. On the back of her left hand was a liver spot as big as a quarter, which he had never noticed before.

"Whatever happened to that picnic we were supposed to have?" she asked. "We kept waiting and waiting for you to call."

Bloomhardt's collar was too snug. He reached to loosen it, but found it already unbuttoned. There did not seem to be enough air in the room, he couldn't fill his lungs. Slowly he pushed himself up and began to inch his way to the door. "We'll be over for a visit soon," he said. "I promise." She followed him onto the porch. "It's just that Annie is so busy these days with this group she's joined, and me, geez, there's a million things I have to do around the house. . . ."

He stood looking at the porch railing, his fingers sliding over the black enamel. When he heard his mother's sniffle and the thick wet glug as she swallowed, he turned. Her face was streaked with tears. "Mom?" he asked, wanting to touch her but feeling too clumsy to raise a hand. "What is it, what's wrong?"

Staring at the floor, she answered, "I know what's going on."

Again he lost his breath. "What do you mean?"

"I know about you and Annie and what you did."

His stomach did a somersault. "What did I do?"

"You moved in with some man."

"With Jake, Mom, not some man. Jake Speers, my old buddy from college, remember? And anyway, that was just until I could, you know, find a place of my own."

She looked up. "You live by yourself now?"

"Well, yeah," he said, and broke the eye contact. "It's a little apartment . . . downtown. Close to the lake."

"You should be home with your family, where you belong."

"I will be. Just as soon as we get things worked out."

"Why didn't you move in here if you needed a place to stay?"

"I don't know, Mom, it's just that . . . I don't know, I . . . I don't know."

She laid her left hand, closed in a fist, against her heart, covered it with her right hand, and began to sob. "Ahh, Mom, come on," he said as he touched her shoulder. "It's not all that bad. You know what marriage is like, sometimes a problem just sort of pops up out of nowhere and the best thing is to get away from each other for a while until you can work things out. That's all this is, it's nothing serious. We'll be getting together again any day now."

She wiped her eyes with the sleeve of her blouse. "Uh . . ." said Bloomhardt. "How'd you find out about it?"

"I called last week. Some woman answered, and when I asked for you, she said you hadn't been there for over three months, and that if there was a God in heaven you never would come back unless it was in a crematory urn."

"That bitch," he muttered.

"It wasn't Annie, it was some other woman."

"Don't worry, I know who it was."

"So I told her that if she ever said anything like that about you again, I'd go right over there and claw out her eyes and stuff them up her nose!"

Bloomhardt laughed softly and kissed the top of her head. "Good for you, tiger."

At each of a dozen apartment houses he was asked to sign a six- or twelve-month lease. "But I only need a place for a couple of weeks," he explained. "Three at the most. A month at the outside."

"Sorry," he was told.

Along the lakefront were cabins, cottages, and efficiency apartments available on a daily or weekly basis, but all were closed for the season. The motels were too expensive. He had only the money in his pocket—a little over seven hundred dollars, now that he had cashed the airline's refund check—and he would use nearly all of it if he rented a motel room for two weeks. It would not be much of a vacation if he had to starve himself. He could not make a withdrawal from his and Annie's joint bank account without alerting her to the fact that he was still in town. So he waved $350 under the nose of the manager of a year-round apartment building and appealed to the man's compassion and greed.

"Look, your rate is three hundred a month, right? So here's a little something extra. I only need a place for one lousy month, that's all. One lousy month, what do you say? It's an easy way to make a quick fifty bucks, tax-free, no strings attached."

But the apartment manager thought Bloomhardt a suspicious character. His clothes looked as if they had been slept in, he was unshaven and uncombed, and there was a glint of desperation in his eyes. "No can do," the man said. "Gotta have you sign a lease."

"Ahh, for crying out loud! Okay, okay, listen, I'm going to level with you. I'm supposed to be vacationing in Europe, see? But I'd rather stay here in town, and I don't want my wife to know about it."

"You got somebody with you?"

"No, there's just me! I'm alone! I am utterly and totally all by myself."

The manager scratched his head. "So why do you want to stay here? We don't even have a heated pool."

"I don't need a heated pool, I don't need anything. I didn't come here to have fun. I'm miserable now, and I fully expect to remain miserable for the next fourteen days, okay? And all I want is a nice quiet room where I can enjoy my misery in private."

"I think you'd better go now," said the manager.

"Four hundred dollars!"

"Try down on the lower East Side. That's where most of the transients stay."

Transients, thought Bloomhardt. I'm a transient in my own hometown. I'm a bum. "Fine," he said wearily. "Thanks for your help."

Half an hour later he spotted a four-story building of dirty red brick with a ROOMS sign posted in a ground-floor window. He went inside and found a spacious lobby empty of furnishings. At first glance he thought the place abandoned, probably scheduled for demolition, but then he noticed a wisp of smoke drifting from behind a scarred wooden pillar. Behind the pillar was a tiny office, a cubbyhole closed off from the rest of the room but for a Dutch door whose upper half had been replaced with thick iron bars. Behind the bars sat a scrawny wraith of a woman, her hair a shock of brittle white straw. A cigarette dangled from the corner of her mouth. But for the wisp of smoke, she was as motionless as a corpse. She stared at Bloomhardt through languid yellow eyes.

"Uh, excuse me," he said as he approached the cage. "You have rooms?"

"Maybe," she answered, which caused her cigarette to twitch and toss its ash.

"By the week?"

"I suppose."

"Thank God." He put his hands on the shelf protruding beneath the bars and slumped against it. "I'll take one, please. For a month, though I probably won't be staying that long. There's no lease, right?"

"No lease," she said. Without taking her eyes off him she raised a hand to her mouth and removed the cigarette, blew a ribbon of smoke through the bars, and stuck the cigarette in her mouth again. "What kind?"

"Kind?" he asked.

"Private bath or no private bath?"

"Private bath," he said.

"Kitchen or no kitchen?"

"Hmmm. Uh, kitchen, I guess."

"How many people in the room?"

"None. I mean one. Just me."

Sucking on her cigarette, she stared at him a few moments longer, then blew smoke out the opposite corner of her mouth. He felt like a curiosity, a man with two noses.

"Where you from?" she finally asked.

He had learned by now that the truth raised too many eyebrows, so even though this woman's eyebrows seemed as lifeless as chalk smears, he told her, "Detroit."

"What are you here for?"

"Looking for work."

She took another drag from her cigarette. "You a cop?"

Bloomhardt smiled wearily. "No, ma'am, I am not a cop. I'm just a guy who needs a place to stay, okay?"

"You want to see the room first?"

"Where is it?"

"Fourth floor. No elevator."

"In that case, just give me the key."

"Two hundred dollars. In advance."

"Naturally," he said.

As he counted out the money and slipped it beneath the bars, she told him, "There's only one phone and it's here in my office and you can't use it, so don't ask. And I don't take messages. There's a booth on the corner if you want to make a call."

"Sounds like paradise," he said.

She pushed a key toward him. "I'll have a girl free in an hour if you're interested."

"You mean the room hasn't been made up yet?" he asked.

She laughed, her first sign of life, a single sniggery grunt, and Bloomhardt realized his mistake. "Oh," he said, jiggling the key in his hand. "Yes, well . . . I, uh, I don't think so. I'm really just too tired right now. But thanks for offering."

The apartment, though so overheated that orchids would have thrived inside, initially seemed cleaner than he had expected. But on closer examination he found the lavender walls greasy to the touch. Because of the meat-packing factory next door, his rooms smelled strongly of raw animal flesh and fat. There was a separate kitchen, just large enough to accommodate a sink and a half-sized gas range and a wobbly card table with its two kitchen chairs. In a cupboard above the sink he discovered five dinner plates, cracked and mismatched, three cups, a saucepan, a greasy black skillet, nine forks, a can opener, and one butter knife.

"More than any man could hope for," he said aloud.

In the bathroom was the cast-iron enameled tub with claw feet, a lavatory with no plug in the basin, and a toilet that only occasionally flushed. Everything, except the lavender walls, was painted pink.

The room between these two tiny ones was actually commodious, with a large, north-facing window. The floor, like the walls, was bare and painted a pale, unripened shade of plum. The only furnishings were a straight-back chair, as wobbly as the kitchen table, and a sofa bed that, when Bloomhardt unfolded it, yielded a moldy apple core, two dog biscuits, and a condom.

There were no curtains on the dirty window, from which he could look down upon the meat-packing factory and its asphalt parking lot, and beyond it the hazy gray horizon of Lake Erie. On the window ledge was a layer of pigeon guano two inches thick.

Finally, in the corner near the window, was a large, lidless packing crate, three feet square by four feet deep. There were no identifying marks to explain what the box had once contained, though it was stuffed with so much brittle yellow excelsior that Bloomhardt doubted anything else could be crammed into it. How the box had come to be there in the corner of the room, through a door too small to accommodate it, he could not imagine. Gingerly he lifted off the top layer of excelsior, expecting to uncover something gruesome, a severed head or arm or at least a nest of squealing rats, but all he found was more excelsior, less brittle and yellow than that on the surface.

Next he went to the window and looked out on the city. The glass was nearly translucent with a gray film of greasy soot. The longer he stood, the more he felt indigenous to this room, as mean as the broken toilet, as unwanted as the discarded condom. This is my home now, he thought. This is where I belong. The radiator hissed as if in agreement and sent a geyser of steam into the air, raising the temperature of the already stuffy room to an oppressive level. The radiator valve was broken and the exposed flange too hot to touch, so there was no way to regulate the temperature. He wrestled with the window but it would not budge. Ten minutes later he surrendered, exhausted, his shirt limp with perspiration, and collapsed on the unfolded sofa bed.

He lay on his back and listened intently for the sound of neighbors, for a squeaking bed, a radio too loud, a fart, a belch, a giggle, a sigh. Any sound would do, any noise at all, just something to focus his attention on so as to keep his own thoughts from engulfing him. He stared at the ceiling and the dusty bare bulbs in the unshaded light fixture, at the spiderweb of cracks in the plaster. *My God*, he thought, suddenly terrified of his future. What have I come to? What have I done to myself?

He sat up quickly, shivering in spite of the heat. On his arms, a thousand goosebumps glistened with perspiration. *Home*, the radiator hissed at him.

The gray of October was ubiquitous, it filled all spaces. During that month the wind seemed never to stop blowing. Bloomhardt walked the streets of his new neighborhood with his collar up, hands shoved deep in his pockets. His eyes stung incessantly, as if from an allergy, though as far as he knew he had no allergies, and he could not understand why his eyes remained so sore and inflamed. Maybe it was because of the steamy heat of his apartment, where night and day he panted and sweated like a fat man in a Turkish bath. Maybe it was the funk of cheap perfume and after-shave that wafted through the halls. Or maybe the myriad of odors outside. There were, of course, the aromas of the meat-packing factory, randomly sour or spicy or stinking of blood, but there were other scents as well, of sauerkraut and onions, of beer from the open door of a smoky tavern, of newly washed clothes hung out to dry in the afternoon breeze.

Bloomhardt took pleasure in this latter group of smells and often paused during his peregrinations to inhale deeply and fill his lungs with them. He even imagined he could pinpoint the very house from which the odor arose, the room and the people inside it, the family gathered round the dinner table. Sometimes as he stood there with his nose lifted and sniffing, a wistful smile on his face, a passerby would look at him strangely and give him a wide berth, as if Bloomhardt's silly smile were evidence of dementia in blossom.

His hours were filled with longing, with regret, with a sense that he had cut himself off from everyone he loved. In an Italian restaurant he bought six age-faded postcards depicting the Tower of Pisa and other Italian landmarks and mailed them to Timmy, hoping the domestic stamps and local postmarks would pass unnoticed.

At least once each day he drove to Fairfax Avenue, parked several blocks away from his house, then crouched behind the hedge across the street. Once he arrved in time to see Timmy step off the school bus and be met at the curb by Annie. As they walked hand-in-hand to the house, he wanted to leap out of hiding and hurl himself at their feet. He also considered diving in front of the bus as it jerked away, making a kind of kamikaze statement of his love for them. All that held him from it was the knowledge of how gleefully Helen Krakow would react when somebody pointed to the bloody smear and told her it was him.

It was not a good vacation for Bloomhardt. He sometimes went two or three days before remembering to take a shower or brush his teeth. He felt uncomfortable in his own clothes, as if they had come from the Goodwill bin. He imagined that his spine had slipped out of alignment, that he was developing a hunched back, that his body was turning against him.

On the Sunday evening before his return to work, he breathed a deep sigh of relief, cleaned himself and his apartment, and even went to a restaurant for a late supper. I've been a fool, he told himself during a dessert of spumoni and almond cookies, a fool to have wasted all this time on worry. Everything is going to work out right at last, everything is going to be fine.

At Universal Steel the following morning, only one thing had changed in his absence: there was an extra lock on the men's room door. Bloomhardt walked into the accounting office at 8:01 and was struck in the face with a ball of paper.

"It's about time you got back to work," Roomy told him.

"You lazy shit," said Smitty. "Wipe that silly smile off your face. This is a place of business."

"I'm not smiling," Bloomhardt said as he checked his seat and desk for booby traps, happy to be remembered.

"Make sure you don't," the Goathead snarled. "You're on company time now."

Nelson looked up briefly, grunted and scowled.

Petey winked and nodded toward the top drawer of Bloomhardt's desk. Cautiously Bloomhardt slid it open, his hand poised to catch the sheaf of papers that, mounted on a compressed spring, were supposed to have flown up into his face.

Smitty glowered at Roomy when the sabotage failed. "You worthless twit, you didn't load it right."

Roomy grabbed himself by the crotch. "Load this, why don't ya."

Bloomhardt settled into his chair and looked gratefully at the accumulation of paperwork spilling over the edges of his desk. Then he turned to glance out the window at the familiar mounds of ore. Flecks of mica glinted from those dark hills, pigeons swooped and soared. A rubber band went *poing!* off someone's finger and stung the tip of Bloomhardt's nose.

"Hey you!" said Smitty.

Bloomhardt turned to look at him.

"Goddamn it, Bloomie. Welcome home."

The Goathead belched, his breath ripe with whiskey.

And suddenly Bloomhardt wondered why, indeed, he was smiling. He grabbed a pink waybill from his stack of papers, squinted at it, and began to pound out the numbers. Tauntingly his calculator sang, Nothing is new, no nothing is new, oh nothing no nothing no nothing is new. . . .

Even after his vacation ended, and with it any reason to avoid contact with the family he so longed to see, Bloomhardt could not bring himself to visit his house, except covertly. On Halloween night he paced back and forth in his apartment, thinking he could hear mice in the packing crate, even though he had checked the excelsior a dozen times and found nothing. On the windowsill was a box of chocolate bars, bought a week earlier in anticipation of this night, which he had hoped would bring a stream of little trick-or-treaters to his door. He had imagined that their rubber masks and painted faces would somehow dull the ache he felt for Timmy. But it was eight o'clock now, and there had been not a single rap upon his door. He had already eaten seven of the chocolate bars himself, washing them down with a pot of black coffee. He was so restless that he itched from the inside out. He stood at the sooty window and drummed his fingers on the glass. He listened to the radiator's hiss. He smelled his own chocolate breath.

Ten minutes more, and he had had all he could stand of himself. He pulled on a jacket, stuffed the pockets with candy bars, and hurried outside.

After the heat of his apartment, the night air seemed painfully cold. The sky was black and moonless and there was a gray breeze blowing, and in that breeze he imagined he could detect the scent of bubbling cauldrons, of wart-nosed witches singeing the air with flaming broomsticks. Hugging himself, bouncing stiffly from one foot to the other, he glanced down the street at the row of shabby homes, weather-beaten houses that looked even humbler and less hospitable by night. In their windows and on their porch stoops sat grinning jack-o'-lanterns, which lent the night an eerie incandescence. From the stunted maple in one front yard a ghost hung from a noose, a stuffed white sheet that fluttered and snapped in the wind. Seeing it, he was reminded of Mickey's ghost flitting like a moth against the tile walls of the men's room at Universal Steel, and he wondered if it, too, had been paroled to haunt the night. A chill crept over him and the hairs rose on the back of his neck, and though his original intention had been to clear his head with a long walk, he now found himself half-running toward his car.

Out of habit, he parked a few blocks away from his house. When finally he climbed out and trotted up the street, teeth chattering, he was dismayed to see the driveway and curb clogged with vehicles. But he would not allow himself to retreat, for he might never find the courage to return. He tiptoed across the yard and onto the front porch. As he reached for the door he heard laughter and music from inside, the pop of a balloon, a girlish shriek.

Tentatively he moved his finger to the doorbell and rang it once, a quick, shy bleat of announcement. The suddenness with which the door popped open caught him off guard, as did the hunchbacked witch who, shaking a straw broom, sprang out at him. As he stumbled backward, nearly falling down the steps, her laughter cackled in falsetto.

"Surprised, little boy?" she screeched, her voice as shrill as a cat's cry.

Bloomhardt blew out his breath and pulled himself erect. "Wow, you bet I'm surprised. That's the best you've looked in months, Helen. You went to the beauty parlor today, didn't you?"

Her long rubber nose quivered as she snarled at him.

"Tell me something, Helen. Don't you ever go home? Doesn't your husband miss you? No, wait, that was a stupid question."

"Coming from you, it had to be."

Standing on his toes, he tried to see inside the house. "What's going on?" he asked. "Where did all those kids come from?"

"You mean nobody ever told you about the birds and the bees?" she said. He ignored this as he tried to peer into the living room. The wart at the tip of her nose bobbed up and down. "What do you want?"

"Not that it's any of your business, but I'd like to say hello to my son. Is he in there?"

"He's in here. And he's enjoying himself. Do you want to come in and spoil the party for him? Maybe try to drown him while he's bobbing for apples?"

Bloomhardt recognized more than a grain of truth in her taunt. "Just do me a favor and tell Annie I'm here, okay?"

"She's upstairs in bed."

"In bed? What's she doing in bed at this hour?"

"Probably having more fun than she ever had with you there. She's got the flu."

"While you're down here having a party?"

"This party was planned long before the germs arrived. Being a germ yourself, you should know how unpredictable they can be."

Another time he might have argued with her, but he had no appetite for it now. Besides, it was Halloween, and the forces that ruled the universe were on Helen's side tonight. He turned toward the steps and told her, "Tell her I was here, all right? And tell Timmy that I hope he has a happy Halloween."

"Now that you're leaving, he will."

Snickering, she stepped inside. Bloomhardt started toward his car, but at the last moment merely stood there with his hand on the door. The longer he thought about it, the more resolved he became to redeem himself. But how to do it, that was the question. He could bully his way into the house, but that would precipitate a shouting match, which would not endear him either to his wife or his son. No, he would have to infiltrate the house without Helen's knowledge, slip behind enemy lines. Such treachery, even if it resulted in but a glimpse of Annie and Timmy, he would deem a victory, and all the sweeter for the subterfuge.

The bathroom window was his only hope. Already well down the street from his house, he doubled back through his neighbors' rear yards, blundering into a garbage can, a clothesline pole, and a birdbath along the way, but feeling more exhilarated by the minute.

At his own back porch, he swung himself up onto the roof, lay still for a moment to catch his breath, then crawled to the window. Kneeling, he dug his fingernails into the wooden sash and pulled it toward his chest. The window moved a quarter of an inch, enough to tell him that it was not locked. He rose onto his haunches, took a deep breath, braced himself, and pulled again.

The window snapped free and whacked him on the chin. Off balance, backpedaling fiercely, he went running backward off the edge of the porch, executed an ungraceful cutaway dive, and landed with a thud on his stomach.

Afraid to move, afraid to stir up the pain, he lay motionless on the soft wet ground. The wind had been knocked out of him and he thought there was a reasonably good chance that his nose was broken. His spine tingled and he was reluctant to test his legs for fear that they were numb, the nerves dead.

But no one, apparently, had heard his fall. As he lay there gathering his breath, he could hear the noise of the party inside. He waited several minutes, then wiggled his toes. Thank God, they worked. He flexed one leg, then the other, and, encouraged by their response, slowly pushed himself to his feet.

Conspicuously less exhilarated than when he began, he climbed onto the roof once more. Wincing, grimacing, and trying to keep his groans to a minimum, he crawled headfirst through the narrow window. Fully inside, he locked the bathroom door and turned on the light. He scraped the mud from his clothes, washed his face and hands, and smoothed back his hair. Then he switched off the light, eased open the door, and stole quietly down the hall.

The door to Annie's bedroom was closed, but light leaked through the crack beneath it. He tapped lightly on the door. "Yes?" said Annie in a voice small and weak.

Grinning sheepishly, he opened the door and stuck his head inside. "Trick or treat?"

Annie was flat on the bed, several blankets piled atop her, her hair loose and fanned across the pillow, an open book facedown on her stomach. She smiled, blinked, and yawned. "I was just thinking about you," she said.

He stepped inside and closed the door. "Anything good?"

"None of your business." But she was smiling when she said it, and her eyes, though dulled by sickness, seemed happy.

"Did you see the party?" she asked.

"How could I miss it?" Casually, as if it meant nothing to him, he went to the bed and sat on the edge of it.

"Are the kids having fun?" she asked.

"Can't you tell by all the noise?"

She nodded. "How about Timmy?"

"I never saw him enjoying himself more."

"That's good," she said. "I worry about him sometimes. He doesn't seem to have many friends."

"Well, he's having the time of his life now," said Bloomhardt.

Annie slid her hand atop his, her palm warm and damp. He bent forward, lifted her hand slightly, and kissed it.

"When did you get back?" she asked languidly.

"Hmmm?"

"From Europe. I thought you were coming home weeks ago."

"Oh, yeah. Well . . . I did, I guess."

"Why did you wait so long to come see us?"

He hung his head and looked at her hand. If he told her he was ashamed, would she forgive him? He was ashamed of his deceit, ashamed of spying on her daily, ashamed of failing Jake, ashamed of being afraid to face her. What would she say to all this if he blurted it out? He looked at her hand in his, her nails glossy and smooth, his ragged and chewed to the quick.

"I wanted to come sooner. I wanted to come every day. I don't know why I didn't."

"I was beginning to think you might never come see us again."

"You must have been delirious," he said.

Still he could not lift his head to look at her, though her hand tightened around his reassuringly. "Did you have a nice time?"

"A wonderful time," he said.

"Tell me all the wonderful things you did and all the wonderful places you saw."

"Geez, there's so much to tell. I wouldn't know where to start."

She squeezed his hand again. "I missed you," she said. "In fact, I'd kiss you right now if I didn't have the flu."

"Kiss me anyway."

"You'll get my germs."

"I want your germs."

She shook her head. "Where did you stay?"

"Stay?" he asked.

"In Europe."

"Oh. Uh . . . Paris. Mostly Paris, anyway. I mean . . . here and there, but, you know, uh . . . I stayed longest in Paris."

"I'm glad you had a nice time. Wasn't it nice of Jake to do that for you?"

Nodding, Bloomhardt stared at the blanket as he pulled out tiny tufts of fabric.

"What about that place where you got the postcards?" she asked. "I'll bet that was nice, wasn't it?"

He smiled guiltily, felt her eyes on him.

"Where exactly was that place?" she asked.

"Down near the corner of Buffalo and Twelfth," he admitted.

She laughed weakly, eyes sparkling. Then, still smiling, she closed her eyes. He leaned forward and, partly to hide his face, partly because he longed for the contact, lay his cheek against hers. "I only made it as far as the airport," he whispered. "I couldn't bear to be away from you."

She did not say anything, but a moment later her hand came up and rested on the back of his neck. He turned his face toward her and kissed her cheek. "Your face is flushed. You have a fever."

"It's only a hundred and one," she said as she opened her eyes and drew away from him. He sat up.

"How did your clothes get so dirty?" she asked.

"I tripped over something in the yard."

"Still as graceful as ever," she said.

He took her hand in his and stroked her wrist. "You're awfully nice to me when you're sick."

"I'm hoping the penicillin will clear it up."

"I love you," he said.

She closed her eyes for a moment. When she opened them again, they were shiny with tears. "Don't start," she warned him. "I'm not strong enough now to resist. I can't fight my emotions and the damn flu at the same time."

He ran his hand along her arm, then kissed the crease of her elbow. "I miss you and Timmy so much that it hurts just to take a breath, just to blink, for God's sake."

"John, don't, please. Don't make me cry, it's not fair that way."

"I'd kill myself if it would make you forgive me."

"I'll think about that one," she said. "Maybe we can work something out."

He leaned toward her again and kissed her mouth, tasted her tears and the fever of her skin. He smelled her hair and the warm, feverish scent of her body. Around the edges of the bed, everything blurred; he saw only her sadly smiling face and the mound of her body beneath the blankets, felt only the gravity that drew him toward her. He kicked off his shoes and pulled back the covers, catching his breath at the sight of her thin body, the soft blue cotton nightgown molded over her breasts.

"What are you doing?" she asked as he slid closer. "John don't, you can't."

"I'm cold, I need to get under the blankets with you."

"Go sit on the stove if you're cold, just stop . . . John, please. If you're cold, why are you taking your pants off?"

"Slide over, I'm freezing to death."

"But I need a bath. And I haven't brushed my teeth all day. There's a cloud of flu germs all around me and I . . . ahh! Oh God, John, oh, that feels good. . . ."

"I love your germs, Annie, I want them all, I want everything you've got."

"Oh God," she said, "oh damn. The light, get the light. And lock the door, hurry up. John, hurry, hurry, hurry . . . ahh! that's it, that's it, slow down. . . ."

Later, as he lay holding her in the warm, musky darkness, Bloomhardt said, "Let me come home again."

She moaned softly, half-asleep.

"I've learned my lesson, Annie. I've changed, haven't I?"

"Ask me when I'm not sick, okay? Wait till Thanksgiving."

"That's almost a month from now!"

"I'm not going to argue, John. I need to sleep. You'd better go now."

Reluctantly he lifted the blanket away, slid out from under it, and sat up. She laid her hand upon his back and said, "By the way, thanks for the house call. I like the way you practice medicine."

"I don't get much practice these days," he told her.

"Really?" she said, only half-teasing.

"I haven't touched anyone, Annie, I swear. A cloistered monk gets more action than I have."

She smiled sleepily.

"But as long as we're on the subject," he said, "how about you?"

"Practice makes perfect," she answered.

"Oh God," he groaned, and dropped his head onto her stomach.

She did not say anything but he could feel her stomach muscles tighten and relax as she held back her laughter.

He decided not to explore the subject further. "Anyway, you're still wearing the necklace I gave you," he said. "That proves that you're still mine."

She thumped her knuckles on the top of his head. "It proves no such thing. It's not a dog license, it doesn't mean I belong to you."

He sat up and rubbed his head. "I can live with that."

Bloomhardt lingered only a moment longer, then he dressed quietly, kissed her lightly on the cheek, and tiptoed from the room. In front of Timmy's door he paused, meaning to leave a candy bar on the boy's pillow, but when he eased open the door he found his son inside, seated at his desk, a study light focused on the pages of a child's encyclopedia. Timmy looked up at him, eyebrows raised.

"Jeepers, Tim," said Bloomhardt as he stepped inside and pulled shut the door. "What are you doing up here?"

"Looking at pictures," the boy said. He pointed to the one on the left side of the book. "This is Jupiter's moon Io. It has volcanoes on it."

"I mean why aren't you downstairs with the other kids?"

Timmy blinked twice. "I didn't like it down there."

"Hmmm. I know what you mean." He kissed the boy's head, then stood behind him with his hands on Timmy's shoulders. He was about to ask to see more pictures when his attention was caught by the bulletin board above the desk. Pinned to the cork were the six postcards he had sent. Bloomhardt felt his throat thicken, felt his face burn with shame.

"I see that you received all my postcards," he said.

Timmy was staring up at him with his head tilted back, and Bloomhardt, when he looked down, could see himself reflected in the glasses. He did not like what he saw.

"You know where those postcards came from?" he asked hoarsely.

"Mommy said Italy."

"Well, Tim, they didn't. Not really. Actually, I bought them in a little Italian restaurant downtown. The waitresses are all blond college girls and the owner is Canadian. I think the cook is Chinese."

Timmy said nothing, but continued to look up at his father. Bloomhardt, groping for words, wanted only to start everything over, wanted to go back in time to the eve of his first mistake, which must have been just a few moments after birth. "I shouldn't have pretended I went to Italy when I really didn't," he said. "It was the wrong thing to do. I just . . . I just didn't want to go."

Timmy looked at him a moment longer, then turned to the book, silent. The longer Bloomhardt waited for a response, the more out of place his hands seemed on Timmy's shoulders, the more resented he knew them to be. Lightly, unobtrusively, he drew them away, then took a step back, ready to slither out the door.

"I pretend sometimes too," the boy said. "It's okay that you didn't want to go to that place. It's probably too noisy there, just like downstairs."

"Yep," said Bloomhardt, his mouth dry. "That's what I figured." He felt like dancing, but barely moved. To keep from grabbing the boy and hoisting him joyfully in the air, he shoved his hands into his jacket pockets, and there discovered the chocolate bars.

"Happy Halloween," he said as he laid two of them on the desk.

Timmy picked up a candy bar in each hand and, turning in his chair, extended his left hand to his father. "You eat one."

"Sure. We'll have our own party, okay?" Grinning, he stripped off the paper and popped a piece of chocolate in his mouth. Timmy did the same. Bloomhardt rolled the wrapper into a tight ball, working it slowly and nodding as Timmy followed suit. Then Bloomhardt said, "Boing!" and tossed the paper off his son's forehead.

Timmy jerked his head back and, startled, blinked several times. Bloomhardt leaned forward to reassure the boy, but just as he did so, Timmy said, "Boing!" and bounced his paper off Bloomhardt's nose.

Eyes wide, Bloomhardt stood up straight. He began to tilt backward, farther, farther, until he fell spread-eagled on his son's bed. He twitched a few times, kicked his feet in the air, then lay very still. For half a minute Timmy did not move. Gradually he pushed back his chair, stood, and cautiously approached his father. Bloomhardt, with eyes closed, began to worry that he might be frightening the boy, but just as he made up his mind to open his eyes and sit up, a small wet fingertip slipped into his ear.

"You little devil!" Bloomhardt yelped as he jumped up and grabbed for him; Timmy ducked away, squealing happily. Bloomhardt snatched up the pillow and sent it flying at the boy, but immediately wanted to call it back.

The pillow hit Timmy on the back of his head and drove him forward, off balance. He crashed into the desk, his head banging against the study lamp, which shot back against the wall, its bulb popping like a gunshot as Timmy crumbled to the floor. A second later, Bloomhardt was on his feet and scooping Timmy up, laying him out across the bed. Annie, clutching at her unbuttoned robe, threw open the door, fumbled for the wall switch, found it, and flipped on the overhead light.

Timmy was trying to sit up, but Bloomhardt kept pushing him down. Both mother and father gasped when they saw the thin smear of blood below the boy's nose. Annie elbowed Bloomhardt out of the way, bent over her son, and daubed at the blood with the belt from her robe. "Sweetheart," she said, "sweetheart, what happened, let Mommy see what happened to you."

"I'm okay," said Timmy, as he tried to squirm from her grasp.

"Baby, lie still, let me see. Let Mommy look."

"He's okay," Bloomhardt said meekly, hating himself. "He just banged his nose—"

Annie spun around to face him. "What did you do to him this time? How did you do this?"

"We were playing," Bloomhardt said.

"Playing? You call this playing? This child is *bleeding*!"

"Let me go," Timmy said. "I'm all right."

"He's all right," said Bloomhardt.

"He's not unconscious, if that's what you mean. He's still alive, so he must be all right—is that the way you look at it?" Her voice was rising steadily, her body trembling. Never had he seen her so angry.

"Get out of here!" she screamed.

"Annie, geez . . ."

"Get out of this house! Go away before you kill somebody!"

Bloomhardt bent to pick up his son's glasses. He cleaned the lenses on the tail of his shirt, then handed the glasses to Timmy. Annie kept her robe pressed to the boy's mouth and nose so that his "Thank you" was muffled beneath her hand.

"I'm sorry, sport," said Bloomhardt as he backed toward the door. "I love you, son. I didn't mean to hurt you."

Timmy's reply was too garbled to be understood. Bloomhardt winked at him, smiled apologetically, and turned to the door. Helen Krakow stood blocking the threshold, three other women and several children, some still wearing masks, crowded in behind her.

"Move aside, children," said Helen as she waved them back. "Hurry, hurry, before the big tough man knocks another child down."

Bloomhardt could see nothing before him but a narrow tunnel of gauzy light. He made his way down the stairs and outside, where he stumbled across the yard and then broke into a run, teeth and fists clenched as he sprinted deep into the unlighted park. When he came upon a thick oak tree, he hurled himself at it and banged his head against the rough bark. Moments later, his vision clearing, he staggered away, out of the park and down the street to his car.

In his absence, all of the car windows had been soaped, rendered opaque by a layer of chalky white. What looked to be at least a bushel of ripe tomatoes had been splattered over the roof and hood. Both rear tires were flat. The radio antenna had been snapped off at its base. EVIL RULES! was scrawled in white shoe polish along the length of his car.

With the elbow of his jacket, Bloomhardt wiped a small porthole on the windshield. He climbed inside and for several minutes merely sat there hunched over the steering wheel. When he glanced into the rearview mirror he saw by the welt of dried blood between his eyebrows that he had cut his forehead. It was an ugly cut, and for a moment he wondered why it did not bother him, but then he recognized the lifeless glaze in his eyes and he understood that dead men feel no pain. He started the engine and pulled away from the curb and, with the rear of his car lurching from side to side, bouncing up and down, he went in search of an air hose, a car wash, and a reason to live.

October became November. Grass browned, trees dropped their leaves, black clouds of migratory birds swept across the sky. The rich smells of autumn, of leaf smoke and cider, blew away, leaving the frosty scent of sterility.

Everything changed, yet nothing was new.

Several times Bloomhardt telephoned his wife, but without measurable success. He sent notes and expensive gifts. He stood shivering on the front porch, exchanging insults with Helen Krakow while trying to look unaffected by the cold. From Annie's lawyer he received a two-page letter advising him that the divorce hearing had been scheduled for the first Tuesday in January. He was advised as well to stay away from his wife, his son, and his house on Fairfax Avenue, until the disposition had been made. The house would be sold; in fact, the local chapter of Annie's organization had already submitted an offer. Finally, he was advised that his movements on and about the aforementioned property were being monitored, that the lawyer was in possession of several photographs showing the defendant, clearly identifiable, engaged in activities of a nonpropitiable nature, i.e., creeping near or about the aforementioned house, peering through the windows of same, and/or crouching behind the hedge across the street with a pair of binoculars to his eyes. Such photographs, he was warned, could have a significant bearing upon the distribution of assets, not to mention the determination of custody and/or visitation rights pertaining to any or all minor children.

Bloomhardt looked up *nonpropitiable* in the dictionary, threw the letter in the trash and sent his wife a CandyGram.

Three days before Thanksgiving, he was served with a restraining order.

Nothing was new, only more official.

his work at Universal Steel became his only palliative. With horseplay and vulgarity he numbed himself, he cloaked his pain for eight hours a day. On the day before Thanksgiving he turned from the water fountain in the corridor only to bump against Roomy's egg-shaped belly. Roomy's breath, as he leaned close and took Bloomhardt by the arm, smelled of coffee and cigarettes, and the chalky smear of an antacid tablet was still visible on his lips.

"You've got to do it for me," Roomy said in an urgent whisper.

"Do what?" asked Bloomhardt.

"I mean, you're a man of the world, right? So what's one more woman to you, more or less?"

This was the kind of interplay Bloomhardt had begun to enjoy of late. It gave him a chance to blow off some steam, be sardonic, churlish, insulting, and rude, which was precisely what his colleagues expected from one another. In answer to Roomy's cryptic statement, he replied, "You want me to service your wife, is that it? Or maybe your daughter, huh? Come on, boy, speak up, don't be bashful."

"Hey, lay off my daughter. She just turned fifteen and she doesn't even know what sex is yet."

"Ugly like you, huh? Can't get a boyfriend?"

"Come on, Bloomie, be serious. I've got a real problem here."

"Okay, okay. So, you want a favor from me? Then first you do a favor *for* me. Get those locks off the men's room door."

"What do you expect me to do, bite them off? I'm not Superman, you know."

"Obviously," said Bloomhardt as he patted Roomy's waist. "But I know it was you who put those locks there in the first place. So go get the keys."

"You're crazy."

"Admit it, Roomy. You can't even walk past that door without hugging the opposite wall. And even then you break into a cold sweat."

Roomy shifted his weight from one foot to the other and glanced nervously down the hall. "I'm not admitting nothing, see? But you don't know what it's like, what it was like that day when I watched Mickey's brains come spilling out the back of his head."

"But it was all cleaned up, right? The whole place scrubbed and painted and disinfected the very same day it happened?"

"You didn't know him, you didn't know poor old Mick. He was my pal, Bloomie. Never a complaint, never a foul mouth like yours. The sweetest man in the world, that's who he was. Geez, I can still remember every detail of the day it happened. Mickey walked over to my desk about noon and asked me for an aspirin."

"I've heard this story before, Roomy."

"But I didn't have any aspirins to give him, see? Because I'd finished off the bottle myself no more than an hour before that. But Mickey says, 'Oh, that's all right, thanks anyway,' and he flashes me that big warm smile of his like *he's* apologizing to *me*. Then he walks over to the men's room, and *ka-BOOM!* Ahh Jesus, I can still see his brains dripping off those tile walls."

"Roomy, be realistic. We can't keep using the ladies' room forever. Between them and the Boss, we never get inside."

"So what? You ever hear anybody else griping about it? No, because they all knew Mickey, same as I did. Christ, I could start crying just thinking about him. So forget it, there's no way I'd take those locks off, even if I was the person who put them there, which I wasn't. No sir, no way. I don't want anything like that happening to me."

"Like what?" Bloomhardt laughed. "You think blowing your brains out is contagious?"

"You think it's not? Tell me something: Where did Mickey kill himself?"

"What is this, a riddle?"

"In the men's room, that's where. But if those locks had been on the door just one day earlier, he couldn't have gotten in. And therefore it couldn't have happened."

"It couldn't have happened there, right, but it—"

"Right! It happened there because he was able to go in there. But now nobody can go in, especially me. And if I can't go where it happens, it can't ever happen!"

"Good Lord," said Bloomhardt. "What logic! It didn't just happen, Roomy. Mickey wanted it to happen."

"What he wanted was a couple of aspirin, and I didn't have any. Besides, it's not as simple as that. Don't you think I've felt like doing the same thing to myself? And Smitty, and the Goathead, we've all thought about it. You have too, admit it. We all get the urge every once in a while to blow our brains out. But as long as that door stays locked, we're safe, you see? Because there's no other place we can go and do it. I mean, would you want your brains dripping off a sanitary napkin machine? Would you want your obituary to read that you were found dead in the ladies' room?"

Bloomhardt laughed softly and shook his head. "I've got to get back to work now."

Roomy grabbed him by the arm and turned him around. "If you ever need an aspirin, Bloomie, I always keep a couple of extra bottles in the bottom drawer of my desk. You just help yourself."

"Aspirin won't cure the problems I've got, Roomy. Not unless I swallow the whole bottle."

"Tell you what, we'll talk about your problems later, okay? We still haven't discussed this little favor I need from you."

"Oh, right, you want me to screw your old lady. What's the matter, is your equipment on the fritz?"

"My equipment is just fine, thank you, and lay off the old lady. No, my problem is this young girl I've gotten friendly with. Actually she's my wife's niece, and she's spending her Thanksgiving vacation with us."

"So what's the point, Roomy?"

"The point, you dimwit, is that ever since she got here two days ago she's been coming on to me. She's so hot that she sets off my smoke alarms every time she walks into the room. But here's the sticky part. This nineteen-year-old beauty queen, this *virgin* beauty queen—did I mention that?—she keeps confiding in me how horny she is. She's been trying all year to get the guys from this fancy college she attends to bang her, but they're either fags or so scared off by her beauty that they won't lay a hand on her. She got so fed up that she even had an affair with one of her female professors, but that didn't do it for her, you know what I mean? She's made up her mind that she needs a man of experience this first time, somebody mature enough not to go limp when she strips off her clothes. And what the hell are you laughing about?"

Clutching his sides as he leaned against the wall for support, Bloomhardt gasped, "And she thinks *you're* the man for the job?"

Roomy tried to puff up his chest, but only his stomach expanded. "I *am* the man for the job."

"Then why aren't you doing it?"

"Well, to be honest with you, I don't want to. Not the first time, I mean. I'm afraid that if I take her cherry I might fall in love with her, and wouldn't that be a fine thing, me crazy in love with a girl only a couple years older than my daughter?"

"But if I have her first, you won't fall in love with her, is that it?"

"Jesus, how could I? How could I love a little tramp who opens up for a guy like you just because she's tired of being a virgin?"

"What do you mean, a guy like me?"

"You know, a stranger, a one-night stand."

"It's more respectable if she screws her uncle?"

"I don't understand why you're arguing about this, Bloomie. I mean, how many chances like this does a man your age get? Hell, if I had any sense I'd be charging you for the privilege."

"You seem to be forgetting something. What if she doesn't want to go along with it?"

"First of all, we won't let her know it's a set-up. I'll concoct some story to get her out of the house, then we'll run into you someplace downtown, and you'll start acting like you can't keep your hands off her, which you won't be able to do anyway. And she won't fight you off, either. I mean, she's no pushover, bear that in mind. She's just crazy to get laid."

"Hmmm," said Bloomhardt, pretending to mull it over. "What's in it for me?"

"What's in it for you? *What's in it for you?* I can't believe you said such a thing!"

Bloomhardt cocked his head thoughtfully and tapped a finger against his chin. After a long pause he said, "I need more incentive, Roomy. I want a shot at your wife too."

Sourly, Roomy said, "You know damn well my wife has a bad back."

"Okay then, your daughter. I'm not an unreasonable man."

"Just forget it, forget it, forget I ever mentioned it. Boy oh boy oh boy, I try to do a guy a favor . . ."

"Simmer down, simmer down, I didn't say no, did I? Just trying to sweeten the pot a little, that's all. You can't blame me for that, can you?"

"Naw, I guess not," Roomy conceded. "It's only natural. And I'll tell you what, if my wife hadn't slipped a disc . . . But hey, we have a deal, right? You'll do it for me?"

"Sure, why not? How about tonight?"

"Tonight? Gee, I don't know, that's kind of short notice."

"It's tonight or never, Roomy. This is the only night I have free."

"Okay, okay, I'll work something out. How does Harrigan's Saloon at about eight sound?"

"Sounds fine," said Bloomhardt, fully intending not to show up. "I'll ask Smitty to join us."

"No way, nothing doing! I don't want that nut within a hundred yards of my niece."

"But Roomy, think about it. With Smitty there, it won't look so much like a setup. You don't want her getting suspicious, do you? She might not take kindly to the idea of you trying to pawn her off on somebody else."

"But why him? I mean, what if he starts grabbing at her? What if he pulls his whanger out right in front of her? He's been known to do those things, you know."

"I'll make sure he behaves himself, I promise. But I'm going to have to insist on this, Roomy. Either Smitty gets included, or you can count me out."

Unhappily, Roomy acquiesced. "You don't give a guy much choice, do you?"

"I'm still willing to negotiate for your daughter."

"Tell Smitty to be on time," Roomy said.

Imagining Roomy's consternation when he arrived at the saloon to find only a drunken, lecherous Smitty to greet them, Bloomhardt was able to settle in at his desk with a smile on his face. But soon Smitty farted, which broke Bloomhardt's concentration. He looked up to see Nelson scowling, a thick finger shoved deep inside his nostril. Bloomhardt turned away, disgusted, just in time to see the Goathead pouring whiskey from a thermos into his coffee mug, filling it to the top, and then gulping it down. Bloomhardt turned again, this time to stare out the doorway at the empty hall. He found the sight of those two strong locks on the men's room door strangely reassuring.

"Roomy?" he asked. "Got any aspirin?"

later that afternoon he telephoned Annie.

"Hello?" she said.

"Hello," he replied.

"You're not supposed to be calling me, remember?"

"But tomorrow is Thanksgiving."

"No kidding."

"I'll take you and Timmy to a restaurant, if you'd like. Or I could come over there and make dinner for everybody."

"If I see you within a block of this house, I'll have you arrested."

"Annie, please," he whispered, not wanting the other men to hear. "You're starting to sound just like Helen."

"Don't you dare say anything bad about her."

He switched on the calculator and drummed his fingers over the keyboard. "I'm sorry about giving Timmy that nosebleed," he told her. "We were playing. It was an accident."

"So was the Chicago Fire."

"For God's sake, Annie, give me a break."

For several moments she said nothing. When she did speak again, her voice was hoarse and shaky. "I can't help it, John. You didn't mean to hurt Timmy, but you did, just the same. And you hurt me too. Every time you call or come around, it hurts me, it hurts like hell, but I can't let myself give in to you. I know it's Thanksgiving, damn it, and I'm lonely too, but I can't help it. So I'm sorry, you can't come over. Please don't call again."

She was crying when she hung up, and the choked timbre of her voice made Bloomhardt feel as if he were suffocating. He dropped the telephone receiver in its cradle, stood up, and started for the door.

"Where you going, Bloomie?" Smitty asked.

"Need some air," he gasped.

"Hey, if you find any, bring some back for me."

because he could not stand the thought of being alone in his desolate apartment on Thanksgiving Eve, Bloomhardt went with Smitty to Harrigan's Saloon and there met Roomy and his unslaked niece. Neither as irresistible nor as rapacious as Roomy had claimed, she was of average height but with a body slightly wider than average, her breasts and hips cinched so tightly in their harnesses that they gave the impression of having been compressed under extreme tension, so that if the seams of her purple dress happened to split, no one within an arm's length would be safe from the eruption. Her name was Donna and she had a voluptuous round face framed by long black hair, but if there was a lingering virginal glow to her skin beneath the heavy layers of rouge and blue eye shadow she wore, Bloomhardt failed to detect it.

For three hours, Smitty, Roomy, and Bloomhardt took turns dancing with her. She seemed alternately bored and infatuated with each of them. Late in the evening, at the close of a slow dance with Smitty, she excused herself to go to the powder room. Smitty returned to their booth, one hand massaging his balls, the other wiping perspiration from his forehead.

He slid in beside Roomy, who, because of his excessive nervous drinking, was now slumped against the wall, unconscious. "Hey, Bloomie," Smitty asked, "what's the story on this guy's niece? He told me she's studying to be a nun, so I've been a regular Boy Scout all night long. But if what she done to me out on that dance floor is what they teach in nun school, then I'm gonna go live in a convent."

"What'd she do?" Bloomhardt asked.

"Man, what didn't she do? I mean, there we were, me holding her at what I thought was a proper distance for a nun. When all of a sudden she throws her box up against me and starts grinding it all around. I open my mouth to ask her if she's having a religious convulsion or something, and she jams her tongue so far down my throat that I felt it licking my toes!"

Laughing, Bloomhardt said, "Sounds like she's warming up to you, Smitty."

"She's got me plenty warm, I can vouch for that. So come on, what's the lowdown? Is she a nunette or ain't she? 'Cause if she ain't, what the hell am I holding back for? And if she is, I'm gonna tell her that she's filled me with the spirit, and then I'm gonna show her exactly where the spirit filled me. I'll worry about my damned eternal soul in the morning."

Before Bloomhardt could answer, Smitty's eyes jerked toward the dance floor again to watch Donna swish and sway back to the booth. In the powder room she had apparently removed her undergarments, for even in the flickering lights from the dance floor, the fat nipples of her breasts could be seen jabbing at her dress front, as could the mounded vee between her legs to which the thin fabric of her dress now clung. She carried her shoes in one hand, her legs and feet bare of the pantyhose she had worn earlier.

As she oozed in beside Bloomhardt, Smitty stared at the twin howitzers of her breasts. "Holy moley," he groaned. "Are those babies loaded?"

Donna giggled and entwined a leg around Bloomhardt's. He was reminded suddenly of Myrna, and felt a panicky urge to escape. As her hand fell nonchalantly into his lap, she said, "Sorry to be gone so long. I smoked a joint while I was in the little girls' room. You boys wouldn't like to go someplace private and smoke another one with me, would you?"

"I've got a joint you can smoke," said Smitty.

"Excuse me," said Bloomhardt as he pushed the table into the aisle, stumbling as he climbed past Donna. "I've got to get out of here, I need some air."

"I'll come with you," Donna said.

"No! No, you stay here and enjoy yourself. Dance with Smitty. I'll take Roomy outside and try to revive him."

He dragged Roomy, who was groaning and muttering insentiently, out of his seat, then ducked his head under Roomy's arm and made his way to the door. Smitty, suddenly terrified to find himself alone with Donna, offered her a wooden grin. A moment later he felt her naked foot wiggling up the cuff of his trousers, and he jumped to his feet. "Uhh," he told her, "hold that thought, okay? I'll be right back."

He shoved his way through the crowd and went running outside. Just beyond the door, he crashed into Bloomhardt and Roomy negotiating the concrete steps. All three men went flying into the frozen gravel of the parking lot, fine silvery snowflakes drifting into their eyes and mouths.

Pushing himself to his knees, Smitty asked, "Everybody alive?"

"What in the world is wrong with you?" Bloomhardt asked as he sat up.

"Listen, Bloomie, sorry about the bump, but there's something I need to know right now. Is his niece gonna be a nun or not?"

"What's the difference? I thought you weren't concerned about your eternal soul."

Bloomhardt glanced at Roomy, who, unperturbed by the fall, lay in a fetal curl, his hands clasped prayerlike beneath his cheek, a satisfied smile on his lips. Bloomhardt no longer wanted to participate in this, not in Donna's seduction, whether of or by another, not in the drunkenness or smoke and noise, not in the desperate groping for sex that was climbing to a crescendo in every corner of the saloon. "I don't know what she is," he said.

"I mean, let's say she is, okay? Do you think God is still gonna let her be His nun, even after I deflated her?"

"Deflowered," said Bloomhardt as he climbed to his feet.

"Whatever. The important thing is, if I go and ruin her future with God, is she gonna hold that against me? Is He?"

Leaning over to pull Roomy up by his arm, Bloomhardt said, "I don't know, Smitty. But in my opinion, an eternity in hell just isn't worth a piece of ass."

"You think?"

"Come on, help me get this lump into the car."

"Why not just leave him there? He looks plenty comfortable to me."

Bloomhardt gazed down at Roomy's smiling face. Ah, to be so dead to the world.

"Hey, I've got an even better idea," said Smitty. "Let's pull the car over on top of him, and when he wakes up he'll think he's been run over!"

It was a clever idea, but a bit too malicious for Bloomhardt's taste. Besides, it would require that they remain at the saloon until Roomy regained consciousness, which might not be until morning. "Let's get him in the car," Bloomhardt said, "before he freezes to death."

Roomy barely stirred as they crammed him into the backseat, his feet resting on the twenty-pound turkey he had picked up earlier at the butcher shop. Smitty immediately tore off the paper wrappings and repositioned the bird beneath Roomy's head. "There, now you have a pillow. Pleasant dreams," he said as he closed the door.

"Don't you think that's just a little too cruel?" Bloomhardt asked. "That turkey is for a family dinner tomorrow."

"Yeah, I guess you're right." Smitty opened the door and reached for the turkey. Bloomhardt turned away to look up at the sky and the hazy moon.

"There," said Smitty as he closed the car door a few moments later. "Is that better, Bloomie?"

"Hmmm?" said Bloomhardt as he turned to look.

Instead of rewrapping the turkey in the torn bag, Smitty had set it atop Roomy's hips, folding Roomy's hands around the drumsticks so as to hold the bird in place. When Bloomhardt saw how the turkey was settled, its rear orifice tucked snugly against Roomy's lap, he said, "Smitty, for God's sake, please tell me you didn't do what I think you did."

"Naw, I wouldn't do that," said Smitty.

But before Bloomhardt could release a sigh of relief, Smitty slapped him on the back and howled, "Like hell I didn't! He's got his pecker up that thing, Bloomie! In there with the giblets! Oh God, look at that smile on his face!"

So convulsed with laughter was Smitty that he fell against the car. "You're sick," said Bloomhardt.

"Don't I know it!" He pounded on the window with his fist. "Ride 'em cowboy! Hi-ho, Butterball, away!"

Even unconscious, Roomy held to the slippery thighs and arched his hips up and down. Bloomhardt reached for the door handle, but the door was locked, as were the others. Smitty laughed so hard that he fell to his knees and rested his head against the fender.

"Where are the keys?" Bloomhardt asked.

"Where they oughta be. In Roomy's pockets!"

Bloomhardt sighed again, but there was no relief in it. "This is the most disgusting thing I've ever seen you do."

"Geez, I appreciate the compliment," said Smitty as he pulled himself up, "but to tell you the truth, Bloomie, I've done a hell of a lot worse than this."

Roomy had settled into a contented stillness now, the turkey slightly askew but in no danger of falling off his lap. Bloomhardt turned away and started toward the building. "Hey, where you going?" Smitty called.

"I'm going to get Donna and take her home and come back with an extra set of keys."

"Ahh, lighten up, Bloomie. Let me have a little fun. I mean, if I can't screw that horny little nun in there, the least I can do is put the screws to her uncle, right?"

"The least you can do is to shut up," said Bloomhardt.

Inside, the barroom was blue with smoke, the music even louder than it had been fifteen minutes earlier. Bloomhardt found Donna not where he had left her but at a nearby table, sitting on the lap of a tall, blond-bearded man, facing him with her legs wrapped around the back of his chair and her hands working inside his shirt.

Bloomhardt tapped her on the shoulder. "Excuse me, Donna. But we're going home now."

"Bye-bye," she said dreamily.

"Your uncle is outside waiting for you."

"Uncle Drunkle," she giggled in her companion's ear.

Bloomhardt slid his hands beneath her arms. "Maybe you'd like for me to carry you out."

"And maybe," said the bearded man, his eyes opening for the first time since Bloomhardt's arrival, "you'd like me to move your nose around to the back of your head."

"She's studying to be a nun," Bloomhardt said.

"I ain't Catholic," the bearded man said.

"Even so, you will very likely roast in hell for all eternity if you don't release this girl."

The bearded man looked at Bloomhardt as if he were something annoying but insignificant. "Sweetface," he said to Donna, at the same time withdrawing a switchblade knife from his boot, "I gotta get up for a minute to do some cosmetic surgery on this jerk, so you be a good girl and sit here till I get back, okay?"

"Um-hmmm," she answered, nodding.

"Hey, you kids have fun," said Bloomhardt, before he spun away and ducked into the crowd on the dance floor.

He had barely had time to think *mox nix* and congratulate himself on his nimble escape when, at the front of the saloon, he came to a groaning halt. His spirits, already low, sagged even further

231

when he spotted Smitty dancing like a leprechaun on a table near the door, hopping up and down with the long pink neck of Roomy's turkey protruding from his open fly.

"Gobble gobble gobble!" Smitty sang as he turned this way and that, thrusting his hips at the wide-eyed women. "Gobble gobble, gobble gobble gobble!"

As Bloomhardt pushed closer, the bartender, a man even bigger than the one with Donna, came from behind the bar, his jaw firmly set, eyes narrow and focused on Smitty, the veins of his neck taut. A second later he made a grab for Smitty, but came up empty as Smitty leapt agilely to another table. "Gobble gobble gobble!" he said as he shook the turkey neck all around.

In no hurry, a patient but sanguinary glint in his eye, the bartender moved toward Smitty's new perch. When he was but a step away, Smitty jumped again, sending ashtrays and bottles and glasses crashing to the floor. "Gobble gobble gob—" he said, cut off in midgobble by a cocktail waitress who, finding herself directly behind Smitty, shoved her tray into his back.

"Umpf!" said Smitty as he lurched forward into the bartender's arms. With his left hand, the big man then held Smitty by the front of his jacket and plopped him down on the edge of the table. With his other hand he landed a series of sweeping blows across Smitty's face, the thick-fingered hand slapping again and again with a precise rhythm that was soon taken up by the cheering crowd.

Smitty swung at the bartender, but his arms were too short and they hit nothing but air. "Oooh, damn," Bloomhardt moaned, close enough to see saliva spraying from Smitty's mouth. Soon there was blood streaming from his nose, and his eyes began to roll. His dangling feet kicked helplessly, his hands fluttered like dying birds, and a few moments later his entire body went slack.

But still the bartender did not stop. The chanting of the crowd grew louder and more enthusiastic. Dispassionately, fatalistically, Bloomhardt picked up the nearest empty chair, moved into position, and swung the chair against the back of the bartender's knees. The barman crashed to the floor, freeing Smitty. Smitty, whom Bloomhardt had thought unconscious, rolled sideways off the table, landed on his feet, and was two steps ahead of Bloomhardt as they raced for the door. A beer bottle exploded against the wall, spraying beer and glass in their faces as they fled outside, a dozen angry men at their heels.

Bloomhardt ran toward his car, fumbling to get his keys out of his pocket. Smitty, already on the street and picking up speed, called, "Run, Bloomie, run! They'll kill you before you can unlock the door!"

A single glance back confirmed this. Bloomhardt altered his course and chased Smitty down the street, bottles and glasses bursting like hand grenades on all sides. Smitty ducked into one alley and then another, Bloomhardt following and praying aloud that he would not be led into a dead end. They ran for five minutes more before Bloomhardt noticed that the mob's ammunition had been exhausted, that the angry curses and threats were fading in the distance. He sprinted to where Smitty, breathing hard and holding a handful of dirty snow to his nose, had paused to catch his breath.

"We'd better keep going," Bloomhardt said, gasping.

"In a second, okay? I can't throw up very well while we're trying to break the four-minute mile."

Gulping air, his hands on his knees, Bloomhardt watched Smitty double up against a parking meter. "I thought that guy had knocked you out," he said.

"Just playing possum," said Smitty between groans. "Sometimes it works and . . . sometimes it don't."

Bloomhardt waited for the city to come into focus again, for the phony stars flashing across his eyes to burn themselves out. "You okay?" he asked a moment later.

"Compared to what?"

"Compared to the dead man you deserve to be."

"Oh sure. In that case I'm in tip-top shape."

"Then let's keep moving. One or two of those Neanderthals might still be following us."

"Sounds like a brilliant idea if ever I've heard one." They had gone only a few yards when Smitty began to chuckle.

"What are you laughing at now?" Bloomhardt asked.

"That was kinda fun back there, wasn't it?"

"Fun? That's a rough place, Smitty. We were almost turned into wall ornaments because of you."

"Hey, there's no greater glory than to die for a good cause."

"What cause might that be?"

"'Cause I'm drunk! What else?"

"Don't talk to me anymore."

"Sure, whatever you say. But hey, Bloomie, thanks for helping me out back there. You're turning into a regular lowlife, I'm really proud of you. Stick with me, kid, and you'll be a sleazeball before you know it. Then we can really start having some fun."

Bloomhardt did not think it possible to sink any lower.

When alone in his apartment during the month that followed, Bloomhardt did nothing. He lay on the sofa bed and stared at the ceiling or out the dirty window, he tried to imagine what was going on in the neighboring apartments, though the women and men who visited there seldom climbed as high as the fourth floor. He continued to telephone Annie from the booth on the corner, but when he said hello and his voice was recognized, whoever answered the phone hung up.

At work he was another person, all restless animation. Not only did he participate in the usual chaos, he became its primary perpetrator. For five days in a row he stole Roomy's lunch bag and hid it in the ceiling panels. He broke into the sanitary napkin dispenser in the women's washroom and on the napkins penned obscene invitations to the receptionist, which he endorsed with Nelson's initials. He lifted a pack of cigarettes from the Goathead's pocket while the old man dozed at his desk, then stuffed the cigarettes with exploding loads. He glued a dead cockroach to the bottom of Smitty's coffee mug. He squeezed the apple jelly from a doughnut, replaced it with mucilage, and returned the doughnut to the coffee cart.

At the end of each workday, he and Smitty would race to a nearby tavern for a dinner of beer, pickled eggs, and pretzels. He would get drunk and happy, then drunker and sad. Later he would pass out on his sofa bed, his shoe box full of notecards spilled beside him. If he awoke before it was time to stumble off to work, he would read a few of the cards and try to force himself to write, but his mind would be as dry as his mouth, his thoughts as dull as the ache that throbbed inside his head.

He lost weight and grew dark circles under his eyes. His skin turned sallow, his hands trembled, he seemed always to be yawning. Every time he moved, he felt his skeleton rattle. When asleep he dreamed that he was running up a slippery hill. When awake, he craved the brief astringency of sleep.

friday, the twenty-third of December. Bloomhardt's fingers tripped blindly over the calculator as he stared out the window at the ore piles. It was 10:00 A.M., and still the Goathead had not arrived. "I'm getting worried about the old Goat," said Roomy to no one in particular. "He's usually not this late."

Nelson said, "If you tried doing some work for a change, you wouldn't have time to worry."

"Shut up, toadface. Nobody rattled your cage." To the other clerks, he added, "If this was Monday I could understand him being so late. But not on the day before a three-day weekend. And a payday, no less."

Petey, eternally optimistic, said, "Maybe he just overslept. I'm sure he's all right."

"Petey," said Smitty, "you're a good kid, so you don't understand this sort of thing. But the Goathead's been in a nosedive now for the last ten years. Haven't you noticed how cheerful and cooperative he's been of late? That ain't the old Goat's personality, it's Jim Beam's. So to tell you the truth, I'm a little worried myself. I got a funny feeling that the old man might have finally hit rock bottom."

"Hey, Bloomie," Smitty said a few moments later. "Call his house and see if he's at home."

"Why me?" Bloomhardt asked.

"You're his friend, ain't you?"

"Of course not. Are you?"

"Ah, come on, go ahead and call. But don't say who it is, or else he'll start thinking we care about him. And then what a pain in the behind he'd be!"

"Bunch of goddamn mother hens," Nelson grumbled.

"Shut the fuck up," came the reply in three-part harmony.

Bloomhardt picked up the telephone and dialed the old man's number. After the fifth ring, a woman answered. "Good morning," said Bloomhardt. "Is this Mrs. Drumbacher?"

"This is Rosalie, the daughter." She had a throaty, sexy, sleepy voice. "My mother can't come to the phone right now. May I ask who's calling, please?"

"This is, uh, Thomas . . . Twiddlebaum," Bloomhardt said. Smitty, stifling a howl, turned to the wall and covered his mouth. Roomy and Petey giggled. Nelson muttered under his breath. "Might I speak with Mr. Drumbacher, please?"

"Daddy is at work," said Rosalie. "Would you care to leave a message?"

"No, thank you. I'll call back later."

"Might I ask the nature of your call?"

Her voice was so mellifluous, so syrupy and warm, that Bloom-hardt extemporized. "Well, Rosalie, I'm senior editor of the, uh . . . *Planet of Poetry Review*, and I called to tell your father that we would be delighted to publish one of the poems he submitted. If he chooses to become a subscriber, of course. For a mere twenty dollars each month."

Smitty, his eyes brimming with tears, nodded enthusiastically and urged Bloomhardt on. "Really?" said Rosalie. "Which poem?"

"Uh . . ." said Bloomhardt.

"I'll bet it's one of his sonnets, isn't it? Daddy has always had a flair for the sonnet form."

"Yes, yes, he certainly does," said Bloomhardt, surprised to learn that there was *any* form of poetry in the old man's life. This discovery, plus the fact that Rosalie sounded so naïve, so *interested*, made Bloomhardt lose his appetite for the charade. "In any case," he continued soberly, "it was your father I needed to speak with. Thank you for your time, Rosalie. Sorry to have disturbed you."

"Wait!" she cried. "I write poetry, too—could I become a subscriber?"

"Uh, sure," he answered, now eager to hang up. "I'll send you a brochure, all right? Good-bye now."

"And would you publish one of my poems? A poem I wrote myself?"

"Well, yes, uh . . . maybe. Perhaps we could discuss it some other time . . ."

But Drumbacher's daughter, in her syrupy sexy voice, began to recite the poem for him. "'When she was young the world was bright, but each day made her older . . .'"

"That's very nice, Miss Drum—"

"'With a further dimming of her light as her supple flesh grew colder . . .'"

"Rosalie?"

"'A loveless life she began to dread; a bride with no guide to ride her . . .'"

"I really have to run now. Honest."

"'Cold ground became her marriage bed . . .'"

"Good-bye?"

"'With her groom all around and inside her.'"

Bloomhardt hung up.

"What's with you?" Smitty asked. "You've gone pale."

"She's a nut," said Bloomhardt. "The Goathead's daughter is loonytunes."

"Like father, like daughter," said Smitty with a shrug. "So the old Goat's not at home, huh?"

"I didn't even know he had a daughter," said Roomy.

"He writes poetry. Did you know that?"

"The Goathead? Naw. Christ. He can barely read."

"His daughter says he does."

"Musta been a wrong number."

It was dusk on the twenty-third of December, and somewhere along the space-time continuum a tiny Jesus was scratching at the womb. The accounting department of the Universal Steel Corporation, minus the Goathead, absent all day, and Nelson, now speeding toward home in his car, stood in the frozen parking lot and warmed their faces in the frosty vapor of one another's breath.

"I'd really like to help look for the old coot," said Roomy. "But my family's waiting for me at home to go pick up a Christmas tree. Besides, after what you guys did to me on Thanksgiving . . ."

"Go on, get lost," Smitty told him. "Go home and give your fat wife a backrub."

Roomy smiled. "Merry Christmas, guys," he said, then ran stiffly to his car.

"I'll help look for him," said Petey. "Just give me a minute to call my wife and tell her I'll be a little late."

"Wait a sec," said Smitty as he clamped a hand on Petey's shoulder. "You're a good kid and everything, Pete, but geez, you don't drink or whore around or anything. You'd only get in our way to-night. You'd better leave this up to Bloomie and me. You go on home and read the seed catalogue and maybe pop that pretty little wife of yours once or twice. You're a good, clean kid and you shouldn't be fraternizing with scum like us. Have a Merry fucking Christmas and we'll see you next week."

"You sure?" Petey said. "I want to do my part."

"Then go on home. A man like you belongs with his family tonight."

A minute later, as they watched Petey driving away, Bloomhardt said, "I've got a family too, you know."

"Sure you do," said Smitty. "Me. I'm the only family that'll have anything to do with you. So come on, let's go, we'll take my car into town."

In the city they wandered the streets like urban nomads, going from tavern to tavern, in and out of the icy wind for nearly three hours. The sky was black and Bloomhardt's soul even blacker. Hands shoved deep inside his pockets, chin tucked into his collar, he felt the chill of his aloneness deep inside his flesh, crystallizing the marrow in his bones.

"Why the hell am I doing this?" Smitty asked. "Christ, I could be holed up in a nice warm dive somewhere with half a buzz on by now, my arm up some floozy's skirt, just having myself a nice relaxed kind of evening. So why do I keep on looking for that old fart, Bloomie? Why am I doing it?"

Bloomhardt had no answer. He watched as yet another young couple, arm in arm, heads bent close together, cheeks almost touching, hurried by. "Tell me something, Smitty," he said. "You ever been in love?"

"That's something like a toothache, ain't it? Only difference is, a toothache is better cause you can get it filled, right?"

They walked in silence for five minutes more. Bloomhardt, still in a pensive mood, was only vaguely aware of his surroundings until Smitty grabbed him by the elbow and jerked him to a halt.

"Hey, wake up, will you? Here's another beer joint. Think we should check inside?"

They pressed their faces to the broad rectangular window and looked in at a barroom that was barely visible through the heavy fog of cigarette smoke. What could be seen was not inviting: crowded, cluttered tables, one with a cat atop it, lapping something from an ashtray.

"Wow," said Smitty. "This place looks too lowlife even for me. What do you say we go down to the Ramada Inn and thaw ourselves out, Bloomie? That's where all the college floozies go. The drinks are two bucks apiece, but the whiskey goes straight to my balls in a place like that."

Peering through the flyspecked window, Bloomhardt felt a surge of pity for the Goathead and everyone else who might frequent such an establishement. "As long as we're here," he said, "let's at least have a look."

Inside the smoky room, nearly every chair and barstool was occupied. Loud, jangling music throbbed from a radio somewhere near the bar, a prickly music that made Bloomhardt's skin itch. "What a dump!" Smitty screamed at him. "But kind of cozy, don't you think? You go on up to the bar and grab us a coupla beers while I check in the back for the Goathead."

The bartender was an ugly brute with a too-small head, tattooed snakes on both forearms, and tattooed daggers showing beneath the sleeves of his sweat-stained T-shirt. Bloomhardt squeezed up to the rail and waited patiently to be noticed. But the barman was in no hurry. At the far end of the bar he stood holding a small gray cat, the same cat Bloomhardt had glimpsed through the window and that he now recognized as no more than a kitten. Holding the animal atop the counter with one hand, the barman was busy creating a pattern of leopardlike spots on its fur by singeing the short hair with a cigarette. The cat lay very still, head on the bar, eyes glazed, as it stared down the counter toward Bloomhardt. He could smell the burning hair and wanted to protest, but there were too many customers cheering the barman on, and the kitten's passivity suggested that it was either too drunk or near death to be experiencing any discomfort.

A minute later Smitty returned, grinning, and elbowed his way in beside Bloomhardt. "He's here, all right. Back there in a booth, all by his lonesome, and passed out stone cold."

"Thank God," said Bloomhardt. "Let's grab him and get out of here."

"You go on back and try to rouse him. I need a drink."

As Bloomhardt turned away, Smitty banged a fist on the counter. "Hey, *garçon!* You work here, or do you get paid just to stand around and look ugly?"

In an unlighted booth in the rear corner of the room, the Goathead sat slumped against the wall. On the table before him were six empty beer bottles and one three-quarters full. Clutched in his right hand was an empty whiskey glass. He sat listing to his left at a thirty-degree angle, cheek flattened to the wall, eyes closed, his plume of white hair mussed.

Bloomhardt slid in across from him. "You dried-up, onion-eating old Goat," he said, not maliciously but with relief and affection in his voice. He sat there smiling at the old man as a father might smile upon a sleeping baby, but as each second passed he became more and more aware of a growing uneasiness.

Smitty returned carrying a huge platter of food and beer, which he deposited on the table as he plopped down beside the old man. "Dig in, Bloomie. We got beer and pickled eggs, smoked herring, pickled pigs' feet, Swiss cheese, pork rinds, chips, peanuts, and pretzels—everything on the menu."

"Smitty," said Bloomhardt, still eyeing the old man, "I don't think you should have—"

"Hey, no strain on me, pal. I snatched a twenty out of the old Goat's wallet. It's the least he can do for us, don't you think? Here, have a beer and enjoy yourself."

But Bloomhardt could not take his eyes off the old man's face.

"Is this the way you found him, Smitty? Just like this?"

"Just like this," said Smitty. "Dead to the world." He folded his hands in prayer and said, "We give thanks, O God, for this old fool of a drunk, and for this bounty his unconsciousness has bestowed on us. Hallelujah and amen. Come on, Bloomie, chow down. I can't eat all this stuff myself, you know."

"I'm not hungry," said Bloomhardt, his mouth suddenly dry. "In fact, I'm beginning to feel kind of sick."

Smitty elbowed the old man in the ribs. "See what you did? We're running in and out of beer joints all night long looking for you, and now poor old Bloomie's got pneumonia." He filled a glass with beer and slid it across the table.

"Drown a cold and fuck a fever, that was my dear old mother's remedy. Hey, how about a nice whiskey, Bloomie? That'll put the gleam back in your eye."

"Sit down, Smitty. I don't want any whiskey."

"Suit yourself." He dropped beside the Goathead again and began eating, alternating noisy bites with slurps of beer. Bloomhardt watched the old man's half-smiling face. In the background was the noise of the barroom, the laughter and hooted obscenities, a woman singing off-key to the crackle of the radio, the barroom odors of beer and smoke and too many warm bodies crowded into the same place.

"Smitty," he said, speaking no louder than necessary, "do me a favor and check the Goathead's pulse."

"Relax," said Smitty with a herring in his mouth. "He's spent half his life in this condition."

"Would you just do it, please?"

"Man, quit worrying. He's fine, he's feeling no pain. Here, I'll show you." Grasping the collar of the old man's jacket, Smitty pulled him several inches from the wall and then released him. The Goathead's cheek banged back to its former position.

"You see what I mean? He's in tip-top shape."

"Don't do that, Smitty."

"He can't even feel it!" Again Smitty grabbed the collar and bounced the old man's head against the wall. "Bong!" he said, doing it a second and third time. "Bong! He's a new kind of drum, Bloomie, he's a one-man orchest—"

Bloomhardt reached across the table and seized Smitty's arm. "He's dead," he told him.

With his hand still holding the Goathead's collar, Smitty's grin went lopsided. "Huh?"

"He's dead. I'm pretty sure of it. He hasn't breathed since we got here."

Smitty drew himself up very straight. Without looking away from Bloomhardt, he eased the old man back against the wall, then, barely moving his lips, he whispered hoarsely, "Move over." As Bloomhardt made room for him Smitty dragged himself across the seat, pivoted while still in a crouch, and slid in on the other side of the table. A second later he screamed and bounded into the air.

"Holy mother of Moses!" he shrieked, as the gray cat flew off his twitching leg.

Bloomhardt laid a hand on Smitty's shoulder and pulled him down. Then both men sat stiff and silent as they gazed at the old man. Half a minute later, Smitty allowed his shoulders to sag. He reached across the table for his glass of beer, raised it slowly to his lips, and sipped from it.

"You rotten old Goat," he murmured. "You no-good, white-haired rummy. Cut out the shit, you ain't dead."

A moment later he moved only his head as he turned to look at Bloomhardt. "He ain't dead, is he, Bloomie?"

Bloomhardt nodded. Smitty set down his glass and began to cry.

The Goathead's family had to be notified, that much Bloomhardt knew. They would be worried, expecting the worst, which was the best he could offer them.

"I gotta take a leak," Smitty had said fifteen minutes ago; Bloomhardt had not seen him since.

By slow degrees, Bloomhardt pushed himself out of the booth and, dragging his feet, made his way to the dance floor, where he pirouetted wearily in search of a telephone. Near the front, a tall man in baggy pants stood on a chair, playing spoons against the ceiling. Another man, crawling on his hands and knees, chased the gray cat from table to table. A fat woman leaned against a wall and, laughing or choking, he could not tell which, poured beer down the front of her T-shirt. Bloomhardt saw it all and for a moment felt wildly drunk, then remembered that he hadn't been drinking.

Finally he spotted the telephone booth, only fifteen feet away in the opposite corner. It looked to him like a windowed coffin standing on end. He wobbled toward it, stepped inside, and pulled shut the door. The interior light was broken, so he dialed by counting the holes for each number. Only after the number had clicked in and rung three times and been answered by a voice he knew, did he realize what he had done.

Quickly he pressed the coin into its slot. "Annie, Annie don't hang up, don't talk if you don't want to but please sweetheart don't hang up, just let me listen to you breathing for a minute, that's all I ask, just hang on for a second and let me listen to you breathe."

He held his own breath as he waited, heart pounding. Half a minute later, having heard no terminating click, he spoke more calmly. "Annie. Sweetheart. How are you?"

Ten seconds passed before she responded. "I'm fine."

"And Timmy? How's my Timmy doing?"

"He's fine too."

The sound of her voice so relieved him that he could say nothing more for a while. Besides, he had not expected to call her, had not done so intentionally, and now found himself at a loss for words. It was Annie who spoke next. "How are you?" she asked.

"Me? Oh, I'm fine, I . . . I just called to wish you a merry

Christmas, that's all. I mean I know I'm not supposed to be bothering you but . . ."

He was surprised, and pleased, to hear a soft moan from his wife. "This isn't any easier for me than it is for you," she said.

He chewed on his lip, wanting to taste blood. "Let me come home for a while. It's Christmas, you know."

"It's not Christmas yet."

"But it's the Christmas season. So how about a little goodwill?"

"Try the Salvation Army," she said.

He smiled in spite of himself and imagined that she was smiling too. Then he remembered what he was doing in that tavern, in that phone booth. "The Goathead died tonight," he told her.

"What? Who did?"

"Al Drumbacher, one of the men I work with. He didn't show up for work today so we went looking for him and we finally found him all alone in a sleazy bar. He's been dead for a couple of hours, I guess, but they just left him sitting there all alone in his booth. That's where I am now, I'm with him."

"Oh, John," she said.

"So now I have to call his family and tell them he's dead. I feel so sorry for them, Annie. Especially his daughter. Imagine losing your father so close to Christmas. That's why I had to call you, sweetheart. I feel so bad right now, I just had to hear your voice again." He was not playing fair and he knew it, but he also knew that he could not play fair and win.

"Why don't you come by on Christmas day," she told him. "Come for dinner."

He wanted to scream for joy, to grab the Goathead and dance a merry jig, but he kept his voice calm. "What about that thing I got from your lawyer? I don't want to go to jail."

"I won't tell anybody if you won't."

He took a deep breath, the first sweet breath he had breathed in a long time. "Come about four o'clock," she added.

"Can't I come earlier and spend some time with Timmy? I'll come with my hands tied behind my back if you want me to."

She said nothing, but he was certain he had heard a convulsive sob before she covered the receiver with her hand. "Sweetheart?" he asked. "Are you all right?"

"You can come at two," she told him. "No earlier."

"Two on the nose, gotcha. But, uh, is Helen . . . you know?"

"Not on Christmas, no. But she will be here tomorrow, and so will a lot of other people. So don't you dare show up around here tomorrow."

"Why, what's happening tomorrow? Another party?"

"It doesn't concern you. But I mean it, John. I don't want you near here until Christmas Day." During this statement her voice was steely and cold, almost that of another person. Then he heard what sounded like a tiny moan, and Annie, sobbing, told him, "Two o'clock. Sunday. We'll see you then." Before he could utter another word, she hung up.

bloomhardt held the receiver to his ear, listened to the Goathead's number ringing, and prayed that the old man's daughter would not answer. What if the Goathead himself answered and invited him over for a cup of egg nog? Bloomhardt was on the verge of hanging up when a voice sounded in his ear.

"Hello?" said an older woman.

He realized suddenly that he had no idea how to break the news to her. Short of breath and unreasonably warm, he asked, "Is this Mrs. Drumbacher?"

"Speak up, I can't hear you. Who is this?"

"Mrs. Drumbacher, would it be all right if I called you back in about five minutes?"

"Who is this? What do you want? If you have something dirty to say, just go ahead and say it, you're not going to get a reaction out of me."

"Mrs. Drumbacher, I'm a friend of your husband's, and I . . . well . . ."

"Is he there? Put him on, I want to talk to him."

"Uh, the thing is . . . he can't come to the phone just now."

"You tell him that that TV he was supposed to get fixed finally busted for good. Six months I've been after him to get that thing fixed, and now it's too late. There's no picture, no sound, no nothing."

"Yes, well, uh, the reason I called is . . ."

"That useless sonofabitch, I told him time after time to get that thing fixed. Put him on, I want to talk to him!"

Bloomhardt leaned against the phone booth wall and took a long, slow breath. Tell her. Just tell her and get it over with. "Please listen very carefully, Mrs. Drumbacher," he said. "Because I'm afraid I have bad news for you."

"You tell that sonofabitch that if he knows what's good for him he better come home with another TV set, and I don't mean one of them dinky portable jobs either."

"Alfred is dead, Mrs. Drumbacher. He died. He's gone. He passed away." Bloomhardt smelled his own breath on the receiver and it nauseated him. An intense wave of heat buckled his knees. "We found him a little while ago, Smitty and I did. I'm sorry, I . . . I'm sorry, I'm very, very sorry."

On the other end of the line there was silence. He steeled himself, knowing that disbelief and wailing would follow. How do you comfort someone over the telephone? he wondered. It was a local call, but that made it no easier.

"How much will I get from his pension?" asked the Goathead's wife.

"Huh?" he answered, caught off guard. "I mean . . . what?"

"He had only two years until retirement, so I oughta get most of it, won't I?"

"I, uh . . . I really don't know."

She breathed like a fat woman. He began to wish that Rosalie had answered his call.

"Ahh, you bastards," she said, her breath full of smoke. "You bastards aren't going to give it to me, are you?"

"Mrs. Drumbacher, I don't know what will happen, I'm not one of them. I worked *with* your husband, right beside him. But I'm sure the company will do whatever's right."

Hearing himself say this, he nearly laughed out loud. "What I need to know, Mrs. Drumbacher, is what you want to do with Alfred's . . . with Alfred. I mean, I don't just want to leave him here."

"Where is he—in a beer joint?"

"Well, I wouldn't exactly call it a beer joint. . . ."

"He only had two goddamn years to go!"

"Please, Mrs. Drumbacher, I don't think you understand my situation."

She breathed a few times, labored, bitter breaths. "Where is he?"

Bloomhardt gave her the address, then repeated it four times while she wrote it down. "You find out for me how much I'm going to get," she said.

"I will, I'll do that. Now, are you sure you got the address right? Why don't you read it back to me, okay?"

"I'll send somebody over," she said, and hung up.

For a long time, Bloomhardt stood there holding the dead receiver, reluctant to abandon the isolation of the booth. He felt guilty and inept, the Goathead's murderer, the company stooge who would never give the widow what she deserved. He thought of Mickey, whose phantasmagoric brains still glistened on the tile walls at Universal Steel, and for the first time he understood Roomy's fear, he understood the paranoia that haunts every man who lives a life of vacuity that only sex and death can fill.

Thinking of death, he was more startled than he should have

been when the door of the booth popped open and a large, grunting mass shoved in against him. Gasping and quivering, he was speechless for several moments. Gradually it dawned on him that the mass comprised two separate bodies, one hard and sweaty, the other soft and sweaty and perfumy.

"Uh, excuse me," he said meekly. "But this booth is occupied."

"Sorry, pal. We'll just be a minute or two."

Bloomhardt recognized that voice. "Smitty, is that you?"

"Hey, Bloomie, that you? Boy, am I ever glad to see you! Listen, hold her up for me, will you? I'm just about ready to get my end in, but she's fading fast."

Smitty shoved the girl into Bloomhardt's arms. "Hold her around the waist, Bloomie, till I get her pants down."

"For Chrissake, Smitty!"

"Hey, I'm hurrying, I'm hurrying, don't be in such a rush, you'll get your chance. Push those panties down a little further, can you, Bloomie?"

"I'm not pushing anything down or holding anyone up. Let me out of here!"

"Stick around, she don't mind. Do you, cupcake?"

Cupcake moaned and rose onto her toes as Smitty wedged a knee between her legs. Soon, Bloomhardt heard a zipper coming down. "Damn it, Smitty, what do you think you're doing? She's practically unconscious!"

"Well, yeah, now she is. But she wasn't five minutes ago when she suggested we come in here. It was all her idea, Bloomie, I swear!"

Bloomhardt reached over the girl's shoulder, put his hand on Smitty's face, and shoved him backward out of the booth. In an attempt to stop his fall, Smitty grabbed for the girl's arm, but only succeeded in pulling both her and Bloomhardt, whose foot was snagged in her fallen jeans, down atop him. Quickly, Bloomhardt squirmed away and jumped to his feet, just as a crowd began to gather around Smitty and the girl.

"Go to it!" somebody shouted, and poured a bottle of beer over the downed couple. Others flicked open their cigarette lighters and played the dancing flames back and forth. Smitty, with his face held up to the trickling beer, sang, "Please help me I'm faa-alling!" which elicited cheers and applause.

Bloomhardt slipped back to the booth where the Goathead waited. The old man had not moved. "Sorry, pardner," Bloomhardt murmured, and patted him on the shoulder. "We'll be out of here soon. I, uh . . . I hope you don't mind, but I'm going to wait outside, okay?"

Can't take it, huh? the old man's smile seemed to jeer.

"That's right," Bloomhardt answered. "I just can't take it."

On his way out, he paused beside the now-abandoned barstools to glance back to the rear of the room. The barman and all of his customers stood huddled in a deep circle, cheering Smitty's antics. What those antics might include, Bloomhardt was afraid to consider. Instead he reached into the beer cooler and helped himself to a six-pack. Then he went outside.

On the frigid curb outside the tavern, Bloomhardt sat with his elbows on his knees, his fourth bottle of beer in his hands. The air was so cold that his bones seemed frozen in their sockets. Even so, he felt no desire to return inside.

When a long black vehicle pulled up in front of him, narrowly missing his feet, he, thickheaded from the beer and cold, thought for a moment that the car was a hearse, a friendly mortician come to fetch the Goathead home. But at a second look he saw that it was a station wagon, a family car. Out from behind the wheel climbed a pretty girl, a girl, it seemed, too young to drive. She had short blond hair whose ends were bleached as white as snow, a small square face, wide brown eyes, a delicate nose, and a full-lipped mouth. She wore a brown vinyl coat whose hem fell at mid-thigh, high-heeled, open-toed shoes, and furry red mittens. Her legs were bare.

As she came around the rear of the car, almost skipping, smiling brightly, Bloomhardt had a sinking feeling that he was about to meet the Goathead's daughter. "Rosalie," he said aloud.

"Hi!" she answered. She hopped up onto the sidewalk and glanced all around. Even though Bloomhardt was sitting slouched forward, he saw that her eyes and his were on the same level. He calculated her height at something less than four and a half feet. He now saw too that she was not a girl at all, but well over thirty, that the illusion of youth was created by her size and the impish sparkle in her eyes, a sparkle not unlike her father's but considerably more moonstruck.

"Have you seen my daddy?" she asked brightly. "He's dead."

Bloomhardt pushed himself to his feet, his trousers tearing loose from the curb with a snap. "I'll take you to him," he said, as he gathered up his beer bottles and dropped them in a trash can.

"Okey-dokey," said Rosalie.

They found the Goathead no longer alone. Sitting beside him was a young woman with her head lolling lazily back and forth and her eyes half open. Bloomhardt thought he recognized her as the girl from the telephone booth. "Where's Smitty?" he asked. She lifted her head, which continued to sway, and squinted at him. "Smitty?" he repeated. "Remember? Where is he?"

She reacted to this by standing up so quickly that, had Bloomhardt not caught her by an arm, she would have tumbled into the Goathead's lap. As it was, she pulled away from Bloomhardt and steadied herself for a moment by resting both hands on the table, one of them in the platter of ravaged food Smitty had bought. She then straightened herself, turned, and walked toward the bar, seemingly unaware of the pickled pig's foot she clutched in her right hand.

Rosalie scooted in beside her father. "Daddy," she said as she stroked his stubbly cheek with her hand.

As unobtrusively as he could, Bloomhardt pulled the table into the aisle. "I'm going to have to pick him up," he said, as if in apology. Rosalie nodded and smiled.

He was surprised by how little the old man weighed. He had been such a compact old Goathead, so full of whiskey and mischief, that Bloomhardt expected more of a strain. But he was as light as a boy. As light as Timmy, Bloomhardt thought. Picking his steps carefully, he started toward the door. Rosalie held to the toe of her father's shoe and led the way.

Just when Bloomhardt began to think that they were going to escape without any further trouble, somebody goosed him. He jumped, lost his footing, stumbled awkwardly for a few more steps, and then crashed onto his knees. From behind came a familiar cackle of laughter—was it Smitty?

With Rosalie's help, he struggled to his feet again, calf muscles bulging, hamstrings ready to snap. Rosalie reclaimed her father's foot and pulled both men along, out the door and onto the sidewalk.

She popped open the station wagon's tailgate, then stood on the curb as Bloomhardt maneuvered her father inside. She seemed as unaffected by the spectacle as if she were watching a bag boy load her car with groceries. The Goathead, on the other hand, was not nearly so relaxed. Half-frozen into a lopsided sitting position, he looked, when balanced on the tailgate, like some weird kind of art deco chair. Using his own body as a shield to block Rosalie's view, Bloomhardt laid him on his side, then pushed simultaneously on the Goathead's knees and shoulders. The old man creaked open like a rusty hinge. Bloomhardt slid him farther inside, rolled him onto his back, and smoothed a wisp of billy goat hair from his eyes.

"Where are you going to take him?" he asked after he had climbed out.

"Home," said Rosalie.

"You mean the funeral home?"

"I mean his home. Our home. *Home* home."

"But aren't we supposed to notify somebody first? The coroner or . . . somebody?"

"Fuck that," she said cheerily.

"Whatever," said Bloomhardt. He glanced at the old man, then took two steps away from the car.

"I'll drive," said Rosalie as she started toward the front. "Hop in."

"Uh . . . I really hadn't planned to come along."

"Have to! How'm I going to get him out by myself? Wanna leave him in there all night long?"

"There's no one at home to help?"

"Nope!" she said.

Bloomhardt sighed, blinked, and shook his head. Finally he stepped forward and closed the tailgate. Just as he did so, Rosalie threw her arms into the air, looked into the sky, and passionately declaimed, "Oh, that it were me as well as him in Death's dark place; for there is on earth no sweeter smell than when Death sits on your face!"

"I'll ride in the back," said Bloomhardt.

at the Goathead's house, after a high-speed ride that had Bloomhardt rolling from one side of the car to the other, trying to hold the old man in place, Rosalie wheeled the station wagon into the driveway, slammed on the brakes, shut off the engine, and hopped out. She snapped open the tailgate and peeked inside at Bloomhardt, whose eyes were still spinning. "We're home!" she said.

With Bloomhardt carrying the old man by his shoulders and Rosalie helping with his feet, the Goathead was conveyed into the darkened house and laid to rest on a narrow sofa in a small square room. Unceremoniously, Rosalie dropped his legs onto the cushions, then spun on her heels and left the room.

The house smelled unpleasantly of staleness and alcohol, and the heavy darkness made Bloomhardt's skin itch. He was anxious to depart, but felt an obligation to arrange the old man's body in a position at least suggestive of comfort. After doing this, after straightening his legs and crossing his hands over his chest, after smoothing down the rumpled hair, Bloomhardt muttered, "Rest in peace, Alfred." He wanted to say more, but could think of nothing that might make a difference. So he turned quietly and, walking on his toes, made his way toward the front door.

From a bedroom upstairs came loud, rasping, snoring inhalations, followed by expulsive moans. Bloomhardt had no idea where Rosalie had disappeared so quickly, but he felt certain that the snorer was the Goathead's wife, for the moaning complaints of her sleep were remarkably similar in timbre and pitch to those she made when awake. He hoped Rosalie had not gone upstairs to awaken her mother, or if she had, that he could slip away before either returned. In the distance, at what seemed the end of a long black tunnel, the yellow porch light shone through a diamond of glass in the door. He fumbled his way toward it, bumping furniture, eager for freedom.

He was less than four steps from the door, his hand reaching for the knob, when Rosalie popped out in front of him from the invisible doorway of an adjoining room. In her left hand she held, navelhigh, a long black candle, its orange flame illuminating the fact that she wore nothing but a thick necklace made from animal teeth and pieces of bone.

"The phallus of Death must penetrate us all," she said in her sleepy, sexy voice as Bloomhardt gasped and clutched at his heart. "It sinks deep, deep, deep," she said while playing the flame back and forth beneath her eggplant-shaped breasts.

"I, uh . . . I wish I could stay, but geez . . . gotta run."

She slid the thick butt of the candle down over her stomach, over the smoothly shaven pubic mound, into the cleft between her legs. Holding the butt in place, she moved the flame in slow, mesmerizing circles. "Filling us with its black light," she intoned. "The black juice of Death."

Bloomhardt reached under her arm and tried to get hold of the doorknob. "That's . . . nice, real nice. You write that yourself?"

Her hand shot out and closed tightly around his scrotum. "Fill me! Fill me with your shaft of darkness!"

Bloomhardt wanted to leap free, but her grip was firm and he was reluctant to leave a valued part of himself behind. The hair was standing on the back of his neck, an icicle climbing up his vertebrae. Upstairs, the obscene snoring sounds continued.

He looked down and saw that the candle was sinking deeper inside her. The louder she groaned, the tighter became her grip on him. He danced on his toes and wanted to scream.

"Let me have it," she moaned as she rubbed her belly against his thigh. "Give it to me, give it to me, give it to me."

"I will, I will, but geez, let me get my pants off first."

Hearing this, she released him and shoved the candle a half-inch deeper. "Ooh yes, give it to me now, now, now. . . ."

"Right," said Bloomhardt. "Just give me a minute and I'll go get it for you." He grabbed her by the elbow and yanked her away from the door, then jerked the door open and plunged outside.

he did not want to sleep, knowing the kinds of dreams he would have after such a night. He made a pot of strong coffee and drank it while stretched out on his rumpled bed, his shoe box full of note cards spilled beside him.

On these cards were ten years of thoughts and impressions,

lines from stories he had meant to write, titles, brief descriptions, snatches of verse. He separated the cards into two piles, one whose prose sounded to him like that of a drunkard or an imbecile, the second, a much smaller pile, consisting of cards on which there was a phrase so honest, so right, that he could not believe he had once composed it.

Eight hours, three pots of coffee, and ten stale Halloween chocolate bars later, at slightly after seven the next morning, he had whittled the smaller pile down to a mere ten cards. From these he chose one at random and read what was written there. *It is a Sunday morning in October and there are dogs shitting on my doorstep.* How appropriate, he thought, that he should begin with a sentence about his past, a past he had once despised but now longed for. He paced the room, reciting the line again and again, pausing only to gulp more coffee, to swallow another chocolate bar in two bites.

Outside, a fine clear mist was falling upon the city, a freezing mist that varnished everything it touched with a lacquer of ice. Bloomhardt thought the scene unbearably beautiful. *It is a Sunday morning in October and there are dogs shitting on my doorstep.* His eyes stung, his back ached, his breath was foul, and his stomach burned with caffeine. His nerves felt laid bare, frayed and sparking. He had seldom felt worse, and never better.

Suddenly he yelped as if stuck with a pin and threw himself down on the bed, where he grabbed the notepad and pencil and began to write. He pressed too hard and broke the point, tossed that pencil aside, and grabbed another. *It is a Sunday morning in October and there are dogs shitting on my doorstep.* Instantly he saw that it was good, probably too good. He wrote impetuously, possessed, impatient for the next word. His hand was moving so fast that his eye could not follow it, the pencil point leaving scorch marks, trailing smoke all the way.

He wrote like this, nonstop, for over an hour, until his vision blurred so badly that the notepad seemed to float in and out of his hand. Finally he leaned back, closed his eyes, and took a deep breath. He felt empty, wrung dry. Not unhappily, he pushed himself off the bed, stretched his arms, and brushed the ceiling with his fingertips. On his bed lay the yellow notepad with a half-dozen pages filled, front and back. He could barely wait to read what he had written. But first he would give the paper time to cool, give his head time to clear, for he did not want to miss a single word of it, not a comma, not a semicolon.

He went to the window again and looked out. Even through the dirty glass the sun as it shimmered on the glaze of ice seemed immaculate and bright. So too every glazed car, every sidewalk and parking meter, every battered trash can. He gasped out loud when the mist changed suddenly to snow, to flakes as big as goosedown, which seemed to hang in the air forever.

Without bothering to look for a cap or gloves, he grabbed his jacket from the closet and pulled it on. Down on the sidewalk he skated across the ice, running and sliding, catching hold of a street sign and spinning himself around. He felt so strong and full of life that, even when, during one fast slide, he crashed onto his hip and spun off the curb and onto a sewer grating, he did not let the shiver of pain diminish his gaiety but quickly rose to his feet and, limping as nimbly as he could, hurried down the street in search of other places to play.

he realized where he was going long before he got there, but he would not allow this realization to linger in his thoughts. He told himself that he was taking a walk, nothing more, simply following his feet wherever they led. When he saw the large white house looming ahead, he muttered, "Well, I'll be darned. Now how did I get way out here?"

Annie's admonition that he stay away today was fresh in his

mind, but he knew she would forgive him when told of all he had accomplished that morning. She would probably be so pleased that she would send her friends packing—he counted six familiar cars lined up along the curb—and then drag him into bed for a congratulatory romp.

So certain of this was he, so enlivened by caffeine and confidence, that he strolled onto the front porch and walked inside without knocking. Sixteen women, all seated around card tables where some were using pinking shears to cut wavy borders on yellow sheets of printed paper, others folding these papers and stuffing them into envelopes, all stopped what they were doing and looked up at him.

He blew on his hands and stomped the snow off his shoes. "Cold day," he offered in greeting.

The woman nearest him, noticeably the smallest and oldest in the room, demanded, "What are you doing here?"

"What are any of us doing here?" he answered, made more confident still by the observation that Helen Krakow was not among them. "Are we put on this earth for a reason? Or is your annoying presence in my life merely coincidence?"

She stared at him coldly, but he was not frightened. She doesn't know I have acid in my blood today, he thought, amused.

"You could be arrested for being here," she told him.

"Thank you so much for that information," he said as he stomped his feet a final time and then started toward the stairs, chuckling. He was invulnerable.

He found his son in his room, seated at his desk drawing pictures in a tablet. "Hiya, sport," said Bloomhardt from the threshold. "Merry Christmas!"

Timmy blinked. Was that a sparkle of happiness glinting in his myopic eyes? "I thought you weren't coming until tomorrow."

Bloomhardt stepped up to the desk and tousled the boy's hair. "You want me to go away until tomorrow?"

"No," said the boy.

"So what are you up to, sport? Drawing more pictures?"

Timmy closed the cover of his tablet. "You can't see it yet."

"Is it a Christmas present? Boy, I can hardly wait! What's it a picture of?"

"I'm not telling."

"Going to make me sweat it out, huh? Okay, then, I guess I might as well leave. See you tomorrow."

"We could play chess," said Timmy. "Or do a puzzle."

"I've got a better idea. Let's you and me go for a walk."

"Mommy said not to go out."

"Yes, but she didn't mean you couldn't go out with me. By the way, where is Mommy? I didn't see her downstairs."

"She went someplace with Helen."

"Do you know where?"

"No," said the boy.

"Neither do I," said Bloomhardt. "So okay, what do you think? Want to take a walk with your old man?"

"It's snowing, isn't it?"

"Sure, but that's the best time to take a walk. Everything is so crunchy and crisp, it feels like you're walking on eggs."

The boy looked at him and blinked. I'm not going to hurt you, Bloomhardt wanted to say. Don't worry, son, I'll keep my distance, I'll walk on the opposite side of the street if you want me to. Just please be with me a while, Tim. Give your old dad a chance.

"Okay," Timmy said.

"Hey, terrific! You get dressed real warm, put on your longjohns and a couple of sweaters and your boots and scarf and hat and gloves, and I'll go downstairs and leave a note for Mommy. You need any help getting dressed?"

"No, thank you," said the boy.

"Great. I'll wait for you downstairs, son."

Bloomhardt felt so good that, had his living room not been full of

hostile women, he would have slid down the bannister and somer-
saulted across the floor. Instead he kept his gaze high and whistled
softly as he wended his way past their tables and into the kitchen.
There was a fresh pot of coffee on the counter, so he poured a cup
for himself, then searched for a pad and pencil. Annie had changed
everything around since he had moved out; nothing was where it
used to be. He was still rummaging through the drawers when he
heard a car pull into the driveway. He went to the window and
looked out and saw Annie's blue Volkswagen coming to a stop in
front of the garage.

Surprisingly, Annie climbed out from the passenger side. Helen
Krakow, the driver, hurried around the car to take Bloomhardt's
wife by the arm. Had both women not been smiling, though Annie's smile seemed strained, Helen's caring and maternal, he
would have rushed outside to meet her as they crossed toward the
front porch.

Bloomhardt stood very still and listened intently as the front
door opened to cheers and applause. What the hell is going on? he
wondered. Next came a minute or two of muffled chatter, but not
so muffled that he failed to hear a few of the epithets directed at
him. He pulled a chair away from the table, sat down, and tried to
look nonchalant. Before long, Annie came into the kitchen. She
moved slowly, as if very tired, and stood with her back against the
refrigerator.

"Merry Christmas," he said with a hopeful smile.

"I thought I told you not to come here today."

"That's true, you did, but I had such a wonderful morning, Annie—I started writing! I actually settled down and wrote something. Once I got started I couldn't stop, it just came gushing out,
and I guess I felt so good about it that I just wanted to tell you and,
you know, share it with you."

"I told you to stay away from me today."

"I know, but geez, it's the day before Christmas and—"

"I know what fucking day it is!"

Bloomhardt jerked back as if jabbed with a cattle prod. Whose voice was that coming from Annie's mouth? Whose icy eyes were those?

Even she seemed startled by her outburst. Sighing heavily, she shook her head, then turned and rested her forehead against the freezer door. "Are you all right?" he asked.

"I will be," she said.

"You look like you might be coming down with something. It's not the flu again, is it?"

She laughed to herself.

"It's been going around," he said.

Again she laughed. A few moments later she opened the refrigerator, took out a pitcher of orange juice, and poured some in a glass. She sipped from it as she stared at the floor. Bloomhardt thought he could detect dark crescents under her eyes, thought she looked smaller, thinner than he remembered. Or maybe it was only the way she was standing there, all huddled into herself.

"Annie," he said, almost whispering, "where were you this morning?"

There was that strained, disquieting smile again. "Downtown."

"What for? What were you doing?"

"I went to see a doctor."

"Then you *are* sick?"

"Not anymore. I had an abortion."

Something that felt like a stone-tipped arrow zipped through Bloomhardt's chest. It sliced through his heart, twisted around the top of his spine, pierced his trachea and esophagus, and paralyzed him from the neck down. "No," he moaned.

Annie smiled crookedly. "Yes," she said.

His vision blurring, he began to pant. A huge bubble of acid climbed into his throat. "Why?" he managed to ask.

"Because I was pregnant. Don't be stupid."

His hands were trembling, but he was only remotely aware of the hot coffee splashing onto his lap. "Did you . . . I mean, do you . . . know . . . who . . . ?"

Her eyes were hard when she looked up at him. "Who what?"

"Who . . . ?"

She stood straight and stepped away from the refrigerator. "Who *what*, John?"

". . . the father is?"

She hurled her glass of orange juice at him. The glass narrowly missed his head, which he had not moved, and shattered against the wall. Most of the juice caught him in the face. He did not have the strength to wipe it away.

"Damn you," she said. "You and your damn Halloween visit. You remember that night? When I was too sick to say no? Well, guess who got the treat and who got stuck with the trick."

He felt himself shrinking, disintegrating, his skeleton turning to dust as the balloon of his skin deflated. "Why didn't you tell me?"

"Why didn't you just soap my windows or pelt the house with tomatoes that night? Why didn't you stay away today like I told you to?"

She had not moved any closer, but he felt as if she were looming over him, shutting off his light and air. Her eyes were as hard as the glaze of ice outside. "My God, Annie, what's happened to you? What have you become?"

"A better person than I was with you, that's what."

"The woman I loved could never have murdered a baby."

"Shut up!" she screamed, and, lunging forward, slapped him across his mouth. She slapped him again—a second, a third time, all the while screaming for him to shut up, he saying nothing, not pulling away, not defending himself, his gaze steady and full of disbelief.

Seeing his pleading eyes still raised to hers, she took a step back. She was out of breath and looked as if she might fall at any moment. Bloomhardt reached up and touched her arm. "Don't," she said, and jerked away.

So he sat there motionless and watched her. She sniffed a few times, went to the sink, drew a cup of water, took a sip, and stared out the window. Bloomhardt looked down at the table. On its surface was a puddle of coffee and orange juice. He could see his reflection in it. He drew his finger through the puddle and stirred the image away.

"Is there somebody else?" he asked.

Her brow wrinkled, but she said nothing.

"I mean if you are in love with somebody else, then maybe . . ."

"No, John," she said, her anger gone. "There's nobody else."

"I don't think I could have taken it if you had said there was. I'm too weak to live with something like that."

"That's probably the first time in your life you've admitted to any kind of weakness."

"I've always been weak," he said, still stirring his reflection.

"Well . . . at least you're strong enough to admit it."

"Not strong," he said. "Too weak to deny it."

His voice was so mournful, so full of surrender, that she turned to go to him, but stopped herself after half a step.

Carefully, too carefully, she set the cup of water in the sink. "Good-bye, John," she said. "I'm going upstairs now to lie down and hate you in private. Don't disturb me again."

She released her breath slowly, head sinking forward until her gaze leveled out, across the threshold and into the living room filled with silent waiting women, all their eyes on her. She then pushed herself forward and walked straight ahead, out of his sight.

Too exhausted to call her back, Bloomhardt squeezed shut his eyes and pressed the balls of his hands against them. When he opened his eyes a minute later he was still seeing stars and did not know whether the hazy figure before him was real or a hallucination.

"Tim?"

"You have orange stuff in your hair," Timmy said.

"Right, I, uh . . . I spilled some orange juice all over myself. Get me a towel, will you, son?"

He took the towel Timmy laid in his hands and then wiped his face and hair. "Are we still going for a walk?" the boy asked.

"Sure. If you want to."

"Mommy said it was all right."

"Did she? Well, then . . . let's go. If you want to, that is. We don't have to if you don't want to."

Timmy put out a gloved hand and took his father's. Bloomhardt stood uncertainly, leaning on his son for support.

"Mommy said to be careful on the ice," said the boy.

"You bet," said Bloomhardt, and, wobbling precariously, blinking in the sudden light, allowed himself to be led outside.

There was snow on everything now, two inches of white powder dusting the city's shell of ice. Just inside the park entrance, in the middle of a snow-covered footpath, Bloomhardt stood with his son. Overhead, branches creaked and groaned, frozen twigs snapped beneath the weight of accumulating snow.

"I don't think we should be standing here," Bloomhardt said, looking up. "There must be tons of snow up in those branches. We could get buried alive."

"Like an avalanche," said the boy.

"Right," said Bloomhardt, still staring up, the dark branches blotting out the light.

"Okay?" asked his son a few moments later.

"Hmmmm? What did you say, Tim?" He looked down at the snow gathering on the boy's cap, and brushed it away.

"I said can we go over there for a while and watch?"

"Over where, son?"

Timmy pointed through the trees to the far end of the park, where children were sledding down a steep knob of land. "Are you sure you're not cold yet?" asked Bloomhardt.

"I'm sure."

"We can go back home if you want to."

"I want to go over there."

They stood near the bottom of the icy hill and watched long toboggans and bright plastic sleds go whooshing by. The hill formed the northern boundary of the park, on its crest a power plant enclosed by a chainlink fence, on its right a baseball diamond and the junior high school Timmy would attend someday, on its left Fairfax Avenue leading out of town to the expressway. A red snow fence had been erected parallel to the street, but in most places it now lay flat against the ground, trampled by children wanting quicker access to the slope.

Here Bloomhardt stood with one hand in his pocket, the other wrapped around his son's. Fascinated by the sledders, Timmy giggled softly after each spill, and sucked in his breath when a fast sled went whizzing by. Every few minutes Bloomhardt asked if he was cold, if he was ready to go home, and the boy always answered no. Bloomhardt watched the sleds too, but he saw them as something else, as tiny lives out of control, insentient lives skidding and spinning in the death grip of gravity. He shuddered and felt sick to his stomach and cautioned himself not to squeeze his only child's hand too hard.

"Can I?" Timmy asked.

"Hmmm?" said his father. Standing beside Timmy was another boy, a chubby twelve-year-old whose clothes were snowy and wet, the cold-stiff rope of a toboggan wrapped around his hand.

"He said I could have a ride if I want to," Timmy explained.

"Do you want to?" Bloomhardt asked.

"I don't know. I think they go too fast."

"Just stick your feet out," the boy told him. "There's nothing to it."

"I might fall off," said Timmy.

"Heck, that's the most fun of all."

Timmy looked up at his father. "Should I?"

"If you want to, sport. You've ridden a toboggan before, haven't you?"

"No."

"Sure you have. Didn't I take you sledding last winter?"

"You said you would, but you didn't."

"Oh," said Bloomhardt.

"Well, do you want to or not?" asked the other boy. "I can't stand around here all day."

"Do you, sport? Want to give it a try?"

"I don't know," said Timmy. Then a moment later, "I guess so."

The older boy pushed the frozen rope into Timmy's hand. "You gotta pull it up yourself. And after the ride too." He shoved a hand out toward Bloomhardt, palm up. "That'll be a dollar."

"For what?"

"One ride, one dollar. Take it or leave it."

Timmy was already moving away from him, trudging up the hill with the long wooden sled in tow, so Bloomhardt, shaking his head, fumbled with numb fingers for his wallet, then laid a one-dollar bill in the boy's hand. "Is your name Dillinger by any chance?"

"Who's he?" said the boy as he stuffed the money in his pocket.

By the time Bloomhardt fell to his knees at the top of the hill, having towed his son on the sled most of the way, he was wheezing and dizzy. Timmy remained seated on the toboggan, eyes wide, fists clenched around the side ropes as his father aimed the sled down the center of the hill.

"Just one ride," said the toboggan's owner, who had tramped up the hill beside them, giving instructions all the way.

"Yeah, yeah, we know," said Bloomhardt, panting. "Ready, sport?"

"I think it's too steep here," Timmy said.

Bloomhardt dragged the sled farther to the left and aimed it to traverse the slope toward the baseball diamond at a forty-five-degree angle. "You won't pick up much speed in this direction," Bloomhardt told him.

"Go on, get moving," said the other boy. "Don't be a chicken."

"He's not a chicken, he's one of the toughest little guys in the world. Aren't you, sport?"

"Then hurry it up," said the boy.

"I don't think I'm big enough for this yet," Timmy said.

"Chicken," said the boy.

"Hey, Dillinger, you got your money, didn't you? So just stand there and be quiet, okay?" Bloomhardt knelt in the snow and laid a hand on his son's shoulder. "Listen, sport. If you don't want to ride this thing, you don't have to. The heck with it. I'd rather go somewhere and get some hot chocolate anyway, wouldn't you? I mean, I'm really getting cold and thirsty, Tim. So how about doing me a favor and forgetting about this ride for now?"

Timmy stared down the hill a while longer. "Will you ride with me?" he asked.

"Sure, that's a great idea. I'll even steer, okay? You slide back and give me some room."

Bloomhardt straddled the toboggan and was about to lower himself onto it when the other boy protested. "Uh-uh, no way. The kid goes alone."

"Ahh, come on," said Bloomhardt as he turned to face him. "These sleds are made for—" But before he could finish, the boy leaned toward Timmy, laid his hands on his back, and shoved the toboggan away. Timmy rocked backward onto his spine, knees and feet in the air, hands clutching the side ropes. The sled was already off course, moving straight down the hill and rapidly gaining speed. Bouncing and rocking, Timmy tried to sit up. He stuck out both feet, but only the left one caught ground, his heel acting as a rudder to turn him even farther to his left.

For the first five seconds of its descent, Bloomhardt was within an arm's length of the toboggan, running behind it, grabbing at air. "Roll off!" he screamed. "You're headed for the road! Roll off!"

"He's a goner," said one boy to another as the sled whistled past them.

Taking giant strides, fighting desperately to remain on his feet, Bloomhardt threw himself after the runaway sled. "Roll off!" he kept screaming. "For God's sake, Tim, roll off!"

Timmy's head banged up and down on the cold wood as the hard, throbbing ground sped by. He held himself as flat as he could; he pressed his elbows and hips and spine to the boards and strained to keep from being jarred off.

"*JUUUUUMP!*" Bloomhardt cried a final time. He was a full twenty yards behind the toboggan now, the trampled-down snow fence ten yards ahead of it. With this cry he gathered all remaining strength and hope into his knees and, with arms outstretched, dove through the air. He landed on his stomach, hands empty, just as the toboggan went *brumpbrumpbrump* over the slats of the fence, over the sidewalk, over the curb, Timmy and the sled separating then to become individual projectiles, both airborne, similarly doomed.

Sliding on his face, Bloomhardt clawed at the ice, kicked with his feet. Scrambling awkwardly, not yet erect, he heard the collision of wood and steel, the heart-crunching thud that followed. Instantly the world changed and became dreamlike, the screech of tires and blast of car horns were like nothing real, the snow, the cold, the sound of his soul turning inside out.

When Bloomhardt finally reached the street, he was running so hard that in trying to stop he fell again, this time sliding across the pavement on his hands and knees, tearing skin at all four points of impact. With stiffened fingers he quickly felt along the boy's neck and back, delicately examined the arm that seemed twisted at a peculiar angle. The driver of the car into which Timmy had crashed, an elderly man with trembling hands and watery, anxious eyes, leaned over Bloomhardt and asked, "Where'd he come from? I never even saw him. I just heard the noise and that was all, I never even saw him until it was over!"

"Call an ambulance," Bloomhardt said, his field of vision so narrow that he could see only Timmy, only the small, unmoving body. When a hand came down in front of him as if to touch the boy's face, he batted it away. "Call an ambulance, damn it! Don't touch him!"

Some other man said, "I called them on my CB. They're on the way."

The elderly driver stood beside his car, its engine still running. He turned to his right and then his left, arms held out, palms up. Slowly he crossed to the curb, then pivoted and wandered between the cars to the other side.

"God Almighty," said the man with the CB radio. "They shouldn't be allowed to play so close to the street."

Bloomhardt said nothing. Everything sounded strange, foreign, miles away. "How bad is he?" the other man asked.

Bloomhardt bent over his son and shielded him from the falling snow. He kissed the boy's cheek. He warned himself that he must not take another breath, not allow another heartbeat, not disrupt the flow of life from his body into his son's until somehow, miraculously, the child might look up at him again and smile.

From the hospital Bloomhardt telephoned his wife. "She's lying down," a woman said. "She's not feeling well." The tone of her voice made it very clear that this was Bloomhardt's fault.

"Get her up. This is important."

"I'll give her a message for you."

"I'll give her the message, damn it. Call her to the phone!"

"I'm not going to wake her."

"Damn it, this is an emergency! Didn't you hear the ambulance siren twenty minutes ago? It went right by the house!"

"My God, what happened?"

"Put my wife on the phone, goddamn it!"

He heard the receiver being dropped, heard a voice shouting excitedly. Thirty seconds later, Annie snatched up the receiver and breathlessly demanded, "What's wrong? What happened?"

"Now, sweetheart," he said, "don't get excited, but I'm over here at County Memorial."

"Oh my God, oh my God, is it Timmy? You sonofabitch, if you hurt that little boy again, I'll kill you—"

"Annie, wait, wait, don't get excited. Timmy's okay."

"He is?" She panted several times, getting her breath back. "Then what's wrong, John? Did something happen to you?"

He was touched by her concern, but at the same time it deepened his sense of guilt. "I feel awful," he admitted. "I wish I were dead."

"Oh, baby, don't say that. Tell me what's wrong, what happened?"

He felt himself getting weak and very small. "I love you, Annie," he whispered, as if these were his dying words.

"I love you too. Now *please*, tell me what's wrong with you!"

"It's not me. It's Timmy."

"You lousy bastard! You sonofabitch! You stupid, stupid, stupid, stupid—"

"It wasn't my fault, I swear! He had a sledding accident. He was just sitting there on the toboggan when—"

"Sledding!" she shrieked. "You were supposed to be taking him for a walk!"

"I know, but—"

"What's wrong with him? How badly is he hurt?"

"Take it easy, it's not all that serious. He's got a broken arm, that's all."

"You lousy lousy lousy lousy bastard!"

"And a couple of cracked ribs."

"You sonofabitch!"

"And a mild concussion. Very, very mild."

"I'll kill you!" she cried. "I will, I mean it, I'm going to find a gun and—"

"Annie please, take it easy. Kids break their arms every day."

"But not with their father's help!"

"You don't know the whole story. . . ."

"What room is he in?"

"Room 109, first floor. He's—"

She hung up.

"And don't bring the goon squad with you," he mumbled into a dead receiver.

She came alone. She marched past him without a word, eyes flashing, as he waited in the corridor outside Timmy's room. Seconds later she came rushing out to back him against the wall. "Where is he? Why isn't he here?"

"Now don't get hysterical, he's still down in the cast room. Where they put the casts on. He should be back in fifteen minutes or so."

She stood before him with her fists clenched, wanting to say more but too angry to speak. Finally she spun away and stood in the doorway to Timmy's room, facing the empty bed. Bloomhardt, leaning against the wall, stared at her back.

"I hate you so much," she said through clenched teeth, shoulders trembling.

"That makes two of us," he said.

"You're not fit to own a dog, let alone be father to that precious little boy."

"Don't I know it."

She turned sharply, eyes aflame. "Why don't you just leave?"

"I will. Right after I see Timmy."

"I mean forever."

"You mean . . . ?"

"I mean go somewhere and fall off the face of the earth. Permanently."

"You don't even know what happened," he said.

"I know that you were with him—that's all I need to know. I hate you so much, I can't stand the sight of you."

"Not long ago you said you loved me."

"I said no such thing!"

"Yes you did, when you thought I was hurt. And you're still wearing the necklace I gave you. Surely that counts for something."

She grabbed the gold chain and tore it off her neck. She was about to hurl it at his face when she spotted the garbage chute a few feet away. She went to it, yanked open the door, and flung the necklace inside. "There. Does that tell you how I feel about you?"

"Jesus, Annie. Won't you at least let me tell you what happened? I'm not the villain this time, honest."

"Well, you're certainly not the hero. Fathers are supposed to protect their children, don't you know that?"

"So are mothers," he said.

"And what is that supposed to mean? I'm not the one who broke his arm."

"But you're the one who killed his brother. Or his sister. Which was it, do you know?"

They stood face to face in the middle of the hallway, eyes locked and full of pain, bodies rigid and motionless, until two nurses came walking toward them and Bloomhardt stepped back to allow them to pass. Annie faced Timmy's room again.

"Anyway," she said a minute later, "that's over now."

Later he and Annie heard the gurney being wheeled down the hall and they both rushed to meet it, one on each side. Bloomhardt touched his son's fingers, so small protruding from the heavy cast. The boy looked at him through cloudy eyes. "Forgive me," Bloomhardt whispered.

Annie laid a hand upon Timmy's face and turned his head toward her. "Mommy's here, sweetheart," she told him as she squeezed his other hand. "Don't you worry, you're going to be all right now, Mommy's here."

Bloomhardt felt the gurney slip away from him. He stood back and watched it disappear into the room. After a while the orderly and the empty gurney reemerged, and finally the nurse. He stepped toward the door, but Annie was there to block his entrance.

"He's sleeping," she said. "You can leave now."

Bloomhardt peered over her shoulder. "I'm his father, Annie."

"If he's lucky," she said, "he won't remember."

VIOLATION! VIOLATION! VIOLATION! said the parking meters as he passed, red flags of disapproval wagging like tongues. It was dusk on the day before Christmas, perhaps the most serene hour of the year, and Bloomhardt felt himself coming apart at the seams, bloated with grief, the very threads of his soul snapping one by one.

His grief was not for himself, however, for he did not consider himself worthy of pity. No, his was a composite grief, a sorrow for the world. He thought of the Goathead, of the old man's wife and daughter, and a thread of his soul tore apart. He thought of his own beautiful son, a mummy in plaster and tape, and a dozen threads popped in a row. He thought of his wife, his parents, of hairy-faced Jake, he thought of Smitty and Roomy and Mickey's restless ghost, he thought of all the people in the world swamped in their private miseries, and the threads of his soul burst apart.

Bloomhardt stood reeling on the sidewalk, clutching his head in his hands. Go ahead and fall down, he told himself. Mox nix, what difference would it make? But he could not let himself drop, though it was what he most longed to do.

Fifteen minutes later there was a screech of tires to his right, but he paid it no attention.

"Bloomie! Damn it, Bloomie, hey!" Smitty, having chased him for half a block, caught him by the arm and spun him around. "Man, are you deaf? Didn't you hear me blowing the horn and yelling at you back there?"

"What? No, I, uh . . . I guess I wasn't paying much attention."

"Well, I got your attention now, don't I? Hey Bloomie, what's the matter with you? You look all cross-eyed and goofy. You stoned?"

"No, I've just been . . . thinking. Just walking and thinking."

"Well, you can stop that right now, pal, because Smitty is here! Come on, there's a bar up the street a little ways. The Glass Punkin—you ever been there?"

"Smitty, I'm sorry, I can't right now, I don't have time."

"Hey, you're not sore at me about last night, are you? You got the old Goat home okay, right?"

"Yes, but—"

"I'm just no good in a situation like that, Bloomie. You understand, don't you? So come on, let's go have a coupla drinks, then I'll take you across town to meet these girls I know. There's three of them, see, and they like nothing better than to get all stacked up in a double-decker sandwich. Or would that be a triple? Gee, I don't know, what would you call a—"

"For the love of God, Smitty, it's Christmas Eve!"

"Yeah? So?"

"So don't you have something better to do? Don't you have a family somewhere? Get drunk and fuck, get drunk and fuck, that's all you ever want to do. For crying out loud, Smitty, what the hell kind of life is that?"

Redfaced, his mouth set grimly, Smitty looked away. A moment later he said quietly, "You think it's easy living like this, Bloomie? Holding off death and reality with one hand while pulling out my pecker with the other? Sure, I admit it, I spend all the time I can avoiding reality. You think you're so goddamn smart, but you don't know what it's like to hate yourself for being a goddamn runty lowlife, do you? With me it's either get drunk and fuck or stay home and blow my brains out. But you, you got everything. You couldn't begin to understand what it's like being someone like me."

"Smitty, I'm sorry, I didn't mean—"

"Ahh, shut up, okay? Christ, all I wanted was to buy you a beer and share some pussy with you, but you have to start spouting that crap about family and loved ones. Well, I'll tell you what, Bloomie, I've got a big family. Every bartender in this city, he's like a brother to me, 'cause all I have to do is raise my finger and he pours me a refill. And the girls I go out with? Maybe they are barflies and whores, but what of it? All I gotta do is smile and they know exactly what's on my mind. We got telepathy, the perfect communication. Can you say that about *your* family? So you see, I *am* gonna be with my loved ones tonight, okay? We're all members of the same family, get it? We know what the world is made of. It's made of food and drink, noise and stink, sex and death. But if you're too dumb to know that, and you're too good to have a drink with me and my family, then screw you, merry Christmas, and have a happy fucking New Year."

"Smitty . . ." said Bloomhardt, but he was already alone. Smitty was several angry strides away and moving rapidly down the street.

Annie is right, thought Bloomhardt, shivering. Whatever I touch turns to dust. I'm a one-man wrecking crew, I'm a demolition derby. All I ever do is hurt people. I'm the Black Death with blue eyes.

In his apartment, he sat close to the window in his straight-back chair, knees against the wall, elbows on the windowsill, nose touching the dirty glass. He altered this position only long enough to take another sip of black coffee or a bite of chocolate bar. Scattered across the floor behind him were the torn and crumpled remnants of his morning's work. He had come home hoping to find solace in his writing and had eagerly read those pages of fevered prose. But it was not brilliant writing, as he had expected. It was drivel. Jumbled, muddy, incomprehensible stuff. Garbage. He tore the papers to shreds and let them flutter to his feet.

And now he sat staring out the window, fingers tapping the glass, a sour pressure building inside him. His fingers began to tap harder and harder. Soon he was rapping the glass with his knuckles. Then with the heel of a fist. When the glass suddenly cracked he jumped up and out of his chair, as if until then he had been unaware of what his hand was doing. He stared in disbelief at the fracture. "Oh fine, fine," he moaned, because now he would have to pay to have the window replaced. The radiator hissed at him, a sneering, spitting laugh. Slowly and deliberately he turned to it. He grasped the back of his chair with both hands, lifted it up, and swung the chair against the radiator.

"Hunnnhh!" he grunted as a chair leg splintered and flew away. Again he swung and again, grunting and straining until there was nothing left in his hands but two short pieces of wood. He threw these against the wall and spun around to face the empty room.

The sight of the torn yellow pages and scattered note cards lying so docilely on the floor infuriated him. He leaped into the air and came down on the paper with both feet, jumped up and down, ground it beneath his heels. *It is a Sunday morning in October,* he read, and kicked that fragment around the room, kicked it into the air and punched it with his fists. When the paper fluttered beneath the sofa bed, he turned the entire creaking thing onto its side, then, with a diving shoulder block, flipped it over.

From there his eye wandered into the kitchen. "Aha!" he shouted as he clambered to his feet. From the kitchen he hurled the two wobbly chairs into the living room. The table had to be thrown three times, but it finally sailed neatly through the doorway, legless, and skidded across the floor to bang against the wall.

Next he emptied the cupboards of their dishes and pans. One by one he sailed them into the living room, some clattering and banging, others exploding in a shower of glass. "There!" he shouted triumphantly when the cupboards were empty. "No more dishes to wash!"

Back in the living room he pounced again on the index cards, the rotten fruit of his dreams. After kicking them a while longer he scooped all the paper into his arms, carried it to the bathroom and dumped it in the tub. Back to the kitchen for a book of matches, back to the bathroom where the entire book was ignited and tossed onto the paper. Soon the bathtub was bristling with flames, smoke stinging Bloomhardt's eyes, heat searing his skin. For good measure he tossed in a few splintered pieces of a chair. Then he stood back to watch the flames dancing and snapping in the tub. The wall tile melted and dripped sizzling plastic. The ceiling turned black with soot.

Mox nix! Bloomhardt told himself. That's my life in there, my gonads and bones, my hair and teeth crumbling and curling and turning to ash. That's me, I'm dead, what's the difference, who cares? Ashes to ashes and dust to dust. If I had any guts I would hop in there myself.

As black ribbons of smoke twisted toward the ceiling, Bloom-hardt watched his morning of ecstasy and gushing blood being consumed, and as the seconds passed he began to regret his impulsive actions. He leaned into the smoke and, burning his hand on the hot metal of the tap, sent a spray of cold water into the flames. Hissing and spitting, the fire died out. But too late, everything was lost. The charred paper, those floating islands of soot—the sight of them pained him more than the ugly blister that was blossoming in his hand.

Finally he shut off the water and stumbled back to the living room, where nothing remained intact but the crate full of excelsior. Noise and stink and sex and death, he heard echoing in his head while perspiration trickled down his spine and made him shiver like a plucked piano string. Noise and stink and sex and death. He stood motionless for a moment and listened. No, there was no noise in his life, only stink and sex and death. He held his breath; smelled nothing. So there was only sex and death. He glanced down at the front of his trousers, but saw no sign of life. So for him there was only death. Only death. The single option left.

But Bloomhardt felt unclean, too despicable even for death. If he was going to his grave, he must clean himself up first—isn't that how it is done? Scrape off the stink and strip away the scum? Ha ha! he thought. I'm a poet too, just like the Goathead's daughter!

In the bathroom he took the scissors from the medicine cabinet, grabbed a handful of hair in his left hand, and *snip snip*, it tumbled to the floor, some of the hairs tickling his cheek as they fell, some landing in the lavatory bowl. He liked the sound of that, liked the look of brown hairs on stained pink enamel. So he did it again, and again, snipping joyfully, tossing handfuls of hair like confetti. Ten minutes later there was more hair on his shoes than on his head. Now he looked as barbaric as he felt, as uncivilized as a wild dog. He snarled at his reflection in the mirror while spraying a thick bonnet of shaving cream over his scalp. With a razor he shaved his skull bald, grimacing with each nick but delighting in the purification of pain.

Blood and lather turned his head pink, so he washed the pink into the tub with a spray of cold water. His scalp stung so fiercely from the crisscrossing scratches and nicks that tears came to his eyes, but he laughed, he enjoyed it, there was cleanliness in that sting and tingle.

Next he shaved his armpits, his face, his eyebrows, his legs. He shaved his chest and, more carefully, his groin. He squatted naked with a hand mirror between his legs and shaved the cheeks of his ass. He scraped the fine blond hairs from his knuckles and toes, shaved his arms and stomach and as much of his back as he could reach, grazed every centimeter of skin where a follicle dared to grow.

When finished, as smooth as an egg, he appraised himself in the mirror. With water glistening on his bald body he looked slippery and sleek, as skinny as an eel. Yet he did not feel one hundred percent clean. Could true purification be so much fun? No, he needed to suffer more, to burn himself clean with pain.

With a bottle of iodine and its glass swizzle stick, he swabbed out his myriad wounds. "Yeeoow!" he screamed as he hopped around the hairy floor. "Ouch! Owww! Holy Hannah, it burns!" Each time the sting of one wound subsided he painted another, sometimes two or three in quick succession, holding his breath until the accumulation of pain made him see stars.

He leaned close to the mirror and examined his teeth. He yanked at a few of them, but with no success. What I need are forceps, he thought, or pliers. Or a monkey wrench. Sadly, he had none of these. He settled for a nail clipper, with which he sheared his fingernails and toenails to the quick. Ahhh, the burn, the hurt—now that was a fire that cleansed! He gargled with a glass of soapy water, swallowed it, and immediately vomited. He dripped hydrogen peroxide into his ears and thought the fizzing would drive him mad. He blew his nose, he bathed his eyeballs in salt water. He straddled the toilet and gave himself an enema.

"Not enough!" he screamed. "Not enough!"

Naked and hairless, as wild-eyed as a lizard, feeling still deficient and unalluring to Death, he paced his wrecked apartment. What he needed now was a torture rack, a thumbscrew, a cat-o'-nine-tails equipped with spikes. But his resources were pitifully limited. Outside, however—yes! yes! there were ways out there to hurt oneself, to get hurt, to cauterize the spirit with pain!

He pulled on a pair of white socks, an overcoat, sneakers, a stocking cap, a scarf to fling dashingly about his neck. Then, with streaks of iodine where his eyebrows once had been, with soap on his breath and acid in his blood, he sprinted downstairs.

Out on the street he turned this way and that, the cold air churning beneath his coat. It was night now, and somewhere across town a cathedral bell was tolling, calling worshipers to service. Bloomhardt felt drawn to the bells and started dancing toward them, moving at a jerky, disjointed gait. The few people he encountered along the way quickly moved aside. "Hosanna!" he said politely. "Hinkadinka doo!"

Finally he spotted the cathedral spire against the gray skyline and broke into a trot. It was a Catholic church and he was a Methodist, lapsed, but sin was sin, right? Guilt was guilt? He arrived just as Mass was beginning, and he bounded up the steps with but a ten-second lead over the police cruiser that had been following him for the last five blocks.

"I confess!" he screamed as he strode down the center aisle.

The congregation stopped singing. The organist stopped playing. The priest stopped smiling beneficently.

"I confess to dastardly deeds!" said Bloomhardt. He paused halfway down the aisle and, to show his respect, pulled off his cap. Behind the priest was a life-size icon of Christ on the cross, and it was this that suddenly caught Bloomhardt's eye.

"Boy oh boy," he said admiringly. "That looks real."

"You confess to what?" asked the priest, hopeful and yet terrified that Bloomhardt might be an actual demon sent to test the clergyman's faith.

"Oh gee, lots of things," said Bloomhardt. "You want me to list them alphabetically?"

This produced a snicker or two from the congregation.

"Hey, don't think I can't do it," Bloomhardt told them. "I might not be able to write very well, but I'm a whiz at alphabetizing. Adultery!" he said. "You see? Right off the top of my head, I didn't even have to think about it. And for *B*?—Blasphemery!"

"Blasphemy," corrected the priest.

"You sure? Well, okay, I guess you'd know. Now then, to *C* . . ."

"Come along quietly," said one of the two policemen who, having sneaked up from behind, now took hold of his arms.

"But I have lots more," Bloomhardt said, smiling at one policeman and then the other. "I can even do a toughie like *Q*. *Q* is for 'quixotic dreams.'"

"*Q* is for 'quiet,'" said the officer as he tightened his grip on Bloomhardt's arm and began to drag him toward the door.

"Not bad," said Bloomhardt. "But can you do *Z*?"

"Zaniness," said the officer on his right.

"Hey, that's pretty good. You're quick. I was going to say 'zoanthropy' and hope that nobody knew what I was talking about. But I like yours a lot better. Do you mind if I use it?"

"Sorry, Father," said one of the policemen over his shoulder. The priest nodded and made the sign of the cross and blessed all three men as they headed out the door.

Okay, Bloomhardt told himself, this could work out all right. Priest or police, what's the difference? Both are adept at administering pain, both are on friendly terms with Death.

"Now then," said the first policeman as they came down off the church steps, "just what was that all about?"

"Food and drink," said Bloomhardt. "Noise and stink. Sex and death."

"Come again?"

"It is a Sunday morning in October and there are dogs shitting on my doorstep."

"Sounds like gibberish to me," said one officer to the other.

"Doggerel," said Bloomhardt.

"You think he's been drinking?"

"Let's find out. Lemme smell your breath, fella."

Bloomhardt blew in the officer's face.

"What do you smell, Ed?"

"I'm not sure, but it smells like soap to me."

"Lifebuoy," said Bloomhardt.

"Hey, Ed, looky here. He don't got nothing on except this coat."

"We're all naked underneath our clothes," Bloomhardt told them.

"Why don't you go call that mental health place," said Ed to his partner. "This guy's not dangerous. Let's see if we can't get him in there for evaluation."

Oh-oh, thought Bloomhardt, this will not do. Two nice cops, just my luck. He waited until the first officer released his arm, then he spun and twisted and in an instant was free of Ed's grasp as well.

"Take it easy, fella," said Ed. "Nobody's going to hurt you."

Like hell you're not, thought Bloomhardt. That's what I came here for. Backing away, grinning, arching his iodine eyebrows, he swayed back and forth and gestured for them to come closer.

"Look at them marks all over him," said Ed's partner. "You think maybe he's some kind of religious nut?"

"Rama rama Krishna, shakka lakka boom," said Bloomhardt.

"Calm down, fella. Just take it nice and easy. We're here to help you."

"Shit," said Bloomhardt. "I was better off with the priest." He leaped backwards, came down on his haunches on the edge of the sidewalk, scooped up a handful of snow, and then pounced at Ed. His hand was barely off Ed's face before the other cop, not as solicitous as his partner, raked his nightstick across the base of

Bloomhardt's skull. Bloomhardt blinked and fell to his knees. Ahhh, he thought as the pain rippled through him. He looked up to see a wall of darkness crashing down from the sky, and grateful for the annihilation, he held his face up to it.

he awoke in darkness, unable to move. Leather straps held his arms, legs, and chest against a hard bed. There was a smell of disinfectant in the air, of hospital sterility and rubber sheets. Somewhere a group of people were singing— "Above thy deep and dreamless sleep the silent stars go by . . ."— and interspersed with this music was the occasional clatter of a bedpan, an elevator bell, a ringing telephone, voices laughing, mumbling, calling out.

Bloomhardt turned his head to the left, wincing as he rolled over the tender knob at the base of his skull. The door to his room was open, and beyond it shone the soft yellow light of the corridor. For a moment he was confused and could not understand why he was there, but gradually the memories came trickling back, vivid and mortifying, as chilling as the air that washed across his naked scalp.

He did not mind so much the way he knew he must look, as ridiculous as a plucked fowl, but that Annie would soon come and see him like this, strapped down, arrested, no doubt, for having assaulted a police officer, and that he would be denounced to Timmy as a crazy man, a nut. He would probably never be allowed to see his son again. He had sought purification—though in a caffeine-crazed, hysterical kind of way—but had achieved only humiliation and a greater guarantee of banishment.

Unable to move anything but his head, he stared at the doorway full of yellow light. Everything, he knew, was lost to him now.

Everything. He could not even find within himself the momentary relief of tears, but was so choked with the terror of loneliness that he had barely enough strength to lie there and pant.

he fell asleep, though for how long he did not know. But he became aware of a shuffling noise near the foot of his bed, opened his eyes, and saw a short bald man standing there, silently reading Bloomhardt's chart. Bloomhardt tried to sit up, having forgotten about the restraints, then grunted when the straps snapped him back.

The little man at the foot of his bed looked at him and smiled. "Got you strapped in there pretty good, huh?"

"Are you my doctor?" asked Bloomhardt. "Listen, there's nothing wrong with me, not really. I didn't have anything to eat for two whole days except coffee and candy and I guess all that caffeine made me go wacky for a while, but I'm okay now, I'm—"

"John Doe," the doctor interrupted while tapping the chart.

"Huh?"

"John Doe. No identification. You're nobody. An invisible man."

"Excuse me, Doctor, but I don't think I understand."

The doctor came padding around to the side of the bed. He leaned over Bloomhardt and tapped him on the forehead. "No identification," he repeated. "John Doe nobody knows. Free as a bird. *Free as a fucking invisible man!*"

What's he talking about? Bloomhardt wondered. He took a closer look at his doctor, and gradually it dawned on him that this was not a doctor at all, just a little bald man in baggy blue pajamas, his breath smelling of Christmas cookies. I'm in the psych ward! he realized, but did not know whether to feel better or worse. Again the little man tapped on Bloomhardt's forehead, accentuating each syllable as he told him, "Free-as-a-fuck-ing-bird."

"Well," said Bloomhardt with a glimmer of hope, "not really. I can't move."

"Fucking straps," said the bald man.

"Fucking right," said Bloomhardt.

"You want me to let you go?"

"I certainly would appreciate it, yes."

"How much?"

"Pardon me?"

"How much is it worth to you, fucking John Doe?"

"Well," said Bloomhardt, "how much do you want?"

"Twelve hundred million dollars," said the bald man.

"Hmmm, well, ahh, okay, I guess I can handle that. Of course, the banks won't be open till Monday, but if you unstrap me now, I, uh . . . I'll meet you back here in three days, all right?"

"No no no no no, no sirree, no fucking way. You want out now, you pay now. Write me a fucking check."

"Oh, okay, sure. Just undo these straps and I'll get up and get my checkbook."

"Now you're fucking talking." Half a minute later, Bloomhardt was free.

"Be with you in just a minute," he said to his liberator. "Have a seat there on the bed until I get dressed." He found his overcoat, stocking cap, and sneakers in the locker and quickly pulled them on over his hospital gown. As he did so, he asked, "By the way, would you happen to know what day this is?"

"Fucking Christmas," said the bald man.

"Fucking Christmas Day?"

"Fucking right."

"Holy Hannah," said Bloomhardt. "And would you happen to know what time it is?"

"Fucking nighttime, that's what."

Close enough, thought Bloomhardt. He had been unconscious, then, for approximately twenty-four hours. Probably sedated, he told himself as he wound the scarf around his neck. He finished dressing, then looked down at his bare knees protruding incriminatingly beneath his coat.

"How much for those pajama bottoms?" he asked.

The bald man thought for a moment. "Another hundred million."

"It's a deal." The little man stripped off his pants and handed them to Bloomhardt, who hastily pulled them on. The cuffs dangled loosely an inch above the tops of his white socks.

Bloomhardt tiptoed to the door and peeked out. The room across from his was 511. Fifth floor, he told himself. The elevator was out of the question, too slow, too conspicuous, and too far to the right, directly across from the nurse's station. To his left, however, forty feet down the hall, a lighted EXIT sign hung from the ceiling. He turned to speak to the little bald man and found him standing but an inch away.

"Where's my fucking check, John?"

"Just a second, okay? Listen, this is an open ward, right? Is the door to the stairwell locked?"

"Fucking no. What do you think this is, a fucking jail?"

"Thanks," said Bloomhardt, and patted him on the shoulder. "You check's in the mail, okay?"

The little man's eyes brightened. He jabbed a finger into Bloomhardt's chest. "Fly, fucking birdie, fly."

"Up, up, and away," said Bloomhardt, and then stepped out into the hall. Once there, he did not look over his shoulder and had no idea who might be watching him. He walked decisively, but not hurriedly. At the stairwell he made a crisp left turn and, still without a backward glance, pushed open the door. Down five flights of stairs Bloomhardt flew, riding the metal handrail much of the way. On the bottom floor he paused just long enough to peek out, determine the direction he wished to go, and get his laughter under control. Between himself and the final exit was a nurse seated at the admissions desk. But could she stop him? Nothing can stop me now, he thought. Nothing!

He stepped through the swinging doors and strode confidently toward her desk. He was two paces from it when she looked up from her magazine. "Good night," he told her, smiling. "Merry Christmas."

She said nothing because she had already seen the cuffs of his blue pajamas fluttering eight inches above his sneakers. As he strolled past her, she looked higher and saw his hairless orange eyebrow ridges, the streaks of iodine on his face and hands. "Security!" she called as she came up out of her chair. *"Security!"*

Bloomhardt shoved open the glass doors and dove into the icy darkness. He ran down the long sloping drive, gulping air, filling his lungs with helium, his sense of direction suddenly as sharp as a bat's. Free! Free! he shouted to himself. I'm an invisible man with wings on my feet! Escape had been so easy, so illogical, that he could not help but laugh out loud. His laughter echoed like applause between the cars in the hospital lot, between the buildings as he ducked into the first side street.

Free as a fucking bird! he thought, and told himself that if he leaped, he would sail up into the sky, could soar as surely as an eagle. So he tried it, he jumped, but landed on both feet again, jarring his knees. Mox nix, he told himself. This is enough, just to be able to run like this, strapless, unconfined. He felt as he ran that he was embracing the world with the soles of his feet. He felt new, reborn, redeemed by suffering, scraped clean inside and out. "The world is a nuthouse," he sang, "and I'm just another acorn!" But he was an acorn itching to grow, and somewhere in the darkness ahead lay the fertile soil of Fairfax Avenue. He could feel it pulling on him, drawing him home. He had wings on his feet and the earth was a trampoline.

The house was dark, the curb and driveway empty. He knew by a clock he had passed along the way that it was not yet 8:00 P.M. and guessed that his wife was still at the hospital. The doors to his house were locked, but this did not deter him. He was, after all, an invisible man, an escape artist. In less than a minute he was on the roof and squirming through the bathroom window, which again had been left unlocked.

Once inside, he closed the window and hung a thick towel over it before switching on the light. He spotted a pair of his wife's panties lying in the corner, picked them up, and pressed them to his face. In their silky texture he felt the velvet touch of her skin, in their odor the dizzying musk of her body.

With the panties in hand he went to Timmy's room, and there found, hanging on the bedpost, the boy's pajama shirt. This he held in his other hand, then pressed both the panties and shirt to his face. The mixture of odors, sweet and subtle and as active as yeast, brought tears to his eyes.

Downstairs he stood in the center of the unlighted living room and gazed at the Christmas tree. It was a huge tree, the kind Annie and Timmy had always begged for but that he, for some selfish reason he could not now recall, had always denied them. An angel stood majestically at its top, her halo scraping the ceiling. The limbs were heavy with glass balls, electric lights, and tinsel. The odors of pine needles and bark and sap washed over him, dislodging the antiseptic smells of the hospital that had seeped into his pores.

He had those three scents now—the panties, his son's shirt, the Christmas tree. He sank to his knees in front of the tree, pushed the presents aside, and made room for himself. He lay on his back, head near the tree stand, and peered into the dark web of branches, the panties and shirt rolled together to make a pillow for the tender spot on his head.

With those three scents he filled his lungs, he oxygenated his blood. He flushed his senses clean and sewed up the split in his soul. He breathed those odors until he could smell nothing more, could remember no others, until finally, as weak as a newborn, he drifted off to sleep.

He awoke violently, sitting bolt upright and smashing a tree ornament with his head, when Annie stepped inside the door and switched on the ceiling light. She gasped, seeing the tree shaking and his legs twitching as he disentangled his face from the branches, then she grabbed a folding chair from against the wall and raised it above her head.

"Annie wait, it's me! Don't hit me, I'm unarmed, I come in peace!"

Still with her panties and Timmy's shirt in his hand, he slid from beneath the tree and sat up. "See? It's only me."

She stared at him a full twenty seconds before lowering the chair. Then she came three steps closer, her gaze moving slowly up and down his body. "What in the world . . . ?"

He pulled off his stocking cap and smiled sheepishly. Again she gasped. "An act of contrition," he explained. "Of purification." He unbuttoned his overcoat and showed her his hairless, lacerated, iodine-streaked body. "An act of penance," he said.

She sat heavily on the edge of the sofa. "Have you gone crazy?"

"I did for a while," he said happily. "And I'm glad I did. Because now I'm saner than ever."

"Which isn't necessarily much, judging by appearances."

"Oh, but it is! Because the old me is gone, Annie, I've skinned him away. What you see before you now is an entirely different person, inside and out."

He knew by the way she looked at him that she was feeling something—whether pity, affection, or contemptuous disbelief, he was not sure, only that something in him had reached her. "So what's the point of all this?" she asked flatly.

"The point is that I'm a new person. I now know things I didn't know before."

"Like what? How many bumps there are on your head?"

He smiled. "The world is a rough place, Annie. People get bounced around and flung here and there, and if they aren't careful, they end up getting broken. But if they have a home like this, and people who love them, then they're protected, and maybe they won't break so easily."

"I repeat, what's your point?"

"This house is my packing crate, Annie. You and Timmy are my excelsior. And I want to be yours."

She looked at him a few moments longer, then pushed herself to her feet. "I'm too tired for riddles, John. I'm going to bed. Go away."

"I need you," he told her. "And you need me."

She paused at the bottom of the stairway, her hand on the bannister. Without turning to look at him she said, "I need you? For what—to make my life miserable?"

"To keep you from ever doing again the kind of thing you did yesterday morning." He saw her back stiffen, her hand tighten on the bannister post. "And to help you forgive yourself for having done it."

Nearly two minutes passed before either of them moved. Finally her hand slid off the post, reached higher along the rail. As she slowly mounted the stairs, she said, "I'll phone the police from up here. You've got about three minutes to get lost."

"How's Timmy?" he asked.

"He'll live. Switch off the light on your way out."

But he sat there, smiling, and did not get up. He listened as she shrugged off her coat and let it fall on the hallway floor. He heard water running in the bathroom, heard the toilet flush, heard her bare feet padding down the hall, the slow creak of the bed as she eased herself onto it. Every sound was music to him, a Christmas carol.

He picked up the pieces of the broken tree ornament, a fragile blue bulb as old as his marriage, and emptied them in the trash can in the kitchen. Then he returned to the living room and switched off the light. He crawled beneath the tree again, lay on his back, and breathed in the rich pine scent. He felt a coolness on his bald head, but instead of pulling on his cap he wrapped Timmy's shirt around his skull. He draped the panties over his eyes. Soon he could feel a warmth, an infrared resonance, seeping into his brain.

"Smitty," he whispered as he clasped his hands atop his stomach and wriggled his toes. "Smitty, my friend . . . you're wrong."

When Annie came back down the stairs a half hour later, he had already rolled onto his side so that he could watch her. The snow reflected just enough hazy moonlight in through the windows that he could see the outline of her body as she descended, paused uncertainly, then sat on the bottom step. She was dressed only in a yellow cotton nightgown and sat with her knees and feet pressed together, hands clasped between her thighs.

"You look cold," he said softly, so as not to startle her.

"I'm always cold."

"You don't have to be."

"I know. Tomorrow I'll buy a fur coat."

He said nothing. He waited.

"Why are you still lying there like that?" she asked.

"To tell you the truth, I don't know. But it feels good. And . . . I guess I was sort of hoping . . . that I could be Timmy's Christmas present."

"We'd have to put you in a box first," she said. "I think a bronze one with a velvet lining would be nice."

He smiled, because there was no malice in her voice. "I think I'm what he really wants," he told her.

"Kids," she said. "They never know what's good for them."

Again he waited.

"Anyway," she began, looking down at her hands. "I just thought I should tell you. Timmy explained to me what happened. That you weren't the one who pushed him. That you didn't even want him to ride that sled. So . . . I guess I owe you an apology. So I'm sorry. About those things I said to you in the hospital. You probably wouldn't be lying there now like a . . . skinned rabbit if . . ."

He smiled, but he was unable to speak. "Well," Annie said. "I just wanted you to know." She took hold of a bannister rung and pulled herself up. "Timmy's coming home tomorrow. You can drop by and see him, if you like."

"I've quit my job," he told her.

"You what?"

"Anyway, I'm going to. Because if I don't, I'm afraid I'll go back to being what I was before. Either that or I'll end up as just another ghost in the men's room."

"I don't think I know what you're talking about, John."

"I guess you had to be there," he said, smiling.

"So what will you do now?"

"I haven't the faintest idea."

"Well," she said after a long pause, "good luck."

As she turned to go back up the stairs, he added, "I want to stay, Annie."

"Don't worry, I didn't call the police."

"I mean forever. I want to be your husband again."

She shook her head. "It just wouldn't work, John. It just wouldn't."

"It would if you'd stop being afraid of it."

"I'm not afraid of anything. Not anymore."

"Geez, I am," he said, then laughed softly. "But I can see that you're right, you're not afraid of anything. You're especially not

afraid of admitting that you love me—if you did, that is, which you
don't. And you're not afraid of admitting what a terrible mistake
you made yesterday morning. And you're not afraid of what your
friends will say if you take me back. And the one thing you're not
afraid of the most is turning back into the woman you used to be. I
know, sweetheart, you're not afraid of a thing. That's why you're
shivering like a tuning fork right now."

"I'm shivering because I'm cold, you asshole."

"Yeah, me too. So what do you say—can we give it a try? We'll
be just like before, I promise."

"We were lousy before. Especially you."

"Good point. But this time we'll be great. Because we're both
really scared to death, and we'll be watching each other every step
of the way."

She said nothing after this. He heard only one long exhalation
before she started up the stairs. "Annie?" he asked. "Okay? Can I
stay?"

Without pausing, she told him, "If you come up these stairs tonight, I'll brain you, I swear."

He smiled to himself and, full of the warm red ache of love,
pressed the panties and shirt to his face. A few moments later he
heard Annie from the bedroom begin to cry—helpless, convulsive
weeping that rattled the bed. He climbed to his feet, searched for
the switch for the Christmas lights, turned it on, and lit up the
room. By the time he reached the stairs he was sobbing as loudly
as his wife, the tears chiming like bells as they fell.

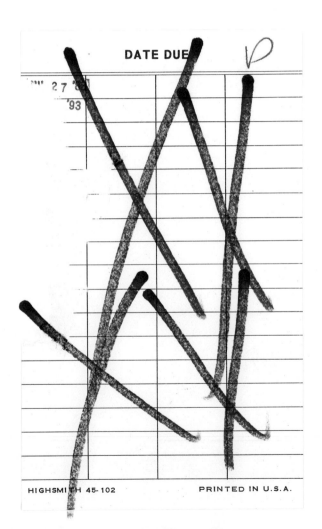

DATE DUE

27 '93

HIGHSMITH 45-102   PRINTED IN U.S.A.